P9-DNH-748

D0014931

Also by Colin Harrison

The Havana Room

Afterburn

Manhattan Nocturne

Bodies Electric

Break and Enter

The Finder

Colin Harrison

The Finder

Sarah Crichton Books

Farrar, Straus and Giroux | New York

Sarah Crichton Books
Farrar, Straus and Giroux
18 West 18th Street, New York 10011

Distributed in Canada by Douglas & McIntyre Ltd.
Printed in the United States of America
First edition, 2008

Library of Congress Cataloging-in-Publication Data
Harrison, Colin, 1960–
    The finder / Colin Harrison. — 1st ed.
      p.   cm.
    "Sarah Crichton Books."
    ISBN-13: 978-0-374-29949-1 (alk. paper)
    ISBN-10: 0-374-29949-8 (alk. paper)
    1. New York (N.Y.)—Fiction.   I. Title.

PS3558.A6655F56 2008
813'.54—dc22

                2007036574

Designed by Abby Kagan

www.fsgbooks.com

1   3   5   7   9   10   8   6   4   2

For my mother

&

In memory of my father

The Finder

Three girls in a car at night, on their way to the beach in Brooklyn. Two are Mexican, about nineteen or twenty, young and pretty—like a lot of Mexican girls you see in New York City. Straight black hair, soft faces, a sweet-eyed optimism not yet destroyed by labor. Dressed in identical blue service uniforms with CORPSERVE patches on the breast, they are nestled in a Toyota two-door subcompact as it flies along the Belt Parkway. The rattling, uninsured car is fifteen years old, carries expired Georgia plates, and has a market value of $125. In New York City you can always buy a car like this and you can always sell one. Who cares about the paperwork? That's for people who have big money to lose. These Mexican girls have no money. They work cleaning offices in Manhattan. Their day begins at seven p.m., so the hour now might be five in the morning, just before dawn. They go out afterward almost every night, a way of saying this work is not yet destroying us. A few minutes sitting in the car at the beach, then they'll swing back to the house on Avenue U, where they live with nine other people. Why drive? *The subway, it don't go where we live.* And the bus, it takes *like forever.* So the girls drive. Often they will smoke a little pot some boys gave them and giggle. Open the car's cracked sunroof, let the smoke drift upward. They are enjoying their freedom, their few hard-won dollars, their provisional American identities. They smoke, maybe drink some too, listen to the radio. Giggling and sweet, but tough—tougher than American girls. In the country illegally. Each carrying some kind of fake green card that she bought for $150. They've made the journey and are not yet beaten down, not yet burdened with children and husbands. They have cookouts and volleyball in one of the Mexican sections of Marine Park. And they have guys, when they feel like it, know what to do to make their men feel *bien*. Sex yet another kind of labor. Their mothers back home don't know—don't know a lot. *Be careful!* they beg, *Nueva York is dangerous for girls like you.* But that's wrong. Mexico is where girls get found in the desert, legs wide open, hair dragged with dirt, dead eyes already eaten out by bugs. New York City is big and safe and filled with rich, fat *norteamericanos.* Maybe the girls won't even marry Mexican men. Why should they? They talk about the office guys. The tall ones who look so good in a suit. You want to do him, girl, I know you do. *No, no, es muy gordo,* too fat. They laugh. They see a lot of powerful people leaving their offices at the end of the day. Men and women in business clothes. Nice haircuts, good watches. *White ladies who think they's better than us.* A corporate world so close they could reach out and touch it with their cherry-colored fingernails. Yet given the stratifications of American society, it is a world they are unlikely ever to know from within. They are like Nigerians in London, Turks in Paris, Koreans in Tokyo, Filipinos in Riyadh—outsiders in their new homelands. Their only advantages are their youth and willingness to suffer, but they will lose these advantages, as eventually they will lose everything, including their lives. Come to think of it, they will lose everything a lot sooner rather than later.

Tonight, in fact. Before the sun is up. Minutes from now.

The third girl in the car, sitting in the back, is older, and not really a girl anymore. She's cute, slim, and Chinese. Yet fluent in English. She's learned to speak a little Spanish, with a Mexican accent. She is the Mexican girls' boss. They were afraid of her at first but now they like her, although they can barely speak English to one another, because of the accents. You speak Chenglish to us, they laugh. Her name is Jin Li, and they call her Miss Jin, which comes out *MeezaJin*. She's very pretty, in that Chinese way. Slender, with a beautiful face. But so *nerviosa!* Always checking on everything. Telling people where to put the full trash bags for the service elevators. What's she so worried about? They work hard, they do a good job. You need to relax, they finally told her. You ever go out? She shook her head and they could see she wanted to. So now, every week or so, she'll go out with them. Keeps things friendly. MeezaJin is studying them, they know. She's quiet, she watches everybody. They are outsiders in America but more at home than MeezaJin is, though she makes a lot of money and reads English. She even has a white boyfriend—or used to, they are not sure. MeezaJin doesn't say much about herself—like she might be hiding something, like she might be some kind of *criminal*, girl, you know what I'm saying?

The work shift has come and gone, as it does each night. The offices need tidying and vacuuming. The trash cans need emptying. There's precious little conversation between the girls and the office people—a few patronizing *thank-you*s, sometimes a perfunctory nodding of the head on the way out. Nobody pays much attention to the cleaning people in a corporation. Why should they? They're *cleaning people*. Occasionally the girls encounter office workers eating pizza and pulling all-nighters. But for the most part all they see is just big-time corporate calm, the hushed rush of money moving through the wires and across the screens. And there is plenty of money, millions and billions, by the look of it. The marble lobby floor gets buffed at night. The elevators get wiped clean, even the steel-walled service elevators that the girls are required to use. The carpeting is washed. The vending company guy refills the free coffee machine with twenty-four kinds of coffee and tea. The Indian computer guys go through like mice, fixing firewalls, loading spam blockers, cleaning out viruses. Every activity is about money. A way to make more money. The windows are washed, the computers are new. *Money.* Being made in every office. You can almost smell it. The girls like being near the money. Doesn't everyone?

To what degree do they realize that the trash they empty out of the offices each day is in fact the paper trail of deals, trends, ideas, conflicts, sensitive issues, and legal wars—some of which, set before other eyes, may have enormous value? The answer is that they have no actual awareness of this. They are only barely literate in Spanish and more or less illiterate in English. This is expectable. Indeed, it has been purposefully expected: they have been hired by MeezaJin for their distinct inability to read English, their unknowingness about the ornate structures of capital and power through which they lightly pass each night. Industrious as they are, their naïveté also has value. Much of New York City depends upon such people. The ones who know nothing. The city needs their labor, compliance, and fear. You could question these girls in a court of law. *Exactly which proprietary documents were you removing, Miss Chavez?* They could never answer.

Jin Li likes these Mexican girls, though. They work hard, they do not complain. She knows that they do not suspect her of anything other than an eagerness to exploit their labor. She knows too that the building services managers who contract with CorpServe, tough guys with keys and beepers and walkie-talkies, see in her a pretty Chinese girl whose English is not so good—she purposefully makes it worse when she speaks to them—and they think she will be a little cheaper. They are right, too. The Chinese are always a little cheaper, when they want to be. They figure out how to do it, how to undercut everyone else, and then they become indispensable. Jin Li's customers are eager to exploit her eagerness to exploit others. People expect the Chinese to be brutal to their workers when they need to be, even in America, and most of the time they are not disappointed.

Tonight the two Mexican girls have worked hard stuffing blue plastic bags into the service elevator of a building near Fifty-first Street and Broadway, with Jin Li supervising. CorpServe is contracted for nine floors of the building: the sixteenth through nineteenth floors, commercial loan processing offices for a bank, and the twentieth through twenty-fourth floors, the national management offices of a small pharmaceutical company. Jin Li runs eight crews at different midtown Manhattan locations each night and floats among them. The office layouts are all roughly similar, with a service elevator that drops into a street-level truck bay where CorpServe's immense mobile shredding vehicle is parked. There an older man in a blue uniform matching theirs tosses the bags into a sucking orifice that shreds them into confetti. This man is Chinese, like Jin Li, and at times she comes down to the truck bay with certain piles of bags, issues specific instructions to him, then watches to see that he complies. The roar of the shredders drowns out their speech. They both know that they are always being watched by ceiling-mounted security cameras, some of them remote-swiveling, and they also both know how easy it is to work around them. You just have to know the angles. The cameras can see the CorpServe truck but not into the truck. You can set aside a few bags marked by hand with a special inch-high Chinese character and the camera doesn't know.

But that was hours past and now the night's work is done and the girls laugh and listen to the Latino radio station and feel the salty mist off the water. The beach parking lot is usually empty at this hour. Nobody bothers the girls, but if someone does—some cracked-out motherfucker, some drunk-ass wannabe punk—they have pepper spray in their purses. Tonight they drink a little cheap jug wine in plastic cups, dance in their seats to the radio. The Mexican girls ask MeezaJin about her white boyfriend. I liked him! So macho for a white guy! What happened? one of the girls asks, wriggling in a seat patched with duct tape. Oh, you know . . . Jin Li laughs but is quick to look toward the water. It wasn't going to work out. But she doesn't elaborate, barely admits the real reason to herself. She was forced to end it. Listened to his phone messages asking her to call. Hated herself for not calling him back. What he did to her in bed—thinking about not getting *that* will just upset her. She's had relationships with *gweilos* before—British, German, Italian. She likes them, much better than Chinese men, and this one was best of all. And maybe that's why she's here tonight, just to forget him.

Now Jin Li feels the wine in her bladder and slips out the passenger-side door to go pee in the sea grass. She has a bit of toilet paper folded in her purse with her and steps over the lip of the parking lot toward a dirt path that leads to a private spot. Private and disgusting. People hang out down there lighting up crack pipes or having sex, and so she is careful before she disappears into the grass. You have to watch out for broken bottles, used condoms, tampons, rotting chicken wings. The girls in the car can no longer see her, so she listens a moment—is anyone lurking down there in the grass? She hears nothing, though the wind is blowing now, rain in it. She braves the dark path and finds a place where she will squat down.

She is just pulling up her pink panties when she hears a low diesel vibration nearby. What is it? She walks halfway up the path and crouches in the grass below the parking lot. Two trucks are pulling into the lot, one a big pickup, tricked out with fog lights and custom chrome parts, and the other a huge commercial vehicle, big as a municipal garbage truck but shaped differently. It's too dark to know what colors they are. The trucks brake to a sudden stop next to the little Toyota. The pickup sits directly behind the car, pinning it against the curb of the parking lot, and the other truck has slipped up on the driver's side, an inch away, so tight the door can't be opened. What are they doing? What do they *want* to do? Two burly men get out, one from each truck, and rush around to the unblocked side of the little car.

Standing in the weeds, the rain making her blink now, Jin Li can see that the two Mexican girls have rolled up the windows and are screaming inside their little car.

One of the men shatters the sunroof of the Toyota with a hammer, then keeps his foot on the front passenger door, in case the girls try to push it open. Meanwhile the second man hooks something on the back bumper of the car—a chain, she thinks—then starts a motor on the bigger truck. Moving quickly, he pulls a huge hose off a spool on the truck and drags it around to the broken sunroof. He shoves the nozzle of the hose downward into the car, releases a lever, and holds the thick hose as it sends its gurgling contents inside onto the girls. The hose bucks and kicks, the flow inside sloshy and heavy.

Behind the windows the screaming intensifies.

What should she do? The car is filling quickly, a line of dark stuff rising against the windows. The only way out is across the parking lot, where Jin Li will be seen. Behind her is the sharp sea grass and sand. Her cell phone is sitting in her apartment in Manhattan, charging. She never takes it to work, on purpose: cell phones give law enforcement a perfect record of your movements. She has an untraceable walkie-talkie in her purse that she uses to call the other CorpServe crews. But its effective range is only about a mile, good enough for midtown Manhattan but no good in Brooklyn . . .

One of the girls is pushing on the driver's door now, banging it against the big truck pulled up tight against the car. But the door will open only a crack, no more. Then a hand shoots out of the passenger window, wildly firing pepper spray. The man holding shut that door slaps the hand and the spray can flies to the pavement.

"Richie!" the taller man calls through the rain. "That's enough!"

Jin Li fumbles in her purse for the walkie-talkie and clicks it on. Nothing but windy static. "Hello? Hello?" she tries in English. Nothing.

Now the lights of the car go on and the engine starts. The car lurches forward to the lip of the parking lot, jolting the truck behind it. But the chain on the bumper holds. The car's back wheels spin violently, burning rubber, the smelly smoke drifting over the sea grass. Then the engine slows, as if in capitulation. Inside the car the girl's foot is slack now. Something is oozing out of the passenger window, dripping down the glass.

"Richie, you fuck, let's go!" the man screams.

The man holding the hose doesn't move.

"Turn it off!"

The man named Richie pulls the lever and withdraws the nozzle. More stuff pours out lumpily from the broken sunroof. The car is full. He replaces the hose onto the truck, then unhooks the chain.

"Go faster!"

The little $125 car doesn't move against the lip of the parking lot, even though its lights are still on and the engine putters. The taller man removes his boot from the front passenger door, jumping back as it opens just enough to release a torrent of ooze. Then he does a strange thing. He reaches around to lock the door and uses all his weight to slam it shut. Then he waits as Richie moves the bigger truck and does the same thing with the driver's door.

He locked both doors, Jin Li thinks. Why?

"Get out of here!"

The bigger man hurries now to his pickup. The whole thing has taken perhaps six minutes. The big truck reverses in a half circle, then shoots forward out of the lot. The pickup truck backs more tightly, swings around, and follows the big truck. They drive without lights, fast.

In ten seconds they are gone.

Jin Li runs toward the car. The wet wind has shifted, and the smell has alerted her. She knows that smell from China, would know it anywhere. The public pit latrines in the smaller towns. The holes in the ground next to huge construction sites in Shanghai where the workers squat over cutout boards. The raw sewage spewing into the rivers. Yes, she knows this smell.

She hurries up to the car and pulls on the doors just to be sure they are locked. Does she see movement inside, a hand flailing through the dark liquid against the glass? She looks around for something to break the window and flies over to the edge of the lot, where she frantically scrabbles around in the grass, her hands raking through plastic bags, old newspapers, beer cans, anything but what she needs. Suddenly she finds a heavy chunk of asphalt. Too much time has gone by! Right? How could anyone—? She awkwardly carries the asphalt back to the car and after three tries breaks the front passenger window. Wet, thick muck streams out, spatters her, the smell horrific. Fecal gases. Fetid urine. She gags, bile burning her throat. She hits the safety glass again and again to make a hole large enough to reach through. Finally. She drops the asphalt and thrusts her arm into the cold, lumpy wetness and feels around for the door lock, the broken glass rasping against her wrist. She finds the lock, pops it up, pulls on the door—it flies open, a great thick black tongue of filth spewing out across the lot.

"Come on!" Jin Li shrieks in Chinese. The stench is sickening, burns her eyes. She reaches in and finds one of the girls. No movement! Too much time has gone by! Seven or eight or even nine minutes! She pulls an arm, and the body of the girl falls limply out to the pavement, covered in muck. Jin Li wipes at the girl's face. Her mouth is filled, black hair tangled and wet with the stuff. She is not breathing. Jin Li rolls her over, clears the mouth, pushes on the back. Nothing! She runs to the other side of the car, breaks the glass there, soaking herself, opens that door, the sewage gurgling as it empties from the car.

The girl is dead weight, slumped against the steering wheel, but Jin Li pulls her free and tries to get her breathing. She doesn't respond. Jin Li is weeping in fear and frustration. Come on, come on! she says, pushing on the girl's back, wiping the stuff out of her mouth. Nothing. Jin Li can't even look at her eyes, which are mudded over with gunk. The girls were scared, they hyperventilated, they inhaled the wet muck deep into their lungs. As they lost consciousness, the stuff oozed down their throats, suffocating them. Same as being held underwater for long minutes. Now the girls both lie on their stomachs on the pavement, still as death while the tongue of filth spreads across the parking lot as the car empties, the rain faster now and forming rivulets that travel toward the storm drains at the end of the lot.

Jin Li hears a woman's voice talking excitedly in Spanish, and she freezes. Who? She looks at the girls. But the girls appear to be—yes—*dead*, bodies already sinking softly into themselves. Yes, it's true, she tells herself. Dead! Now comes Latino dance music. The radio is still on in the car and the muck has drained below the dashboard speakers. *"Yo te voy a amar hasta el fin de tiempo!"* wails a singer's voice.

The first light of day is on the horizon, showing the rain gusting across the lot.

Jin Li understands now. Someone knows. Someone knows what she was doing. They saw her get into the car in Manhattan and followed. They wanted *her*.

She runs. Fleeing over the pavement, wet black hair streaming behind her, eyes wide, she runs for her life.

The seats directly behind home plate in Yankee Stadium are so close to the field that the usual metaphysics of baseball spectatorship are warped by reality. What was distant becomes near. What was giant becomes life-size. What was fantasy is observable fact. You are so close that you can see the calm face of Alex Rodriguez as he steps up to home plate. You can watch the clay fall off Derek Jeter's spikes as he taps them with his bat. You can see Jorge Posada, the great Yankee catcher, tighten his meaty fingers around the handle as the pitcher begins his windup. An aisle rises from field level directly behind home plate, perfectly centered. The seats to the immediate left and right of the aisle are thus the best positions from which to judge the perfection of a pitch, especially if one leans into the aisle to get a centered look over the backs of the umpire and catcher crouching behind home. From this perspective it seems that the pitcher is throwing the ball at *you*, and spectators in these seats find themselves leaning back as the ball pops into the catcher's mitt. It's that close. You are here, you are in the game.

These seats are also notable for the population that occupies them—the city's power hitters and those whom they favor. Corporations own large blocks. The Yankees management itself doles out tickets to sponsors, celebrities, and major league officials. The half dozen or so eye-level seats on either side of the aisle that afford this opportunity are thus, for true fans, arguably the best seats in the stadium, better than the plush corporate boxes and the media suites above them. The proof can be discovered by who sits here: the select few often include a scout from the archenemy Boston Red Sox, armed with a radar gun to measure pitch speed and a clipboard on which to record the subtle patterns of each player's behavior. That the man sports a fat World Series Championship ring on his hand is a sacrilege to the Yankees fans around him. They remember how the Red Sox stole the championship from the Yanks back in 2004. But these are not the cheap seats high in the upper deck, where men hoot madly when the Yanks score, belly bumping and sloshing their beers in tribal frenzy. No, down here in the realm of money, such an enemy figure is in no danger. Everybody is *always* safe in the good seats, because the security men in their blue blazers are nearby, *always* watching—

Who, exactly? It really *isn't* celebrities and politicians, not day in and day out. Who, then? The complete game-by-game information as to who possesses the tickets to particular seats is available only to the management of the New York Yankees, but to someone who frequently sits in this area, the season ticket holders would be apparent—there is the Citicorp section, the Time Warner section, the Goldman Sachs section, and so on. Ford, ExxonMobil, HSBC, DuPont, Pfizer, Google, Japan Airlines. This dense clustering of corporate power adds a second layer of prestige to the seats; one is *among* the elect, which would appear to prove that one is *of* the elect as well—a pleasant conclusion few can resist. Sprinkled through these official and corporate blocks of seats are smaller blocks—two, three, or four seats, usually—held by wealthy individuals who treat their family, friends, and business associates. The section is also notable for its density of attractive young women, who are not shy about how they bounce up and down the narrow aisles. Indeed, many of these women observe a baseball game dress code, which combines a pink Yankees cap—excellent for holding a ponytail aloft in flirtatious display—sunglasses, and a Yankees shirt insouciantly short about the midriff. Their inhibitions weakened by cups of beer, well aware of the acres of male flesh around them, and frequently harboring not-so-secret fixations on the famous millionaire athletes on the field, these women often perceive the booming musical entertainments on the public address system as an opportunity to stand and dance with unabashed stripperish zeal, arms over their heads, shaking this and grinding that, their collective abandon—dozens! hundreds of dancing girls!—a kind of ritualized female offering within the great echoing male temple of baseball.

Thus, for the male corporate executive alert to his changeable status in the world—down as well as up—the small patch of real estate behind home plate offers so many rich, interlocking pleasures that it is not unusual to see such men sit back in their seats with a deep sigh of gladness and expectation, eager to receive what they know they so rightly deserve.

Which was why Tom Reilly used his corporate seats as often as possible. His job was to make rain for Good Pharma and that meant wooing and wowing a steady stream of potential investors. He himself loved the Yankees—though how many baseball games could a man see in a year?—but what he *really* loved was how great seats at the game put people in a great mood. And he made sure to keep that mood going. After the game he had the limo take his group straight from the stadium to one of the best night spots, maybe a hot little lounge crowded with models, maybe a jazz club downtown. Always something to do in New York, folks. Affable Germans, clever Brits, fake-relaxed Japanese, high-tech cowboys from out west in $7,000 snakeskin boots or gumbo-guzzlers from down south—gimme anybody! They *all* had a blast with Tom Reilly. Show them a good time, make sure they get back to their hotel exhausted with fun. Good *fun*. Good *Pharma*. The first equals the second. They were no longer just a small company. Last year's revenues topped $800 million. Market capitalization now $33.2 billion. Growing steadily. Twenty-eight percent last year. See what happens when you whip *that* out of your pants! New drugs in the pipeline. Emphasis on lifestyle improvement therapies. Good stuff coming out of Good Pharma. That was the message, and the message was the medium, baby. Good Pharma was a new enough biopharmaceutical company that it needed to keep hustling investors. Nibble on our stock, graze on our bonds, get a taste of it. Rub a little of that surging market penetration on your gums, snuff a bit up into your nostrils. Like that? *Taste* that . . . *feel* that—that stream of patents, the awesome products under development? The new applications, the category killers, all aimed at global use? Good stuff, right? Then gobble some of the pills or, better yet, just inject the stock right into your bloodstream. *Good* Pharma! Nine million dollars spent on branding research, too: respondents liked the postironic pun in the company title. Seemed hip, new, futuristically cool in its faux–Big Brother cleverness. "Big pharma" (derogatory but perceived as powerful and efficacious) plus "good karma" (retrohippyish, naturalish, organic or Hindu or religious or *something* kind of humane and nice) equals Good Pharma! They had drugs coming along that were going to make the aging baby boomers start cha-cha-ing all over the golf course. Make them remember their sixth-grade homework, hump everything that moved, lose weight while they slept, dunk basketballs. That was true, in fact, even if anecdotal. The Good Pharma researchers in one of the cartilage-therapy trials had enrolled a couple of *old* NBA players, geezery black giants who felt so good they started dunking the ball again. The stuff was based on some kind of Brazilian tree frog bone cells that they'd cloned. Think of when that hit the market, think of the clip in the webcast commercials when a seventy-year-old black man dunks a basketball! Millions of thick-hipped white women would *demand* prescriptions! Score with Good Pharma!

But now it was time for baseball. The pin-striped Yanks were on the field, expertly whipping the ball around, warming up under a soft seven p.m. sky. Tom had the tickets ready in his hand and settled down in the seats with his two guests, a sixtyish Cuban investor from Miami named Jaime "Jim" Martinez and his protégé, a young man who knew enough to say nada.

"You were right!" agreed Martinez, seeing how close they were to home plate but expecting no less. "Very good seats."

"Absolutely," burbled Tom, the message being *you guys are worth it.* That was half of making a deal, getting that symmetrical rush of greed started. And he should know, he'd made a lot of deals for a guy who was just a few years over forty. Tom Reilly, Senior Executive Vice President for Schmoozing Big Investors. Corporate responsibility for the Manufacture of Extremely Valuable Hype. Skills include Smiling Through the Pain, Showing No Fear, and Lying When Necessary and Sometimes When Not. Good with bankers, researchers, stock analysts, the media, anybody. The public face of the company. Handsome but not too handsome. Not pretty. Manly. Solid. Healthy-looking. Confident. Wife a successful Park Avenue internist in private practice. Children: none yet. Stated reason: Too busy. Real reason: Lazy sperm. Weak, undersexed, insecure sperm. Dud bullets, wet firecrackers. Solution: Maybe in vitro, which his wife, being a doctor, wasn't crazy about; she knew the low odds of success and comparatively higher odds of having preemies. State of marriage: Could be better.

But why think about such things? There was money to be made! And in Jim Martinez next to him, Tom Reilly sensed worthy prey. Martinez possessed a full head of silver hair slicked back Pat Riley–style and a charmer's smile, no doubt useful as he fronted for a venture-cap group trying to diversify into biotech projects. The group's funding came from Cuban doctors, lawyers, and real estate developers in southern Florida and Latin America. Hard-core capitalists, Castro haters. Many of them were on their third or fourth wives, had boatloads of getting-whiter-with-every-generation grandchildren who'd grown up with BMWs in the driveways and going to private schools. The pressure to make more money never stopped, even for rich men! Especially for rich men! The group was looking to take a $54 million position in Good Pharma's new synthetic skin project, which was also to say they expected to get a discount on a purchase worth more than $62 million—a chunk of business that Good Pharma would prefer to sell for $69 million or so. Thus the purpose of the evening. Martinez and Tom were creating an atmosphere of bogus informality and cold-blooded heartiness in order to facilitate the knife-fight negotiation to follow.

So it began! The game, the chatter, the corporate foreplay. Three men in blue blazers and good slacks. Tom ordered beers and hot dogs from the attendant and then set about entertaining the Cubans. The first inning blew by, then the second. Yanks up 2–1 over Baltimore. Good tight pitching, a couple of great plays in the infield, one by Jeter.

Then in the third inning the overpaid Yankee sluggers murdered the Orioles' starting pitcher for five runs. The game suddenly threatened to become a laugher, but now Martinez was on his third beer and had become so relaxed that he'd started to explain how the wealthy Cuban investors in Miami were getting frustrated with all the hurricanes that damaged or slowed their real estate projects and hadn't yet figured out how to wire the post-Castro Cuba for their benefit.

"We're tired of risk," Martinez admitted. "So maybe we try something else. Maybe we see what your company can do for us."

"I think you'll find we have a lot to offer," Tom breezed back. "You know, it's not *quite* public knowledge yet, but some of the early research results coming out of these trials show a very promising—"

At this moment an attendant appeared at the end of their aisle. He checked something written on an envelope.

"Tom Reilly?" he asked Martinez.

"He's right here," Martinez said.

The messenger handed Tom the envelope. "I was told to give this to you."

"Thanks," Tom said, quick fingered with a twenty-dollar bill as a tip. The messenger darted away. Tom threw his guests a smile. "Not enough to have e-mail and a phone in your pocket, now they've got to send actual pieces of paper . . ." He tore open the envelope and withdrew a single sheet of yellow stationery with a blue border. He could stand and read his message in the aisle, but that was rude and also suggested a crisis, exactly what he didn't want to suggest. So he unfolded the paper enough to glance quickly at the message, felt it gore him in a soft, private place, and yet had the presence of mind to nod as if merely receiving confirmation of what was expected.

"Anything good?" the foxy old Cuban from Miami nudged.

"Better than good," Tom lied, half a smile on his face as he slipped the message into his breast pocket. "We try to avoid using wireless for very sensitive info. My secretary sent a messenger . . . it's a big, big deal that just got approved and we need to keep hush about it—you understand. Can't announce anything yet."

He nodded conclusively in response to himself and returned his gaze to the game. How convinced were the men? Maybe not enough.

But he bluffed his way through the end of the inning, then rose to go use the men's room, where he waited urgently in the long line, then bolted to the toilet, closed the door, and sat studying the typed message again.

> Tom, we know that you know there is a problem. We have asked politely but you have not responded to our inquiries.
>
> We are talking about real money. And real consequences if we don't get it back.
>
> Tell us now, while you still can.

For a moment, he felt sick. Hot dogs full of crud, mixing with the beer. A feeling he had too often lately. But he fought back the urge. *I still have some good moves to make*, he muttered bitterly to himself, *a lot of goddamned good moves.* Like the New York Giants quarterback ducking out of the rush from a couple of enormous linemen intent on sacking him. A quick step sideways, backpedal to get a moment of safety, then throw long into the end zone. Escape doom with the great play. His mind was a blur of sports images and Good Pharma spreadsheets. He crumpled the yellow paper and threw it into a bin full of beer cups.

When he returned to his seat, the two men from Miami were—what? Gone? He looked up and down the aisles for them.

An older man in the row ahead of him turned around.

"You see those Cuban guys who were here with me?" Tom asked.

The man nodded. "That messenger came back while you were away. He handed them another letter." The man pointed under the seat and Tom leapt to pick it up.

> Gentlemen, your affable host this evening, Mr. Tom Reilly, is in deep trouble. He may be an accessory to large financial crimes. We suspect that it is not in your best interests to be seen with him in such a public venue.

A great cheer went up. Rodriguez had lifted a giant homer into the center field seats. The crowd stood, roaring exultantly as the big man loped around the bases. No one saw the pharmaceutical company executive curled in his seat, fetal in his dismay, at last vomiting at what he knew was going to happen.

Her name is not important here. She was in her late thirties and working as a legal secretary for a firm on Park Avenue. The attorneys there, men and women alike, disgusted her with their self-importance, their preening fatuousness. But she kept this to herself. She had tried the single life and mostly found disappointment. In her early years some of the young associates tried to date her and she let herself be taken to dinner and then into bed, but these men were, whether they knew it or not, auditioning wives. They talked love and devotion but were in truth matrimonial credentialists; they wanted a wife to have a degree from a good college at the very least and an advanced degree as well. And this she did not. Within a few years it got around the firm that she was easy, that she opened her legs after a few dates, and this, of course she knew, was true. So what? If you liked a guy, why wait? Why is it called *easy*? Why not *eager*? Yes, eager. Once in an associate's office after a late-night race to prepare a court document. Bent over on the windowsill, watching taxis fly down Park Avenue. It *was* exciting. So she liked men, *eagerly*. Liked their muscles and penises and whiskers. Hands and shoulders. Even a man's Adam's apple could be sexy. Who could blame her? But once she'd been labeled, the associates of any promise and discretion steered away from her, and this meant that the younger associates, new to big city life, took their shots, as did some of the older partners, the divorced, almost divorced, and never married. Mostly a disgusting lot, wheezers and nose-hair neglectors. Her boss, one of the most senior partners, pretended not to notice, and in time the associates and the younger secretaries cycled away to other jobs and people forgot who she had been and began to see her as yet another unmarried, now aging, and lonely woman, which, even though she was only thirty-eight, was true.

As her boss got on in years, he had come to depend on her more and more. She began to catch important errors in his memory and in the letters he wrote, and to his credit he recognized that she was extending his career. But more to his credit, he quietly siphoned off part of his yearly bonus to her—a secret cash arrangement that occurred outside of her regular salary. She worked longer hours and by degrees realized that she did not have the energy and hope necessary to sift and sort through the men still available to her, the thin-fats, the optimistic depressives, the probably/actually gay, the pervomaniacs, all of them. How disappointing! How tiresome! The men in their forties were looking for thirty-two-year-olds, the men in their thirties looking for twenty-five-year-olds. She knew the drill; she'd *been* those women once, enjoyed the attention of older men. Swooned over their *sophistication*, their *power*, their sexy salt-and-pepper hair. Good grief. What was wrong with her now? Her breasts hadn't dropped much. She was still juicy, still *wanton*—maybe. Some of her unmarried friends who suffered from perenially disappointed ovaries had decided to have babies without men, buying sperm on the Internet, lighting a bunch of candles in a dark room, lying back and inseminating themselves. But she didn't want to be a lonely single mom. She didn't know *what* she wanted, except that something interesting, anything, had to happen before—before she turned into her mother!

So she moved from her cozy, so-totally-hip apartment on Twelfth Street in Greenwich Village, where everyone white under the age of fifty was addicted to the Internet, to a three-bedroom house in the Bay Ridge section of Brooklyn, one of the many little tribal neighborhoods that fed the city each day. Still largely Italian but now everybody was living there—Brazilians, Chinese, Russians, Indians, Mexicans, Vietnamese, Africans, even Iraqis. All working crazy hours trying to squeeze onto the jammed, hot-breathed dance floor called American turbo-capitalism. Rang your doorbell, asked if you had work. Painting, roofing, cut grass, you need car washed, lady? Bay Ridge was also the same neighborhood where her parents lived, so she could keep an eye on them. She bought the house using the money the old partner had funneled to her, and this pleased her. She could walk to the subway and always get a seat going into work. Easy, a little shopping on the way home. But her life became quieter and even lonelier. She paid her bills, she planted marigolds and peas and lettuce in the spring, she drank a glass of wine with the news and another before going to bed. The months flew by. She perused the newspaper but forgot what she read, she never remembered her dreams, she bought sensible shoes, she didn't bother to masturbate. Nothing was happening. She considered actually going to church, for the social interaction. How terrible was that?

Certainly she never expected to meet anyone. But one warm Saturday afternoon she opened her door and saw a man in a baseball cap and green T-shirt standing in the yard next door. He was shielding his eyes and inspecting the roof, a short yellow pencil and clipboard in one hand. Meanwhile, she inspected him. "Hi!" she suddenly called, surprising herself. He turned toward her and slipped his pencil into his breast pocket. They got to talking. His father owned the house, he said, and he was just taking care of it, for now. His old red pickup truck sat in the driveway and she realized she'd seen it there a few times before. His name was Ray Grant, he told her. She liked Ray, liked him in the way women will sometimes like a certain man. He seemed unaware of how his shoulders and arms looked in the T-shirt, the way his jeans hung on his hips. She didn't see a wedding ring. His fingernails were clean. His eyes were the bluest blue, which she always loved, and she saw both confidence and aloofness in him. He wasn't going to tell her anything, or not much, even.

Okay—she threw herself at him! Invited him in for coffee, and she heard his heavy boots behind her as they went up the stairs into her kitchen. Coffee became a late lunch. He wasn't in a hurry, didn't check his watch. Didn't say much, either. She just talked and talked, got herself more excited.

"So your dad owns the place next door?" she repeated, when the conversation paused. "Maybe I've seen him a few times, come to think of it, but not in a while."

Ray nodded. "He's sick, so I came back to be with him."

"Sick?"

"Very sick."

"I'm sorry—is he, will he get better, I mean?"

At this Ray cut his eyes to the floor in quiet sorrow. Lifted his baseball cap and put it on again. Full head of hair, she noticed. She could see the pain in him, how he tried to keep it inside. I kinda love this guy, she told herself, what's wrong with me?

"No," Ray finally said. "He's not going to get better."

She just looked into those blues eyes. "I'm so sorry."

"It's a rare blood-vessel cancer. Angiosarcoma. They went in looking, thinking it was something in his kidneys. But it was all through him. He's got, I don't know, a few weeks maybe. Hard to judge."

She'd just met this man. Don't pry, she told herself.

"Came back?" she said anyway. "I mean *you*. You came back from where?"

He looked at her in a way that meant he wasn't going to tell her. "I was away," he said. "I've been back about three months."

"Oh."

"I've been mostly overseas the last five years or so," he added. "Don't need to say much more than that."

"Even if I'm dying to know?"

"Even then," he said, but gently.

She played with the edge of the tablecloth, folding it back, smoothing it, folding it again. "Sounds sort of glamorous."

"It's in no way glamorous."

Time to change the topic, she thought, time to stop acting like a schoolgirl. "What did your dad do before he got sick?"

"He's been retired a long time. Before that, a cop."

"Are you a cop?"

"Nope."

But there was something in the way he said this, a pause that meant something. "You just look after your father's house?"

"Yes."

"He has just one rental?"

"Six."

"All kind of like the one next door?"

"He kept buying them, back in the eighties when they were cheap."

She did the math. The houses probably weren't fancy, but with the staggering rise in real estate prices in New York City, the sick father was a wealthy man by everyday standards.

"Six rentals?"

"Yes."

"So you're here in the city," she ventured. "Are you trying to find gainful employment, are you dating five girls at once, are you reading any good books lately?"

Ray smiled. "You want those answers?"

"Girl doesn't mind knowing a few things."

He nodded playfully. *Game on.* "Okay, sure. I'm not looking for work. I'm taking care of my father, nothing more than that. I'm not dating five girls at once. I was seeing someone but she told me we were over a few weeks ago—"

"Was your heart totally broken?"

He studied the question. "It presented an opportunity to think."

"That sounds like a lot of you know what."

"It might be. But I try not to be too attached to anybody or anything. I fail but I try."

"Are you Buddhist?"

"No, but they have interesting ideas."

She just studied him, this Ray Grant. He was earnest. No spin, no attitude. She liked this.

"And as for the books, yes, I'm reading a couple of good books right now. Does that answer your questions?"

"Yes, thank you."

He nodded. "So," he said matter-of-factly, "what are we doing here?"

"What are we doing here?" she repeated, knowing exactly what he meant.

Ray looked at her, into her. She saw his intensity, the thing she had sensed the first moment she saw him. Now it was focused on her. She wanted this but it scared her.

"What do you want to do?" he said.

"What—do what?"

He just gazed into her. She couldn't lie to him.

"You seem like you want to do something now," he went on, more softly. "I could be wrong, though."

"Yes," she whispered, then nodded. "I do. Yes."

There was a silence in the kitchen, a silence through which many messages traveled. Outside the afternoon had become cloudy and the kitchen was shadowed. She felt nervy and excited now.

"Go take your clothes off and get in your bed," Ray told her.

She couldn't even manage a little ironic smile, like *who do you think you are?* He was being truthful. He knew who he was and he knew who she was—and in her case that was somehow already naked. "What are you going to do?" she began, breathing a little too quickly. "I mean, what are you going to do while I'm removing all my clothes and becoming even more vulnerable?"

"I'm going to make a phone call and then I'm going to walk straight into your bedroom and we will get to know each other, is my guess."

"Then what?"

He smiled. "Then—what do you think?"

"Are you going to kill me?"

Maybe she was joking, maybe not. Actually she wasn't.

"No," he said.

"You promise?"

"I promise."

"Okay then." She tried to sound breezily confident. "I'm trusting you, Ray Grant."

She stood up slowly, then turned into the hallway. I must be crazy, she told herself. This is the stupidest thing I've ever done in my life.

She pretended to walk down the hall but stopped. She heard the little musical chime of his cell phone being turned on.

"Hi," came Ray's voice, echoing from the kitchen. "I'm going to be late . . . no, no, the house is fine. The roof has a few years to go. I'll be there before nine . . . Did she clean you? . . . Good. How's the pain? . . . Remember, the doctor said you could—I'll come home now, Dad, if it hurts too— . . . well, okay, but I want you to please please take it if— there's no reason to—okay? . . . I think they're playing Baltimore again, just turn it on . . . Yeah, okay, I'll see you then."

She heard him snap the phone shut and she hurried to her bedroom. She kicked off her shoes, pulled back the covers.

"Hey there," Ray said in the doorway.

"Hi." She turned around. It had been years since she'd been undressed in front of a man. She didn't look as good as she used to, no getting around it. "You promised, remember?"

He flicked off the light. They kissed in the darkness, then she pulled away and sat on the bed to finish undressing. "Honestly, I never do this," she protested aloud. "It's not like me at all."

He didn't say anything.

"Is your silence judgmental?"

"Nope."

"What is it?"

"Confessional," Ray said.

"That's a funny word. What are you confessing to?"

"My own weaknesses."

"You don't look weak to me."

He had undressed and came now and stood before her. She put her hands on his chest first and felt the warm firmness of the muscles there. He was relaxed, which relaxed her.

"You surprised me," came his voice. "Didn't see it coming."

"You might be lying," she whispered. "But I appreciate the attempt." She leaned into him and kissed his belly and drew her hands down the rippled flank of his stomach and felt a long section of puckered, knotty flesh.

"Oh," she said. "What?"

"Scar," he answered in the dark, voice soft. "Old scar."

"What did it?"

"Something very hot."

But she barely heard this. She drew her hands around the hard arc of his buttocks, felt the muscle there. Now her eyes were closed. She felt a little dizzy. Someday I will be an old woman and will need things to remember, she told herself. This makes me happy. She moved her hands again.

"That's good," he said.

Later, after he had not killed her, she rolled in the damp sheets. Rolled ecstatically, as if at the edge of a far dream. I had forgotten, she thought, I'd actually forgotten.

"You hungry?" she murmured. "We never had dinner."

"Absolutely."

They stood languidly, in no hurry. In the half-light she saw the scar on Ray's stomach. Patchy skin grafts, maybe a couple of operations. What did it feel like to have the front of your stomach burned off? Don't ask him, she told herself, he doesn't want to talk about it.

She pulled on a robe as he slipped into his pants. In the kitchen he sat in a wooden chair while she made pasta and a quick salad. He also knotted his shoes, slipped his cell phone into his pocket, and put his baseball cap back on. For a moment she worried that he was eager to leave, that she had disappointed him somehow. But then he leaned back in the chair and her anxiety passed. She lit a candle and opened a bottle of wine. I'm going to make a little toast to the pleasures of sexual intercourse, she thought. She took out two glasses, poured wine in them, and set the table, feeling better than she had felt in—oh, God, in *years*. Maybe we'll do it again tonight, she hoped. I'm going to keep this guy here to the last minute. She glanced at the clock, knowing her mother would call before too long, exactly what she didn't want. This reminded her of Ray's father.

"Do you need to call your dad?" she asked.

"He's probably watching the Yankees game. I'll need to check in, though."

By phone? Or did he have to go back to his father's house? She was about to ask when she noticed car lights slide up her driveway.

"Weird."

"What?" asked Ray.

Holding the steaming pot of pasta, she glanced out her kitchen door.

"It's a limousine in the driveway. A man is getting out. More men."

She took a step backward.

"You're not expecting anyone?"

"No." She looked again. "They're checking out your truck."

"I forgot to lock it."

"They're not opening the—they're coming *here*, I think!"

The large figure knocked on the glass of the door. Ray stood up. Now a hand pounded the glass.

"Hello?" she called anxiously. "Who is it?"

The pane of glass above the door handle shattered. She screamed and jumped back behind the kitchen table.

A gloved hand reached in past the broken glass and unlocked the door. The hand disappeared. In stepped a big Chinese man in a black suit. He moved to one side and three more Chinese men came in.

"Ray," said the first man, pointing. "You go with us."

Ray moved between her and the men, protecting her. "Who are you guys?"

They didn't answer. The first Chinese man pulled back his coat to show his gun. Two of the others slipped behind Ray.

"Miss lady," said the Chinese man. "Do not call the police. Or we will come back here and"—he saw the pot of pasta in her hand—"and we will eat up your bad noodles."

The two men put their hands on Ray's shoulders. A tremor ran through him, she sensed, a desire to respond violently that he repressed right away. He looked at her. "It's all right," he said. "Don't call the police. I mean it."

But she knew it wasn't all right. She stood at the kitchen door as they dragged Ray down the steps and into the limo.

Was this really happening?

She wanted to scream, she needed to scream. They were taking him away! The doors shut, and the long car reversed smoothly out of the driveway, then disappeared.

What to do? Shouldn't she do *something*? She gazed down at the broken glass on her kitchen floor. Her hands shook. They could have hurt her. What were they going to do to Ray? He didn't know the men, but—but what? He accepted their presence, she realized, as if he had quickly figured out who they were. She picked up the phone. Ray said don't call, so I won't, she thought. No, actually I will. She started to dial the police. But stopped . . . maybe it would make things worse for Ray, and she couldn't take that chance.

Instead she slipped the phone in her robe pocket and went out the kitchen door. Ray's red truck sat in the same place in the driveway parallel to hers, and she tried the passenger door. It opened. She stepped up high and climbed inside, aware that the cab light inside illuminated her to anyone driving by or looking out a window. She was expecting to find fast-food wrappers, coffee cups, all the usual guy-in-a-truck junk. Instead she found a clipboard with Ray's father's name and address on it and notes Ray had taken on the house. She inspected his tight, careful handwriting. Under the clipboard lay three books, one on the effect China was having on the global economy, another a philosophical treatise on death and consciousness, and the last a thick history of Afghanistan published in London in 1936. I have absolutely no idea who this guy is, she told herself. She popped open the glove compartment. Engine repair records, clipped carefully together. Beneath them lay a ten-inch bowie knife, the handle worn and taped over. She slipped the knife out of the sheath an inch or two. The blade gleamed. It scared her and she slipped it back.

From there she looked under the seats. Beneath the driver's side was a standard roadside emergency kit, with flares, flashlight, and jumper cables. Under the passenger's seat she pulled out a girl's yellow canvas tennis shoe. Everything about it suggested flirty sexiness. She set it next to her own foot. Too small for her. A fine dainty foot. A *thin* sexy foot attached to *thin* sexy ankles. Not worn at all, new. She felt a little jealous now, a little mad. Ray had definitely had sex with the woman who'd lost this shoe. You just *knew* these things. That was what he meant when he said the word "confessional." Maybe this woman was the one who'd broken it off. But why? Who would dump a guy like Ray? she thought. She suddenly remembered the gasping noises she'd been making in bed, her hands clutching the sheets.

Frantic to know something, to *do* something, she swept her hand all the way under the truck seat. Her fingers found a Tupperware container. She popped open the top. Inside was what—a dead animal? No, it was hair, thick and curly and black. How disgusting! A note was tucked inside. She pinched it up, careful not to touch the hair. The note said:

Hey Ray-Gun, I told you I'd send you my beard. What did you do with yours? I'm riding the surf here in Melbourne. Come visit me if you want. I'm with you—given up e-mail. It's too fast. I need to slow down, a lot. I'm just waiting for the next assignment. Also I got some weird head pains from those pills they made us take. I am having my usual postmission meltdown. It's the little bodies that do it to me most. You understand, I know you do. Sorry to hear about your dad. I know you love him so much. Not sure if I can keep doing this. Will drink and whore my way to higher consciousness. Maybe you survive it better than me. Maybe not. I don't have many ideas anymore, not sure if I'm actually a genuine American. Might not be. Can't see myself going home, just too weird. You get any good ideas, send them to me. Let me know if you get a new assignment. All right, surf's up in like an hour.

Z

Beneath the scruffy hair was a photograph of two muscular men with long beards. Ray and another man, presumably Z, the one who'd written the letter. Deeply tanned, in dirty T-shirts, mountains behind them. Soldiers? she wondered. She didn't see any weapons. Her eyes lingered on Ray's arms and shoulders, their obvious strength. She knew what they felt like against her fingers.

The phone in her pocket rang, startling her. She folded up the note and shoved it and the photo back into the Tupperware and the shoe back under the seat, as if the caller might be able to see her. It was her mother, ready to have the usual conversation. She hopped down from the truck and went back into the kitchen.

"Mom, let me call you back."

But her mother wouldn't. They got into it from there. The doctor's visit. Your father's arthritis. Another ten minutes of her life gone to this. She found herself drifting into the bedroom to look at the rumpled bed. The sheets seemed to still have some of Ray in them. But he was gone.

"You sound like you're *crying*," her mother said. "You crying? What's the matter?"

She hung up. All right, she was crying. She meets a great-looking guy in *her driveway*, lets him screw her brains out for an hour, and she's happily cooking him dinner when—*hello?*—a bunch of gangster-ish Chinese men drag him out the door? Who wouldn't be freaked out by that? Of course I'm going to cry! In the kitchen, she found a flashlight in the drawer. Maybe there was more stuff in Ray's truck. She went to the kitchen door and opened it.

The old red pickup truck was gone, like it had never been there. Like Ray had never been there, never been with her . . . and she knew, with that odd true knowledge that sometimes reaches far beyond one-self, that she would never see him again.

They took the Belt Parkway toward Manhattan, gliding at a smooth seventy, the open water to their left. One of the big ocean liners was leaving the harbor, portholes lit up in the dark, a silent enormity. The four Chinese men around him didn't seem to notice. They appeared lost in their own thoughts, as if Ray were an inanimate package they were transporting. He told himself to relax. What were they going to do—kill him? He doubted it. There was just the beginning of a logic to all this. Jin Li had told him one night at dinner she couldn't see him anymore, that she was very sorry, there were things she couldn't explain. Yes, it had to do with her brother Chen, she admitted, the one who lived in Shanghai and considered himself a big-deal businessman. She'd sounded anxious. Ray had tried calling. They hadn't fought. He'd been worried about her, cursed himself, and called a few more times. But nothing, no communication, for two weeks. Long enough that you think it really is over. Long enough to get lonely. Maybe the men knew why Jin Li hadn't answered her phone. How had they found him? They must have located his father's house, forced him to tell them where Ray was, gone to that address, seen the truck, seen the lights in the nice woman's kitchen. Seen Ray sitting at the table.

"Guys," he said. "I need to call my father, that okay?"

The men looked at him silently.

Ray pulled out his phone. "He's sick and I have to check—"

One of the men grabbed the phone and handed it to the man who had spoken to Ray in the kitchen. He scrolled through the numbers. He looked up at the others and said something about Jin Li.

"Yes, her number is in there," Ray admitted. "I've called her a lot."

"Who else did you call?" asked the man.

"Not too many people," said Ray. He waited. "So let me call my father, guy."

They didn't answer him and he counseled himself to be patient, not to overreact to what was obviously some kind of kidnapping. He hoped that his father had pushed the button on the little electronic box that delivered a preset bolus of Dilaudid, which was synthetic morphine only much stronger. The machine, which had a tube that went straight into his father's arm, provided dosages at regular intervals but also allowed his father to receive a limited number of optional doses when the pain became too great, which happened more frequently now. Ray prayed his father had taken the extra doses and been knocked out, would sleep through Ray's absence. He'd said he'd be home before nine, and that wasn't going to happen. His father got anxious when Ray wasn't there and pawed the blankets in worry, twisting his head painfully toward the doorway. Ray was just going to have to assume that Gloria, the night nurse who had cared for hundreds of terminal patients, would be sure his father was comfortable. He'd set up the hospital bed in the living room, which had more space for equipment and chairs for visitors. Ray was paying for private-duty hospice nurses around the clock, $10,000 a week to care for his father. The policemen's medical insurance didn't do enough. The six houses together were worth at least a couple of million. So spend it. All those windows fixed, crummy bedrooms repainted and repainted again, more than twenty-five years of dealing with deadbeat tenants, busted water pipes, broken refrigerators. Now it was payback time. His dad deserved the best. Ray had gone down to the local bank where his father had first gotten his mortgages, long paid off now, and explained the situation. He'd cashed out one of the houses, and even at $10,000 a week, the money would last many months. It was his father's time that was running out.

"Hey," Ray tried again. "What about the phone?"

The Chinese man in the suit looked at Ray, pushed a button that made the window drop, and flipped the phone into the rushing darkness outside. The cool air swirled around inside the car, then the window went up.

The permanent government of New York City, the true and lasting power, is found in the quietly firm handshake between the banking and real estate industries. Nearly every other business—television, publishing, advertising, law firms, hospitals—is comparatively insubstantial. Only the banks and the developers can tear out a section of the city and replace it with something new. Can alter the feel of a neighborhood, where people walk, eat, and live, and thus actually change what New Yorkers say and feel about themselves, remap their minds even as their city is remapped beneath their feet. The developers destroy the past to improve the future, they make nothing into something, they push away humans they can't use and pull in new ones they can. Who else could gouge a hole large enough for five thousand swimming pools at the southwest corner of Manhattan's Central Park, then erect the Time Warner building, a garish twin-towered, tuning fork of an edifice, stuff it at the lower levels with the very same luxury-junk stores found elsewhere, then charge $40 million for enormous apartments above it?

Of course the apartments were all quickly bought by aging movie stars who didn't care about being hip anymore, Saudi princes with dyed beards, London speculators, the newly rich Spanish, Russian oilmen who'd gotten their money out before Putin stopped them, computer company execs from India. Moguls near and far, not all of whom realized that the "eightieth-floor" penthouses were quite an achievement for a building only sixty-nine stories high.

The limo pulled to a stop outside this building and the men walked Ray to an unmarked side entrance manned by two guards. The intercom buzzed them through and a moment later they stood in an enormous elevator. The men kept the floor display panel hidden from Ray, so he counted seconds. He knew from his training that they were rising about forty feet per second, which put them close to the forty-eighth floor when the elevator stopped. They proceeded to a marbled foyer and arrived in a huge living room with a view over Columbus Circle and northeast to Central Park.

A Chinese man of about thirty, very slender in a tailored black suit, emerged from another room. His eyes flicked over Ray's work boots, old jeans, and green T-shirt.

"Thank you Mr. Ray for coming to see me," he said, waving at the sofas, an enormous gold watch around his wrist.

They sat. The other men moved to the back of the room and stood.

"My name is Chen," said the man. "I have big problem. And I want you to fix this problem."

Ray was silent.

"This is my problem," he went on. "You were boyfriend for my sister, Jin Li. She works for me in New York City. She tells us about you. Everything about you. She loves you very much, everything like that. Then maybe four days ago, she not appear."

"Disappeared?" said Ray. "How do you know?"

"Let me finish talking to you."

"Fine."

"That's right," Chen growled. "Fine for you, fine for me."

Ray started to say something, thought better of it.

"So I will talk now. You listen. Jin Li calls me in China. Very upset. Like that. Two girls that they are with her get killed in their car. The men in the Brooklyn village, they put the shit in the car. But not my sister. Nobody find her. This does not surprise me too much, Mr. Ray. She is, what do you say, self-reliant. Too self-reliant, maybe you know. She leave our family and come to United State. I give her job running my company here and then she not appear. That is my problem. The American police do not know who kill the two girls."

"I wouldn't be so sure."

"I am sure. I pay people to tell some things."

"You can pay people, but that doesn't mean they know."

"I am paying a man who knows all these things!"

Ray shrugged.

"Do you know about this bad thing that happened?"

Ray shook his head. He wasn't following the news much these days.

"The American police do not know my sister was in that car. I read the New York City *Daily News* on the Internet in my country. You can still do that if you know what to do. China government say one big thing, everybody do the other thing, the little thing. The paper only say two Mexico girls, where they put the shit into the car. Very bad. Jin Li, she call me and then she does not go to work, like I say before. I have to tell somebody to run my business. That is big problem just like that. Where is Jin Li, I say. She is good at the business for me. I talk with my lawyer in Chinatown. He say if you ask American police to look for Jin Li they will ask too many question. Just like China! I do not like too many question. I am boss, I have the question. In China we do not like the police. We do not trust them. I do not trust polices anywhere. I want to know where is Jin Li but I cannot find her in this city."

"I'm sure there are plenty of good Chinese private investigators in the city, retired detectives, people like that."

"That is what my lawyer say. Are you a lawyer, too?"

"No," answered Ray.

"So my lawyer get some man to look in her apartment, look at her bank, look at her money, and everything. We do this, we do what he say. Nothing. She is really really hiding, you know what I mean? Or maybe she is dead but how come they do not find the body? I do not think she is dead. She call us, like I say to you. She is upset. This is what she is. Then she did not call anymore to us. But I ask myself why her white boyfriend does not look too much for her? Why he not asking her friends, where is Jin Li? Have you seen her? Maybe he does not love her so much today. That is what my lawyer say. White boy, Chinese girl, no big deal, right?"

"You want me to talk now?" Ray asked.

"No." Chen pointed at one of his men and said something in Chinese. The man left the room. Then Chen turned back to Ray. "Here is what I think. She is hiding somewhere-place and you know where, Mr. Ray, you help her now."

"I don't. I have no idea where she is."

"Then why you do not ask about her and everything like that?"

"I didn't know she was missing."

"I do not believe you."

"I haven't spoken to her for a couple of weeks, and she stopped returning my calls. In America, we call this getting dumped. And you know, we only saw each other a few months. She didn't tell me much about herself."

Chen smiled hatefully. "Maybe you were too busy fucking my sister in the pussy to ask so many question."

"She didn't seem to mind."

"You like the Chinese pussy? You like how tight it is, Mr. Ray? Not like the big fat white—" Chen's interest was distracted by the return of the man who had departed; he carried a cardboard box. The man set it down in front of Chen, who inspected its contents, nodded, and then looked back at Ray. "Let me tell you some extra things. We know many informations about you, Mr. Ray Grant. We pay lot of money to retired NYPD detectives who tell us about you. We know your father was New York City detective. Sixty-three Precinct. There are many people who do not like him. Right now someone could walk into his room and shoot him."

"He's dying. He might even prefer to be shot."

"Maybe yes. But you do not. You want to be with him," Chen ventured, watching Ray's expression. "You need this man, your father, I think to myself."

They'd been watching him for the last few days, Ray realized, running groceries, in and out of the house. Knew when he was there and when he wasn't. Did they also know he was with the woman, then put their plan into motion? Possibly. Barged in to find his father peacefully in bed watching the Yankees game, Gloria sitting next to him. Ray had let himself get distracted. How he hated himself for that now. "I can't help you," he said. "I'm just the guy who was banging your sister, no more, no less."

"I am going to pay you to find her."

"Sorry, not interested."

Chen's right hand played with the gold watch on his left wrist, his small index finger rubbing an intimate circle on the face. "I will pay lot of money. I have lot of money and I will pay lot of money to find her."

Ray looked at Chen directly. "Not interested."

"What will motivation you?"

"Nothing will motivation me. I'm not interested." This wasn't true; he was now quite interested in finding Jin Li, but on his terms, not her brother's.

Chen didn't respond. Instead he pulled a toothpick from his breast pocket and picked at his teeth. Finished, he inspected the toothpick for dental residue, then laid it carefully on the glass table. One of the beefy men standing at the back of the room came forward with a wastebasket and plucked the toothpick up and dropped it into the basket. Then he took out a tissue and wiped the glass table clean.

Chen pointed over Ray's head. "When they sell me this apartment they say the window do not open too much. They say something about cold air-conditions and the architect design. Special glass that is shiny. I say I pay so much American money for this apartment, you say I cannot have window that is open? Everybody say New York is big deal, number-one city. I say no. New York no big deal, too old. Not too smart. China smarter. Shanghai much more smarter. You come to my country, you find out. In Shanghai I get window that is open when I push it. I say this to big New York architects. They say this is one-billion-dollar building, most expensive in New York City ever. I say one billion dollars is very small piece of money in China. They say okay we will fix, we will make you special window, just for you. So now I have special window."

Chen nodded to the men behind Ray. They slid open one of the panels of glass. The night air swirled coldly into the room and the sounds of traffic drifted up from the street.

"We throw you out the window now."

Ray looked at him. "I don't know where your sister is."

"Yes, I possibly believe you."

"Then what's the problem?"

"The problem, Mr. Ray, is you say you will not look for her."

"I don't think I can find her."

"We know you can find her. Jin Li say you have very big military training."

"I don't."

"Jin Li say your passport is stamped Afghanistan, Turkey, Malaysia, places like this."

"She interpreted those facts incorrectly."

"You will look for my sister?"

"No," he said.

"I see. Okay, like I say, okay." Chen pointed at the window. "Out."

"Can I tell you why this is a very stupid idea?"

Chen spoke to his men in Chinese. They stopped.

"This building is new," said Ray. "It's full of extremely rich people like you, Chen. It certainly has one of the best security camera systems in the city. The Saudis and Israelis would never buy in unless the security was good. They have things to worry about these days. Cameras watched you all the way up the elevator. If you throw me off the building, I will hit the street and die—instantly, I hope. Many people will notice this. My death flight might even be captured on video, which means it would be on the Internet an hour later. They will use their cell phones and call the police. One of the Midtown North rolling units will be here within a minute. Meanwhile you will have to escape, going right past all those cameras. The police will probably seal off the building, which is standard procedure when someone falls out of a window, especially when the place is loaded with celebrities and rich people. But let's say you get out of the building. Are you going to escape by limousine? I don't think so. So you would have to take a cab, a hired car, or even walk. Where would you and all your men go? A hotel? The airport? Central Park? You see, there's no—"

"Out!" said Chen.

He didn't bother fighting them. They lifted him up and carried him to the window, then threw him headfirst out of it, face up, his knees bent over the sill, with each man holding one of his feet. His baseball cap fell off. By instinct he grasped the edge of the window. One of the men smashed his hand with the butt of a gun.

"Don't break window!" yelled Chen from within the room.

The men lifted him and pushed him farther out, so that only the heels of his shoes touched the building. He felt their tight grip around his ankles. He weighed about 190 pounds. How long could they hold that? His hands fell below him, blood rushed to his head. His back touched the face of the building, the sheer clean line of windows, most lit, a few dark, dropping below him. I'm upside down, he thought stupidly. Some change in his pockets shook loose and he watched it tumble brightly toward the lighted streets below, taxis flowing around an upside-down Columbus Circle. The yellow pencil fell from his breast pocket. He closed his eyes to calm himself, slowed his breathing. Release your desire, he chanted, for desire causes you to struggle and be fearful. *You desire not to die.* He'd been in worse jams than this one. Far worse.

"Do you agree?" shouted an angry voice.

He said nothing and instead concentrated on his breathing. They wouldn't drop him. It was a matter of outwaiting them, not letting himself be terrorized.

"Mr. Ray! Listen to me. Listen now!"

Something touched his face. He kept his eyes closed. Don't break, he told himself, don't you break.

"You see, you look!"

His eyes stayed closed. He breathed through his nose to slow his heartbeat. It worked. He knew from experience that he could last five minutes upside down if necessary.

"You look!" they screamed. "You see this!"

The thing brushed his face again. He opened his eyes.

"Do you see what that is?" he heard Chen yelling from above.

At first he did not. A box with tubes, hard to focus on while hanging upside down, swinging back and forth in front of his eyes, the tip of one of the tubes attached to a bloody needle.

Then he understood.

His father's morphine pump.

They'd taken it, yanked it right out of the vein in his father's right arm. He needed a forty-milligram bolus of Dilaudid every hour, or the pain was—

"Yes, yes!" Ray screamed. "I'll do it! Yes, get me up!"

When the limousine returned Ray to his father's semidetached house in Brooklyn, two of the three men got out slowly, watching him, but as soon as he was free he bolted toward the front door, carrying the Dilaudid pump. His red truck was back in the driveway, he noticed. He flew in through the cluttered entrance, past all of his father's gardening equipment and landlord supplies, and into the living room, surprising the guard, who jumped to his feet and drew a .45 pistol.

Ray froze, raising his hands. The other men arrived in the room and the guard lowered his gun. The nurse, Gloria, sat next to the hospital bed holding his father's head in both her old hands, bent close to him, lips on his forehead, whispering lovingly to him as he arced his back in pain, digging fitfully at the bed with his shrunken legs. His upper lip was drawn back, showing his old worn teeth, and the lids of his closed eyes fluttered in torment, the brows above raised in disbelief and wonder at the canyon of pain through which he traveled. Ray had seen his father suffer, but this was different; this was an old man on a steel hook.

"Oh!" cried Gloria, seeing that Ray held the drug pump. He handed it to her. "He's been so good, so brave. God has been helping him in this terrible hour."

She plugged in the machine, keyed in the restricted access code, checked the drug supply, and quickly inserted a new intravenous line into his father's arm. The two other Chinese men appeared in the doorway.

"You are the one who did this to my father?" Ray asked the guard.

"He is old," said the guard.

"Would you do this to your own father?" said Ray, smelling alcohol on the man.

"Father never get old."

"We are leaving now," said one of the others. He pointed at Ray and then at the front door. "You go first."

He felt the three men behind him as he walked to the front door. As he passed through the cluttered hallway, Ray let his right hand trail to the side and find a spray can of rust-preventative paint. The left hand grabbed a pair of hedge clippers he'd dropped into the umbrella stand the day before.

He popped the top off the paint, found the spray button with his finger, wheeled, and sprayed the first man behind him right in the eyes. The man screamed and clawed at his face. Ray clubbed him with the paint can and he went down.

As the second man reacted, Ray grabbed the clippers with both hands and clipped savagely at the man's face, taking off the tip of his nose—he cried out and instinctively covered his face with his hands. Ray clipped again, this time sinking the blades into the man's fingers. The man fell to his knees, blood streaming onto the floor.

The third man had his gun out now and fired wildly past Ray, shattering the light fixture. Ray clipped at the outstretched hand holding the gun, missed, then went low and tackled the man, pinning the gun with one hand. His other hand pulled down the hall table and he swept his fingers blindly through its contents. The man was punching Ray in the head with his free hand, grunting with the effort. Ray found a roll of cellophane tape. No good. Loose batteries, a box of tacks. Nothing he could use. He took several blows to the head. The guy was really hitting him. Then his fingers felt a narrow key used to open paint cans that the hardware store on Eighty-sixth Street gave away for free when you bought paint. Shaped like a curved screwdriver. This Ray jammed into the man's ear, the first time into the cartilage, the second time right into the auditory canal. He buried it to the hilt, pounded it with his palm. The pain of a burst eardrum was such that the man went slack, urinated, and began to weep. Ray pulled the gun from his hand, jumped up dizzily, and swept the gun at the three men, all of them balled up in pain.

"No kill! No kill!" the one with the missing nose tip begged.

Ray put the gun to the neck of the third guard. "You understand English?" he screamed.

The man nodded.

"Don't hurt my father! Do not *ever* hurt my father!"

"Okay, boss, okay," the man coughed.

Ray yanked the man to his feet, took the guns from the other two, and kicked them out the front door. The limo driver, a white man, no doubt hired with the car, stared ahead, studiously ignoring the injured men stumbling into it. Their wounds were not life-threatening, Ray knew. He'd seen nearly every kind of injury a human being could suffer, and these were not serious. A phone call would be made, a private doctor found, perhaps in Chinatown in Manhattan but just as likely in one of the enclaves of Chinese doctors in Queens or Brooklyn.

Ray quickly retreated into the living room and saw that the Dilaudid had pulled his father into a deep sleep. Gloria looked up from her book, noticed the guns in his hands, then found his eyes. "I gave him double. He's fine now."

"You?"

She pointed at her Bible. "I got my reading."

Ray checked the window. Two blocks away, the limo sped through a red light. Already the men would be calling Chen and Chen would be calculating his response, wondering if Ray's actions confirmed him for the task of finding Jin Li or whether such sudden violence suggested a reckless lack of judgment. In either case, Ray had revealed himself to Chen, and this in itself constituted Ray's first disadvantage, his first mistake.

Stupid, he berated himself, you can't be so stupid and expect to survive.

It was a good hiding place but she hadn't slept well. Every hour or so she woke as a siren flew by, or someone hollered murderously in the street below, and she found herself hotly disoriented all over again, not sure whether to hang her head out the window and look down or wait soundlessly where she lay. Who would know about the building? A few people. But who would know *she* knew about this building? No one. No one in the world should know, Jin Li told herself. So why am I so nervous?

The night was warm, and thus the five-story building, one of a series of former factories on West Nineteenth Street, had become aromatized by the humidified essences of mold, dust, dead flies, cardboard, and dry-rotting wood—seemingly the layered odor of time itself expiring without end. The structure and six just like it had been built in the early part of the twentieth century; successive waves of real estate speculation had passed through and around these buildings, converting most to loft apartments, offices, showrooms, fancy restaurants that invariably failed, and the like. But a few remained unrenovated, and the reasons usually had to do with structural damage to the building, either from fire or water or, more often, because the building itself was a neglected holding long entangled in a lawsuit, estate matter, or family dispute.

Alone among the seven factories was the building where Jin Li sat up now in the half dawn, thinking she'd heard something. This building was notable for the implausibility of its continued existence;

the place should have collapsed long ago. Why? All five floors were crammed with heavy useless matter, the crème de la crème of junk. The top floor was filled with claw-footed iron bathtubs and pedestal sinks, many of them tagged with information explaining their origin: "Hotel Edison, 1967 renovation," and so on. The fourth floor contained engine parts not only from vintage American cars and trucks of the 1930s, '40s, '50s, and '60s but, even more obscurely, utterly impossible-to-find motorcycles from early German, French, Italian, and British companies long defunct. The weight of these parts alone should have compromised the floor joists decades earlier. On the third floor could be found close to two million pairs of women's nylon stockings, still boxed, ranging in size from "petite" to "queen." The freight elevator was forever frozen on this floor, its bearings finally burnt out. Just to empty the building, either for demolition or renovation, would have required the replacement of the elevator, a considerable and demoralizing expense. Moving downward, the second floor contained thousands of boxes marked "Property of U.S. Department of Housing and Urban Development/New York City Regional Offices." These lost records documented the marginally successful attempt by the federal government to house hundreds of thousands of low-income residents in Queens, Brooklyn, and the Bronx during the economic downturn of the early 1970s. And finally, the ground floor was piled with spools of obsolete fiber-optic cable, bought when the city was rewiring itself in the speculative fever dream of the 1990s.

From time to time people asked about renting cheap office space in the building and these inquiries were fielded by the custodian, a Russian man with strange, faded Cyrillic tattoos on his knuckles who did little more than sweep up the sidewalk once a week and remove flyers advertising art-house movies and new rock bands. He handed the prospective renters copies of the keys to the steel door to the building, told them to use the stairwell, and to go in the middle of the day for the power was off and no lights worked. "And please you drop key in mailbox." But whether the key was returned was a matter of character—as was whether the Russian custodian noticed. He generally didn't, for he noticed very little in life now. He followed the rankings of his favorite European soccer teams, he drank not vodka but four bottle-inches of Sambuca each night from the same crusty glass, and if asked whether he really cared about who came to and went from the cramped and dirty building on Nineteenth Street, he would have admitted he cared not at all.

Returning to that building by way of the stairwell to the second floor, one could easily discover that Jin Li had pushed around some of the boxes of federal housing records to create a small room within them; in this dim space was all she carried with her: an inflatable mattress, a fat wad of cash, her Chinese passport, a small green suitcase containing not only her blue CorpServe uniform but also one nice cotton dress (why she'd hastily packed this, she had no idea), a bag of toiletries, a cell phone now carefully turned off, and a Styrofoam ice box. On the mattress lay Jin Li, looking at the ceiling, thinking again she had heard something downstairs.

What? Anything?

She listened. Nothing—*maybe.*

At least she had planned ahead, Jin Li told herself, keeping the key that the Russian had given her when she'd come looking for cheap office space for CorpServe a few months earlier. The place had been all wrong for her purposes, but its obscurity and neglect had struck her as potentially useful in other circumstances. In China nowadays buildings like this were soon demolished and someone like her brother would put up a cheap apartment building three times higher. The Russian had never asked for the key back and so she'd kept it—in her purse and in the back of her mind as a place she could hide. No one would want to rent space in a firetrap that had no electricity or heat. But still she was anxious. She could have been followed—that was possible. The men at the beach in the big trucks had followed her, after all, had been looking for her and her alone. She was sure. The Mexican girls didn't know anything. How did the men identify Jin Li? She had been so careful. Did they plan on coming back? Were they still looking for her?

And then there was her brother, Chen. As soon as she'd called from a pay phone, he jumped on the first flight he could find to New York

City and started asking around for her, making things worse. Usually it took forever to get a visa to visit the United States, but Chen knew people, was owed money and favors by men and women all over Shanghai and even in Beijing. He'd panicked when she'd called him—not over *her*, but that his clever international criminal enterprise was endangered. "What did you do?" he'd screamed at her in their family's Mandarin dialect. "How did you fuck up?"

It was a question Jin Li couldn't quite answer, though she'd thought about it constantly. CorpServe had been carefully created by Chen with one devious purpose in mind, but in order to appear to be a conventional company it contained three divisions, two of them legitimate business units operating in the open. The first division cleaned New York City offices at conventional rates, bidding for contracts with management companies and corporate operations people. This part of the company ran daily crews in thirty-two buildings, the number naturally fluctuating as contracts were won or lost upon expiration. The crews dutifully cleaned, collected, and hauled dry waste—paper, cardboard boxes, printed matter, coffee cups, and so. on—down to the service bays where the refuse was loaded and removed by one of the city's private carting companies, another distinct business so cutthroat and residually mobbed up that one entered it only at great risk and with even greater connections. It would be a good two generations before anyone with a Chinese name operated such a company in midtown Manhattan.

The second part of CorpServe, which serviced seventeen buildings, both collected dry waste and provided onsite "chain-of-custody" document destruction. The company owned nine forty-four-foot mobile units, each of which was divided into a shredding equipment area and a payload space for storage of the shredded materials. Each unit could handle up to eight thousand pounds of paper per hour and could shred not just boxes, files, paper clips, and rubber bands but also CDs, DVDs, identity cards, hard drives, even uniforms. CorpServe provided shredding as high as the level five standard, used for commercially sensitive and top secret documents, which mandated a maximum particle size of 0.8×12 millimeters. The mobile units generated their own electrical power, and everything was shredded and baled in one simple operation, the bales then trucked away in volume to paper mills where the paper and extraneous matter were separated by particle-weight blowers and recycled. Each mobile CorpServe shredding unit was equipped with a New York State–certified scale that weighed the material to be shredded and came with a complete video system that recorded the actual shredding. After each night's work, the CorpServe technician provided the building services manager a copy of the scale tickets and a video of the shredding. This was usually a big selling point, but in truth these tickets and videos soon piled up and were eventually shredded along with everything else. Document destruction, just like office cleaning, was an incredibly boring business. There was no tangible product except a blur of confettied paper. The customer paid to make something into nothing, literally for the creation of emptiness. The mobile shredders were loud; no one wanted to watch them for very long. On long-term contracts, client oversight eroded away then vanished. The uniformed CorpServe crews—all of them Mexican, Guatemalan, and Chinese women—unfailingly showed up on time and did their jobs. Trying to get a handhold on America, the workers generally felt lucky to be employed, spoke English poorly, and affected a submissive mien, rarely even speaking to office personnel—not out of a quest for efficiency but on the assumption that no one had anything to say to them. Which was true. Faceless, nameless, they were more or less invisible.

From an organizational viewpoint, these two CorpServe divisions were remarkably "flat"; one person ran each, supervising the work crews and schedules from the company's run-down warehouse in the Red Hook section of Brooklyn. Jin Li had picked this location because it was cheap and out-of-the-way yet relatively close to Manhattan. No one much bothered with the CorpServe trucks coming and going there. Another person handled the bookkeeping and payroll for the two divisions. These operations were sufficiently profitable to justify the existence of CorpServe.

But it was the third function of CorpServe that both Chen and Jin Li fixated upon. This part, which generated no organizational paperwork, and indeed was never mentioned or described in writing, combined select elements of the other two. The idea was simply to steal useful information. When the cleaning division worked in offices that generated wastepaper that looked potentially valuable to Jin Li, she tried mightily to underbid the shredding contract for that building, if there was one. Sometimes she was successful and thus gained legitimate access to the stream of desired waste information. This meant that her company not only removed the information but also controlled it after removal. Then it was a matter of segregating the material that should not be shredded. Of course sometimes she was not successful in underbidding the shredding contract and no information could be removed on a regular basis. One of Chen's principles was that no nonrefuse documents be stolen from offices, a directive she agreed with. That was too risky, would draw attention if discovered. Theirs was a quiet, subtle play in which companies were *paying them to remove valuable information.* If there were ever a question about a particular bag of waste, why it had not been shredded, then Jin Li could just say a mistake had been made, bags had gotten mixed up. But no mistake had ever been made.

Until now, that is. What was it?

Jin Li had supervised all three operations, only occasionally appearing at one or another of the legitimate cleaning or shredding locations, but five nights a week riding with mobile shredder #6 (a lucky number for the Chinese) as it appeared at the small number of locations she wanted to plunder for information. She always wore a baggy blue CorpServe uniform, removed her makeup, tucked her hair up under a cap, and presented her company ID if asked. The security officers in the buildings either recognized her as the supervisor or knew that cleaning company staffs had a lot of turnover and didn't bother to question a diminutive Chinese woman in uniform with an ID clipped to her breast pocket. Except for the driver of #6, the other CorpServe staffers didn't know her true role. She was just the shift supervisor who sometimes removed waste herself. The promising stuff made it into the "blue bags," as they were called, and these were set aside for careful scrutiny later. If any of the cleaners seemed too interested in Jin Li's activities, Jin Li quickly praised the woman on her excellent work, shifted her to one of the legitimate cleaning operations, and gave her a marginal raise.

As she prowled the target businesses at night, Jin Li moved with light-footed efficiency, for if you clean offices every day, you know a lot about them. Typically she received plans of the floors that CorpServe cleaned and made a point always to ask if there were any sensitive elements of the job, such as a CEO who stayed late, which offices needed to be vacuumed daily because of allergies, which vacuumed less frequently, etc. All in the guise of providing excellent service, which in fact CorpServe did. Very often the response by management pinpointed exactly which office or offices were *most* valuable. Jin Li had learned that secretaries and assistants had better trash than their supervisors, because they made drafts of responses, copied e-mail, and so on. But that was not all! CorpServe could also provide, if asked, another service: secure, lockable plastic bins marked TO BE SHREDDED, an assistance that companies liked, since it efficiently segregated sensitive documents away from the eyes of their own not-so-trustworthy employees. Of course these bins usually contained the *very best* information Jin Li most wanted, or, put another way, CorpServe's clients were paying it extra money to more efficiently steal the very information they most wanted destroyed. She had keys that fit all of the different makes of these bins, and it was a matter of quickly emptying them into a bag that she would later inspect. People were amazingly sloppy with paper, especially now that everyone used computers. Companies spent enormous sums on their internal and external computer security, hiring an endless string of geniuses, wizards, and solemn soothsayers to implement every manner of state-of-the-art antihacking protocols. Paper, however, was by definition superfluous, since every document and e-mail existed somewhere on a computer. And because things were not "saved" on paper anymore, they were less likely to be "filed" away. Paper had become the temporary, disposable manifestation of the electronic file, convenient for carrying around but not worth being careful with. You could always print out another copy.

All this was true from one office to the next. Some had security procedures, but these were rarely enforced with any regularity. People in New York offices were too busy, too pressured, too ambitious to worry about their wastepaper. It was someone else's problem.

Which was also to say it was Jin Li's opportunity. She had learned to avoid certain industries and to target others. Law firms had some value, especially if they had a mergers-and-acquisitions department, a fact easy enough to determine. But the short-term value of these papers was so obvious, not to mention subject to SEC security regulations, that the law firms generally went to great lengths to destroy their paper. Publishing and media companies, by contrast, had absolutely no value. Retail banking was useless. Insurance companies were useless too, except if they had a corporate liability department, which had the potential to be a gold mine if documents revealed a company facing huge undisclosed problems, such as product lawsuits. The companies underwriting corporate bonds had some value, since they evaluated the underlying creditworthiness of the companies whose debt they peddled. Pharmaceutical companies were good, when you could find one with interesting product research, but the best offices were financial services firms, which evaluated stocks, because what she wanted most was time-perishable information that immediately affected the price of a publicly traded company—stock prices generally reacting to information faster and more dramatically than do bonds. The information had to be so good, so privileged, that the analysts, journalists, stock pickers, inside leakers, and anyone else interested didn't already have it.

The global stock markets ran on the quaint theory that they were efficient, that is, that crucial information about publicly traded stocks was available very rapidly to any interested party; the reality, of course, was different. Companies lied, cheated, inflated profits, hid debts, booked phony business, and smilingly pretended that their exalted leaders were not dying or ineffective or irrevocably insane or, most typically, widely hated by insiders. Companies "smoothed" their data to appear more steadily profitable, developed products that bombed, suffered internal wars between personalities, between divisions, between the directors and management, between management and the

rank and file, between stockholders and management. Internal dis-
agreements could be mild, festering, explosive, litigious, even potentially violent. As one of Jin Li's professors at Harbin Institute of
Technology had said, no matter how large and bureaucratized, no matter how rigid and repressive, corporations were ultimately just collections of human beings, subject to everything that both afflicted and
elevated them—not unlike, the professor had reminded them, the collective farms created by Mao in the 1960s which, though meant to be
efficiently productive, were disasters.

So what had been Jin Li's mistake? This was the question that had
haunted her since she'd run through the rainy dawn away from the
shit-flooded car and the two Mexican girls sprawled out next to it.
Hurrying to the parkway and flagging down a cab on its way into
Manhattan. Hunched in the back clutching her purse, terrified,
smelling the excrement on her clothes and skin, trying to keep her sob-
bing quiet. Someone must have seen what she was doing. Who? This
would take some analysis. Every night she received the blue bags culled
from the night operations, each bag tagged by floor and company and
day. These were trucked to the building in Red Hook, where by day Jin
Li and three trusted other Chinese women separated them into their
respective piles, arranged by company. One night's trash was usually
useless, but as the record accrued, a context was revealed. Jin Li
watched divisional struggles, executives attacking each other, results
exceeding expectations, projects being canceled or accelerated—everything that happened in a corporation. As conflicts heightened, or as
she became more fully aware of their possibilities, she focused the paper collection on the respective desk, office, or floor. Perhaps a dozen
time-lapse narratives played out continuously on paper. Often there
were gaps in information and she would have to infer what had happened. She kept notebooks on each company and updated these regu-
larly, and included newspaper stories and chat room conversations that
confirmed or conflicted with the inklings revealed in the corporate
garbage days or weeks earlier.

A laborious process, this sifting for flecks of gold in a stream of data, but perhaps once or twice a month Jin Li found a genuine opportunity. In the ebb and flow of possibility, there inevitably arose companies that were approaching a merger, a new product launch, a phase of "restated" earnings, or quietly confronting a government investigation. She scanned all useful documents, along with her written commentary, onto an encrypted disc that each week was sent hidden in a fat bundle of last month's computer magazines that she bought in wire-wrapped bales at three cents a pound from a New York company that was paid handsomely to falsify circulation figures for glossy national magazines. Many of these magazines had promotional computer discs bound into them, and it was a simple matter to swap her disc into a certain issue, fold over the corner of the front cover, and send the entire wire-bound bale of magazines to her brother. The Chinese authorities generally smiled on any activity that created the free transfer of valuable information from the West to China and were happy to wave the computer magazines through. Of course it was easier, faster, and cheaper to send the information by e-mail, but her brother was rightly terrified of the American government's electronic surveillance programs, which sniffed phone and Internet chatter for keywords or word patterns. And then there were the filters that the Chinese used on all incoming e-mail. The people's government went through waves of greater and lesser repression of e-mail, but it was safe to say that Chen was not so well connected that he could be sure when the periodic tightenings would take place or how good the filters were. He had seen friends arrested for merely having the word "freedom" appear in their incoming e-mail.

So better to smuggle information the old-fashioned way—physically. Each week Jin Li reserved space on an air cargo container that left JFK on Thursday night and arrived in Shanghai the next Saturday at dawn local time. Twenty-seven bales of the computer magazines, arranged in a cube, shrink-wrapped on a wooden pallet, went into the huge container. The container was off-loaded within an hour of arrival, and one of Chen's men would take possession of it. The bale containing the correct disc was always in the center of the pallet, and thus it was a simple matter to remove this bale, cut it open, and search the stack of magazines until the one with the folded-over cover was found. The plan was elegant in its simplicity. If for some reason another magazine cover had been folded over by accident, then the discs in the two magazines could easily be compared. The disc would be driven at high speed to Chen's apartment complex in one of the newest and most outrageously expensive high-rises where impoverished newcomers from the far provinces skulked around hoping to cadge errands from the smartly dressed Shanghai professionals too busy to pick up dry cleaning or polish their new cars. By Saturday morning, Chen had booted out whatever hookerish women he had entertained the night before and set to work, downloading the disc and following Jin Li's instructions as to what certain documents might reveal. He employed a small group of dedicated analysts, some of them trained by and stolen from the same large American and European venture funds and banks trying to spin money out of China, and they would collate the information against conventionally available research, sometimes deriving perception where she had not but mostly corroborating her judgment.

By Sunday evening Chen had selected the strategies and supporting documents that he found most useful, and on Monday, while seated in a private dining room in one of China's most elite banks, he would explain to a small group of investors what he had discovered. Sipping their turtle soup, they listened intently, nodding solemnly if the opportunity appeared especially promising. Chen was transparently motivated by a mix of greed, hedonism, and national pride; older men, especially those who had lived in the time of Mao, found him easy to read, since the satisfaction of all his desires required outward behavior. Every week or so Chen had a nugget to display, and when he didn't, the group reprised the week's news about the companies they followed, speculated upon, or manipulated. If they wanted to take action, their position on the globe helped them. Most American stocks traded thinly in the off-hours when the European and New York stock exchanges were closed, and it was possible to quietly take a sizable position before the main action began hours later on the other side of the globe. The fact that Chen was mining data directly out of New York

City appealed to the nationalistic aggressions of his Chinese investors. To a man, they hated America, or said they did.

A most agreeable business, cheating the rule of law and the playbook of Western capitalism.

Chen and his coconspirators knew what they were doing, too. China had first allowed the public trading of stock in the nineties, and so the older men all had years of experience feeling the whims and drift and anxieties of markets. They had reached a level of intuitiveness that rested upon having had fortunes lost and larger ones won. In recent years stock market mania had reached deep into the Chinese middle class, and the opportunities to pump and dump stocks were now routine. The government's warnings and attempted restrictions on the frenzied trading of stocks had only served to embolden that same behavior, for the Chinese people knew that good times were often followed by bad. Life was luck—but you didn't wait around to be lucky, not when a thousand others wanted what you had. Thus did desire in the many create opportunity for the few. Very often Chen and his group determined how to first make money off a stock against the Western markets and then how to make money off it again, a second time, within the Chinese markets. Together they discussed the bets to be made, very often finishing the discussion with the ceremonial ringing of a small brass gong, a sound that reaffirmed their Chinese culture and mocked the opening bell that would start the trading on Wall Street hours hence.

After this moment, a great feast followed in one of the city's private clubs, at which drinking was accompanied by the attentions of the dozen or so girls brought in not only to help the men forget their anxieties about having just committed millions of hard-currency dollars but also to confirm their impression of themselves as masters of all they surveyed. There was one girl particularly skilled at manipulating the back of her throat and her tongue simultaneously. Jin Li had heard her brother discuss with great excitement this seemingly rare and remarkable ability. The girl, who had arrived in Shanghai penniless but quickly achieved significant wealth, was not particularly beautiful, but her services were highly sought after and the men had been known to bid drunkenly against each other until one man persevered past any reasonable limit and purchased his pleasure. The lucky fellow then retired to a private room with his consort.

Pigs, thought Jin Li, fucking pigs, all of them. And here I am, over in America, helping them do such things, and in trouble. She could hate herself for it—almost, except that, yes, she had agreed to her brother's proposition and had even explained to him how she was the best person to carry it off. She would do it for their family, she'd said, for their parents. And, to be fair, Chen had risked a great deal. As the Mexicans said, he had *huevos*, eggs—balls. The start-up money for the project required nearly $6 million and her brother had gone to a series of investors, describing the scheme—nothing on paper, of course— using terms either oblique or specific, depending on his audience. Yet the scheme had been quickly funded. So quickly, in fact, that Chen had worried that someone else might steal the idea and set up a competing operation—if not in New York, then in London or Paris or any other Western city where the Chinese did a great deal of business.

But that was then and this was now. Which company had gotten wind of what she was doing? Which company had sent the two men and the big truck after her? Why had they also killed the two Mexican girls? I am partly responsible, she thought sadly, I endangered them. Who had claimed their bodies? Who would tell their families in Mexico? They would want to know why this had happened.

Could she have expected the attack? There were no complaints on file, and the accounts receivable were more or less up to date. Her company had been aggressively stealing information from eight firms in the last six months, and she could easily check the recent stock prices of them, but that would tell her almost nothing. Her brother and his cronies could be building a conventional position in a stock, they could have bet that it would fall, or they could be dealing with a company's competitors or suppliers. They could even be using her good information to sell disinformation. The one thing she did know was that they preferred smaller American companies for which the trading volume was low enough that they could move the price with their buying or selling.

The CorpServe ploy had been in business for four years now, and in that time it was fair to say they had been spectacularly successful. Her brother had purchased three large buildings in Shanghai, built himself a new house, bought an apartment in Hong Kong for one of his mistresses, and started getting his face massaged each morning.

And had Chen given Jin Li much in return? No, not enough. A good salary, by New York standards. By Chinese standards, a fortune. But no security. The opposite of security, even as he'd gotten rich. *She* was the one who could be prosecuted in the United States, thrown into federal prison or deported. The one the men had been after. Her brother needed to find her now, she knew, because his whole empire ran on the stream of information he received from her. No one else at CorpServe knew what to do, what to look for. No one else could be trusted to be loyal. Chen and his investors had taken huge speculative positions that required that Jin Li's hands and eyes be connected to their minds—to their *money*. A discarded scrap of paper on one side of the globe could conceivably be convertible to millions of dollars on the other side. Chen could not afford to lose touch with her, lose control of CorpServe, or have her disappearance known about. Her brother, she knew, was desperate now.

But maybe she didn't want him to find her. And maybe he would figure that out. Chen would call Mr. Ling, an old Hong Kong lawyer who still worked in a little office above Canal Street in Chinatown, and Mr. Ling would figure a way to get into Jin Li's apartment and find her bank statements, credit card activity. Well, let them do that. She had plenty of cash set—

Wait! A noise?

She crept to the window, slid it open higher. Did she dare look out? Someone gazing up would easily see her.

She hazarded a peek out of the window.

Nothing.

She glanced at her cell phone. She wanted to turn it on but knew not to. Chen would have called, just to see if she picked up. To talk, yes, but to continue their ongoing argument. That he had sex with Russian and Eastern European prostitutes meant nothing to him, but the fact that Jin Li preferred not to sleep with Chinese men was an insult to him. Why are Chinese men no good for you? he had screamed. She didn't have an answer. It was no one particular thing. She liked the whiskers on American and German men, she admitted it. She liked how they were taller and heavier than most Chinese men. You have a colonial mentality, her brother said, in your head. It is deep in your head, like one hundred years ago. Can you not see that? Her answer to her brother: Fuck you, you do not understand women. Not at all. She liked some of the American men and the European men because they did not know her Chineseness. They knew she was Chinese but that was all. When she said the word "father" or "mother" in English to them they did not know what she meant. They knew what the words meant in their languages but not hers. Their language did not have her pain in it, her heaviness. A strange thing, admittedly. I have a Chinese part of me and I have a me part of me, she told herself.

Was this why she liked Ray? Yes, among other reasons. He was like her in some ways, secretive and quiet. Most of the American men she'd dated wanted her to get to know them as soon as possible, as if that was a great honor they were bestowing. Not Ray. He spoke but somehow stayed reserved. He was "reticent," one of her newer vocabulary words. They had fun, walking down Broadway at night, going out for dinner. He knew the city; it was where he'd been born. She often had the feeling he was looking at the individual buildings but he never said why. Inspecting them somehow. Often they took a drive in his red pickup truck. She might have left a pair of yellow tennis shoes in the cab, she remembered sadly. She found the big scar on Ray's belly interesting, its little mountain ranges of swirling tissue, the squarish skin grafts like fields below. Strangely beautiful to her, though she would never say that. Because he wouldn't believe her. She knew that he had traveled a lot. She had poked through his papers and found his passport and seen the stamps from China, Australia, Malaysia, Indonesia, Vietnam, Afghanistan, Sudan, Thailand, lots of countries. She noticed how good he was with chopsticks. Not careful with them, but bringing the bowl close to his mouth and flinging the food into his mouth like a peasant.

But what else did she know about him? Even less than he knew about her. He lived with his father in Brooklyn, spent some time overseeing his father's rental houses. Caring for him until he died, but also waiting for something, waiting to be called away. Never talked about his work, either. She'd asked once, but he'd just smiled and shaken his head softly. But he wasn't "morose"—another vocabulary word—he was energetic and fun. He read a lot, she saw. Which she liked. Mostly philosophy and history, topics that didn't much interest her, though the fact that they interested him intrigued her. He had a physical regimen that he performed each day, like the old Chinese ladies exercising on the flat roofs of the apartment buildings in their cities, except tougher. He'd hung a long rope out of his father's top window, secured it, and then climbed straight up from the garden below to the window, feet flat against the clapboard siding, then rappelled downward and done it again. Five times a day he did this. No belts or harnesses, no rock climber's equipment. Fearless, and maybe stupid, yes, but she *had* been impressed. All arm strength. This explained his arms and shoulders. Rock hard, even a little scary. But he wore loose shirts, never showed himself off. How could a man be so strong like that? And more to the point, why? What dangerous exploit was he preparing himself for?

Jin Li had her suspicions but no answers. The closest she had come to learning had been a few weeks earlier, right before she'd broken it off. They had been walking along Fifth Avenue after eating when a fire truck had raced by. Like most New Yorkers, Jin Li had become inured to the sound of fire truck's sirens, seeing them as a noisy irritation as they passed. "Goddamned things," she'd muttered, then turned to Ray.

He'd looked at her, saying nothing, eyes cold.

"What?"

But he didn't answer. Stood there rigid, as if bracing for an attack. His teeth were set against each other, his eyes unblinking, feet spread apart. An instinctual response. She'd said something he found ignorant, and she sensed that whatever had happened to him—the scar, the unwillingness to say why he'd drifted around the third world for years—related to this very moment. She felt him capable of violence.

"Ray? What is it?"

He stared at her, traveling great distances in his mind.

"Don't look at me like that. *Please!*"

Then his face eased, blue eyes warm again. Ray had nodded to himself, the emotions put back in the safe place in his head where they'd been, and took a step along the sidewalk with her, as if the moment had never happened. But it had. She had seen *into* him. Finally, she knew that Ray—

A noise! This time for certain! A door opening downstairs.

She slipped over to the window again, looked out. Two Chinese men were standing on the street below, waiting.

Now she heard noises in the stairwell. Two sets of feet stomping upward. They passed her floor and continued higher. Searching from the top, she thought.

Jin Li gathered her small number of things into a pile, pushed a dozen boxes around, and created a tiny hiding hole within the expanse of crumbling cardboard. Here she squatted down into a cannonball position and waited, the smell of dry-rotted paper in her nose.

She did not have to wait long. The two men pushed through the door, the old floorboards creaking under their weight. The Russian custodian, from his voice. And another man, whom she watched through a crack between boxes. Another Chinese man. With a big bandage taped on the end of his nose.

"It is very big room," said the Russian. "Many boxes."

The Chinese man did not answer. She could no longer see him but she could hear him walking heavily along the floor. She smelled a cigarette and assumed the Russian was waiting while the other man finished his inspection. But then she noticed that the Russian had moved to the window behind her. She held her breath and twisted her head around. The Russian was casually sliding the window shut, his tattooed fingers gripping the frame. She'd forgotten to close it! She watched his face. A grimness there. The window was the old kind with iron sash weights that rattled in their tracks, but the man was deliberate and slow, easing the window down with minimal noise, his mouth pressed tight as if trying to hold its sound within him. When he was done, he let his hands drop to his sides. But they opened and closed and opened again expectantly, each hairy finger marked with a bluish spider of ink. Then he stepped forward quickly, making it appear that he had been standing elsewhere.

He knows, Jin Li realized, he knows I'm here.

Pain, pain, go away, come back and kill me another day. Bill Martz rose as he always rose now, with pain in his back and knees and feet, not to mention pain between his ass and his balls, which meant his prostate gland was acting up again. He winced as he stood, found his slippers, then inspected his naked self in the bathroom mirror. You look like a hairless orangutan, he thought. He pissed with great relief into the bathtub, which he did whenever he could. No aiming, just fire, let the maid clean up after him. Pissing with freedom was an increasingly important activity to him, even imbued with existential significance, and he cared little what anyone thought. At cocktail parties and dinners at private homes, he often pissed into the bathtub instead of the toilet. Or even in the sink. What were they going to do to him? Nothing! He was Bill Martz!

Connie was making breakfast. His fourth wife. He often wondered why they were together. Once a month or so he forgot her name. She was twenty-eight years younger than he was and the difference showed every day. One of those women who had collected and instituted into their regimens so many beauty secrets that they appeared to be aging at one-tenth the rate that normal people did. Glowing! Bubbly! Peppy! He resented her youthfulness even as he absolutely required it as a condition of their marriage. Soft, bouncy, firm. And he wasn't just talking about her breasts or face or ass. Nope. It was a grim and insufficiently recognized truth that as women drifted into and out of menopause, their sexual selves suffered mightily. No matter what the women's magazines chirped. Looseness. Dryness. Discomfort. *Pain.* Connie was old enough that menopause was out there, lurking on the horizon in a few years, but he was confident that her ob-gyn had all sorts of endocrinological tricks up his sleeve. He'd better. Bill Martz had seen (wife number two) what happened otherwise and it was not a happy thing. He was too rich to be afflicted by a dry vagina!

Why had he married Connie? Why, really? She was beautiful, but so were lots of women. She made him feel good. Well, sure. But why had he actually married her? They weren't going to have any children and he had gotten the snip back in his fifties between marriages two and three, when he was running around so much that he couldn't keep the women straight in his head. He had married Connie because he was lonely and she was there. Simple as that. He didn't love her, not really. He was fond of her, yes. Terrible word, "fond." He had loved his first wife passionately, but she had died of breast cancer at forty-two, and thereafter he had been able only to approximate a decreasing percentage of that original feeling with subsequent women. So, no, he didn't really love Connie. And he doubted she loved him, not if he knew anything about women, though he appreciated her willingness not to make it an issue. Why *should* she love him, anyway? He wasn't particularly lovable. He wasn't particularly anything, except rich. And nasty. *Vanity Fair* had once devoted a whole article to how nasty and rapacious he was, and not one word was libelous. He was a nasty, rapacious orangutan who pissed into his bathtub instead of the four-thousand-dollar toilet. I used to be charming, he reflected, back when I cared what people thought of me. Why'd Connie marry him? The *moan-ay*, of course. The security. But Connie was still just young enough to have children. And why shouldn't she? She had every right to have them. He understood that marrying him might have been a disastrous decision for her. At this he felt a distinct sadness for her, what she'd missed. He had four grown children and they were his only consolation. The rest of it all could go to hell.

Really, his wife was wasting her life by being with him. If he had any courage he would tell her this. She was still pretty enough to go out on the remarriage circuit and grab a reasonably decent guy—someone with, say, eighty or a hundred mil. He and Connie had sex about twice a month, thanks to the beautiful pills science provided to guys like him, but he had to admit it wasn't great. Connie wasn't the problem. She was fine, or would be fine. He didn't have it, the juice, the mojo, the mustard. The act itself was ghostly, a tissue of sensation atop thousands of earlier iterations. He couldn't feel the pleasure in its originality, his cock no longer the time-travel device it used to be. His rational mind was never overwhelmed. In fact, he smelled death on himself—a sour, exhausted whiff. Whether this was mere aging or his problem in particular didn't matter. There was no pill for it, no woman for it, no end of it, no antidote for it—

—except big action! Making decisions, risking, winning, taking the hit when it came, feeling the force of money. Money as wind, fire, stone! Money as beauty, ugliness, and pain! Money as fear and hatred and love! Only with money were his instincts perfect, his reflexes untouched by age, his passion endless. He couldn't explain this and it certainly wasn't admirable, but it was true.

He pulled his robe tight and shuffled into the kitchen. Connie was there with two plates of eggs. The house staff arrived at nine, so she usually made breakfast. He sat carefully. Connie had put cushions on every chair in the house for him. She knew his prostate hurt. They'd fought about him not going to the doctor. Drove her nuts. And maybe that was why he didn't do it. Forcing his old guy's death-smell decrepitude upon her, a kind of rich man's sicko dominance. I didn't used to be like this, Martz thought, poking his head out the open window and looking down. He could see the morning runners in Central Park, the maples leafing out in the late spring.

He pulled his head back in. "I want to give you some carefully considered advice," he announced grandly. God, did Connie look good. Five hundred sit-ups a day, yoga, tennis, swimming three times a week in the pool in the apartment house, free weights—all her old habits from her modeling days.

She bustled about happily. "I like your advice."

"I think, number one, that I am very lucky to have you around.

This isn't about what's good for me. Number two, I think that you are probably wasting your life hanging around an old man like me who can't really fuck you decently anymore, who is crabby and achy and full of his own compacted, neurotic, self-important, and irresolvable bullshit. Okay? You are young enough that you could go find somebody and five years from now you could be feeding a couple of beautiful little children some breakfast, instead of an old man. This is the truth, lady. I'm turning into a rotting bag of meat, Connie, and somebody is going to have to wipe the drool and the shit off of me. Why should it be you? The answer is that it shouldn't. My advice is that you get a quick divorce, nothing contested, and start meeting guys. I'd give you enough money so that you didn't have to worry about anything. Hell, I'll double whatever is in the prenup that *you* made me sign, and you could actually have a decent life and not hang out with an old bum—admittedly quite rich—like me. Who isn't even *charming* anymore." He patted his place mat. "That's my morning speech. Now, where's my coffee?"

Connie silently set a cup down in front of him, along with a neat stack of the *Financial Times*, the *Wall Street Journal*, the *Asian Wall Street Journal*, the *New York Times*, and the business sections of the *Los Angeles Times*, *Miami Herald*, *Chicago Tribune*, and *Washington Post*. He read them each day as a rich man, which was to say as if they were the sports pages. Across the city, no more than a few hundred men like him, all possessed of meaninglessly grand wealth and old enough to feel as he did, played the game against each other, against younger men, against technology, information, and the passing of days. They played it as long as they could, and then, if they were smart, they took their winnings at the right moment and retired to Normandy or Palm Beach or a ranch in Montana or someplace nothing much mattered anymore. If they stayed too long in the game, they got cut open, even wiped out. That insurance guy, what's his name, lost $600 million. Should have eased out, let the scandals fall on the shoulders of younger men.

And maybe Bill would do this. But not *yet*. He had to fix his little huge problem with the hedge fund. He had leveraged his flagship,

Martz New Century Partners Fund, into a goddamn $352 million position on Good Pharma and needed to unwind the position before something bad happened. He no longer cared whether he made money; he just wanted out even, or at worst with just a haircut. Lose $20, $30 million, okay, he could live with that, make it up elsewhere. That kind of money could be hidden from the investors easily enough. But he was down $107 million in just over thirty days on the position, and against the prudent and obvious advice of his young, high-priced princelings, he had doubled the bet late, thinking the stock would bounce up, but it had only drifted down further. The kind of error an amateur made. Pure gambling. Now they were whispering about him, he knew it, talking behind his back, saying *Big Bill is sucking on a land mine right now . . . Big Bill's lost his fastball . . .* Something was wrong with Good Pharma and somebody knew what it was. And wasn't telling Bill Martz. Somebody like that slick fuckwad Tom Reilly. I'm too old to be worrying about being vulnerable to the fate of one small bullshit drug company, he told himself. Too old, too rich, and too smart. Or certainly one would think so, except that he'd taken an unnaturally large position in Good Pharma, expecting that it would give him a fat boost by year's end. All his researchers had reported it was on the verge, great stuff in the pipeline, synthetic skin, cartilage pills, things like that.

Connie put his eggs down. "I put in that dried red pepper we found in Mexico last winter."

"Hmm. Thank you, these look great."

She let her hand linger on his shoulder. "I like old rich bums, by the way, just to finish the conversation."

"What about young rich bums?"

"Not charming enough."

He ate with gusto. At least he hadn't lost his appetite. When he paused, he looked up and said, "Seriously, Connie. I say this all the time but I am serious."

She was waiting for him. "You say *that* all the time, too. I'm *very* happy, Bill."

"That's because you are wasting all your maternal energies on a sixty-nine-year old baby. I've had four children. I know how great they are. A few more years go by you can't have kids and I'm out there at the wheelchair showroom."

She smiled, but her eyes were wet. "Please, Billy, this does kind of hurt me when you say this."

"I'm sorry."

"It makes me happy to be with you. Maybe I'm not so wrapped up in the future like you are."

"Probably because you have a lot more of it."

She looked at him straight. "Yes, I do. But so?"

He went back to his eggs. It was an old conversation. Not an untrue conversation but unsolvable, almost comfortable in its familiarity.

"What's really bothering you, Bill?"

He tasted the coffee. Perfect. "Bothering me? I'm bothered by the fact that I've taken a huge bite out of Good Pharma, expecting it to be a takeover candidate. I thought it was cheap. No, not cheap, but reasonable. They have half a dozen drugs in the pipeline. Some will bomb but we think two are huge. But it's too early to get good information yet. We just have inklings. And the market is craving new products. You get the right new product, you get a new demand, okay? People want something that never existed before! I know the number-two guy, Tom Reilly. He's not the CEO but he's the guy who knows what's really going on. Real slick fuckwad, let me tell you. Good Pharma's stock is down thirty-seven percent in the last few weeks. I want to know why. I've asked, and nobody can tell me or will tell me."

"Why don't you ask this Tom Reilly?"

"I have."

"Well?"

"He's avoiding me. Hiding in the weeds."

"So?"

"I'm starting to make his life difficult. I had him followed to a Yankees game two nights ago and messed with his head. Sent him a little message from old Billy-boy."

"Has he called you?"

"No, he's scared. I expected him to call me after the game, but he didn't."

Connie frowned at him, pressing her breasts forward aggressively. "You need to kick some ass, sounds like."

"Think so?" It excited him to hear her say it.

"You're *good* at that, Bill."

"I can be."

"No, you listen to me," she told him. "Nobody fucks with Billy Martz, right? I've heard you say this to me a thousand times. You're tougher, you're smarter, and you're definitely meaner. You are a *mean* old bastard, Bill! Get that information out of him so that you can fix the problem. You hear me, Bill? Frankly I don't think you've really given it much effort yet."

He nodded. "I could turn up the heat."

"You could?" she said, her voice disgusted.

"I *will* turn up the heat. I'll roast the asshole."

"Then go *do* it, Bill, and stop telling me how fucking miserable I am!" His beautiful wife put her hands on her hips and looked ferociously at him, and in that moment they both knew, again, happily, why he had married her.

She was in more danger than he realized. Ray put down the phone. One of his father's old friends from the job, Detective Pete Blake, now on the brink of retirement himself, had filled Ray in on the murder of the two Mexican girls. A loner who'd never married, Blake used to come to the house for Thanksgiving dinners, throw a football in the alley with Ray while his father raked leaves before going inside for the feast Ray's mother had cooked. "Yeah, we found them laid out on the parking lot," Blake had said. "Couple of days ago. Aerosol mace dispenser on the pavement. Somebody filled the car with sewage. The guys had to have a pump-out truck, some kind of vehicle that holds septic waste."

"I thought the whole city is tied in to the sewers."

"It is, but people still need pump-outs when their pipes are clogged or break. Plus you got some old septic tanks still in operation here and there."

"So you look for one of these trucks?"

"The thing of it is that the state Department of Environmental Protection shows computer records for 918 such vehicles licensed to operate in Brooklyn, Queens, and western Suffolk County. Take a long time to knock all those out. Course, the truck could be unlicensed, too, maybe even be from Jersey or north of the city. So maybe it's smarter to work it through the girls. They'd been drowned before being pulled out of their car. Smart way to kill somebody in some respects. There's no DNA. I mean, there's too much DNA, all of it contaminated. Plus we don't really know who these Mexican girls were. They had ID but it was all fake, fake green cards, everything. No driver's license, of course. No bank accounts, used one of those check-cashing places, probably. Telephone is in the name of somebody who doesn't live there anymore, utility bills paid by money order. It's like that with all these people. Might be a drug thing, girls smoked a bit, there were boyfriends in the trade. Lots of Mexicans selling drugs in Brooklyn these days. We know who some of them are. The thing of it is that all these organizations are always fighting for turf, showing how fricking vicious they can be. The Albanians are very tough. So are the Salvadoran kids. Last month we had a dead guy, they put him through a band saw, put the top half on a pole like some kinda Mexican scarecrow. So killing a couple of wetback girlfriends is good advertising. Your girlfriends are shit, you are no-body—this is the way these people think. We found traces of stuff in the trunk of the car, glove compartment. Car is still drying, we'll see if there's anything else. We got people to talk to, snitches, rats, nice people like that."

"Didn't see it in the news."

"Didn't nobody tell you, Ray?"

"What?"

"There's no news in Brooklyn. You want news? Commit your crimes in Manhattan, and try to do it south of, like, Ninety-sixth Street. No, actually we kept it quiet, to help us with any informants. One of the tabloids got it but ran it small. Anyway, someone broke the two front side windows with a chunk of asphalt to open the doors, failed to save the girls, then disappeared. That means the car was locked from the inside, and that means that either the girls were al-ready incapacitated or were trapped in the car and someone locked the doors after they were incapacitated. There was a wine bottle in the car, maybe they had passed out, we don't have complete toxicology and au-topsy body weight back yet, which is disgraceful, if you ask me." Blake made a coffee-sipping sound. "Still too hot. Anyway, whoever tried to save them is probably too scared to get involved, and who could blame them? Rain fell pretty steadily on the bodies for maybe an hour, washed out the car like that." Blake paused, and when his voice came back, it was professionally softer, a little slower, slipping in a question. "Why you interested, anyway?"

Ray wasn't going to mention his evening with Chen and his men— not yet, anyway. "My old girlfriend works at the same company they did. I think she saw them earlier that night."

"Then we might want to talk to her."

"That makes two of us. She's not around, if you know what I mean."

"You find her, let me know. She's a person of interest. What's her name?"

"Jin Li."

"Chinese? Real Chinese?"

"Yes." Ray knew this fact would stick in Blake's brain.

"Off the boat, I mean?"

"So to speak." He wanted to change the topic. "So how do you go after the guys who did it?"

"Tough—nobody saw nothing, so far, anyway. Right before dawn. We'll work the drugs, see what we get. Trucks can't go on the Belt Parkway legally, but if it did, we got cameras. Sometimes they work, sometimes they didn't get serviced. Course, if you know the side roads you don't have to take the Belt." Blake barked a laugh. "Your father'd be tearing up the parking lot drains, looking for whatever he could find."

"You do that?"

"Not yet. We can't go into the drains."

"Why?"

"Federal wetlands. That's a tide zone. Environmental regulations. We screw up the drains, then we can pollute the ocean, something like that."

Blake was fastidious, Ray remembered, but also methodical. He collected New York subway memorabilia: hats, badges, uniforms, tokens, subway signs, regulation booklets, all displayed in frames or binders. He had a copy of almost every New York City subway map ever published, quite an accomplishment considering the subway had opened in 1904, its maps updated every year or two as the system grew and the original private subway companies consolidated into the Metropolitan

Transit Authority. He'd seen Blake's collection: each document was kept in an archival Mylar folder and thoroughly cataloged. A weird pursuit for a middle-aged man. Maybe not so strange for a detective who lived by himself. "That's the reason, the ocean?"

"Nah, the real reason is that if we tear up that pipe we got a big traffic problem in that parking lot this summer. People can't park, you got flooding, a mess. Also, no cop is ever going to crawl up a drainpipe stuffed with sewage, especially since it will all wash out into the gulley there anyway." Blake gave a long sigh. "How's your dad doing?"

"Not too good, Pete."

"You want me to come around, say hello?"

"He might like that."

"Honest with you, he told me he was dying and that he was saying good-bye to me. This was like three weeks ago."

"Drive by in a couple of days. Mornings are better."

"You got it."

After the call, Ray stared at an information sheet that came with the Dilaudid going into his father's arm. He'd grabbed it when the nurse wasn't looking. Effects of Dilaudid to the general and central nervous systems, said the flyer, include "sedation, drowsiness, mental clouding, lethargy, impairment of mental and physical performance, anxiety, fear, dizziness, psychic dependence, mood changes (nervousness, apprehension, depression, floating feelings, dreams), light-headedness, weakness, headache, agitation, tremor, uncoordinated muscle movements, muscle rigidity, paresthesia, muscle tremor, blurred vision, nystagmus, diplopia and miosis, transient hallucinations and disorientation, visual disturbances, insomnia, sweating, flushing, dysphoria, euphoria and increased intracranial pressure."

I'm going to lose him to drugs faster than the cancer, Ray thought, heading toward his father's bed. But of course Dilaudid was amazing stuff; he'd received it himself, to help with the pain of his stomach burn and the skin grafts. The drug made you feel warm and heavy, removed all hunger and pain. Removed sexual desire, too. Eight times more potent than real morphine. People called it "drugstore heroin." He wouldn't mind sampling a tiny bit again sometime, either.

In the living room, his father lay in his hospital bed, now a small body under the sheet, his eyes shut, chest rising and falling faster than was natural. It was his heart working hard at the dying. Ray nodded at the morning shift nurse, a young woman named Wendy, and she left the room.

"Hey, Dad," he said.

His father opened his eyes, blinked, shifted his gaze toward Ray.

"I'm sorry you suffered so much last night."

His father shrugged. "Not suffering now," he whispered. "Fine now."

"Were you asleep?"

No, his father mouthed, eyes falling closed.

"Thinking?"

Yes.

His father opened his eyes, picked at the morphine tube to be sure it was not pinched or bent. There flickered in his expression a serious intent, a flash of concentration that told Ray that his father was still mostly here.

"Thinking about what?" Ray asked.

"Worlds."

"Worlds?"

"Yes," his father whispered, "worlds within worlds."

Ray glanced at the automatic Dilaudid pump. He had a few minutes before it sent another bolus into his father's bloodstream, knocking him out.

"Dad, the reason that everything happened last night was I have a girlfriend who has disappeared. You haven't met her. She's Chinese. We broke up a few weeks ago. Her brother wants me to find her and what he did was his way of telling me how serious he was."

His father nodded calmly. "Threatening."

"Yeah."

"Studied you, I think."

"I think so."

"Figured out your vulnerability. Me."

Ray exhaled by way of agreement.

"I was hoping you might meet that nice lady who lives next door there." He cracked a slow-motion smile. "She needs a husband, fast."

"I did meet her."

"Oh, then—"

"I was talking to her when they grabbed me."

His father's mouth pulled at one side. "You had a long *talk*."

Ray ignored this. "These guys weren't messing around."

"You could call the cops," his father noted.

"Should I?"

A long pause. His father shook his head weakly. Licked his lips.

Ray handed him a cup of juice. "But they could maybe protect you."

"Not me I'm worried about."

"I think I should move you, Dad. Somewhere safe."

"Hospital?"

"I was thinking, yeah."

He sipped his juice. "People die in hospitals, son."

"Dad—"

"I want to die in my own house, in this room. And I don't really care how I die, Ray, or when, so long as it's in this room, in this bed."

This was a speech he'd heard before. "Yes, but these guys will come back, Dad."

"Let them. What's the worst they can do? Murder me? They'd be doing me a personal favor."

Ray hung his head. Six weeks earlier, when he could still walk a bit in the house, Ray's father had told him he wanted to end it sooner rather than later. Did Ray mind if he shot himself? "Why put you through what's coming?" his father had asked then. "Why put *me* through it?"

"Why? I want every minute with you, Dad."

His father had nodded silently.

But Ray hadn't been convinced, and so within an hour, he had gathered all of his father's guns and ammunition and taken them out to the shed in their small backyard and hidden them in a waterproof wrap beneath a couple of bags of peat moss. A shotgun, a rifle, two

Glock 9 service pistols, always kept oiled and clean, plus the boxes of ammunition. Then he'd put a new lock on the shed and hidden one copy of the key inside the rotten birdhouse outside the kitchen window and put the other on his own key ring. If his father had somehow noticed the absence of the guns, he hadn't mentioned it. Of course it was possible his father had not only noticed the absence of the guns but had also discovered or deduced their new location. Ray had leaned a shovel up over the new lock so that it couldn't be seen from the house, but he knew that his father missed very little. The man had been a detective, after all.

But that was weeks ago, and his father had gone steadily downhill ever since. Now the Dilaudid pump clicked; the stuff was going into the tube in his father's wrist. Ray wouldn't have much more time to talk, so he returned to the topic of Jin Li's disappearance. "Her brother told me she was in a car with two Mexican girls who died a few nights ago, and I just spoke with Pete, who told me about it."

"So you *did* call the cops."

"Sort of. It's Pete."

"He's a detective second grade, with thirty years on the job. Method of homicide?"

"It was a car full of shit. Dumped it in the car, drowned them. Pete said his people hadn't gone into the drains yet, because of environmental issues, traffic—"

"Bunch of crap. They just don't want to go in. You have to have hazmat suits, dysentery shots. Case like that, you *got* to go into the drains."

"Why?" Ray asked.

"Think about what the cops found . . . two dead girls . . . aspirated human excrement . . . the bus takes them away. Then the FD hoses out the car for them."

"They found drug traces in the trunk and glove compartment."

His father shrugged. "Pete's gonna think it's drugs. Maybe. I think the shit is the best clue."

"How?"

"What you got to do is find out where the shit came from."

"I know where it came from, it came from human beings. Pete says there are something like nine hundred septic trucks in the area handling loads like this."

"No, no, *listen* to me, there'll be stuff in there, information. There'll be information in the shit."

Now Ray watched the synthetic morphine course through his father, softening the tension in his neck and forehead. His large fingers, bony and thin now, eased against the blanket.

"You did hear me, right?" croaked his father.

"I did."

"I don't want to be moved. I want to die in this bed in this room in this house. Then I will be with your mother."

"Dad, we could easily call the precinct and they'd put a car outside the house."

"Nah."

"Why?"

"I got all the advantages, son."

This made no sense. *Mental clouding,* the Dilaudid sheet had said, *euphoria.* "Like what?"

His father shrugged. "You, for one. Might be interesting. Plus there's another reason."

"What?"

"Might give me some satisfaction. I can still think, buddy-boy, when those angels of mercy don't pump too much of this stuff into me."

"It's so you don't suffer."

"There's lots of kinds of suffering. Your mother heard you were under that building, *that* was suffering. I never seen suffering like that."

"I have."

"When?"

"When she was dying, Dad. I saw you."

His father's eyes drifted upward in remembrance, and he munched his mouth a bit. "Funny how we forget some things."

"You want anything to eat?"

His father shook his head. "Not for me. I got a little applesauce." His eyes were closed now, but he smiled, gums yellow. "You know what this is, don't you?"

"No, what."

"My last case."

"This is serious, Dad."

"I know it's serious," he whispered. "My last case, and I get to do it with my son. Couldn't be better than that." His father pushed the pain button, getting an optional bolus to chase the one just delivered. Upping the dose, wanting more, addicted. "If I were you I would get down in there in those pipes today before the guys down at the precinct maybe decide to do it after all. They won't crawl around in pipes. They'll bring in a backhoe and tear those drainpipes right out of there and look at every inch. But you get in there first, might be just as good."

His father's head lolled a bit, fading fast, and Wendy reappeared in the doorway.

"I'm going to clean him now," she whispered. "So he doesn't feel me moving him around."

Ray nodded. "How's he doing?"

The nurse tore open some antiseptic pads. She moved down to the foot of the bed. Ray followed her.

"The kidneys are barely working . . . he's losing weight," she went on. "I think I know what you are asking."

"That's exactly what I'm asking."

"He's got a strong heart, which isn't helping now. His hands and arms still have strength, too. Sometimes things can go on . . . but I'd say a week, maybe ten days."

"He's not eating much."

"He'll take applesauce, a little yogurt."

"Gloria told you about the men who came last night?"

She nodded. "Your dad won't move, you know."

"What about you? These guys could come back."

She considered him. "This is what I do, Mr. Grant. I stay with people who are dying and bring them what comfort I can. Your father is a lovely man. I don't see a lot of family, his wife is dead, you are all he's got—"

"What about Gloria?"

"We've been in many situations. You'd be surprised what we've seen."

She returned to the bedside and lifted the covers to expose the nephrostomy tubes that were draining his father's kidneys into clear plastic bags. The sight of these was bad, but not as bad as the original incision from the exploratory surgery running up his father's torso, a huge knife cut. Ray couldn't bear to see this, how poorly it had healed. He had seen things far worse, but those hadn't involved his father. He swallowed his terror and sorrow and stepped outside.

Like many men of his generation, Ray Grant Sr. had built a workshop in the basement, where he listened to baseball and football games on the radio while tinkering over more or less useless projects. The shelves held screws and nails in old jam jars, tools he used in the minor repairs he made on his rental houses, a hodgepodge of lumber, metal screening, boxes of doorknobs and hinges, cans of unknown metal parts for unknown appliances—in sum, the same loose, useless crud that had accrued everywhere else in the house, shed, porch, and backyard. He had dragged an old armchair down the stairs intending to strengthen it, and after doing so had left it down there as a more comfortable place to listen to the games on the radio.

Ray poked around in the workshop, gathering the tools he might need in the parking lot drain: gloves, goggles, rubber boots, flashlight, metal saw. Crawling up into a pipe full of shit wasn't exactly a good idea. He'd given himself a shot for either amebic dysentery or Japanese encephalitis in a dust-blown field hospital on the other side of the world six months earlier, but he couldn't remember which. He found the tools but wasn't quite ready to climb the stairs, for whenever he spent any time in the workshop he learned something about his father.

It was a room that showed how methodical and disciplined his father had been. Books on real estate management, electrical wiring, plumbing, building management, all carefully underlined, annotated even. Records of his buildings, going back twenty-five years. On the other side of the shop stood a row of rusty file cabinets containing copies of every one of his case records, going back to 1982, the year he made detective, got the gold shield. Completely illegal to have these records, but no one in the NYPD minded. Part of the institutional memory. Old cops remembered things, after all. Ray had read hundreds of these cases, including the unsolved ones. You read a few dozen, though, and soon saw how tedious police work was. He opened a drawer for the 1983 cabinet, pulled out a folder at random. Flopped it open, started to read a DD-5 form, the basic report detectives filled out: "Suspect walked south to Grand Central Station, where he was observed making a call from the last phone on the left in the east exit, and then suspect was observed exiting on 42nd Street, where he stopped at a newsstand for three minutes. He then walked . . ." And so on.

Ray slipped the folder back, shut the drawer. He didn't want this jam-up with Jin Li to be his father's last case. His father had already solved his last case, a blackmail that involved a young woman and a banker in his fifties. He knew because he'd read the file: the older guy had screwed the woman for a couple of months in one of Manhattan's better hotels, and when he got tired of her, she got tired of pretending that she liked him. Happened all the time, except that she expected real money for her trouble. The executive had paid her a few times, then warned her he was sick of it and to back off. By this time she was fucking a lanky, well-spoken Dominican who needed extra funds for his coke habit. At his urging she went back for more money to the banker, who told his wife they were going to New Zealand for the summer. She would fly there first and he'd meet her, which he did, after telling Ray's father everything about the affair. Yes, he preferred it be kept quiet. By the time the girl was arrested, the Dominican had left town for Santa Fe, escorting a young heiress with a drug habit. The girl could afford only a cheap lawyer, and when the banker and his wife finally returned from their restful sojourn in New Zealand, the girl had already accepted a quick plea bargain and was doing her two years. "A stupid last case," his father had said at the time. "But there it is."

But of course there had been more cases. Once a detective, always a detective. It was a way of thinking about human reality. After his retirement, his father had occasionally helped out his friends who now ran private investigation agencies, mostly by making a few calls or going along on a car ride to talk to someone, his service revolver tucked in his coat. Or setting up on someone, waiting in a car for six hours sipping coffee and pissing into a bottle. But mostly he had run his houses and once a year indulged in a fishing trip down to the Bahamas. He'd had a few girlfriends, after first asking Ray's permission if he could take off his wedding ring. He wanted to keep it on, he admitted, because it made him think of Ray's mother, but he was never going to find any companionship that way. His hand was the first place the women looked. Ray understood that. And so the wedding ring had reappeared in the little silk cuff link box in his father's underwear drawer, where he kept his military and police medals, his gold detective shield, his own father's watch, and other sacred items.

His father had gotten about five good years. The fishing trips, a cruise to Alaska. A couple of girlfriends who kept him busy, insisted he take them to Broadway shows, out to dinner, a few trips to Atlantic City. Companionship, laughs. Ray hadn't asked much about the women. He didn't want or need to know about them. Maybe they would help with his father's loneliness, and if so, then good. He wasn't much use to his father, anyway, being so far away and often out of touch. And in fact it had been one of the old girlfriends who called Ray while he was in Malaysia to say that his father had just had emergency surgery for blocked kidneys except that they had found a rare cancer everywhere and would Ray please come home, it didn't look good.

He didn't tell me he was having problems, Ray had said.

He didn't want to worry you, came the reply.

Ray stood now looking at his father's framed commendations and badges, as well as the inscribed photographs with Mayors Koch, Dinkins, and Giuliani. The letters from men and women thanking him for locating their children or finding the murderer or solving the robbery. His father had once put on a coat and a tie each day and taken the subway into Manhattan, where he'd done most of his tours. He had worked his way steadily through the ranks of the city's four thousand detectives, never accepting a promotion to manage other detectives and become part of the bureaucracy. Never getting caught up in the intrigues and petty betrayals, a relentless fact of police work. Staying out of the cop bars, avoiding any contact with Internal Affairs. Accepting reassignment from precinct to precinct, squad to squad. "Just do the work, son," he'd always said. "Just do the work and the rest takes care of itself." He stayed on foot, in the car, and on the phone. Or free, as he saw it. A bad fall off a wet fire escape when he was in his early fifties had slowed him a bit, but worse, when he was fifty-six, off duty and sitting in a neighborhood bar watching a Yankees game, he tried to step in between two fighting patrons, one a short fat man who had started it. His reflexes were gone and he had taken three punches, one a roundhouse flat to his cheek, a second into his solar plexus, doubling him over, and the third an uppercut beneath his jaw that broke six teeth. He fell over and had the presence of mind not to draw his service revolver, given that he was in no condition to use it properly. The assailant was caught two days later, and it was discovered he been a pretty good club fighter ten years before, in his twenties.

But the bum knee and the bad jaw led Ray's father to have a long think. He had his pension coming to him, he had his rental houses, he was set. More than that, he'd been a cop too long. The cop life was a hard one and had worn him down.

"You could do this, you know," he'd said to Ray many times. "You have the whole package. The judgment. Good with people. Tough. I should know, too."

"I don't think so, Dad," Ray had said every time back. "I'm not ready to do it."

"That's why you'd be good."

"No."

"There's still time—I could call a few—"

"No. I'm not able to—" *Kill people,* he'd never quite been able to say, something police officers very occasionally had to do.

"You'd be surprised what you're able to do."

"Not shooting someone."

"You'd shoot if it meant saving others' lives."

"Maybe not."

And in time his father had let it go, disappointed certainly but perhaps relieved, too. Lot of cops ended up as damaged men, one way or the other. There were some lost years in there, what with what happened to Ray, his mother getting sick, the beating his father took.

Ray climbed the basement stairs with the equipment and dropped it all into a box in the hall.

"Mr. Grant?"

Ray looked up. Wendy stepped into the hall. She wore a trim white nurse's dress and an unbuttoned blue sweater.

"What's up?"

"Your dad is comfortable now, sleeping."

"He seem pretty lucid to you?"

"In and out." She smiled in understanding. "That's normal. We expect that."

"It's the painkiller?"

She nodded vaguely. "Mostly."

"Please just tell me. Tell me the facts."

"Okay. It's a lot of things. The Dilaudid, yes. But the brain is an organ, too, and it's subject to the stresses of the disease. The cancer could be in the brain, in fact. He's not getting enough nutrition and that has its effect. But also there are the emotions. He is dying and he knows he is dying and he is worried about you."

Ray studied her. She was young and earnest, much different from Gloria, the night nurse who'd seen everything.

"It'll be like this, in and out?"

Wendy nodded. "As the pain gets worse, we'll have to increase his Dilaudid, and as that goes up, he'll be out more. He'll sleep a lot, too."

"How much longer?"

"So hard to say." She kept Ray's gaze, almost aggressively, it seemed. "As I said before, his heart is very strong for a man his age and the lungs are clear. It's not in the next few days. But sometimes these things take a turn."

"Yes."

She ducked her head, then lifted it. "I wanted to ask you if you had any family—who might make this easier."

"He outlived his only sister. My mother died years ago. He asked that no friends come. One guy might show up, but that's it."

"I see." The nurse seemed hesitant to conclude the conversation. "So, it's on you."

"Yes."

"If I may, Mr. Grant . . . ," she began, edging a touch closer to him. "I want to say that it is hard to be with a person who is dying and I am just wondering what your sources of emotional support will be in this difficult time."

"Thank you. I'll be fine."

But Wendy persisted, her eyes troubled, even unprofessionally moist. She smoothed her hands along her nurse's dress. "Have you been . . . please pardon me for asking, have you ever been with someone who is dying, Mr. Grant?"

He looked at the young nurse but was unable to answer. Instead a wind of memory passed through him. Mountains. Villages. Fields. Dust. Collapsed cities. Babies crying. Smoke. Years of memory. All the years he had been away.

"Mr. Grant?"

He found her eyes and then he found a bit of his voice. "Yes, miss, yes I have seen human beings die. I have seen my share, anyway."

A minute later Ray eased into the garden with a bundle under his shirt and opened the shed lock. With a glance back at the house, he slipped inside. He hefted the bags of peat moss. His father's guns were right where he'd left them, along with the boxes of ammunition. He lifted the Glock, always surprised by how heavy it was. Swung it around, dry-fired. His father had taught him how to shoot, taken him to the NYPD firing range in Queens. But he'd never liked guns. Nor the men who worshipped them, fetishized their power. He put the Glock back, added the guns he'd taken from the Chinese guys, ammo removed, then reset the bags on top. He thought of the two Mexican girls. Who would do that, what kind of sick person would kill that way? And Jin Li had been in that car? If the killer or killers knew that now, then she was still in danger. What if they had been after her in particular? This hadn't occurred to him before. A wave of protective fury went through him. I will find her, he thought. I'm going to find Jin Li and then I'm going to find the man who wanted to kill her.

The Russian was coming back for her, climbing the stairs with a slow, ominous tread, and he pushed open the door that led to the room full of boxes. He carried a paper bag with him. Jin Li had moved her small bundle of things to another part of the second floor, far from the window, in case he came looking. And now she was glad she'd done that. She watched him through a crack in the wall of boxes. He was in his fifties with slicked-back hair and the strange tattoos on his hands. She didn't like the tattoos; they looked like bugs. He hoisted his pants and looked about.

"Yes, I know you are in here, Chinese girl," he called. "I know you are hiding. I know you understand English, all these things I say."

The Russian went directly to the spot where she'd been before, inspecting the boxes carefully. He stopped, bent over, and picked up something. "You left something, Chinese girl," he called. He seemed to be holding something between his fingers, but she could not see what it was from across the room. "I have it right here," he called tauntingly. "You left long very nice black hair."

Instinctively she touched her head, as if to feel the hair's absence.

"I like this hair," called the Russian. "It is beautiful thing. But not as beautiful as you."

These words sent a ripple of dread through Jin Li's stomach.

"You see, I remember you, Chinese girl. I remember when you looked at this building. Maybe something like four months ago. You were wearing fancy clothes and shoes. Big businesswoman clothes. You never give back key. I know that. For most people, okay. But I notice this thing. Of course I do! I notice it because never has pretty Chinese lady come to look at building. Now I know you are here and I know those men are look for you. They told me the place where they stay."

He sat on one of the boxes and lit a cigarette. "I think you need to talk to me. Those men will pay me to tell them you are here. They told me one thousand dollars if I tell them you are here. But they look like bad men to me. And you are pretty girl." He smoked contemplatively, holding the butt up as he spoke, as if he were speaking to the cigarette itself. "Why do they want to find you? There seems to be so much pressures with this Chinese man with the funny tape on his nose, you know? Why are they look for you? I ask myself this interesting question. So I think maybe you want to talk to me a little bit. Talk to lonely Russian man. Russian and Chinese people, it is good thing. I am kind Russian man, you will see." He opened his bag. "There is juice and bagels and apples in here," he said, setting down the bag. "This is good for energy. Help you think a lot. I want you to think about being friendly to lonely Russian man. If you are friendly to me just only one time, then I will tell Chinese man you are gone, you not here. This is good deal for you, I think. I think maybe you liked me a little bit before and so you will think yes, maybe this is good deal. Just one time. There is good mattress downstairs, I put blanket. I am going to come back in a little while, maybe one hour. This time I will lock the door downstairs. You cannot get out now."

She listened to the Russian leave the room, his heavy footsteps making the warped old boards creak. Did she dare to come out? Maybe he was waiting behind the door! How did he know she was hungry? Then she crept over and inspected the bag.

Apples, in a bag. Smelled good. Delicious. And yet the worst thing, too, the saddest thing . . .

She had come such a long way, so far that she no longer remembered every step of the path, dared not think of the distances. Born in the arid plain, on her parents' farm. They did not have running water, only a town pump. Her father had grown up on the farm, never liking it. And he wasn't much of a farmer, either. The hogs got strange diseases that made their noses drip. Her grandfather was allowed to have three apple trees behind the barn. These he fertilized with chicken droppings he gathered from the road with a shovel. Her father had borrowed money from the town council and then had struck off for Shanghai and sold mealworms in the bird market for three years before sending for her mother. Then, a year later, after her mother had prospered selling mealworms and her father had built a little business hauling bamboo scaffolding from one building site to another, they sent for her and Chen. Her grandmother had wept and taken to her bed, saying she had been abandoned by everyone and it was time for her to join her ancestors. Her grandfather, whom she loved more than anyone, *ever*, more than anyone in the past and anyone she would ever love in the future (except for her children, of course—oh, how she hoped she'd have children someday), had taken Jin Li and Chen in the wagon down to the train station with a little sack full of his own apples, rice balls, and dried pork. He explained that they would be taking a *very* long train trip. Almost three days. He gave Chen some money— a handful of old bills—and told him that he would have to buy them water and sweets during the trip. Then her grandfather asked her brother to check to see if the train was coming, and when he ran excitedly to look, her grandfather showed her the new bills in his hand. *Take off your shoe and sock, quick,* he said, and he slipped the bills into her sock and pulled it back on. *Do not let older brother know you have this money,* he instructed gravely, *or he will take it and lose it. I gave him the old bills for water and sweets. Give this new money to mother. If brother loses all his money and you need money, take only one bill out of your sock and tell him you found it. Do you understand?* her grandfather asked, the skin folded over his old eyes. Yes, she said, eager to please him, anxious he know that she would do anything he asked of her. *This is all the money that I have saved in my life. It is for you and for older brother and for kind mother.* She nodded eagerly but did not want to leave him now. She felt suddenly scared. She saw what was happening. *You are my little bird and you will fly far,* he said, making a little cough. *I will never see you again but you will always be my little bird.* Then the train came and they rode hard-class on a bench seat for fifty-six hours. It was crowded and the people smelled. The train stopped and you had to go squat in the weeds. Her brother spent all the old bills on sweets and gum and water, but she did not pull out any of the new bills her grandfather had given her. Years later, when she had been a merit student at Harbin Institute of Technology, she had come to understand that each bite of the apples in the bag was the last she'd had of her grandfather. She'd never seen him again. And certainly he was dead now, it had been so long. That was the saddest thing and yet she would never cry about it, ever. She and her brother had lived in a little apartment in a crumbling block in old Shanghai, one room with mold on the window side, long since bulldozed to make way for an elevated highway now clogged with new cars, trucks, city buses. Her mother found work in a factory where she affixed a tiny piece of plastic lettering to the front of DVD players all day long. She used an electric hot-glue gun and had to do eighteen thousand pieces per twelve-hour day if she wanted to be paid at the end of the six-day workweek. About one piece every two seconds. Within two years, as Jin Li and her brother went to school, her father built up the scaffolding company enough that he was able to buy a small plot of ground and build a three-story apartment house. That same year Jin Li's mother became so tired and sick from the long hours of work and the smell of the glue that she fell asleep as she worked and the hot-glue gun shot a long wad of burning adhesive onto her cheek. She was fired from the factory and came home, and Jin Li took care of her. The wound became infected and a doctor they paid came and cut out the infection and cauterized it. It healed but left a jagged, rippling scar and nerve damage that made one side of her mother's mouth droop. Her mother retreated into their house and would not come out. Jin Li and her brother did the shopping. Her father chose to sleep in the fold-out bed in the front room and rarely spoke to her mother. He no longer let her cut his hair and meanwhile began to wear better clothes. Soon her father was dining out with minor government officials, sometimes taking Jin Li's brother to these meetings, where he began to learn the ways of business as it was done in the new China. Meanwhile, Jin Li learned English in school and studied as hard as she could, without passion, she saw now, but as a way of escaping—escaping something, *everything*. When she was fifteen she received the third highest score on the school tests in all of Shanghai District and that included the children of rich parents who had tutors who knew whom to pay to get a copy of the previous year's test. Her best score was in chemistry. Her mother came to the ceremony, but her father did not. Then came her proudest day: she was admitted to Harbin Institute of Technology, one of the finest universities in all of China, specializing in astronautics, mechatronics and automation, hot-working technology, communication and electronic systems, physical electronics, and optronics. Her team built the first plasma immersion ion implantation equipment in China! But in her third year her professors encouraged her to study American capitalism and information technology. We might need you for something different, Jin Li, they said. And of course her father and now her brother had been behind this, with his government connections. They wanted to use her to make money. Her English, her good looks, her ability to mix. Sometimes we send special people to work in America, they said. Very secret. So she studied American corporations, she read the history of New York City, she translated old copies of *Time* magazine, and she listened to radio broadcasts about traffic on the Brooklyn Bridge, the Abraham Lincoln Tunnel. She read a funny, old-fashioned novel about New York called *Bright Lights, Big City* that made no sense to her. She learned about taxis and subways and the Chrysler Building and why Greenwich Village was famous. And then—

How exciting it had been to come to America! But so strange. With every passing day, every week, she had felt herself changing in ways she did not understand. America was much different from what she'd expected. People were so . . . so *free*. They had the freeness *in* them. She hated them at first, thought them foolish and weak. But then a few years went by. She began to make a lot of money—what Americans called "big money"—for her brother and his fellow pig-men investors. The government supervisor from the consulate who was supposed to check on her every two months seemed less interested in checking up on her. China was changing rapidly, and yet she was not supposed to return. I am so dislocated, Jin Li thought, so "disjointed"—another vocabulary term that maybe wasn't quite correct. I am not in my country, I am not in my own self. She read the newspapers relentlessly, finding the *New York Post* and *Daily News* easy enough, and then after a year moving on to the *New York Times*. Always she was careful, especially on the phone. She knew about the American government computers searching for information, listening to phone calls, seeking word patterns, filtering through e-mails and search strings, linking hundreds of variables to hundreds of other variables. That was cutting-edge, major league. Although China's population was much bigger than America's, and Shanghai much larger than New York, she understood financial scale better now, after sifting through all those pieces of corporate trash. The American companies were so large! They operated all over the world! How tiny was her brother's enterprise! So small it should not be noticed. But someone *had* noticed. Who?

Now she heard shoes on the steps. The Russian, coming back, as he'd promised! She pulled her most precious items into the small green suitcase, as well as the bag of apples, and darted out the fire door and up the stairs. Third floor, fourth floor, fifth.

"Chinese girl!" came the Russian's voice behind her, this time deeper, with more of a breathy, slurry growl in it. "I know you are there on stairs, heh, I can hear you."

Jin Li reached the top of the steps. He was coming up behind her, his footsteps heavy but determined, his rising cigarette smoke reaching her first.

I am not scared of him, she decided, not very much.

"Chinese girl," came the voice, clearly drunk, "I am going to give you very good excellent Russian fucking." His wheezy cackling echoed in the stairwell. "I am going to give you good old Soviet . . . going upstairs, heh? Okay. I go faster."

She pushed open the door to the fifth floor and hurried around and through the iron bathtubs and pedestal sinks. Thousands of white people had washed themselves in these tubs and sinks, all of them now no doubt long dead. A room of naked ghosts soaping their crotches.

She was looking for the wooden ladder that led to the roof hatch, and she found it, climbing easily, suitcase in one hand.

"Chinese girl, now is time you will have very good sex with me, heh," came the boozy, excited voice, confident of its own intentions, eager for satisfaction. "I am excellent at good fucking, you like to fuck, I can see it in your eyes and the Chinese man say you like to fuck white men, so now I will—"

The roof hatch had a blue wooden door kept shut with a heavy steel padlock. But the lock was held by old screws in boards that had been rained and snowed upon for almost one hundred years. And anyway, Jin Li, honor graduate of Harbin Institute of Technology, had quite cleverly pulled out those screws the night before, using the hard edge of her nail clippers, while making her silent investigations through the building. Now she pushed against the blue boards with her fingertips and the door sailed open, caught by an evening wind that carved over the uneven flat tops of the connected buildings. In an instant she was out on the tar-papered roof, lifting her dress as she scampered past the old brick chimneys, many crookedly bent as if they'd melted ever so slowly over the many decades. The sky was not quite dark yet, and she could see where to quickly place her feet, where to avoid the angled black vent pipes that jutted up like elongated metallic mushrooms as well as the other rooftop clutter of telephone wires, satellite TV dishes, rusted cans of roof cement. By the time the Russian man lurched into the open doorway of his roof hatch, Jin Li was many buildings away, hiding behind a chimney with her little green suitcase and bag of apples. She breathed easily, even feeling a bit of defiant triumph, dark eyes flashing, but she knew that he would tell Chen about her now, which was also to say that she was in more danger than ever.

8 You do what you gotta do, and he was going to do it. Ray pulled his truck into the beach parking lot just as the sun went down. There was nothing special about the place except for the vista of water in front of it and a few red-hulled container ships out on the horizon. Trash and bottles. The kind of place teenagers used for drinking and screwing around, like he'd done when he was a teenager. Why would Jin Li be here with two Mexican girls in the wee hours of the night?

He parked in the far corner of the lot, away from the few cars there. He'd waited until dusk because he didn't want people to see him, and anyway, it was dark in the storm drains all the time. The lot was large enough that it had eight drains, and the question, he supposed, was where they went. Pete Blake had said they emptied into a gulley. Under most circumstances in New York City the drains would empty into the sewage system. But the elevation of the parking lot was four or five feet lower than the parkway fifty yards back and itself not much higher than the waterline, which meant that in a heavy fall storm when the tide was high, the waves probably flooded the parking lot. You couldn't have seawater draining into the New York City sewage system.

Each side of the lot had four drains, two on the corners and two centered in the middle. There was indeed a gulley of brackish water parallel to the lot, and Ray stepped through the high weeds and found a sizable pipe of corrugated aluminum. It was screened. He detected a thin whiff of excrement. He walked back to his truck and retrieved a pipe wrench and hacksaw from his toolbox. The pipe wrench was use-less on the screen bolts, which had long ago rusted tight. He dropped into the grass. A sediment of rotted organic matter pressed against the screen. No one, including any New York City detectives, had opened that screen in a long time. But the screen mesh would be easy to cut. He sawed a large upside-down U and pulled down the flap. He peered in with the light. A long, dark, tight colon of a tunnel. The idea of crawling into it sickened him. But I'm just fucking crazy enough to do it, Ray thought. Plus my father was a great detective. He'd be doing this if he could. He left the tools on the grass, set out his flashlight ahead of him, and crawled in, the flap in the screen snapping back after he let it go.

Go, Ray, go, he chanted. The storm drain was a standard three-foot width that rose steadily as he crawled. The bottom of the drain was silted with sediment, as if he were crawling along a moist streambed. His pants were soon damp and then soaked through. The light re-vealed leaves, trash, and at least one dead squirrel. He came to a junc-ture where the large pipe split in two pipes, one going left, the other right. These, he assumed, drained from the two sides of the lot. Which one should he take? His nose told him the answer. The one on the left smelled of shit, plain and simple. He crawled into it and found the smell getting worse. He estimated that he was halfway to the parking lot. The firemen washing out the car would have run their hoses long enough to clean off the lot but not so long that they would driven the excrement all the way through the drains. The subsequent rainfall had been light, but even a few hours of it would have created a fair volume of runoff.

He crawled farther. If he switched off the light, the corrugated tunnel was completely dark. A wet, increasingly odorous dark. He switched his light on again and then began to find what he wanted to find. A tampon. A cigarette butt. He shined his light on the bed of the pipe and saw a toothpaste cap. What do people put in toilets besides waste? Damn near everything. He noticed a scrap of paper and picked it up. Too dark to see what it was. He stuffed it in his pocket. His coat would smell of shit when he was done, he knew. He crawled farther.

Saw another scrap of something and put that in his pocket. The flashlight now revealed a long slick of rotting excrement, perhaps six inches deep, and at the far end, perhaps seventy feet away, a tiny square of pale night light where the drain opened to the world above. He would have to crawl seventy feet through shit. But guess what? he said to himself. This is nothing. You've seen much worse, pal. Just use some of the usual tricks. He pulled out two plugs made of tissue paper that he had dipped in mentholated jelly and put these into his nose. Then he unwrapped a wad of pepper gum and started to chew it. Last he pulled an air filter mask around his head. Just do it, Ray told himself. He shimmied forward on his belly, inspecting the detritus lodged in the shit. More tampons, then a baby's pacifier. People drop things in the toilet and think they magically disappear. He pulled a wiry thing and out came a woman's eyeliner brush. He dropped it and moved on. He came upon a slip of paper, a soggy colored napkin, and stuffed both into his pocket. Something else with numbers on it. Into the pocket. As he approached the tiny square of light, the shit became deeper, clogging the drain enough that he couldn't go farther. He reached out with his gloved hand and swept it across the shit. He felt three things. He pulled them to the flashlight. One was the end of a man's necktie. He discarded it. The second item was a dead mouse. A mercy he couldn't smell it. And the last item, he reminded himself. To the left. He swept his hand over the muddy shit until his finger found a child's sock. Useless. He stuck it in his pocket anyway.

He had reached to within ten feet of the drain and could even feel a weak draft of air from it. But the pipe was now clogged with vines. He took one last look around before retreating. What was this? A wet wad of shitty napkins with some kind of writing on them. He stuffed them in his jacket. Time to go. The pipe was too tight to turn around in, so he dutifully shimmied backward, feet first, until he reached the larger storm pipe, and there he could pull himself into a cannonball position, rotate, then shimmy face forward as the pipe fell in elevation before him. Downhill went much faster. He pulled himself through the U cut in the screen, then lay in the grass a moment, next to the tools he'd left there, apprehending how much human excrement he had caked on his knees, thighs, stomach, chest, forearms, and gloves. It was on his mask, cheeks, and forehead.

Things could be worse.

Back at the house, he removed the items from his pockets, set them on the back porch, then stripped to his underwear, left his clothes and shoes outside, and went into the house. After showering and pulling on clean clothes, he placed the items in a pan of warm water, rinsing off the shit and mud that adhered to them. With a bit of soap, the sock proved to be white, with ROBERT PETROCELLI JR. hand-lettered in indelible ink on the sole. The napkins were all cocktail napkins, the kind found at better restaurants. They were printed *Jeannie & Bill's Wedding* and, below that, *Sammy's*. A wedding reception. The paper with numbers on it was a credit card receipt issued to one Flora Silverman. Another piece of paper proved to be the soggy business card of one Fareed Gelfman, a sales associate at a used car emporium in the Bronx. On the reverse was written "Call me at home" and then a cell number. The last piece of paper was crumpled around a wad of chewing gum. The paper was so saturated that to pull on it would tear it. This Ray took to the kitchen. He put the wadded-up piece of paper on a plate and set the plate in the microwave. Ten seconds was probably enough to loosen it. When the timer went off he removed the plate and set it on the table, where he gently pulled the edges of the paper and found a photograph of a skinny white man with dozens of ear piercings performing fellatio on an obese black man. Very interesting, except that it was useless to him and he crumpled the paper and threw it in the trash.

The other pieces of information might tell him something. He made a big cup of coffee, then got out his father's old street maps of Brooklyn and Queens. Both were served by the municipal sewerage system, but to the east, as the two boroughs met Nassau County and building lot sizes got larger, making the transition from dense row housing to the classic suburban grid, some houses and businesses still used septic tanks. He looked up Robert Petrocelli and found one listed in Ozone Park, Queens. He marked the Petrocelli address. Then he looked up Flora Silverman in Queens and Brooklyn. There was no listing. But the place of business on her credit card receipt was a sushi restaurant in midtown Manhattan. The sewage certainly hadn't been picked up in midtown Manhattan. She'd crumpled up the receipt and thrown it into a toilet in Queens or Brooklyn. Not much to go on. He looked up the name on the next piece of paper: Sammy's Catering and Music Hall, *We Do-Wop Weddings, Anniversaries, Bar Mitzvahs, Birthdays.* This address was a mere nine blocks from the Petrocellis, also in Queens. My shitty information is pretty good, he thought.

He dialed Sammy's and spoke to the receptionist. "Hi," he said. "I'm new to the neighborhood and I saw you do a big business."

"We're always busy," came the reply. "What can I do for you?"

"Well, actually I'm wondering if you can recommend a sewage service."

"This some kind of joke? It's eight o'clock at night!"

"No, no joke. I saw you had a truck out there maybe a week ago and I can't remember the name on the side and figured if you used a service it would be—"

"We mostly use Victorious," said the voice. "Sometimes Town Septic. I can't remember who it was last week. It's a big truck, that's all I can tell you."

"Thanks," said Ray.

Next he dialed Fareed Gelfman.

"Yo," came a voice with rap music in the background.

"I'm trying to reach Fareed Gelfman."

"He's in the hospital."

"What?" said Ray.

"Yeah, some dude went upside his head, beat him down *bad.*"

"Why?"

"Oh, you know Fareed, man. He's alway poppin' on the women. Seems he gave his business card with his cell number on it to some girl who had a boyfriend and the dude went apeshit on him."

"Where'd she live?"

"With her boyfriend. Queens, Brooklyn, some shit like that."

"Thanks." Ray hung up. He dialed the Petrocelli number. A little girl answered.

"May I please speak to your mother or father?"

"Wait a minute."

"Yes?" came the voice of a busy woman in her forties.

"Mrs. Petrocelli, I'm calling from Town Septic."

"Yes? So late?"

"I'm wondering if you would consider using our services."

"We always use Victorious. Says Vic's on the side of the truck. Annie, go wash your face."

"I realize that, but I hope you'll consider our services."

"Vic's has same-day pump-out. We have pipe problems in the basement, and with all the kids, it clogs up."

"I see."

"We been using them for years. Also, Richie plays on my husband's softball team. Annie, you're a *mess*."

"Richie?"

"The driver for Vic's."

He sipped his coffee. "I see."

"So I'm sure your prices are like competitive and all, but we're not interested." She hung up.

Crawl around in some shit and you learn some things, he thought. He went back to his father's phone books. There were eight Vic's in Queens, but none were sewage operations. Brooklyn had twelve businesses with the name Vic, including barbershops and deli and pizza places, and one of them was Victorious Sewerage, located in Marine Park—not exactly close to the service addresses in Queens.

He dialed the household he'd called earlier.

"Hello?" came the voice of an exasperated mother. "What is it?"

"Hi, I called from Town Septic, earlier."

"I thought we were done."

"I'm just calling to clarify. You use Victorious Sewerage in Brooklyn?"

"Something like that. They got trucks all over out here. I have no idea if it's Brooklyn. Now please don't call again, I got kids to put to bed."

He hung up.

"I want the report," came a voice from the living room.

He found his father lying back staring at the ceiling.

"I crawled in, found some stuff. They suggest a Brooklyn company called Victorious Sewerage."

"Local?"

Ray told him about the map and phone calls. "Maybe I should tell Pete Blake."

His father waved a disgusted hand. "He'll figure it out sooner or later. Plus, you don't know much, anyway."

"I know the shit probably came from pipes or septic tanks cleaned by this Victorious operation."

"You go there tomorrow, ask questions, find this Richie guy."

"Just walk in?"

"Yeah, just walk in, Ray. Find him, follow him. Exactly what I would have done."

Ray studied his father. This was the face my mother kissed as a nineteen-year-old, he thought, this was the face that had walked the beat, voted for Nixon in '72, with most of America, then been glad when he resigned, who had questioned hundreds of suspects, heard every line of bullshit and weaseling, was an awkward dancer and a moderate drinker, a man who often visited his wife's grave, took a little fold-out chair and battery radio with him, sat there an hour listening to the Yankees game, his hand on the tombstone.

"Dad, you need a shave."

His father grunted. "You drinking coffee?"

"Yes."

"Gimme some of that. Haven't had coffee in—"

"Is it all right?"

"What's it going to do, kill me?"

He handed his father the cup. He drank slowly. "Mmn."

"What'll it be, electric razor or a blade?"

"Blade. Who is the barber?"

"Me."

He got a basin of hot water and a towel and shaving cream and a safety razor. He wet half the towel and softened up his father's face. His father closed his eyes and sank back into his pillow. "Feels good," he muttered.

Ray lathered up his father's neck and cheeks. It had been many years since he'd touched his father's face so much, maybe since he'd been a boy.

"You know, I worked a lot of missing persons cases," his father began, as if he'd been thinking of Jin Li since the morning. "Maybe forty or fifty. And what you see with them is that the people who are missing because they are hiding don't stay hidden for very long. They start moving around, they get restless. Folks get—"

"Hold still." Ray went under the chin with the safety razor.

"—lonely. I used to map out who a person knew, who the family was, the best friends, the old girlfriends."

The coffee was making his father talkative. "So how does this apply to Jin Li?"

"There's no family in the city?"

"No. She's from China."

"Friends?"

"I didn't know her very long before she broke it off."

"Boyfriends?"

"I have no idea."

"How long from the moment you met her until the first event in the bedroom Olympics?"

Ray remembered. "Two days."

"Don't think you get any credit for that, either." His father rolled his eyes toward the window. "Has orgasms easily?"

He nodded, feeling too embarrassed to say this to his father. "Do I get any credit for that?"

"No, of course not. It's the woman, always. How long was she in the country before meeting you?"

"Three, four years, maybe."

"Pretty girl, new in town, lonely. There've been plenty of guys, is my guess. She might have gone looking for an old boyfriend."

The idea made him wary. "Maybe."

"Easy on the cheek there. You see her apartment?"

"Little place way up in the nineties on the East Side. Very small."

"Not in Chinatown."

"Hated Chinatown. Too Chinese."

"Anything in her apartment?"

"Usual stuff. Dresses. She spent most of her money on clothes."

"No car?"

"No."

"Did you ever stay in her apartment?"

"Lots of times. Ate breakfast out."

"What did she read?"

He patted his father's cheek. Smooth. "Everything. She reads English perfectly."

"But spoken not so good."

"Spoken very good. It's the pronunciation that is hard."

"The palate hardens at some young age."

"She can understand any spoken English, except perhaps any really hard accents, like a deep Southern accent."

"So really she could go anywhere in the States easily enough." His father lifted the coffee cup again.

"That's what I'm saying."

"Did she have a secretive nature? Don't think, just answer."

"Well—"

"Just answer yes or no."

But before he could, Wendy came in, her long shift about to end. "Coffee!" She turned on Ray. "He can't be drinking coffee!"

"I asked for it," said his father.

"I am *sorry!*" the nurse said to Ray. "I think you just don't *understand* here. I think you need to be a little more sensitive to the situation. I realize that you have not spent much time with people who are"—she glanced at Ray's father—"who are sick and dying, yes, we can say that, but—"

"What was that?" croaked Ray's father suddenly. "What did you say about my son?"

The pretty young nurse turned to him and spoke more gently. "I said, I *know* he has not spent much time around people who are—"

"That's exactly what I thought you said." His father lifted both arms in excitement, pulling on his tubes, turning his fevered eyes directly upon her. "Let me tell you something, lady, my son Ray there has spent *years* around the dead and dying, he has seen *fields* of the dead, laid out in rows by the *hundreds*, burnt, crushed, drowned, he has seen the dead buried by the *thousands*, he has held the tiniest little babies that were—"

"Dad, Dad, that's enough!"

His father glared at the young nurse, who, for her part, looked at Ray in stunned wonder, at last realizing—as had another woman a few nights earlier—that she had no idea who he was.

They'd been happy once. And this was just the kind of rainy spring Manhattan evening he used to like. "Your wife is in the car downstairs," his secretary would say. Then came a quick brush of the hair in his private washroom. Adjust the silk tie in the mirror, shoot a look at Tom Reilly, guy on his way up. Then, downstairs, the company car would be idling by the curb, Ann waiting expectantly, and soon they'd head to yet another swanky dinner party. He'd let his hand slide along Ann's long firm thigh, eager to show her off, eager to hit the evening hard, plunge unabashedly into all the falsely earnest conversation, the self-congratulatory mannerisms, the grinning and groping, the money ogling and power sniffing, drinking neither too little nor too much, all on the happy glide path of intimacy with people *who made things happen.* He still remembered the night when Bill Gates was in the room—*the richest man in the world is in this room, Ann, right now, the richest man who ever lived*—and the time Jack Welch dropped by to pay his respects . . . but now, tonight it was different, now both of them were lost in their thoughts as the wet night slid by the windows outside, Ann next to him but with zero idea what he was walking into, that he was feeling weird spiders of pain crawl over his chest and left shoulder. Should he tell her, his doctor wife? She'd ask him what was wrong, why he was so stressed out. Nothing, sweetie, just a dinner party at Martz's mansion in the sky, twenty rooms thirty stories up in the air. Martz, the man who is stalking me. Tom had to go, no matter what, pretend nothing was wrong. The invitation had come yesterday. A straight-up test to see if Tom was avoiding Martz. Well, fine. He'd just swallowed a couple of beta-blockers at the office to zap out his anxiety. Martz would find the opportunity to take Tom aside and say, six months ago you were begging me to buy your stock and I do and so now what? Sniffing him for the anxiety that had been zapped out. There was something diseased and awful about Martz. Predatory, vulturish, his many hundreds of millions made by buying and selling the work of others, never had created or produced or invented anything himself, just slithered in when companies were weak or underfunded or down on their luck and sunk in his money-sucking fangs. And that was when Tom was going to look him in the eye and say, *Bill, you know as well as I do that the market is irrational sometimes, and the best we can see somebody has been driving down the price, maybe selling on the way down in order to buy back everything at a lower price later. Now you must stop hounding me . . .* Well, he'd say something like that, flat-out lie, just knock it back at Martz in a moment of high-stakes poker . . .

But Tom was unconvinced by his own line of bullshit and so felt around in his head wondering if he could feel the absence of anxiety. How long did beta-blockers take to kick in? He should know the answer, given all the drug efficacy reports he'd read. He could ask his wife, but she'd want to know why he was taking them, how he'd gotten them. Why was he so worried? It was not just Martz, no sir. There was more, much more, *bad more.* His fate, Tom understood all too well now, teetered upon a mere four words, words that were vague and deeply unimaginative: *send them a message.* Yes, he had said something like that, *send them a message,* send CorpServe, the office-cleaning and paper-shredding service, a message that he did not want them snooping around in his executive suite or anywhere else at Good Pharma. They were very thorough and got their cleaning done between the hours of seven and four every night as per the contract, but over the last few months several of his people had reported that they wondered if their papers had been pushed around a bit on their desks. The service's workers seemed unresponsive to a few casual questions. Like they were trained to be that way. Were they stealing? Looking for inside information? Hired by a Good Pharma competitor? It was all subtle, unprovable stuff, unless you installed hidden cameras, hired corporate espionage experts, the whole nine yards, a paper trail that eventually could be subpoenaed by a disgruntled, big-shoes investor like Martz or the neat freaks at the Securities and Exchange Commission. He had ordered that the IT department actually enforce the mandatory shutdown of all network workstations after six-thirty p.m., as well as upgrade the instant encryption of intracorporate and outgoing e-mail. Did this give him a margin of security? *Not necessarily.* So when a new report came that there was a particular question—just a question, mind you—about the service, something about some of the bags of paper for shredding maybe not quite all getting into the big mobile shredder parked at street level, he told his building services chief the words he had repeated to himself nearly every hour since he had vomited under his seat at the Yankees game: "I don't want people screwing around with our information! Send them a message that we want cleaning and paper waste removal and if we have to worry about them, we will tear up the contract and not pay them a dime. But frankly, I don't want to have to go find another service at this time of year. This outfit is cheap. So have a talk with them. Send them a fucking message they won't forget."

How he wished he had a recording of this comment. It would prove that Tom Reilly was innocent of anything. A bit nasty, perhaps, but innocent. *Send them a fucking message they won't forget.* He'd said it to James Tonelli, his facilities and operations manager, an eager, overly aggressive forty-year-old who prowled the building constantly checking on heating, cooling, plumbing, fire alarms, you name it. James, who was from Brooklyn, had simply said, "Don't worry, I'll take care of it," nodding as he did so, maybe some idea half hidden in his eyes, and so Tom had done just that, he had not worried, because James had said he'd *take care of it.*

They had not discussed how that might be accomplished, which Tom suspected would probably mean that James would have a ferocious little chat with the representative of the service company, a good-looking Chinese woman, he thought he remembered, having maybe met her once, and question the company's procedures and on-site supervision practices. The usual stuff. But then, a few days ago, he reads in the tabloid newspaper that two Mexican girls working for that same company have been found murdered out by the beach in Brooklyn? Still wearing the company uniforms? That sounded like *a fucking message they won't forget.* The girls had been recognized by some Good Pharma staffers, and the corporate relations office had confirmed they had worked in Good Pharma's offices *that very night.* Tom had simply nodded when told this and said, "If there's any inquiry, just please refer it to legal." At least the company name hadn't made it into the news. So far, anyway. And the next day James Tonelli calls in sick, and the day after that. Was this something to worry about? Was that a message Tom *wouldn't forget?* He wasn't sure. Well, yes, he was sure. He could construct rational reasons that might prop up his hopes, but his gut told him the two things were connected. There had always been a bit of talk about whom James knew in Brooklyn, whom his family was connected to. The Lucchese family, the Gambinos. These were just names, right? Did they really mean anything anymore? What was Tom, an expert in the Mafia? Wasn't the Mafia finished in New York, wiped out by RICO prosecutions? Just a joke that you enjoyed while watching reruns of *The Sopranos?* We actually kill people, ha-ha. Everybody thinks we are gone, ha-ha-ha. He realized that the Metro section of the paper sometimes had stories on organized crime. He should pay more attention to these things! The speculation about James had actually added a positive aura to his presence, and in general he got things done quickly—solved union issues, city inspector issues, anything that came up. He seemed to know whom to call and how to talk to them when he did. A very valuable skill set.

So Tom could worry about James. But Martz, the man who would be his host in ten minutes, didn't care about James or two dead Mexican girls. He cared about Good Pharma's stock price. In the last two weeks it had taken another dive, dropped another 17 percent. Why? Anyone's guess. Too many sellers! Usually companies knew why their stock was going up or down. Analysts issued reports, made recommendations, knowledgeable people commented in the newspaper, and companies themselves were required to make forward-looking comments about their projected earnings. It was a strange thing when a company didn't understand its own stock price, and by strange he meant very bad.

Why would so many people be selling Good Pharma's stock? Maybe they had a good reason to think his company was not as valuable as others thought it was. Maybe they had a good reason or maybe they had an *excellent* reason. And what could that be? Good Pharma had six major drugs in final development. Of these six, one was a major hit, three were minor duds, one was unknown as yet, and the sixth was a major wipeout. It had been Tom's intention to sequence the news of these developments very carefully. Unfortunately, the rate of progress of each drug in development did not match the optimal order of the announcement of its success or failure. So he had started to mess around with their progress, trying to speed up the big success, slow the duds a bit, and put the catastrophic wipeout into deep freeze: to be announced in fragments, even as the company also announced new initiatives, the ongoing successes of its major hit, and so on. He'd intended to play by the rules but certainly bend every opportunity to the company's advantage. There were things you could do—

—*if* you controlled your information! If you assumed that the data and reports in your office, lying around on people's desks, in their computers, and of course in their heads, were protected.

If not, hell's bells.

But what was he to do? If he started a formal internal investigation into how certain critical drug trial information had been stolen or released, then he might accidentally draw attention to the problem itself. He'd be creating *more* problematic information. *That* could be stolen, too, or leaked. All you needed was one Good Pharma exec chatting to an outsider at the wrong moment and you could have a hundred news stories inside a day, virally proliferating to the bloggers and investment websites. The stock price would crater. You would also draw attention to the company's information control processes—how faulty they were. How faulty the oversight was. Tom Reilly's oversight, that is.

Martz, of course, was already on to him, seemed to have sensed the problem, started to harass Tom. That's what this evening was all about, getting a chance to get close to Tom and make his threat even clearer. Tom saw that. Oh, yeah. But Martz would not be the last. Tom knew that the major shareholders—the mutual funds, the banks, the hedge fund operators—were not going to give him that opportunity. They had started to call, pressing for appointments. Lots of folks owned part of the company: German banks, French banks, English banks, their German pharmaceutical competitors, the Japanese conglomerates, South Korean real estate magnates, the Hong Kong shipping and manufacturing magnates. Lots of tough, unsentimental bastards. Cared not a whit for Tom Reilly and how many beta-blockers he was popping. Or anyone else at the company. Lose a quick 17 percent on $100 million, that's $17 million. Need to then get a 20 percent return to make yourself whole again. And Good Pharma didn't have a nice fat dividend protecting the stock price.

He felt the beta-blockers kicking in. He felt . . . well, *calm.* Cool, clear. His heart beating more slowly. Wow. *Wow.* He was calm enough to return to the unhappy topic of James Tonelli. Pretend for a moment that the cleaning service had in fact stolen some valuable information, such as the early rotten results on the synthetic skin trials. Pretend you can prove that. Now pretend that James spoke to somebody else who told somebody else to scare those two Mexican girls out of their minds—self-importantly intensifying the meaning of "send a message"—and they did something stupid, or something worse—like go and kill them. Then pretend you are the *New York Times* or *Wall Street Journal* reporter and you find out that some kind of important secret research information leaked out of a company and the stock price cratered and then the company—a company in the *health* field—apparently somehow caused the murder of the people working for the company that took the information. What might be the outcome of *that*? Tom felt calm! The outcome? A blizzard of bad press, shareholder outcries, God knew what else. His career would be shit-canned. And no severance or golden parachute, if he was found to have broken federal laws or company policies. Prison, even, if people testified a certain way. Once there was a problem, companies cut people out of their ranks within hours, like a bad spot on an apple. Under questioning, James would report that he had done exactly what he had been told to do. Mr. Thomas Reilly, let me see if I got this right: *You are the vice-president of a company doing cutting-edge research into how to save people's lives, your father was a doctor, your wife is a doctor, and you ordered or condoned or intimated that two helpless Mexican girls who cleaned your offices be asphyxiated by a tankload of human excrement?*

Maybe he *had* said something more to James. Was it possible? Maybe he had said something like, "Play rough, if you have to." To which James had given a solemn, tight-faced nod. Had Tom said that? Could he have *actually* said that? (He felt calm!) "I know people who know some people." Why could he now hear James saying that to him? Why did it sound like something James *would* say, with a touch of the Brooklyn streets in his voice? They'd talked early one morning, at around eight a.m., when the caffeine was pushing Tom along, jacking him up. *I know people who know some people.* That was bad. *Play rough.* That was bad, too. Had these things really been said?

Tom looked over at Ann. She spent the day with patients. Blissful. Had no idea what he was walking into. He felt calm.

As soon as she'd stirred that morning, they'd come to her: Mrs. Thompson, with the heart disease; Mr. Bernard with the bad liver; Harriet Gorsky with end-state renal failure; her patients, all 1,690 of them, a milling, shuffling, coughing, anxious crowd in her mind, divisible by age and sex and of course illness as well as probable illness. Her lung cancer patients, for instance: the patients who in all likelihood might have it, pending tests; did have it and were realizing they would die before too long; and those who were in the bed now, coughing weakly. Or there were the many women with anxiety disorders, who ranged from mildly obsessive to those needing immediate hospitalization. Put her in a room with all of these people (no, please don't) and she would be able to drift from one to another sensing disease in many cases, suddenly recalling the string of data that came with each patient, the hemocrit level, the path report, even height and weight at the last checkup. And their histories, their secrets—an enormous psychic bur-den she tried not to carry but always did. She cared for them, she found them interesting, this selection of humanity, skewed of course toward those who had health insurance and women (men so obstinate about caring for themselves). A few she genuinely didn't like, a few she might cry over when the end came, and a few she even loved, from afar, mostly, chastely, no hint betrayed, of course. Some of the older men who'd lost their wives came in wearing a coat and tie, as if still working, and they often were stoical and silent as she described their conditions, what the problem was. They pursed their lips and nodded, rubbed their dry hands together like it was just a financial matter re-quiring they write out a very large check. Broke her heart. Maybe they reminded her of her father in his last years. How could they not? They were human beings. They stood nearly naked before her (the men with their loose underwear lowered as she felt for hernias, common in older men and potentially quite serious if infection set in, or testicular swellings), they had odors (women generally wore perfume and cleaned themselves better), they burped softly, farted, grunted. Very occasionally they urinated by accident, especially during an anal exam. She never betrayed any emotion at this, never showed that such behav-ior was in any way shameful. Because it wasn't. We are animals and subject to the mortification of the flesh. Born so that we may die.

She looked over at Tom in the car. Lost in his thoughts. Seemed calm—for him, anyway. Hadn't asked her about her day. Had barely kissed her hello when she got into the car. Was she angry with him? Yes, but more than that, discouraged. They each worked too hard, they carried too much . . . and with that the day came back to her . . . after lunch she'd seen a young married man who complained of chest and stomach pain but admitted that he had just had an affair with his wife's divorced younger sister and probably given her herpes. Ann nodded patiently but thought, *You creep.* Ann had handed the man a prescrip-tion and told him to tell his wife, who was also her patient. Next was a young woman who'd asked to have her antidepressants adjusted up-ward. The woman was clinically obese, so much so that the fat had reached the last knuckle on each of her fingers, and was a heavy smoker. Ann had spoken sternly to her about her lungs and heart but doubted it would have any effect. The next patient had been an elderly woman whose lower spine and pelvis were deteriorating because of severe arthritis. She moved slowly, apologizing unnecessarily as Ann inspected her lumbar region.

So different from one another, these human beings. If you are a doctor, you have secret knowledge of these differences. And if you have secret knowledge, then you are always at risk of knowing things about people you love, knowing the very thing that you prefer not to know. And now there was something about Tom that was bothering her. She didn't know if she felt this or knew it, or if she felt it as his wife or as a doctor. He was, to all outward appearances, an utterly healthy forty-two-year-old man, six foot one, perhaps 230 pounds, which was too heavy, but vigorous. Yet there was something, a twitch in his eye, a distracted irritability. The animal was under stress, unusual stress. He'd said nothing. Either he knew what was wrong or he didn't. But she sensed that he knew exactly what was wrong. Underneath that affable glad-hander was a sharp mind. Tom could be very tough with people. He compartmentalized, internalized, rationalized. Valuable abilities in a corporate setting, she knew. But the animal always won. This is what she'd learned from her patients. The brain was an organ that privileged itself before other organs, arranged the perception of reality for its own comfort. But it could not control the body's reaction to its own perceptions, the secretion of hormones, the cellular flux. Tom was acting like nothing was wrong. He seemed calm, but she knew he was not. Something *was* wrong. Right now, as he was staring out of the window of the town car, telling her nothing. Why?

"This is it," he said to the driver.

A lovely apartment! Huge! High in the air! Some of the people were actual billionaires, not that it mattered to Ann. She chatted, drifted, let Tom do his thing, talk to the big wheels, over in the corner, each holding his drink. She'd shaken hands with some people but found her way to a huge sofa and sat there happily, half hidden by a giant spray of lilies, accepted a glass of white wine. The servants were all *tiny* Guatemalans. She was too tired to be of much use to Tom. So she watched. She'd been introduced to Connie, the youngish wife of someone important there, so Ann studied her. The woman sported a very expensive boob job. How natural and yet grotesque! How *impossible* yet marvelous! One hardly knew who was most responsible for this aesthetic state of affairs, men or women themselves. And yet, equally strange to Ann was the fact that the fake tits *worked*. Men who were otherwise among the most sophisticated and brilliant, worldly and perceptive, lawyers, bankers, artists—men who had buried parents, friends, spouses, even children, and who thus knew the essential tragedy of the flesh—were themselves so often rendered helpless before these unnatural yet unarguably beautifully executed falsies. Smart men! Thoughtful, sensitive men! Doctors! Yes, *doctors*, who should know better, who were well informed about infection rates, adhesions of muscle tissue, immune system response, nerve damage, tissue scarring, ligament failure, the complications of burst implants, and so on. Yes, even doctors. The male response was hardwired in, kicking off testosterone pulses in the endocrine system. Couldn't help themselves. Helpless. Helpless *men*. They lost the power of discernment and resistance. They lusted, and in the glare of that lust, women gained power, if for only a moment.

Now Connie spied Ann across the room, turned, and came to her, smiling with professional hospitality.

"Are you—you seem to be—"

"I'm sorry—bit tired. Long day."

This admission was on the outer edges of Manhattan dinner party protocol. You never admitted weakness or insufficiency. "Oh, are you—what—?" ask Connie politely, one eye on the room.

"I'm a physician and I just saw a lot of patients today, that's all."

At this Connie's posture softened, and she drew nearer, seeming to reappraise Ann with both admiration and a bit of fear, for people know that doctors know things the rest of humanity does not.

"May I ask your specialty?"

"I'm an internist. Internal medicine."

Connie sat down, intimately next to her. "I keep telling my husband he must see a doctor."

Ann nodded. Many wives said this.

Connie leaned closer, whispered. "Can I talk to you about this? He pees too often in the night. Maybe six or seven times."

"That *is* too many times."

Connie leaned closer. "And he has *pain*."

"When he pees?"

Connie winced, as if sampling such pain. "Don't *think* so."

"Trouble peeing?" Ann asked.

"Maybe. He's so private. I know he has pain you know, down there, down *under* there."

Benign prostate hyperplasia less likely, malignancy more so, she thought. PSA test. New inflammation test. Eliminate false positive. Biopsy probable. "Pain all the time?"

The question triggered alarm in Connie's beautiful face. "Maybe, but I think *yes*, all the time!" she whispered.

"Between his anus and scrotum. Sensitive to touch?"

"Well—" Connie drew a breath of surprise at the sudden clinical *frankness* of this question. And made a quick check that no one was listening to them from behind the lilies. "Well, *yes*. It worries me so much!"

Ann wondered if she had seen Connie's face before somewhere, an advertisement, perhaps. "He should see a urologist as soon as possible—I mean tomorrow—and get a digital exam."

"That's what he doesn't want . . ."

"He's going to have to get over that."

Connie was nodding frantically, eyes wet, apparently having forgotten the party.

"It's no big deal, frankly. As a woman, you know that, the way gynecologists poke into us."

"I've *told* him."

"He's never had one?"

"No."

Ann nodded. "Afraid?"

"Yes."

"You really should have a talk with him."

"Yes. He's so very tender down there."

"He needs an exam *tomorrow*."

Connie became tearful. "Doctor, do you—do you do them?"

"Almost every day."

"And the men—do they mind the fact that—"

"I'm a woman? No. They accept it."

Connie looked at her, a question seeming to tremble in her big beautiful eyes. "Would—would you, would you do it for him?"

"Of course, he can call my—"

"No, no, he's going to Germany tomorrow for four days, he's being picked up at six . . . no, no, I mean would you, could you now? Here?"

Here. Now. Not what she wanted to do but it was her duty, always her duty to help. Connie led her down a hallway to a sumptuous bedroom filled with Picassos on every wall, Manhattan sprawling below from two sides. *This is real money,* Ann breathed to herself. *This is what Tom wants.*

"Do you need anything?"

Yes, Ann said. Connie nodded. She picked up the phone, pushed one button. A servant was dispatched to an all-night pharmacy for rubber examination gloves and K-Y Jelly.

"I'll go get him," Connie called. "Please just wait—"

More than a few minutes went by. Was Tom wondering where she was? Not necessarily. He could easily be locked in a conversation on the far side of the room. She sat perched on an upholstered bench with her purse, which had a very small doctor's bag in it.

"—to do it, Bill, I absolutely insist."

Connie appeared at the door. "He thinks he's humoring me."

Martz stepped into the room, glowering. "I am."

"I said it would only take a minute."

Connie handed Ann a white bag from the pharmacy and pulled the door shut.

"Well, Doctor—"

"Please call me Ann," she said, "given that I am your guest."

Martz nodded obligatorily, his expression indicating he had no idea who she was. "Where do you practice?"

"I have my own office practice and I have privileges at Beth Israel."

"How many exams of this nature have you performed?"

"I don't know. Several thousand, perhaps."

Martz's eyes, yellowed by decades of golf, hung open as he stared at her. She could not decide if he found her attractive or whether his interest lay elsewhere. Maybe he hated his wife for asking him do this, maybe he hated Ann for agreeing to do so. Most likely he was examining her for signs that might tell him what she was learning about him. This was typical of patients; they studied the doctor who studied them. Up close she saw that he'd had dozens of tiny skin cancers removed, including on the outer edge of his lower lip. The divot in his lip suggested a healed knife wound, even a disregard for danger.

"I told your wife I'd do this," Ann said, "but of course, it's your decision."

"Let's do it. Then she'll let me alone."

Martz dropped his pants.

"Bend over, put your hands on the table," she instructed.

"How did she find you?"

"We got to talking."

"What a topic of conversation."

"Well, you know women," she said, lubing her fingers. "We do talk about *everything*."

"I didn't meet everyone," he growled, being polite, making conversation. "You came with—?"

She went in with the forefinger and middle finger together in one firm motion. He grunted. They all grunted, except the men who'd had anal sex; they anticipated the sensation and evaluated it. She moved her fingers up the inside of his rectum and felt the lateral and posterior walls for any rectal masses. Then she identified the prostate on the anterior wall and swept her fingers from side to side, noting smoothness, consistency, lumps, asymmetry, and size.

There was a lot of swelling, bad swelling.

"Excuse me," she responded, "what? Oh, I came with Tom Reilly. I'm his wife."

"Aah, I see." Martz stiffened, actually tightened his asshole. "Good to know that, Doctor. That is, *aah*, informative. I want you to know exactly what would make me . . . *better*, would reduce my difficulties."

In general she preferred that patients not self-diagnose. They were inevitably wrong, usually erring on the most dramatic side. She'd once had a woman come in with numb feet and insist she be tested for multiple sclerosis, when in fact the problem was that her shoes were too tight.

". . . the change in my life that would be most *prophylactic* would be if your—"

She paid little attention to what he was saying, instead carefully feathering her fingers against the lumpy surface of the prostate, probing softly, seeing if she caused pain. The basic rule was that you pressed no harder than you would push against an eyeball. She arced her fingers back to the edge of the prostate to see if she could feel the shape of the swelling better, whether it involved one lobe of the prostate or both.

"Dr. Reilly?"

"Yes?" she answered.

"I *said*, if your husband—"

Martz's hand shot back and grabbed her own, pulling it out of his rectum, making a wet sucking sound. He turned toward her, underpants still at his knees, shirt and tie hanging down, and drew close, uncomfortably close to her. His large, loose-skinned hand lifted her smelly, gloved fingers up between them as his eyes stared into her face. "If *Tom* would do me the courtesy of telling me—" She fought Martz and tried to pull away, but his big hand held her fist tight, her authority as a physician gone. "—what the *fuck* is going on at Good Pharma." He saw her confused reaction. "Oh, your bright, ambitious husband *knows* something, Doctor. But he isn't telling me. Tried to pretend nothing is going on. Tried tonight, to my face, lied directly to my face, Doctor Reilly. Isn't telling me or anyone else, as far as I can see. I have *hundreds of millions of dollars* invested in his company. Do you understand? That is a lot of money, even for me. Other people's money, Doctor. The stock was going up. But now it is not. There's a piece of information I don't have! Tom has it, Doctor! Tom *knows* it! And I want him—" Now Martz was crushing her hand in his, leaning into her with the color rising in his face, his lip curled in anger, a primate showing his old teeth, her fingers with his blood-streaked shit on them an inch from her nose. "—to tell me!"

The pain woke him. As always at this time of night, just a few minutes before the machine sent a shot of lovely wonderful morphine through the tube in his arm. He loved the drug more than he could say, craved it, yes, of course—no wonder people destroyed themselves for it. *I'm addicted.* But these minutes were when he was most clear, the pain rising quickly yet bearable, the veil of the morphine pulled away just far enough to let his mind work. Precious seconds to him. Precious time to think, think about the only thing he had left now: his son. All else was lost to him—his body, failing further every day; his spirit, which needed a body to be manifest; his physical belongings, which he could no longer use or even see from where he lay; and his memory, weakened by suffering, medication, and time. And of course he had lost his wife, Mary, years ago, he had lost the fellowship of his brother detectives when he retired, he had lost so much, nearly everything now.

And yet, he knew, this was in the way of things. Everyone lost everything at the end. You became unified with every human being who had ever lived and who ever would live, including his parents, his brother and sister, Mary, of course, and even Ray. Perhaps that was consoling. You know again the people who have died and you feel they know you now. Dying slowly, you think about death, you study its approach. You imagine the world after you are gone, you see the enormity of time, the final privacy of consciousness. He'd sat with Mary in the last weeks of her life, her mouth pulling back day by day into an emaciated mask, her breath fouler each day, too, and he had gazed into her dull eyes and spoken to her and she to him and he knew now that he had no idea then what she was thinking. She had tried to share it but known she could not. They'd held hands for hours and that had been everything. Worlds within worlds. He saw that no one alive knew what he was thinking. Even the nurses, the lovely professional death watchers.

But he was not dead yet. Not *quite.* He turned his head to see that it was just after two a.m. Ray was upstairs. The night nurse slept in the next room. Sometimes he heard her talk in her sleep, which made him smile. Such an intimate thing, a sweetness.

Now he lifted the sheet to examine the long incision where the doctors had cut him open trying to find out what was wrong with him. Right through the stomach muscles. They had closed him up, knowing there was no hope. The incision had not healed well and kept getting infected. The nurses left the wound unbandaged with the wish that the air would help. How it hurt to lift his head, but he did, just to see the giant cut, which ran from his breastbone to the top of his public hair. The edges of the incision did not meet, had dried and puckered back from each other. Beyond that lay his penis in a nest of gray hair, a white plastic catheter stuck in it to drain any incidental urine that dribbled through his blocked kidneys. He could barely feel the catheter anymore. He had stopped missing his penis, years earlier, in fact. It had become a mere hose. Old men didn't talk about this, not even to each other. Just bore the truth of it, the change of life. You learned something about the world when you lost your sexual desire, you saw things differently, how tormented young men were, how stupid and out of control.

He could feel the liquids gurgle inside him and he could feel them gurgle out. The nurses measured his urine, the watery mud of feces that came from him. Not that it changed anything. They meant well and were trying their best. Just quietly helping him, hour after hour. Few men honestly confronted the superior unselfishness of women. Because to do so unraveled their entire belief systems and that was something they could not endure. He always tried hard to follow the nurses' directions—*please, lift your legs . . . here's the spoon, Mr. Grant . . . we need to turn you so we may clean you . . .* He was not afraid of the pain. The little box worked quite well and he had been very clear with Ray that when the time came, Ray was to push him softly into oblivion. It would be hard for his son, he knew his son would resist doing so, especially given his training, but he hoped Ray would do what needed to be done, in the end.

He hoped his son would have the strength to kill him.

And yet, to repeat himself—as he was doing, he knew, repeating his thoughts over and over, slowly wearing them into nothing—and yet his son was here and would go on. But there was trouble for Ray now. The Chinese girl. The men who had taken away his machine. Ray had explained the problem. And he had been able to respond, to nod his head a bit and say yes. Ray was very clever. But the father always knew the son's flaws. Ray could be too impulsive, too instinctive. This might change as he got older. He had a weakness for women, too. Not a womanizer, not exactly. His weakness was that he cared for them easily, without remembering to protect himself.

Ray's other weakness was more serious. It was that he assumed that he was lucky. He had done so since he was a boy. Lucky how? Not that good things always happened to him but that bad things wouldn't. He'd been buried alive and lived. You were that lucky only once in a life. And maybe that used up all the rest of your good luck.

As for what Ray did while he was away, the old detective didn't quite understand all that. Foreign countries, he didn't know about. He knew about Brooklyn, Queens, and parts of Manhattan. The trouble with the Chinese girl was real enough. It was New York City kind of trouble. He sensed it. Somebody wanted something badly. Probably had to do with money, maybe the half-dead Mafia in some way, given the neighborhood. Mob carting services, truck companies, garages. He'd never dealt with Chinese gangsters but knew they could be tough, ruthless. Ray was mixed up in it now . . . he'd find that sewage company tomorrow and somebody there would know a few facts. Or Ray would sense a lie. He had that gift. As a detective you told yourself that people were telling the truth unless you had reason to think they were lying.

Otherwise you would drive yourself mad with suspicion. But nonetheless you could tell. The brain knew. Something in the voice, the eyes, the facial muscles. Scientists had studied this, proved it. But as a detective you just got very good at sensing the lie. You listened to hundreds of people lie, you learned how human beings do it. He'd forgotten—oh, yes. This Chinese girl had gotten to Ray somehow. Ray was in this thing now, whether he wanted to be or not. It was going to get worse for someone, he was sure. Two girls had died, and if he knew anything about how these things went, they wouldn't be the last. He knew Ray had moved his guns to the shed and put on a new lock. He knew that Ray had hidden the key in the birdhouse. And he knew that Ray had checked on the guns yesterday. This was unlike him. It meant Ray was preparing himself, worried. And the nurse had told him about what Ray had done to the men in the hallway, the savagery he'd displayed.

Does all this scare me? thought the old detective. Maybe. Well, yes. But I have to believe in Ray, because otherwise I am dying for nothing. I have to try to help him. Be *victorious*.

And that was when he thought of something, something important that Ray needed to—?

The Dilaudid pump clicked and sent him a bolus. The warmth of it was so beautiful . . . *I'm addicted* . . . But wait! What was the thing he had just thought of, the thing Ray had to know? The morphine was taking it away from him . . . something important, having to do with Ray's problem, the kind of information that he used to . . . the exact sort of thing a detective always wrote down in his . . . just so he couldn't possibly . . . And here he . . . he had *forgotten*, the morphine warming his eyes, slowing his heart, pulling his breath deeper toward painless sleep . . . oh, he had thought of . . . it was . . . the thing that his son needed to know . . . what was it?

"Yo, I'm Richie's cousin."

Too fast.

"Hey, guy, I'm Richie's cousin."

Better. Get that Brooklyn thing into the voice.

He was sitting in his truck down at the corner of Fourteenth Avenue and Eighty-sixth Street, pulled over by Dyker Beach Park, where he could see old Italian guys playing bocci, rolling the weighted balls along the packed-dirt alley. Lot of good times playing baseball in that park. Across the street was a deli that once been a joint called the 19th Hole, a notorious Mafia hangout. Dozens of murders had been ordered, planned, requested, or approved there by the Lucchese crime family. His father had once said to him that Ray was never to set foot in the 19th Hole under any circumstances, no matter how old and tough he thought he was, and if he knew anyone who frequented the place, Ray was to drop the acquaintance immediately. But now the Mafia was mostly broken up, scattered, on the run. So they said, anyway.

The city kept removing pay phones, but there was one outside the deli, he'd remembered. He didn't want to use the house phone, plus the sounds of the street would add authenticity. The phone was free. He jumped out of the truck, crossed Fourteenth Avenue, slipped in the quarters, dialed.

"Victorious," came a woman's voice.

"I'm trying to get in touch with Richie."

"He's not around."

"I kinda need to talk to him."

"Call him on the cell," she said.

"Don't got the number."

"Who is this?"

"Richie's cousin." There, the leap into the lie.

"Well, he's out on a job."

"Just tell me where he is, I'll go talk to him there."

"Can't do that."

"Listen, I'm trying to help the guy out with something, see what I mean, like?"

A long pause followed. "Hang on."

Then he heard the woman talking into some kind of radio or squawk box. "Richie, where you at?"

A garble of static came back that Ray couldn't understand.

"I got a guy says he's your cousin."

More static.

"Hello? He says what's this about?"

Ray looked down Eighty-sixth Street, drew in a lungful of the place. "He knows what it's about. I ain't talking about it on the phone."

She repeated this, and the squawk box answered.

"All right," she told Ray. "He's out on a job down in the Rockaways, 123rd Street right before the boardwalk."

"Thanks." He was about to hang up when he heard a man ask, "Who just called for Richie, who was that?"

The line went dead.

Ray listened to the far buzz in the earpiece, then hung up. He lifted the receiver again and inserted a bunch of quarters from his pocket, not even counting them. She didn't answer, but her cell phone message came on, then the beep. "Jin Li," he said, "this is Ray, the guy who used to be your boyfriend. I'm not calling to talk about what happened between us. I'm just worried about you, okay? Your brother is in New York and found me. He's got a bunch of guys with him and he's looking for you . . ." What else to say? Don't mention the police, he told himself, that will just freak her out. "He explained to me about what happened to you with the two Mexican girls. So I'm looking for you, too. You can call me, but not on my cell. It's gone. Call me at home. You have the number. If a woman answers, remember it's my father's nurse. I know you are scared. All right, I hope you are—" The phone chimed, time was up. He replaced the receiver. If she wasn't answering her cell phone, well—it could mean several things, all of which gave him a bad feeling.

The Rockaways was a big sandbar that hung below Brooklyn, with a village clustered at either end and miles of fabulous beach in between. Technically it was part of Queens, though it felt like Brooklyn, because you could get there from Flatbush Avenue, the zigzag thoroughfare that people had been using for more than three hundred years, starting with Dutch farmers driving their pigs and cattle to market until the present, when you were just as likely to find a Pakistani hauling a load of fake BMW carburetors made in Vietnam to be installed by a Jamaican mechanic in a car owned by a Nigerian. The future of New York City was often found in the cultural mixology of Brooklyn and Queens long before arriving in Manhattan. The Rockaways, however, had always been hard-core Irish, a place apart, dominated by policemen and firefighters, more or less segregated. Once known as the "Irish Riviera," the Rockaways was a place where working-class New Yorkers once rented bungalows for fifty dollars a summer. Jigs and reels were danced in the bars, beer five cents a glass. That was all gone. Now it was high-rises and million-dollar homes. He'd once spent a lost weekend there when he was eighteen, drinking, running around, driving on the beach. How naïve he'd been at that age, obsessed with a girl whose name he could no longer remember and, even more important at the time, preoccupied with his summer league baseball team. He'd been a pretty good catcher, could take the beating of the position. But, like most American teenagers, he'd been utterly oblivious to almost everything beyond himself. Boys were different in other parts of the world; they became men sooner, were accelerated toward their fates. Example? Sure: Once, in Mogadishu, Somalia, he'd had a fifteen-year-old stick a Chinese-made AK-47 into his face while a crew of younger boys swarmed over his supply truck, stealing water, medicine, foodstuffs, motor oil, water purification tablets, children's clothing, and three dozen crank-powered radios. Ray had spent two days loading the truck, and in a matter of minutes, it was plundered. The boy made Ray lie on the ground, and when his crew was done he had fired a bullet into the desert sand next to Ray's head. Then left. Ray had taken his sweet time getting up and, before doing so, it occurred to him that he could dig up the bullet, which he did, about a foot deep in the sand. It was still warm and he touched it to his lip religiously, why he didn't know. The next day, after he had returned to camp with the empty relief truck, he heard that the boy who'd held him at gunpoint had, that same evening, had both arms macheted off by a rival group stealing the supplies from his crew.

Here and now, Ray told himself, *be here and now. Don't be haunted.* He made the turn for the Rockaways, the Atlantic to his right. He reminded himself that all he knew about Richie was that he'd probably been the man who'd pumped out the household waste in Queens that had found its way into a parking lot drain in Brooklyn. Not much to go on. But not nothing, either.

The Rockaways—the name suggested a faraway place where you might rock a chair by the ocean. Which was correct. On 123rd Street big houses sat on narrow lots, the kinds of places families could stay in all summer, kids going to the beach every day, dad out back with the barbecue. He spotted the big green sewage truck pulled up on the curb, passed by, found a parking spot, and walked back. A large man in coveralls with a blond crew cut stood next to the truck, letting a fat rubber hose run through his gloved hands as it mechanically spooled itself onto the truck. He was just finishing.

"Hey," called Ray, walking up. "You got a minute? Let me tell you my problem. I live couple streets away. Kinda embarrassing. My wedding ring went down the toilet. Barely flushed, though."

The man nodded warily, inspecting Ray up and down, no doubt wondering if Ray's presence was related to the earlier call about the "cousin."

"Happens all the time," he said. "Earrings, watches, dentures. All kinds of stuff."

Ray felt jumpy, a little strange. "How do I get it back?"

"Could still be there. Turn off all your water. Give us a call, we'll pump you out, see if it's there."

Ray pretended to watch the hose. "You got any kind of screen on that, find things caught in it?"

"Yes. But we only use it if we're looking for something. It'd get jammed every three minutes, shit people put in there. I mean the stuff that *ain't* shit, if you see what I mean."

Ray nodded. "How fast these trucks fill up?"

"Day or two. Lot of shit in the world."

"Holds what—?"

"On the side of the truck it says eight thousand gallons but we try not to fill it quite that much. Gets too heavy. Hard to go uphill. You can crack a guy's driveway."

Ray pointed at the name on the door: Richie.

"They give every guy his own truck?"

"No, only us top guys."

"What if the truck breaks down?"

A pause, the mood shifting. "What if I don't feel like answering any more questions?"

"Hey, just being friendly," Ray said.

Richie grunted. Then he looked at Ray, mouth tight. "I don't know who you are, buddy, but you're fucking with me. I can feel it. So get the fuck away from me and my truck and just take your bullshit elsewhere. Either that or we got a problem, and if we got a problem, then I got a lot of ways to fix it."

The two men held each other's gaze. Indeed, Ray thought, we've got a problem.

But he played it cool. "No sweat," he said, "not a problem." He put up his hands meekly, backed away.

But now that I know what you look like, Richie-boy, he thought, I'll be watching you.

"Sir, we are *honored*. But before we begin I just want to say that we know a man like yourself has many options, of course, so I have personally supervised this research, not only for the confidentiality issue—one can never be too careful—but also because I want you to know that we are dedicated to providing you excellent service."

The man, who was named Phelps, got no response, and his voice seemed to echo around the large room full of antiques and paintings thirty stories above Central Park and then get lost up near the high ceiling of concentric ornamental plaster medallions. The kind of ceiling no one built anymore, not unless they had a few extra hundred thousand to spend. Probably not the kind of room where Phelps usually presented his findings. Dressed in a gray wool suit, he had a salesman's fastidious grooming and eagerness to please. With a whiff of a military background, or perhaps law enforcement. His partner, a younger man named Sims, also in a gray suit, blinked constantly, like a timekeeping device. Martz, dressed in a yellow bathrobe and fleece booties, didn't like either man. Literalists, detail men. Pin pokers who found existential reassurance in confirmation of the obvious. Incapable of seeing the big picture. Then again, the world ran on such people. He himself employed dozens of them. These two came highly recommended and after canceling his trip to Germany he had ordered them to come to his home so that no one would see any "security consultants" arriving in his office.

"Go on," he said, irritated by the man's lip-licking obsequiousness.

"We have tracked the trading of Good Pharma back through the various brokerages using our contacts and friendships," Phelps began, opening an electronic display monitor, "and we would like to present what we feel is a thorough analysis of what has happened." A computer graphic appeared on the large screen. "What you are seeing is a time-lapse flowchart of the trades made in Good Pharma from January first of this year through May eighth, the day the stock took its first big hit. We have taken as our baseline the one-hundred-day trailing average trading volume in order to then factor out the typical trade volume originating in the large institutional accounts, whose management is known to us, as well as the retail level trades originating in storefront discount brokerage operations, Charles Schwab and so on, that mostly cater to those few older investors who don't use the Internet. We have also done our level best to filter out the automatic dividend reinvestment buying and scheduled buying by firms for their retirement accounts—in short, anything and everything that creates *normal* trading volume in Good Pharma. Only by knowing the normal does one quantify the deviant."

"Sounds kinky," Sims suddenly interjected, seemingly to his own surprise.

Phelps shot him a look of amazed hatred, then went on. "Anyway, this still leaves some eleven million shares of Good Pharma stock traded *here*—on May eighth, which is nine times the trailing average daily volume." The screen jumped to a multicolored chart detailing the eleven million shares. "We have traced these trades backward through the floor traders and clearinghouses and found that most of the trades were made on Internet accounts flowing through Asia. Now then, you see here"—the screen's time-flow graphic showed a rising mountain of sell orders superimposed with a jagged downward red line tracking the drop in price of Good Pharma—"that the trading volume shows nine thousand sell orders made in a four-hour time period. The first sells hit the New York Stock Exchange as strike price orders and the price dropped immediately, and yet one can see a few institutional traders came in thinking they had a quick chance to pick up a bargain, but these buyers were soon overwhelmed, about eight or nine minutes later, with another wave of sell orders, these again smaller than before but greater in number, as presumably news of the sell worked its way through private networks. A lot of sophisticated day traders in Taiwan run proprietary computerized trading models, some of them quite good. One can see here that the sell orders mostly came through Hong Kong, Beijing, Taipei, and even Ho Chi Minh City brokerages. A few through Tokyo. The wave of selling was completed in about nineteen minutes. At this point, news of the enormous price drop had flowed through the financial news networks, and the major institutional customers froze, not knowing whether to buy and pick up a bargain, or sell along with everyone else. The hedge fund guys froze, too. The problem was that the analysis on the stock was generally positive, of course, with buy recommendations running about five to one over sell recommendations."

"For Christ's sake, I know all that," Martz muttered.

"All right, then," Phelps said. "Yes, you know that. We have a very friendly contact high up in China Telecom who was able to collate the sources of the calls to the various Asian brokerages, and then using regression analysis we traced them back to five individuals residing in Shanghai. I'm afraid that we were forced to relinquish a very considerable sum to get the phone records, but once we did, we can see that the probable source of the entire wave of selling originated with these five men or their representatives. They happen to be principals in a variety of real estate projects in Shanghai and the surrounding areas and have made quite a name for themselves. One of them is a Shanghai government official, by the way."

Martz had a bad feeling about what he was soon to hear. "Any legal recourse?"

"Doubtful. We violated private brokerage agreements, clearinghouse confidentiality agreements, American securities law, Taiwanese security law, and Chinese security regulations. That's why our information is so good."

"It's not *that* good—I mean, I basically already knew something like this had happened."

"Yes, sir, I understand that a man of your experience would certainly intuit the basic structure of causation." Phelps smiled ever so indulgently, then thought better of it. "When I worked for the government we were often able to make educated guesses about the causes of illegal trades, but it was the detail work that really showed how people operated. So please give me one more moment. Now then, one of the five Chinese businessmen originating these trades is named Chen. In his early thirties. He has some two dozen holding companies that he controls and we were able to trace one of them, using a confidential source at Hong Kong Banc Trust, to a privately held company here in New York. This small company, which is called CorpServe, provides cleaning, waste removal, and paper-shredding services to a number of office buildings and corporate clients around town. One of the contracts is a midtown address, and you will recognize it as the corporate offices of Good Pharma."

"Oh, those fuckers!" Martz yelled.

"Yes. Now then, I have asked my colleague Bert Sims to give us the backgrounder in paperized information security."

Sims, still blinking constantly, stepped forward, shooting his cuffs like a comedian on television. "Thanks, Bob. Pleasure to help out, Mr. Martz. Heard you were one of the richest men in New York City. Wow, I said to myself. Quite an honor for me. Now then, the great bulk of information security has to do with computer files, text encryption, wireless security, and so on. As it should. That stuff is complicated and you need smart people to protect it. But then one must ask, where else in the universe is important information found? In two other media. The first is brain cells. People walk around with a lot of valuable information in their heads. Its value and accuracy are generally in decay. The other medium, of course, is paper. Good old paper. We have become very—pardon the expression—*promiscuous* with paper. We once thought we'd have paperless offices but of course that never happened. That's a joke. People print out e-mails, they make copies of reports online, they distribute charts in meetings, and so on."

Sims blinked as he prepared to expound again. "There is only one way to remove the problem of paper, from a security point of view.

You destroy the paper itself. But what is destruction? That's an interesting question."

"To you," Martz said.

"Yes, to me but also to my colleagues in the paperized security industry who are charged with the task of analyzing paper destruction issues and related methodologies." His eyes lost contact with Martz as he wandered through his interior landscape of abstraction, his voice dropping its synthetic heartiness and becoming the affectless droning of a man who lived for and only loved information. "You can burn paper, which causes smoke, and if you are running a legal, commercial operation, that smoke has to be cleaned, by federal statute. Has to be scrubbed, because most inks have PCBs in them. Ink is a pretty bad substance once you start spreading it around in gas form. You can also destroy paper by dissolving it in acid or some other kind of solvent, but this is smelly and expensive and very messy. You can hide paper, bury it or lock it away, but this only postpones its fate. If you lock it away, somebody can always break in and steal it. Plus the costs of secure storage are enormous. Just ask the U.S. government. Our country spends ninety-eight billion dollars a year on the storage of undigitized government records. Did you know that? What about burying paper? Well, there are landfill issues. Plus people could always dig up the—"

"I am paying for information I can use, not a complete regurgitation of everything you've ever learned. Get to the point."

"Of course. Yes. So, okay, the last way you can destroy information on paper is by shredding it. There are different methods and standards of shredding security, from long strips to confetti. You have your strip-cut, cross-cut, and particle-cut machines, grinders, disintegrators, and granulators. One concept is that you turn, say, one hundred pages of valuable information into ten thousand pieces of confetti, and perhaps mix it with fifty thousand pieces of the same size that have no valuable information, and no one in his right mind would or could reassemble those pieces.

"But things, Mr. Martz, are not always as they seem. Shredded documents can be reassembled. The most famous case was the 1979 takeover of the U.S. embassy in Iran, when the Iranians hired local carpet weavers to reconstruct shredded embassy documents by hand. Nowadays the computerized document reassembly business is well developed. Confetti is small only because you are big. If you were tiny, then you would see it very differently. Let's say that piece of confetti was as big as a pizza box, or even bigger, as wide across as the rug in your living room. At that size it would seem fairly thick, and there would be lots of details about it on all of its surfaces. Well, you know what? We can make that piece of confetti large—informationally, I mean. We can microscan it and get a very detailed image of it. Very detailed. That itself is digitized, labeled, and stored. Kind of ironic, actually. The digital becomes paper, becomes digitized gain. Now, with a computer program that reads all those pieces of paper and puts them back—"

"What are you getting at?" asked Martz, hearing the door open in the hallway.

"You could read the documents. But it would take a lot of labor and a lot of computing power. Yet in China, both of those things are almost free now. The cost of labor is actually still dropping in some areas, as more and more people come off the farms and search for work. And most computing programs in China have been pirated from Western companies. You literally have small Chinese companies running on software they got for free that cost their original owners millions of dollars." Sims's eyes noticed something behind Martz, something that unsettled his robotic composure. "The government supports, I mean *sees*, no I did mean *supports*, this—this activity I am—"

"Hello!" Connie pranced into the room across the Persian carpet on shiny high heels, carrying a shopping bag and wearing a wicked little black cocktail dress that showed her every gigantic and fabulous curve. "Pardon me! I'm so sorry! Bill? What do you think?" She whirled around, displaying her impossible convexities. "Do you just *love* it? Please say you do!" She looked back coyly at the security men. "Oh, please excuse me, I just had to show my husband." She flung her hands up and bent one leg, an old model's pose. "See?" She pulled the hem up one side of her steel-hard thigh. "Perfect fit. Here, *feel.*" She stepped forward, her leg grazing Martz's yellow robe, touching his pale hairy calf, and took his hand and put it flat on her stomach, made him rub it, his fingers making incidental but not unnoticed contact with the round underside of the firm shelf above. "Nobody produces this kind of silk, no one. Don't you just *love* it?"

Martz nodded, not sure who in the room was the most humiliated, he or the two men. Connie was capable of this kind of behavior, he knew all too well, and it came in part from her awareness that she would never have children, that her sexiness was her only hold on him, and also from her unacknowledged desire to be attractive to men other than her husband. Younger men, more attractive men, *vigorous* men. Christ, he'd been married four times and humped sixty or seventy women, he knew a thing or two about female human beings. Connie needed a good banging, really *needed* it, and he hadn't given her that in a long time. So, no wonder. Poor girl. Now she bent down to his ear, no doubt flashing her perfect rear side at the men waiting patiently. "Oh, Bill, don't be mad," she breathed. "I wanted it for *you.*"

She stood and flounced away. The men sat there a moment, collectively stunned.

Martz broke the silence. "Gentlemen, that was my wife, and after you reel your tongues back in, we may resume."

Sims nodded obediently, his blink rate suggesting a rapid mental rewinding until the point of interruption was found. "As it turns out, computers can recognize shredder patterns and perform best-fit sorting by shape not just by—"

"Stop talking," Martz commanded. He turned to Phelps. "Thus far all you guys have done is waste my time and ogle my wife. The first thing I can't stand, and the second I forgive you for, since you had no choice. Now, get back to Good Pharma's stock price. Can you get any kind of phone logs here?"

"This would require lawsuits and subpoenas, in my opinion," said Phelps. "Even with my connections in the Justice Department and the Southern District's offices, it would take weeks, minimum."

That was too long. Martz wondered about Tom Reilly. Did he know about this Chen? Or did he know there might be a security problem?

No wonder he wouldn't talk. And, more to the point, what did Chen know about Good Pharma that Bill Martz did not?

Phelps waited, his eyes bright with secret knowledge.

"Go on, tell me the rest," said Martz.

"The younger sister of Chen is listed on CorpServe's website as the contact person for Manhattan sales."

"Chen's sister works for the shredding company?" Martz asked, voice rising in furious amazement. "Why didn't you say so? It's her!"

Phelps nodded. "It would appear so, yes."

"Can you find this Chen person?"

"We anticipated that question, and using our contacts in the Department of Homeland Security we have traced his movements."

"Where is he? Some casino in Macao raising a toast to all the American investors he's burned?"

"No, sir," said Sims. "Actually, he's here in New York."

"*What?*" Martz stood up and his robe hung open, revealing the hairy landslide of flesh that was his chest and stomach.

"He received an expedited clearance to travel here, and when one of these requests comes from a Chinese national, we automatically—"

"I don't care about the paperwork, tell me where he is!"

"Short answer, we don't know."

"Why not?"

"It wasn't clear that you might want us to find out, sir."

He flung his open hands at them in exasperation. "I want you to find out! Christ on a cracker, man, I want that information!"

"Yes. We can use our contacts in the U.S. Immigration Service to—"

"Now, today! As soon as possible!"

"We will do everything that—"

He pointed at the door. "Go! Get out! I want the answer as fast as possible! End of day!"

They packed up their equipment and left, though not without, Martz noticed, a furtive pivot of the head by Sims in the hope that he might catch one more eyeful of the bewitching Mrs. Martz.

He stood at the window, thinking of this treacherous Chen and his sister planted in New York. He recognized their type. They were the hungry generation. Every family that ever made a fortune had started with a hungry generation, the one that worked harder, hustled, cut corners, jumped earliest. The Martz family wealth had begun in this way, too. His own grandfather had started the family fortune in 1922 when he and his younger brother went out for a picnic in Central Park, enjoying some hard cider and sandwiches from a basket and watching their wives and children play in the grass. The younger brother, a twenty-three-year-old electrical engineering draftsman, had fallen asleep in the grass because, his wife said, he had been working too hard. What was all the work? Martz's grandfather had famously asked his sister-in-law. His brother, he learned, had been assigned the design of a power station in a copper mine in Chile. The Manhattan engineering firm had ten men working on the drawings around the clock. Enormous power requirements, no one quite understood why. Rush-rush, hush-hush. *Inside information, not yet public.* Martz's grandfather had woken up his brother, asked him the name of the copper mine. His brother had boozily muttered a word that sounded like "Chuckee-Moma" and fallen asleep again. Martz's grandfather had written the funny word with a fountain pen on his pretzel napkin, excused himself, and walked straight south from Central Park to the New York Public Library. "Chuckee-Moma," he learned, was the closest his brother could get to "Chuquicamata"—the name of the largest copper mine in the world. Two months later it was acquired by the Anaconda Copper Company. But not before Martz's grandfather had purchased or borrowed every last share of Anaconda stock that he could get his hands on. Thus was a fortune created and a family legend born—just as this Chen was doing now.

Martz returned his attention to Good Pharma. It seemed apparent now that Tom Reilly suspected there had been an information breach. He might have had his own analysis of the stock-trading patterns performed. That Reilly had not reported this publicly was grounds for his removal and perhaps prosecution under federal securities law, but Martz was quite happy that Reilly had wisely not upheld any of his legal responsibilities; it meant there might still be a quiet way out of this mess.

The Chen kid had robbed him—millions, right out of his wrinkled hand. Martz was old and tired and it hurt every time he sat down, but he wasn't too far gone not to defend himself. Chen had stolen a mountain of gold from him, and now, with Tom Reilly's help, he was most certainly going to steal it back.

The Crown Royale Hotel on Park Avenue above Sixty-ninth Street requires many fresh sheets for its customers. And fresh pillowcases, towels, face towels, and tablecloths, to say nothing of table napkins starched to near rigidity. The hotel's laundry facility, a room nearly forty yards long two floors below street level, consumes tens of thousands of gallons of water a day, pallets of bleach and detergent. No working laundry, no happy hotel. The man who ran the Crown Royale laundry, Carlos Montoya, had, for a Mexican, lived in New York City a very long time. Long enough that his shiny black hair had become gray, that his face had sagged into a mask of tragic sensibility, and that he was a grandfather many times over. He appeared to all who might wonder to be a tired, industrious, law-abiding member of society who perhaps should lose forty or fifty pounds and consider having his shoes shined more often. A naturalized United States citizen, he paid his taxes, had a nice new car in his driveway in Queens, voted for both Republicans and Democrats, and was, by far, the most powerful Mexican crime boss in the city. Which is to say, not very powerful, if compared to the Italians, Chinese, Albanians, Vietnamese, or Russians, but not so bad compared to the Pakistanis, the Haitians, what was left of the Irish, and whatever the Muslims in Brooklyn were up to these days with their shops selling Islamic books, oils, clothing, foodstuffs, and everything else the FBI's informants kept buying from them. Nonetheless, Carlos's distribution network crossed all five boroughs, and with his connections in the hotel and restaurant business, he controlled most of the retail Mexican marijuana business in New York. He had dealers everywhere. And two of them were in trouble, being hassled by the police for the murders of two Mexican girls, murders they did not commit. Two very beautiful daughters of Mexico who were killed in a most disrespectful way. A murder a Mexican could not have committed. Not in Brooklyn, anyway.

Carlos's office, if it could be called that, was a cubicle at one end of the massive laundry room. It was here that he pondered his predicament, smoking a cigarette in violation of hotel policy. (He had no fear; he could not be fired, he knew.) The two boys, muscular and carrying faces of insolence, had been taken in for questioning by a Detective Blake of Brooklyn. Blake had developed their names within *one day* of the murders, which suggested that the Mexicans in that part of Brooklyn were having trouble keeping their mouths shut, or that Carlos's boys had a lot of enemies on the street, or, most unlikely, that Detective Blake was unusually effective. Carlos liked the idea that this detective might be working hard to solve the murders but not if it meant getting the false conviction of Carlos's boys. The two of them were guilty of *muchas cosas*, yes, but not of killing the two girls, both good hardworking girls from central Mexico who had fled north to the States to find jobs. He'd driven out to Marine Park and been told their story in the back of a pizza parlor that he partly owned—how they'd been smuggled through a Texas safe house, how they lived out in Brooklyn on Avenida U, drove a bad car, smoked a little of his *producto*, supplied for free by the boyfriends, kept a clean apartment. Carlos felt a kind of paternal responsibility for all the boys and girls coming to New York. They needed older Mexicans around to see how they could make it in America. He considered Mexico a lost and dying nation, but he knew Mexicans to be a beautiful people who were not understood by the rest of the world. He had read about Mexico's history and had actually purchased in an expensive Manhattan antiques shop a vintage map that showed Old Mexico, which stretched well into California, Arizona, and Texas. *We were here before they were,* he always said, *and we will be here when they are gone.* The disrespectful way the girls had been killed, asphyxiation by human excrement, made him burn with hatred.

But his immediate problem was his two *caballos*, who, he worried, would start cracking under the pressure of the detective's inquiries, perhaps choke out a few names they should not, especially his. And there was another thing: one of the busboys in the hotel's restaurant had a younger brother who worked in a sewage-service yard on the eastern edge of Brooklyn. Word had gotten around about the murders. The brother remembered seeing the two girls at a picnic in Marine Park. He had noticed that one of the trucks had discharged its contents into the yard's emergency overflow tank, which was large enough to hold two loads, then been hooked up to another truck and received its load directly. The second, now empty truck had then been refilled with the contents of the overflow tank. A most strange activity, the perceptive young man had noted. Why switch loads of shit from one truck to another, especially when it all went to the same place, the sewage treatment plant? It wasn't like the stuff was valuable. The first truck then went to the county sewerage facility and discharged its load. Very strange, said the kid, like they were playing three-card monte with loads of *caca*. That night, the same night the girls died, the second truck had left the yard late and been driven out to the east end of Long Island, to a dumpy little town called Riverhead, driven not on the Long Island Expressway, which was always monitored by Suffolk and Nassau county patrol cars, but along the rambling country roads stretching east-west on Long Island. A hundred-mile drive, *comprende*? The truck had discharged at a Suffolk County facility out there the next morning and then been driven to Queens, or maybe New Jersey, and had never returned to the yard in Marine Park. Vanished. The first truck was power washed inside and out, then returned to regular service.

Had the yard's owner been aware of all of this activity? Carlos wanted to know. *Sí, sí.* He told us to do it. Carlos had asked the young man to come to him, found him believable, even wrote down a few notes. "You must now forget all this," he said, "forget you told me." But then he grabbed the boy's hand. "If you see something more, you call me, yes?"

Detective Blake had asked a lot of questions but had not yet arrested Carlos's dealers. Maybe he had other suspects. But to be safe, perhaps Carlos should send his boys on a little trip to California in the back of a laundry truck, tell them to stay away for a few months over the summer, go north, work the apple harvest in Washington. Don't tell me where you are, he'd say to them, don't call me, don't call anybody you know in Brooklyn. The boys wouldn't want to go, but they would. Of course their disappearance would appear to confirm their guilt. Which he didn't terribly mind, since they were hotheads who might eventually cause him trouble, anyway.

But if now he had a problem, he also had an opportunity. He took the service elevator to the nineteenth floor, had a quick word with the Mexican housekeeper counting out fancy little bottles of shampoo and bars of perfumed soap that the hotel guests threw by the handfuls into their suitcases, and then, using his hotel custodian's passkey, entered the room of a British Airways executive in the city on business at JFK International Airport. Carlos touched nothing, not the minibar, the nice clothes on the hangers, the fat wad of pounds and dollars on the dresser. *You touch nothing, nothing touches you.* Instead he picked up the phone to make a call, the cost of which would be buried in the airline executive's charges and perhaps look like a call to the airport. The hotel had almost three thousand phones, which were routed through four hundred lines by a computer on a next-free-line basis. Then the call was tagged with a dummy phone number so that people receiving the call who had caller ID could not get a number inside the hotel that they could call directly. If you called the dummy number you got a not-in-service message. (Very smart, these Indian phone guys, Mexicans should learn from them.) Carlos had thought this out long ago. The log matching the room phone to the trunk line was maintained in Bangalore by the hotel information services vendor. It would require a subpoena and weeks of digging to produce the actual room where any given call had been made from. Meanwhile, the guest who had used the room was long gone and would have to be located in order to be asked about the call that he didn't make. Meanwhile, too, the room would have been vacuumed and cleaned thoroughly fifty times. No fingerprints, *mami*! The room maids were instructed to wipe each phone once a day to control for germs that might cause an outbreak of sickness in the hotel—one of hotel management's nightmares.

He dialed the Brooklyn sewage service.

"I would like to speak with your owner, please." No trace of an accent, when he wanted. He'd learned by watching Lou Dobbs on CNN.

A minute passed.

"Yeah, who is this?"

"I am someone who knows you," said Carlos.

"Who?"

"I am very familiar with your business," he said.

"Oh?"

"I am very familiar with what you put in your overflow tank. What you put in and when you took it out."

"What d'you want?"

"I think you might know."

"Fuck off." The phone went dead.

Carlos called back. The man answered.

"Why do you hang up on a polite caller?" Carlos asked in his best CNN voice.

"You call back, I'm going to hunt you down and kill you," snarled the voice. "Then I'm going to rape your wife and children."

Now it was Carlos who hung up. I think I have a little project now, he told himself, savoring a nasty happiness in himself. Yes, I have a little game with a white man who kills Mexican girls.

Okay, so I panicked, thought Jin Li as she waited for the ferry. I never should have hidden in that old building downtown. She wore big sunglasses and a Yankees cap pulled low, on the assumption there were security cameras in the terminal. Well, she *had* been scared. Instead, she should have first done exactly what she had just accomplished the previous night, which was to rent a room and private bath in Harlem from an old black woman named Norma Powell who owned a five-story brownstone carved up into a boardinghouse. Jin Li's room was just large enough for a bed, a dresser, and a wall mirror. The paint was no good and a mold stain that looked like Australia stretched across the ceiling. But the room had a good door made of real wood and a brass dead-bolt lock. But even better was the fact that Norma Powell's middle-aged son sat in the front room all day watching television. He appeared to live in the front room, in fact. He weighed perhaps four hundred pounds, more than half of that fat, but he projected a kind of elephantine protectiveness toward his mother that Jin Li found reassuring. Anyone breaking into the house would have to get by or over him. On the other hand Jin Li didn't really like Harlem, which was also her way of admitting that she felt uncomfortable in a black neighborhood, but that was its advantage. Harlem wasn't where you'd first look for a Chinese woman.

Jin Li had said that she was a Korean exchange student at Columbia University, an explanation that had seemed unnecessary to the widow

Powell as soon as she counted Jin Li's cash: $300, per week, payable every Monday morning, put your envelope in my mailbox, honey, and no gentlemen callers after seven p.m. or it's out you go. But Norma Powell did want the phone number of the previous landlord, so she could follow up and confirm that Jin Li had been a good tenant. Fine, *whatever*, as she'd heard the American teenagers say; feeling only somewhat sly, she gave Norma her own phone number in her office in CorpServe's Red Hook building. If she really bothered to call, Norma would find this number useless, since it had no greeting on it and after three rings automatically kicked over to a fax machine—set that way so Chen could send her written information that avoided the Internet. As for her name, Jin Li had actually given her real one, since it matched her forms of identification, but said her hometown was Seoul, South Korea, where her father worked in a Kia Motors factory. It was both amusing and a little disgusting that she was pretending to be a Korean, especially since her name was in no way Korean sounding, but Norma Powell didn't know that. Anyway, there was an American phrase for this she liked: Ya do what ya gotta do. That's me, Jin Li thought, I'm doing what I gotta do. She had unpacked her meager belongings from her suitcase and taken a very nice long hot bath in her bathroom, attended by three cockroaches. They didn't bother her; in Shanghai their building had been infested with Asian water bugs, which were much worse. She'd scrubbed her face and later done her nails and altogether felt a lot more determined about everything. Maybe the police had caught the men who killed the Mexican girls. Or maybe she would call them up anonymously, not using her cell phone, and describe what had happened.

Maybe, but not yet, because she had a plan. After all, she had been trained to think, trained well at Harbin Institute of Technology, by professors in logic, systems analysis, data management, and probability analysis. CorpServe had many crews leaving jobs the night she was attacked, yet the crew singled out was the one carrying Jin Li. Why? The only plausible reason was that she was the person who knew exactly which offices were being plundered for information. The response by the assailants, or rather by whoever had hired them, was crude, indeed, stupid. There were many other approaches they could have taken. They could have changed the access to their facilities. They could have fired CorpServe. They could have called law enforcement or a private investigation agency. They could have spoken to her in person, called, written, or threatened legal action. Such actions would be morally and legally defensible, would have created a useful paper trail, and had the benefit of remaining controllable from an executive position. When two guys dump shit into a car in the dark in Brooklyn, she reflected, a corporate executive is not there to supervise. The actions may not be what he ordered, what he would accept, or what he is subsequently informed about. He has almost no control. Executives, she knew from reading thousands of pages of their correspondence, craved control, because they believed it was the essence of power. The attack in Brooklyn, from a corporate perspective, was insane, almost suicidal. It created negative information and initiated events outside the corporation.

It was the action of someone who had panicked.

Who? With this question she had a distinct advantage. Whoever had ordered the attack could not know that she alone knew which eight companies CorpServe was actively probing. In three of them, the stock price had recently gone up, creating great wealth for her brother and his associates. In another four, the stock price had drifted sideways for several months, awaiting developments. The last one was a relatively small pharmaceutical company, Good Pharma, which had suffered significant erosion in its stock price, something like 30 percent, in the last few weeks. She'd been feeding Chen information about the bad news regarding its synthetic skin product, which was due to receive FDA approval. The expected market for the product was enormous; it wasn't just burn victims who needed new skin—at this her thoughts traveled to Ray's stomach, the grafts and scars there that formed some kind of mysterious, erotic calligraphy on him, an accidental tattoo she had come to love—not just burn victims, no, but old people with wrinkled, sun-damaged skin that was thin now and tore like tissue paper. The product wasn't for vanity but for health. As the baby boomers aged, the nursing homes and life-care facilities would be crowded with people confined to their beds, where bedsores were a major issue.

Bedsores were simply spots of necrotic tissue—skin that had died from being under continuous pressure, which cut off the circulation of blood. Existing techniques for avoiding bedsores, frequent turning and shifting of the bedridden, couldn't prevent them. The synthetic skin product, which did not yet have a trademarked name, was meant to be grafted atop the fragile, thin skin of the bedridden, providing an extra layer of protection, and causing a minimal immune system rejection response. But the product was not working very well in clinical trials, a fact that Jin Li had reported to Chen.

Her brother, ambitious pig-man that he was, did not really understand America, she realized. Now that Chen was here, Jin Li knew, he would probably blunder about, intimidating the CorpServe employees, making clumsy inquiries. He'd be a little too excited to be in America, would run around feeling important. And spend a lot of money, too. Just because you were big in Shanghai didn't mean anybody even held the door for you in New York. The people of New York considered themselves to be living in the center of the known universe. They generally loved the other great cities of the world, especially London, Paris, Berlin, and so on, but they were quite opinionated about New York. You had to prove yourself in New York, she'd seen, prove you belonged, were good enough. Smart people came to New York from all over America to compete with one another for the city's riches and pleasures. This was how the Americans did it. Chen might not understand. Much as she hated the responsibility, he probably needed her help.

Now the gate opened and she was allowed to walk onto the ferry to Staten Island. She'd never taken it but it seemed familiar to her, one of the old ones with wooden benches—a lot like the creaking, romantic ferries that churned back and forth between Kowloon and the island of Hong Kong. She'd been there with her father, who'd gone to look for financing for one of his projects.

The time was nearly five p.m., a late spring evening when the air was fresh and cool, the season that the city renewed itself, and she watched the early commuters find their favorite spots and open their newspapers or handheld devices. The ride was certainly long enough for her to accomplish her plan and take the return ferry to Manhattan.

The announcement came over the speaker and the ferry moved. From her seat at the open stern she could see the skyline of Lower Manhattan shrink before her. Where had the World Trade Center been? She didn't really know, could sort of picture the two boxy towers. That seemed so long ago now. She'd watched the first reports on the television monitors in the university's dining hall, along with a knot of other students, some of whom cheered at the sight of Americans being incinerated.

When the ferry reached halfway across the harbor, she took out her cell phone, planning to activate it for the first time since the morning before the attack. Should she really do this? Her hands trembled. She knew that as soon as the phone went on, its signal pinged the nearest cell phone towers and that the police could at any later time identify its location, which was why she wanted to check the phone while moving across New York Harbor. Should she do it? Maybe not. But she felt so cut off now, so alone. She pushed the On button, heard the trill as the phone powered up. She had three messages. The first was from her brother, who said, "Jin Li, you must call me so I know you are fine. Mother and father have asked about you and I said you were good but they know I am not telling them something. Also, of course, we must keep the business going and I want to talk about that. I am paying your boyfriend, Mr. Ray, to help find you. All he cares about is money, he asked for so much. I had to pay double. I am at the new apartment in the Time Warner building. Call me, Jin Li."

Before she had a chance to figure out how many lies her brother had told her, the next message came on: "Jin Li, this is Ray, the guy who used to be your boyfriend. I'm not calling to talk about what happened between us. I'm just worried about you, okay? Your brother is in New York and found me. He's got a bunch of guys with him and he's looking for you . . ." She listened to the rest of the message, something about calling him at his father's home. She turned off the cell phone, unnerved by the sound of his voice, almost crying now. I miss you, Ray, she thought, I want to be with you. Why had she ever listened to her brother and let herself be told to break it off with Ray? On the night of the attack she probably would have been with Ray instead of riding in the little car with the two girls. Ray took her places, they ate all over the city, they walked in Central Park. He never probed too much, asked her why she worked so hard for CorpServe. He didn't want to possess her, she realized. She liked that. He never asked for any promises from her, either. They always had sex in her apartment. A wave of sad desire ran through her. She liked it when he turned her over onto her stomach, lifted up her hips, and began that way, his big hands holding her, sometimes running his finger up and down her backbone. One night as he did this, she'd said, do you count the strokes in and out? And he laughed and said, why do you ask? Well, it goes on for a long time, she said playfully. Yes, he answered, sometimes I do count the strokes, just to see. I knew it, she said. How many tonight? You tell me, he said, beginning again. No, you tell me, she'd answered, beginning to breathe hard. Fine, he'd said, hundreds, that's all I'm saying. She dropped her head down on the sheet, felt dizzy and a bit crazy, too, like she didn't exactly know who she was. Not exactly a bad feeling. Maybe she whispered *go slow.* Maybe she didn't.

Jin Li sighed and squirmed a little on the bench. What had she been thinking? Now she was living in a room in Harlem, afraid to go back to her apartment or work. There was one more message on her phone, she remembered, and maybe it was from Ray.

A strong male voice, not Ray's: "Hello, this is Detective Peter Blake of the Brooklyn Homicide Division of the New York City Police Department. I am looking for Jin Li, and I believe this is her phone number. Jin Li, you are a person of interest in a case involving the homicide of two Mexican women. We know that you were the supervisor of these women and may have seen them shortly before their deaths. I would personally appreciate a call from you at your earliest convenience at the following number." Which he gave, then added, "It would be in your best interests if you found me before I found you. Thank you very much."

The police? She snapped the phone shut in terror, looked around suddenly as if they could see her. How did the police get her name?

Chen would not contact them; he wanted to find her first. But he and Ray had spoken. Each had referred to the other. Chen must have told Ray about what happened in the car.

And Ray—Ray had told the NYPD. She couldn't believe this but it was true. He'd betrayed her.

He remembered her foot, her ankle, her thigh. He set the little yellow sneaker on his truck's dashboard, a shiver of misery going through him. Oh, God, I miss Jin Li, Ray thought, every part of her. He sat parked in the lot of a check-cashing operation across the street from Victorious Sewerage, which was no more than an odd-shaped muddy lot surrounded by a twenty-foot fence topped with concertina wire, all this protecting a battered construction trailer at the rear and ten enormous, virtually identical sewage trucks parked in a haphazard line, including the one that Richie had driven into the lot twenty minutes earlier. A hulking cement-block building lay behind the trailer but it wasn't clear whether this was part of the operation. The day was done, past six p.m., and time was passing, he knew, clocks ticking everywhere, one on Jin Li, another on his father, a third on how long it would take Richie to get deeply paranoid.

A small Mexican man—a boy, really—with a red hose was standing atop one of the trucks, running steaming water into a valve. Murky water ran out of another valve at the bottom. Richie emerged from the trailer, walked over to a pickup truck, a certain spring in his step, like he was a man with a plan, and rolled out of the lot—

—with Ray following him. At the light, Ray pulled up close enough to jot down the license plate number. Then he saw Richie looking up at his rearview mirror. Ray pulled down his windshield shade. The idea was to follow Richie home.

The light was still red but now Richie sped across the intersection, barely missing three teenage girls on foot, each talking on a cell phone. Richie turned at the next corner. Ray was disgusted with himself. When the light changed he sped to the corner, turned, looked for Richie's truck—it was gone.

His father opened his eyes dully. "The report, please."

Ray ran through it.

"I thought you knew to sit back on a tail."

"At least I got the plate."

"Give me the phone. No, first get me some illegal coffee."

A few minutes later, his father had on his old half-frame glasses that he hadn't worn in a month and pointed a bony finger at a phone number for Ray to dial. He held the phone near his head and closed his eyes, summoning a voice he hadn't used in a long time. "Ellen, this is Ray Grant . . . no, no I'm doing great, thanks." The coffee sharpened him up fast, thought Ray. "A little chemo and that's it, but thanks for asking. Listen, this is the thing, I'm on a private job here and could use a little . . . we got a plate number and need the registration address. Yeah, yeah, sure." He read her the plate number then waited. "I've known her thirty years," he said to Ray. He returned to the phone. "Number two Sixth Street? South Jamesport? All the way out there?" He nodded. "Great. Hi to everyone."

His father dropped the phone, panting now. "This guy lives way the hell out on the east end of Long Island!"

"That's where I'm going, then."

He looked accusingly at Ray. "These Chinese guys want the sister, not some bullshit sewage-truck guy!"

What was wrong? "Dad, Dad, I'm going to break into her apartment tomorrow morning."

"What took you so long to have that brilliant idea?" But his father didn't wait for an answer. "Anyway, it's not good enough! You got to start figuring out what that girl is *thinking*." He pointed his finger at his own head, shaking it like it was a loaded gun, and stared ferociously at

Ray, eyes unblinking, teeth bared. "Either you or somebody else! Fact, let me tell you something, you gotta go like hell, Ray, you go twenty, maybe twenty-one hours *at a time* now, drink coffee, get ahead of it, see, things are—this Vic, I keep *almost* remembering! I don't get it, something—" His father looked around wildly, like there were other people in the room, shades at the door. "Hey! Hey! Get out of here!" He looked back to Ray and beckoned with his hand, his voice in a low conspiratorial whisper. *"I got a feeling that together you and I, we can—"* His eyes shot over Ray's shoulder, became terrified. "No, no I can't!" he yelled, "Not yet! I got my gun here!" He pawed the covers frantically. "Ray, Ray! Get them!"

But Ray had reached for the Dilaudid machine and pumped two boluses straight into his father, who in a minute or so looked at him with sudden passivity, his mouth munching in wordless speculation—before his eyes rolled up in his head and he slumped backward into the pillow, hawing the breath—the stench—of the near dead.

Ninety miles, rainy road. Long Island, the largest island in the United States, split at the end, the South Fork leading to the swankfest Hamptons, filled with people who wore white clothes to expensive summer parties, and the North Fork, which was traditionally more working class, populated by farmers, tradesmen, retired NYC cops, and firemen. South Jamesport was one of the first few towns on the North Fork as you drove east. Ray found the house, a little bungalow ranch on a corner, Richie's pickup truck in the driveway. Hell of a drive into the city every day, but then again, you get to leave the city every day, too. Guys like Richie lived in their trucks, anyway.

Ray parked next to some woods and walked back to the house along the dark road. What exactly was he going to do? Not sure. He carried a short crowbar in his jacket, mostly as a weapon. He also had a battery-powered speed drill with a carbide saw attachment. Two-inch rotary blade, goes through anything until it gets dull. He slipped along the road. It was a quiet neighborhood, which meant people minded their own business. Ray edged along the back side of the house, found a window. Richie was sitting in front of his television in clean clothes, hair wet. He had a beer and a bowl of oatmeal on the arm of his chair.

Can you tell if a man is a murderer just by watching him? Of course not. So his father would say. If you know a hundred other things about him, then maybe.

The phone rang. Richie muted the television, kept watching. "Yeah," he said. "About ten minutes."

Ray eased around the side of the house. A moment later Richie came out, smelling of some kind of aftershave, climbed into his truck, and drove away. On his way out for the big date.

Now or never, Ray thought. He considered going through a window, but a neighbor, or even someone driving by, could easily see this. Same with the front door. Instead, he hunched down among some unkempt boxwoods and thought about breaking into the metal ground doors leading to the basement. You made a four-inch box cut, then reached in and pulled back the slide bolt. The carbide blade worked perfectly. A little noisy. Thirty seconds of noise. Couldn't be helped. The box of steel dropped away and Ray waited for the edges to cool, then reached in and opened the door. Then he lifted the door, slipped inside, and let the door fall soundlessly back into place. He found a light. The basement was jammed with boxes of mildewed clothes, broken furniture, sports equipment, and empty beer bottles. A weight-lifting machine sat in one corner. Ray turned off the light and scooted past a washer and dryer piled with dirty laundry—the smell of sewage distinctly noticeable—and up some internal stairs that led to a small living room dominated by a wide-screen television. All the lights were on. Why? This worried him. He kept moving. The small bedroom was taken up with a big bed. More dirty clothes. A couple of golf clubs on the floor. In the bedside table drawer he found four dirty pistols and several ammunition boxes. He didn't touch them.

He poked his head into the bedroom closet, meeting a strong whiff of shoes. What am I doing, he asked himself, what am I looking for? Even assuming Richie was the guy who killed the two Mexican girls—

just a speculation—what connected him, a meatball who lived in this low-rent dump, to Jin Li, a highly educated, stylish Chinese woman who worked in midtown Manhattan ninety miles to the west?

I need to find something, Ray muttered to himself. In the kitchen he opened Richie's refrigerator: beer, milk, orange juice, batteries, a baggie filled with unidentified pills, several cartons of muscle powder, perhaps $200 worth of nice steaks, and, in the freezer, what appeared to be a giant frozen rat wrapped in a plastic bag.

A sound?

No. *Yes!* A truck had pulled into the driveway, speakers booming. Ray wasn't sure he could make it to the basement stairs. He back-pedaled blindly and was confronted with a choice of the bathroom or Richie's bedroom.

" . . . shoulda cleaned up," he heard Richie say, coming inside the house.

"I like it," came a girl's voice. "It's cozy-like."

He chose the bedroom, nearly tripping on a golf club. Where to go in such a small room? The closet. He opened it and stumbled atop a pile of golf shoes and balls. He pulled the door shut. The crowbar was tucked by his side. It was a good weapon but not in a closet.

The minutes passed and Ray felt himself becoming stiff. Maybe he should have tried for the basement stairs. He could hear a low murmur of voices, a little music. The bedroom light, he realized, was on. Had he turned it on? He couldn't remember.

" . . . waiting for?" came Richie's voice, as he walked in to the bedroom. He flicked off the light.

A girl followed.

"I redid your *totally* terrible drink." She giggled.

"Yeah?"

"Yeah, I made it better, too."

"So I never went to bartending school. Come here."

"I will," she sang back. "I like this bed. Wait, let me just smoke. The train was so slow! I really needed a cigarette. Drink your drink and I'll smoke one."

"I thought that was for after."

"Gets me in the mood. You guys are always in such a hurry."

Ray could smell the cigarette. He felt a golf ball under him and quietly put it into a shoe.

"How long you lived here?"

"Four years."

"Rent or own?"

"Rent. Shoulda bought a few years back."

"Tell me about it."

"But you know, I pull down some good dollars, make a little on side jobs."

"You haven't told me if you like the drink."

"I do, I do."

"Good, or else my feelings were gonna be hurt."

"So this is kind of nice," Richie ventured. "This isn't in a hurry."

"That feels good," came the voice a few moments later.

"Want to roll over there?"

"You seem pretty relaxed," she said. "I mean, *most* of you is relaxed. Some guys, you know, they get nervous . . . first time out of the gate."

"Yeah, you know, whatever." The great lover, shrugging humbly at his own talents of seduction. "Plus, I got the home field advantage."

"I *guess*. Why don't you lie back, let me start relaxing you."

"Can't argue with that."

"First finish the nice drink I made you. I worked hard on it, too, just so you know."

"—right?"

"Yeah, that's it. Just lie back . . . good . . . take a breath . . . so, you been living here long?"

"Four years, remember? Come on, give me a little action here."

"Keep your pants on, guy, I'm getting there."

"Thought you wanted my pants *off*."

"I do, definitely."

"I'll take them off."

"You go, boy."

Sound of clothes, a belt buckle.

"So you were saying about living here?"

"That's better."

"Good."

"You're good at that."

"Just relax, Richie."

"I am, very."

"Good, good."

"You?"

"Right here."

"Sleepy, kinda."

"It's okay, it's nice to lie here with you."

The room was quiet. A minute passed.

"You—" came Richie's voice.

"Shhh, it's okay."

"Wait, wait . . . fuckin' *sleepy*."

"Shh, don't worry."

"Did ya—? I'm very . . ."

Ray could hear Richie breathing. It slowed, deepened, and a rasp of a snore introduced itself. He hadn't heard the girl move. Maybe she'd fallen asleep, too.

Then came trill of a cell phone. It scared him and he had to stop himself from reacting. She picked up quickly, after just one ring.

"Hey. He's asleep . . . you owe me. I had to touch his *dick*! Goddamn dis*gus*ting. What? No, the door is open. I'm not moving, in case he wakes up. Just get here fast, okay?"

She hung up. More cigarette smoke.

The snoring had become a deep sawing gasp that reloaded and gasped again.

Ray tried to slow his own breathing and concentrate on not moving. Someone was coming to the house, and it made him nervous. If the girl left the room, he could run for it—maybe. Golfballs all over the floor. The room had a window. Maybe it opened easily, maybe not. He felt one foot slipping, pulled it back. Once the girl stopped watching the drugged man on the bed, her attention would begin to drift and she would notice Ray. She might not consciously hear him but she would feel him. It was a proven thing. Tibetan monks with their ears plugged and eyes covered with a satin sash could be led into a room, breathe a few times while turning in a circle, and identify in which corner of the room another monk sat motionless on a prayer rug. You see that once, you never forget it.

The girl was just sitting there in the dark. He heard her slide open the drawer.

"Guns!" she whispered aloud.

Then the door to the kitchen opened. Ray heard the heavy footsteps through the walls.

"Hey, Sharon?" came a man's low voice.

"Here!" she whispered loudly. "In here!"

The steps approached the doorway. "He's really out?"

"Think so."

"Get in the car."

"Let me put on my shoes."

"Did you let him fuck you?"

"*No.*"

"I think you did."

"No way, he's disgusting."

"You touched his dick, Sharon."

"He *made* me. I was doing it for *you.*"

"Blow job?"

"No, I swear."

"You're fucking lying."

"No, no—"

"You just better get in the car."

She left. Ray could hear the unconscious man breathing loudly. He thought he smelled something like cinnamon.

"Fucking douche bag."

"Come on," came the girl's voice down the hall, "what are you doing? There are guns in the drawer, by the way, mister jealous motherfucker."

"You touch them?"

"No."

"Get in the car!"

She left. Ray could hear the back door open and close. The lights flicked on. A line of light ran between the closet doors now. He heard the drawer slide open, the clatter of the pistols being taken, followed by the boxes of ammo.

"Hey, hey, fuckwad," came the voice. "Look at you, Richie, try to fuck my girl. Plus you fucked up, which means now you're going to fuck *me* up."

There came the lowest groan in the bed, as if Richie had heard this accusation and was trying to respond.

An ominous silence followed. Then came a whipping crack.

Richie gagged out a delirious, inchoate howl. The golf club, thought Ray. Another crack, this time wetter, more awful.

"Fucking made her touch your—!" Then came two, three, four, six, eight blows, in rapid and savage progression, each making the same wet cracking noise, the assailant breathing quickly, panting in a frenzy, grunting at the effort, the splatting blows ending after twenty seconds at most, whatever ability to respond that Richie might possess now obliterated.

"Ugh, fuckin' . . . fucked *up*," breathed the voice. "I fucking *told* you, Richie. Somebody calls me, then some guy is looking for you! You blew it, you fucked up!"

No answer came back.

There seemed to be a deliberative pause—as if the assailant was weighing what he wanted to do next versus what he needed to do. Ray heard him shift his weight from one foot to the next, lining up the swing. Then the blows came, another savage series, wet-wet-wet, so fast Ray knew the club was being whipped up as fast as it was whipped down, ten-fifteen-twenty blows or more, the assailant grunting in spasmodic exaltation, taking pleasure again and again—and then, just as abruptly, the wet whipping sound stopped, the club flung heavily against the wall.

Footsteps disappeared through the doorway, through the kitchen, and out the door. Ray heard a car start up and disappear.

Silence now.

He smelled blood.

Just wait another minute, he told himself. *Be sure.* Finally he pushed open the closet door and stumbled out to the floor, legs numb, pulling golf balls and shoes with him. On the bed lay Richie, his face a bloody mass—no nose, no cheeks, a hole that had been a mouth. His smooth chin had been driven into his windpipe, and in general the oblong spherical shape of the head had been flattened. Nearly every blow had hit Richie's face, cratering his skull. The few errant swings had glanced off the wet mass onto the pillow, leaving golf-club imprints. For the brief period that Richie's brain had continued to deliver information to the heart, the left ventricle had kept pumping blood up through the aorta and out the crushed face, leaving Richie's head in a pool that now faithfully followed every wrinkled depression in the bedspread, soaking downward as it went. After the heart stopped beating, lividity occurred—the seepage of fluids from the highest part of the body to the lowest, which meant in this case that blood and other fluids would continue to leak from Richie's ruined head for some time to come. Indeed, Richie's crushed forehead had now paled to a purplish white, the flesh drained. His popped eyeballs seeped blind tears of viscous matter.

Richie had never had a chance, his shirtless body still sprawled in the position of deep sleep, hands out, shoes off, his boxer shorts askew, belly soft, a tattooed lightning bolt adorning his hip bone. Next to him, the bedside table drawer had been yanked open. On the floor lay the bloody golf club, bent in the middle now. Blood had sprayed the walls and ceiling. The police would have no difficulty re-creating what had happened.

The police. The Suffolk County detectives knew what they were doing, would be all over the place sooner or later. No doubt Richie's killer and the girl had left all sorts of indicators of their presence—her prints on the edge of the glass, etc., but maybe there was an explanation for that; they visited Richie earlier in the evening. *It was Ray who was the anomaly in the life of Richie.* So now he took the trouble to find the Clorox in the basement, wet a rag with it, and wipe every surface he had touched. Clorox destroyed DNA. Nerve-racking as hell; he had to remember every one of his steps in the house. He felt a thin trickle of sweat begin under his arms. Of course he'd left skin cells and hair fibers around, especially in the closet. The cops would swipe hundreds of different surfaces. His DNA was on file, too, somewhere. The department took it in case they needed to identify your remains.

He forced himself to find a vacuum cleaner and vacuumed out the closet, every golf ball and shoe, and then threw them in again. The problem was that flecks and spots of blood were all over the floor and he was walking in them. Blood on my shoes, soaking into the minute scratches in the soles, he thought, I have to get rid of them. Didn't help to have the dead Richie behind him, watching, sort of. He flicked off the bedroom light, in case a neighbor looked in and saw the faceless body on the bed. He pulled the bag out of the machine, then dropped it, the Clorox, and the rag into a trash bag and took it with him, right through the basement again and out the ground doors.

He let the door close quietly, aware that he had not turned out any other lights in the house or checked to see if the front door was locked. Was that good? He wasn't sure. But the fact that he had broken into the basement doors disturbed him. It suggested the entry point of Richie's murderer. The police would examine the minute edges of the place where the metal was cut and see no weathering, that it was fresh. Ray had accidentally created a false clue—one that could point at him. He knew that the paint on the carbide blade would match the paint of the metal ground doors. Another thing to get rid of, he told himself. Shoes and saw blade. Also get rid of the saw itself; the matching paint dust would have been sucked into the motor; they'd find that in five minutes, match it using gas chromatograph tests. Wait! he thought. There would be matching paint dust on his clothes, too. Shoes, bag, saw, all clothes, he told himself, get rid of them.

He retreated into the woods again, half expecting police cars to pull up any minute. The night breathed a soft warm breeze. He slapped at a mosquito. A car passed. He had not seen Richie's killer. Maybe I should have jumped out of the closet and stopped him, thought Ray. But the guy was swinging a golf club with murder in his heart. Ray wasn't quite satisfied at this line of rationalization. He would've had a moment of surprise. It was at least possible he could have saved Richie. But then what? He'd have to have fought the guy. He thought he remembered the guy taking guns out of a drawer, the sound of it. Yes, the girl told the guy about the guns and opening the drawer was the first thing he did. Were the guns loaded? If so, Ray could have jumped out of the closet and the guy could have wheeled and shot him in the face.

Maybe it was better he'd stayed in the closet.

When he reached his truck, he took off his boots so as not to wipe blood on the pedals and floor mat. I'm being careful, Ray thought, but something is bugging me, something I missed. He put the shoes and the saw in the big plastic bag, along with his coat, and tied it off, then dropped it in the back of his truck. He could dump the bag here but preferred to do so elsewhere, maybe separate the items first.

I'm thinking like a criminal, Ray realized. He sat in his truck and forced himself to take long breaths. I might have stopped it, he thought. He couldn't tell the police much about the murderer. I don't know his name, I never saw his face. But the girl was called Sharon. They could find Sharon and then the murderer. But Sharon could just say she was elsewhere the whole night, with the murderer. Ray was the one without the alibi. Even if the cops believed him, he would have to tell them everything, back to the Chinese guys and then crawling in the pipes. They'd probably arrest him, too, since he'd then also be connected to the deaths of the two Mexican girls. The stranger your story, the more likely the police would put the cuffs on, get the wacko off the street. He wondered whether he should tell his father about Richie. The advantage would be that his father would understand the situation better, how dangerous it was. But it might make him worry. It also might make him want to kick the whole thing over to his old NYPD colleagues and be done with it. And then they'd arrest Ray, no matter who his father was.

No, no, he thought, I can't tell Dad about this. The man can't be lying in his deathbed thinking that his son is a murder suspect.

He started the truck and turned it around on the dark road, unable to resist driving by the house on the way to the highway. It had been, what, an hour or more since he'd crawled out of the closet? He approached the house—not sure why he wasn't seeing it.

Then he did see it. The lights were out, every one.

Ray pushed the accelerator in fear, sped past. *The lights.* He'd left all the lights on and now they were *out.* But wait—he'd turned off one light, in the bedroom. If it was the killer who had returned to the house to turn off the lights, had he noticed this? Or smelled the Clorox? Seen the blood smears on the rug? Maybe even seen the cut basement ground door?

I know about him, Ray realized, but now he knows about me.

He was exhausted from his drive back to the city and he was anxious, too—unusual for him. Seeing Richie dead like that had shaken him up, loosened up some old stuff he'd thought he'd carefully tied back together a while ago. The old loose fucked-up stuff in his head. The *bad* stuff. He needed to soften it fast, blur it out. And to do that he wanted something more than getting quietly buzzed on a few beers, something deeper. He'd smoked opium a few times in Pakistan, never got hooked. At midnight, he remembered, Gloria cleaned the Dilaudid machine.

So he waited, sitting next to his father, who was asleep. She went into the kitchen to prepare and, in that moment, Ray quickly pulled out the shunt that was inserted into the intravenous line that went to his father's arm and slipped it into a needle line he'd stolen from the nurse's box of supplies and put into his own wrist. Then he punched the drug delivery button. The machine gave him the last discretionary dose of the twenty-four-hour period. The machine kept track of how many times the patient pushed the button, and if the nurse had been checking, she might notice.

He felt a warm pressure go into his arm, the dose delivered. Then he pulled out the shunt and slipped it back into his father's line. There was no danger of contamination for him or his father because the shunt itself never touched anything other than sterile plastic. He gently pulled the line from his own arm and slipped it into his back pocket.

Gloria returned, gave him a second look, unplugged the machine, disconnected it from the line going into Ray's father, and took the machine to the kitchen.

Ray dropped heavily into the deep chair next to the bed. A faraway thought came to him that his father had built up a tolerance over the weeks he'd been taking Dilaudid, whereas Ray had no such preparation . . . but so what? The thing was hitting him now . . . a warm wash that dropped him into collapsing pools of stupefying pleasure. . .

What phantasms dance in a man's head while clutched in a morphine dream? Does he witness what never happened? Or does he redream what he otherwise wishes he'd forget? Does the mind billow florid sweetness or release its darkest horror? Do the most recent images (Richie, dead before him) and thoughts (I could have saved him) and smells (blood) find their antecedents within his memory? Does one nightmare recall another? It must be possible . . . Do the sounds come back . . . the roaring above them as they searched the subbasement for anyone trapped behind fire doors? Wickham in front, Ray shining his flashlight along the dark corridors, all electricity turned off, walking in their heavy boots and unbuckled bunker coats and helmets in the subbasement looking for people trapped behind jammed fire doors . . . those sounds of footsteps always in his mind, the last footsteps before everything, before Wickham had stopped, cocked his head . . .

Hear that?

No. Wait. I do.

A roaring had begun.

Let's get out of the footprint.

Wickham nodded. He shined his light down a long hall filled with pipes. That way.

The roaring increased. The concrete ceiling was cracking.

It's collapsing!

They ran as fast as they could in their heavy, clinking equipment, their flashlight beams bouncing crazily up and down. The horizontal pipes on the ceiling started snapping like sticks, water bursting from them. A wave of dust hit their backs, then smoke. They pulled on their air masks.

Ray followed Wickham. They turned a corner. It was blocked with concrete.

The header had collapsed. Wickham swore behind his mask.

They stopped. Ray switched on his radio.

Company Ten, Team Alpha, we're trapped down in the service hall running west on the sublevel.

No answer.

Now a wave of dust and debris was blowing steadily at them. Somewhere above them was enormous downward compression.

Wickham said something in the noise . . . pulled him close and yelled in his ear.

Under a T joint. *Reinforced.*

Ray nodded. They trained their lights along the ceiling. The dust was so thick that both flashlights were necessary. Ray grabbed Wickham and they held each other close until they found a T joint in the corridor. They squatted under it. Ray turned on his radio. All he could hear from it was roaring. No voices. Just an open mike somewhere.

The ceiling collapsed ten yards away, right where they had been standing, pancaking flat against the floor. Then five yards away the ceiling collapsed and hit the floor with such force that debris spat at them like shrapnel. They lay flat on the floor under the beam.

It's coming!

They could hear the roaring above them, the tremors shaking the floor. Then the floor collapsed beneath them and Ray grabbed for Wickham and they fell together, holding each other, spinning as they dropped through the darkness. Ray landed on something hot that burned away his overalls and T-shirt. The hot thing slid along the muscles of his stomach, instantly charring his flesh. He moaned in shocked agony, as did Wickham, and they fell off the hot thing and tumbled another six feet, Ray landing flat on his back, Wickham facedown on top of him, heavily, crushing him nearly, pinning him, Ray's nostrils filling now with the smell of burning rubber and burning flesh, his belly a flank of torment, the pain of a thousand knives hammered into him.

Atop him Wickham writhed. Oh! No! No!

A hissing sound.

A groan. Panting. Groaning. No. No, please, no.

Wicks . . .

Ray was pinned with his left arm under his back, Wickham on top of him.

Something burning in the darkness, hissing.

Meat burning.

Oh, God, please, please . . . No more, please, God. Mother of God . . . I'm begging! . . . No, no . . . Molly, I'm—I'm sorry . . . oh . . . oh.

Wickham's head lay on Ray's chest, his body jerking. Ray moved his right hand down to Wickham's head, felt for the helmet, the visor, then slipped his hand down the neck, found the shoulder, ran his hand along Wickham's upper arm, and pulled on his arm. Ray squeezed Wickham's hand.

Molly!

I'll tell her, I promise. Don't worry.

He let go of Wickham's hand and tried to feel what was pinning them. His ribs hurt. He worked his gloved hand down over Wickham's back until he came to the metal pipe that had crushed Wickham's backbone. It was so hot it seared through Ray's insulated glove just at the touch, and he yanked away his hand even as his fingertips began to burn. He worked his hand back to his torso and found the flashlight jammed beneath him. Then he switched it on, only to see a cement girder four inches from his face. By crooking his neck he could see the top of Wickham's helmet, his shoulder, and beyond that, the pipe, which wasn't a pipe at all but a heavy-duty electrical cable that had fried off its insulation and was still burning downward into Wickham's back, cooking the bone and flesh as it sank through him.

Every movement an agony, back, ribs, stomach, Ray brought his hand to Wickham's. He squeezed it again.

No response.

Oh, Wicks. What will I tell Molly?

He realized his goggles were dusted over. He brushed them off. He found the flashlight again and lifted his head just enough to see that he and Wickham were trapped between two giant cracked slabs of concrete sandwiched atop one another. Sweeping the beam back and forth, he saw an immense horizontal landscape of debris: what looked like part of a car, electrical wiring and panels, popped and flattened drums of unknown content, dripping water pipes, all compressed within the irregular two-foot gap between the slabs. Anything higher than two feet had been crushed to that depth, a depth that, when you thought about it, would just about accommodate the thickness of one man lying atop another.

He found his radio using the flashlight and turned it on.

Company Ten, Team Alpha.

No response. He switched it off. What is left of my stomach? he wondered. He closed his eyes. A tightness in his lungs. Ribs hurting. The air was bad, filled with dust. He wiggled his right foot, then his left. He couldn't feel his left arm pinned behind his back, though the pain in his left shoulder told him the joint was being stretched beyond capacity. The pressure of Wickham . . . he couldn't get a deep breath. He felt himself get cold, the onset of shock. He might have internal organ damage that he couldn't feel yet.

Had he passed out?

It seemed so. He felt wetness between his legs. He had urinated while he was unconscious.

Wickham was soft now on top of him. Ray felt down toward the hot cable, touched it with his glove. It had cooled.

He tried to wriggle out from beneath Wickham, but it was no good. The space was too tight. He wasn't quite getting enough air. He could not fully expand his chest; he wasn't getting full use of his lungs. If the rubble above them settled another inch, Wickham would crush him to death. His flesh would split. Well, maybe that was already happening. He felt a claustrophic anger toward Wickham now, a fury to survive. The other problem was that the circulation in his left arm was impeded; eventually this would cause swelling and even tissue death.

He had to assume that part of the tower had collapsed from the plane hitting it, which was surprising; the building was engineered to take a direct hit. The squad had gotten there right away, helped the thousands streaming down the fire stairs dazed and panicked. The women who had taken off their pumps and were walking through glass. Then the bodies had started to land on the street.

That seemed like a long time ago now.

It would be many hours, perhaps days before they dug him out, if they ever did so.

He realized that he was dehydrated. There was a water bottle in the pocket of his bunker coat, but it was trapped beneath him. Another reason he had to get out from beneath Wickham. He worked his left arm free then hugged Wickham upward, like a man lifting a sagging dance partner, and after many minutes of effort, dragging the weight inch by inch against the resistance of the cement beam above, he was able to shift the heavy, nearly severed torso to the side, where there was enough room to slide it wetly a few feet away. The flashlight showed Wickham's open eyes, their surface already glazed dull by dust.

He felt the pressure against his chest and burnt stomach release. A tremendous difference.

He could actually breathe now. He panted with his eyes shut. His ribs hurt. His head pounded as the blood came back to it. Now perhaps he could work his legs out. He pulled on his legs one at a time, bending his knees upward to see if they worked. They were fine, right? No, one leg hurt. In fact, a lot of him hurt, he realized, especially where the front of his stomach was burnt away.

The pain rode up and down and through him and he had to tell himself not to give in to it, but he did nonetheless, feeling himself falling toward unconsciousness. He needed water badly, he realized. Water would save him, if he was to be saved. He awkwardly pulled up Wickham's bunker coat and found the water bottle there, a full liter. He drank half of it. He felt around in the pocket some more and found two packets of peanut butter crackers. That was Wickham, always ready. He ate the crackers slowly and washed them down with the rest of the water.

Then he examined his burn, holding the flashlight above him. The flesh was seared down to and into the muscle and wept blood and lymphatic fluid that itself had mixed with the fluids of Wickham and the dust that covered everything. I don't know what to do about this, Ray thought. He found his own water bottle and considered washing out the wound. But he might need that water, he realized. He could clean the wound and find it still became infected. In burn victims, he knew, survival was based on the total percentage of skin area affected. His burn was deep but not wide. He decided to save the water.

Now he turned on the radio.

Company Ten, Company Ten, go ahead.

No answer.

Had there been a complete loss of radio transmission?

It appeared so.

He wondered if he could hear voices above him, faint sirens, something. Maybe not.

He glimpsed at Wickham. If Ray had been on top, he'd be the one dead now. It was that simple. Because he landed below Wicks, he'd survived.

Lucky, thought Ray. I can't be luckier than that.

The limp fireman recovered from the rubble sixteen hours later was rushed by police escort to St. Vincent's Hospital, intravenous saline lines inserted in both wrists and both ankles. His nasal passages and esophagus were plugged with cement dust. His heart was beating weakly once every two seconds. In addition to his severe third-degree burn and the sepsis that had quickly set in, he was found to have a collapsed lung, fractures of the tibia, nine ribs, one vertebra, and a finger on the left hand, cartilage damage to the left shoulder, and a ruptured spleen. When he awoke two days later, his mother and father were seated next to him. The president was going to attack Afghanistan, they told him, the war against terrorism had begun.

An hour later the deputy fire commissioner for legal affairs appeared in his room and shut the door. The short fat man with white hair pulled up a chair close to Ray's head. We need to have a little talk, Firefighter Grant. I apologize to you for pressing this matter upon you only hours after you have regained consciousness. But it's an important matter that we need to get straight. Ray nodded vaguely, not knowing what else to do. We see no reason why his wife, Molly, needs to know how much Firefighter Wickham suffered. She saw most of the body. That was difficult enough. We had our own people work on him before the funeral home came. She was told he was killed before he was burned so badly. We had to tell her something. But we don't want anyone knowing the particulars. This department lost more than three hundred men, Firefighter Grant. We will be finding bodies for weeks to come. I am ordering you as a fireman in the brotherhood of firemen and I am asking you as a man of honor that you never discuss Firefighter Wickham's suffering and injuries. The men who found you and Wickham are all sworn to secrecy on this matter. You do not need to fear that others will speak of it. And if they somehow do, the fire department will never comment on it except to say that Wickham was killed in the heroic line of duty. No one needs to know he was nearly burned in half by a hot cable. It would hurt individuals and it would hurt the morale of this department in a time of great suffering. In addition to your injuries and trauma, this will be an extra burden to you. I recognize that, the department recognizes that. Furthermore I ask that you never tell your father, not because he is your father and from what I understand a very honorable man but because he is a policeman, and you know of the very difficult relationship between the two departments in this city. You should also know there was one newspaper reporter who was nearby when Firefighter Wickham's body was recovered and had a question, but we had a little talk with him. I expect that this information will perish with you. That you will never tell anyone, ever. Especially the news media. Are we agreed about this, Firefighter Grant?

Yes.

Firefighter Wickham's suffering was a sacred sacrifice that must not be polluted or cheapened by public discussion of it. Are we clear about this?

Yes.

You're sure. Including your father?

Yes.

They shook hands.

He stayed in the hospital six weeks and was unable to attend Wickham's funeral, the flag-draped casket carried on the back of a pumper truck, as was the tradition, followed by row upon row of his brothers in their dress blue uniforms.

Had he been in the chair all night? He opened his eyes, felt stiff in the chair. Did I wake up before? wondered Ray. I thought I woke up. His head felt light. He needed coffee, sugar, something.

"Did you enjoy your trip?" asked Gloria, about to go off duty.

"My trip?"

"Your little drug trip."

He shook his head, blinked. "You knew?"

"Of course."

"But said nothing?"

She was waking his father, breakfast ready on a tray. "Nothing to say, once the juice was in your arm, except that if you do it again, I'm going to report you."

Ray sat up.

"Plus it wasn't like you were going nowhere on me."

He sat up some more. His head felt filled with sand.

"Very unfortunate," croaked his father, eyes open.

"What, why?" Ray answered.

"This house has many nice beds upstairs that I worked hard to pay for," his father said. "I wish you'd slept in one."

"I'm fine."

"Well, while you were sleeping I did a great deal of work for you."

"You did?"

"Sure."

"Well?"

"She gets mail at her apartment?"

Ray thought. He remembered locked mailboxes inside the apartment house foyer. "Yes."

"Did she have a regular phone there, a landline, we used to call it?"

"Yes. Mostly for international calls to her mother."

"And a cell phone? She's not calling China on a cell phone."

"Yes."

"Two phone lines," observed his father. "Billing cycles every thirty days. Two bills in thirty days. Cell phone and regular bills tend to be separate, they are for me."

"She's been missing something like five days."

"If the bills were perfectly distributed fifteen days apart, you have about a one-in-three chance that there's a fresh bill sitting in her mailbox showing who she was calling. Might be very useful information. Only other way to get it is with a court subpoena."

"One in three aren't bad odds."

"They could be worse or better."

"Maybe she had her mail forwarded."

"No." His father winced. "People running for their lives don't *do* that. Plus it generally requires a trip to the local post office. You have to give a new address. She didn't *have* a new address."

"Maybe she had the post office hold her mail."

"No!"

"I'm just trying to think of—"

"No! She was attacked at night. She fled. The post office doesn't open until eight in the morning. She was long gone by then."

Maybe, thought Ray. But one-in-three odds were pretty good.

"So I get into her building. I've got my old fireman's keys."

"Make sure you break into her mailbox."

"Just break into it."

"Yes," his father said, waving at Gloria now for breakfast. "Hell, man, this girl's life could be on the line here."

"I know, Dad."

He waited for his father to respond. But he didn't, and instead just stared into space, eyes unblinking and mouth tight, like a cop confronting a suspect for the first time, knowing he was guilty.

16 What is the Marine Park Athletic & Social Club of Brooklyn, New York? By law it is a nonprofit organization that happens to own the land and trailer used by Victorious Hauling & Sewerage, precursor organization to Victorious Sewerage Services, LLC, precursor to the current and not yet bankrupt company, Victorious Sewerage, LLC, which enjoys a thirty-year lease at $100 a year. Simple enough, it would appear. On a map, the Marine Park Athletic & Social Club is an irregularly shaped lot on landfill near the Dead Horse Inlet of Jamaica Bay. Its baseball field, dugouts, and small clubhouse are heavily used by summer-league baseball teams, most of which have an affiliation with local Catholic schools. As a nonprofit organization, it pays only nominal real estate taxes. A good third of the property is devoted to the sewerage company, a muddy lot of trucks, the office trailer, and a huge two-story cement-block warehouse originally built to house the regional inventory of a national paint company. Judged to contain enormous environmental damage from thousands of leaking cans of paint, the entire lot was sold in the 1960s by the company for $1, with the proviso that all future liabilities would pass to the new ownership. The president of the Marine Park Athletic & Social Club is also the principal owner of Victorious Sewerage, one Victor Rigetti, Jr. The company has been known to engage in commercial activities far outside the scope of its state license, such as buying untaxed #2 home heating oil from various freelance purveyors, providing parking space for the fuel trucks of those same purveyors, supplying warehouse space for "discount" clothing merchants wishing to store inventory temporarily, and so on. The large warehouse includes a three-bay truck garage, as well as several small windowless areas in back, one that is used to store tools, restricted-use chemicals, harsh solvents, cleansers, and other materials used in the sewage and cesspool business, and one that contains two bunks, a toilet, a sink, a refrigerator, and an illegal unvented stove. Another appears to be used to store tires and engine parts, but if you know where to look, which almost no one does, you may find behind the piles of truck tires a spring-loaded, four-foot-square floor panel that lifts up to reveal a homemade ladder that descends into a deep, small, ill-lit room that has in it a bathtub, a chair, a mouse-gnawed mattress, a pile of chains, and a hose.

You could call this a never-used fallout shelter built in the atomically paranoid 1950s or you could call it an infrequently used dungeon. Take your pick; both are right. Anyone with just a hint of claustrophobia would soon be reduced to frenzied panic in this windowless, underground room once the floor panel was replaced and its true smallness had become evident. The room, however, is wired for light (one bare bulb, with a pull chain) and electricity and has running water. At the center of the room is a floor drain. The drain leads to an illegal septic tank directly beneath the hidden room. This room has been carefully vented not to the storage area above it but through the walls and to the roof directly. Any malodorous effluvia issuing from this room are thus released well above the level of human beings and instantly mix with the diesel exhaust of the large trucks leaving or entering the property.

The bathtub, by the way, is a rather elegant old-fashioned enameled one, enamel being useful for its imperviousness to acid and solvents. Oddly enough, its drain is sealed. Yet there is a small hole drilled near the top lip of the bathtub, with a tube attached to it leading from the outside of the tub, and close inspection reveals that the tube is pure copper, oxidized green now, and leads directly to the drain in the middle of the floor. Further inspection of the room shows that the water pipe entering from the wall is divided into three separate uses: one a common hose bib attached to a hose that is neatly coiled in the corner; the second a smaller-gauge tube that runs directly to the drain in the middle of the room; and third, another small tube of equal diameter that runs directly to the old bathtub, providing it with its only source of water. The stopcocks that connect the main pipe to the smaller tubes are welded to set positions: one can turn on only so much water through the tubes and no more.

Once the tubes leading to both the tub and the floor drain are comprehended, it becomes apparent that the tub is slowly filled from the water tube. The tub's contents drain at an equal rate at the top of the tub through the copper pipe that leads to the floor drain, and these contents are further diluted by the second water tube that leads to the drain.

The tub, it should be noted, is full, and its soupy contents are a dark, reddish brown. The water tube leading into the tub trickles perhaps a gallon an hour, which means a gallon an hour of the soupy brown mixture exits the tub to the drain, there to be diluted by the flow of water from the second tube.

Next to the tub are a dozen-odd canisters of various solvents, acids, and caustic jellies, some empty, a few half full, the rest unopened. Each variety of canister has its own respective implement: a glass measuring cup and a tin scoop for dry powder, a steel ladle for jellied matter. The neatness of the canisters and the careful placement of the implements is suggestive of habit, orderly procedure, and thoughtful intention.

Standing overly close to the tub causes one's eyes to water and soon thereafter one suffers from a raspy cough and light-headedness. The chemical stench is bad enough to prevent anyone from wanting to plunge a rubber-gloved hand into the odorous murk in the tub, but if one did, and stirred around a bit, one would find not only that it was hot, because of the exothermal chemical processes at work, but also two dozen metal grommets, such as are typically found on men's work boots, a pair of mushy Vibram soles, a number of tooth fillings, a piece of a jawbone, some slippery, degraded pieces of skin, perhaps one with a lightning bolt tattooed to it, a handful of vertebrae, their most acute tips and wings blunted by the action of the chemicals, a set of large

scapulae, male from the size of them, and a complete pelvis, also originally belonging to a large male, already so eroded by the chemicals in
just a few hours as to appear to have been lying on a beach for a
decade. Within only a few days, all the bones and the skin will be gone,
leaving just the rubber shoe soles, the metal fillings, and perhaps some
indistinct sandy granular matter. This residue, it may be assumed, will
be wiped up with a paper towel and discarded in the local McDonald's
in a McDonald's bag retained for this purpose. Meanwhile, the water
will continue to trickle into the tub and drain for hours to come,
slowly washing away all traces of the tub's contents. Then three gallons
of bleach will be poured into the water and this, too, will be allowed to
drain away.

If the building and lot used by Victorious Sewerage represent the
most tangible assets of the Marine Park Athletic & Social Club of
Brooklyn, New York, then the most valuable intangible asset owned by
the club would unquestionably be the baseball diamond, flanked along
the third base line by aluminum bleachers. Intangible because of the
goodwill and great times to be found here. Each summer Victor Rigetti
watches his team, Vic's Marine Park Angels, compete on this field. It's a
motley team, filled with misfits, delinquents, fatties, and goofballs, but
most summers they win two-thirds of their games and usually feature
a pitcher stolen or bought from one of the elite teams. The fathers of
the boys are often owners of local businesses and otherwise known to
each other, and thus it is impossible to eavesdrop on the conversations
there unless you are sitting on the bleachers themselves.

Victor Rigetti knows everyone who sits on his bleachers, however,
and if a parent of a player on the other team somehow mistakenly as-
sumes that the bleachers are for anyone who wishes to use them and
thus finds his way onto them, then he is assaulted with cold stares and
silence until the point is made and taken. Victor is a big, handsome
man with a full head of black hair, thick as a brush, wide in the shoulders and chest. At work he generally wears a Carhartt jacket, dark blue
work pants, and Timberland boots he replaces three times a year.
Clean, always clean. Fingernails, hair, clothes, teeth, watch, car, house,
everything. Doesn't touch the shit anymore, no sir. He's done his time.

That's for the drivers and their helpers. He runs the business. It goes up and down, generally down, but he's branching out, wants to buy the gas station at the intersection of Flatbush and Avenue J, just has to figure out how to scare the Turkish owner into selling to him. Guy does a hell of a business without even trying. The attached convenience store is a gold mine, too. People load up on junk food while they gas up. Kids cry for candy. Vic has stood there and watched the dollars fly. Gas prices are going to keep going up, especially because of the Chinese. Building cars like mad over there. You own a gas station in Brooklyn, you have it made. And an American gas station should belong to an American, not a fucking Turk. Lot of these outsiders stealing the bread and butter from guys like him in Brooklyn. People whose families have put in generations of work and then these other dark people from other countries come in and swoop down on the decent businesses. Not good in his book, and his book gets updated every day. Never forgets. You go to the park, it's like visiting fucking South America. The Mexicans, well, okay, they're good for your basic labor, grunt construction work. Though he's noticed they're getting into the stone trades. The American blacks are mostly finished in Brooklyn, pushed out by the foreigners, as far as he can see. Well, not him. He's hardworking and has a plan. Presents well, he knows. Stands tall, answers questions, knows things. Knows people, lotta different kinds of people. Knows what he's got to do and, if necessary, he does it and doesn't complain. Is he law-abiding? Whose laws we talking about? Men generally fear him. Women aren't sure how they feel. They find the basic package attractive—the size, the strong face, the full head of hair—but there's something about him they pick up on, makes them hesitate. Maybe back away. He's never married. Never wanted to, never *needed* to. He always has a piece of beaver on the line, usually a younger woman, one of the fuckomatics, he calls them, doesn't know much yet, thinks it's exciting to be with an older guy. Endless supply of the fuckomatics in the bars of Brooklyn. Italian, Irish, Polish, Puerto Rican, whatever. Often have a bad relationship with their fathers, easier to bag if they do.

Then, of course, there is Violet, and that's a whole other story, and even he doesn't understand it.

As president of the Marine Park Athletic & Social Club, Vic controls access to the baseball field, controls who plays there from March to October. Which, actually, is a lot of people, teams from all over the place. The field is thus a setting of utterly plausible conversations. One can meet there and have conversations that have meaning or don't. One can have such conversations while appearing to root for the baseball team, and these important conversations can be woven through half a dozen conversations of no import, as well as general commentary on the progress of the game, the quality of the umpiring, the reflexes of the infielders, and so on. It was, in fact, such a conversation a few weeks back in which Victor had listened to Jimmie "Ears" Molissano make him a proposition. Ears wasn't going to say who had first approached him. There was a problem, and it needed a solution. Although the problem couldn't be discussed, except in the most general of terms, the solution merited conversation, and Ears said that he was hoping that Victor and one of his best men, someone like Richie, would be willing to follow a certain car with certain employees of a certain company and send them a message. He would tell him exactly how to find the car in midtown and where it went next to the beach just off the Belt Parkway almost every night, especially if the weather was good. It was not a difficult job, Ears said, and certain people would be grateful.

"I appreciate this gratitude," Vic had said, "but what I really need is some friends who can help me with getting a gas station."

"This is the kind of thing that my friends can help you with."

"Somebody needs to talk to that Turkish guy on Flatbush."

"People can talk to him," said Ears. "People can influence him."

"A vague promise doesn't help me much. You know I been wanting that station for going on five years now. Place has got four gas bays. He can handle sixteen cars at a time. People gas up there right before they go to Jersey, the shore, whatever. I don't understand how these guys right off the boat end up with a gold mine like that. Pisses me off. Makes me crazy."

"I understand."

"No, no, Ears, you don't understand. You don't understand how the

Turkish guy does it and you don't understand my frustration. You have the lumber yard your father left you. Life is easy. Me, I'm not asking for much. Couple of your best guys talk to him and he agrees to sell. He sells, I buy."

"Maybe we take a piece of that."

"The sewage business only takes me so far, you understand? I'm ready to diversify."

"I want to get back to this other thing. If it's done right, I think we're talking twenty K," Ears had said, sitting on the bleachers. "If it's done right."

"Twenty thousand is shoeshine money. How much are you getting paid?"

"Hey, Vic, come on."

"Tell me."

"The job's worth thirty-five, I'm taking less than half off the top."

"Twenty-five."

"Shit."

"Twenty-five and I'll take you to a club in the city, pay for a few dances, how's that? Plus you explain to the Turk how it's gotta be."

Ears said nothing, shook his hand. "You'll pay Richie yourself?"

Victor nodded. "All right, tell me more."

"Easy stuff," Ears had said. "You follow a car out of midtown, near Rockefeller Center. It'll be a little Toyota with Georgia plates. It will have a couple of employees in it from a paper-shredding company."

"I should get into that business," Victor interrupted.

"It's trickier than it looks," answered Ears. "The shredding trucks are expensive and need a lot of maintenance. Anyway, you follow this car. It's going to Brooklyn. Lot of times it goes to the beach. Same lot every time. Same spot in the lot. Most nights. Very late, no one else around. Workers there party a little, smoke a joint, something like that. Then you show up."

"And do what?"

"You send a message."

"What's the message?"

"You don't say anything. You terrorize."

"Who's gonna be in the car. Guys have guns?"

"No, no, it's a couple, three Mexicans. No guns. Nothing to worry about."

"I'm terrorizing Mexicans?"

"We want them very scared. We want them to never go back to this business again. We want the message sent that they better stop what they are doing immediately."

"But you don't want me to talk to them?"

"No—the actual message will be sent another way. All you do is terrorize."

"You care how I do it?"

"No."

"You want creative terrorism?"

"I don't care what kind of fucking terrorism it is, so long as nobody is left around to talk about it."

"You want no talking afterward."

"Yes. We want a long period of silence. Like forever. But it can't look like a hit. No guns."

"You want these people dead."

"We want endless silence."

"Fuck you and your mystery bullshit. I want endless gas station profits, let's be very clear about that. And speaking of terrorism, you sure these aren't some kind of Islamic motherfuckers? I don't want to start messing around with that shit, we got all kinds of funky little mosques all over Brooklyn now, you never know where these guys are. I heard those guys are building bombs."

"Naw, it's just a couple of Mexicans in service uniforms. Don't say anything, just scare them to death. Send a message to their whole organization."

So he did. He had Richie ready with an old beater tanker with stolen plates and all the business lettering scraped off. The truck barely drove anymore and he needed to get rid of it anyway. They'd switched around a watery tankload from Queens. Richie had been told to strain the load, get out all the pieces of paper, tampons, anything that could identify it. Pure shit, Vic had told him, I want nothing but pure shit.

Then Vic had positioned his pickup truck at Sixth Avenue and Forty-eighth Street in Manhattan, gotten the call that the Toyota two-door with Georgia license plate beginning with H7M had pulled down Fifth Avenue at Fifty-second. Victor had eased over to Fifth along Forty-eighth and looked to his left, north up Fifth Avenue. All he could see were sets of headlights, but the hour was so late that they were irregular, the traffic down the avenue running light. No one was behind him so he sat at the green light, waiting for the downtown traffic on Fifth to get caught by the red light, which it did. Then he spotted the Toyota two-door. Piece of cake. He pulled out as it passed, ignoring the red light. He'd followed it downtown, then east on Canal Street, over the Manhattan Bridge, looping around to the Brooklyn-Queens Expressway, onto the Gowanus Expressway toward Bay Ridge, then the Belt Parkway through Bath Beach, Gravesend, Sheepshead Bay. The car stayed in the right lane, was being driven both cautiously and inexpertly, the speed varying. He hung back most of the time, then blew past to have a look. The car had smoked glass, tough to see in. He thought he saw two, maybe three figures, though, caught a tail of music out the top of the window. He eased off, let the Toyota pass him, let a car get between them, then moved up again and called Richie on the cell. Richie had the truck ready, knew how to get to the lot. And then—well, Victor remembered what happened next. Who wouldn't? The figures inside the car, flailing at the glass. Too bad that they were girls. That was unexpected. Ears should have told him but had been smart not to. Because Vic wouldn't have taken the job. But there it was, a done thing. They'd driven the old truck out to Riverhead that same night, dumped the rest of the load in the morning, then driven it into Queens, taken off the stolen plates, and sold it to a scrap dealer for $400. Dirt cheap, no questions asked. The dealer wanted the truck for the tank, and the rest of it went to a yard. That truck was gone, forever, chewed to pellets and sent in a hopper by rail to Pennsylvania for recycling.

But Victor had a bad feeling. The strange phone call telling him that the caller knew what he did. The also very strange phone call for Richie from "his cousin." Richie had never mentioned a cousin! The way Richie had been acting, like he knew something was up. The way some of the Mexican workers looked at Vic. He didn't like it. He got the feeling there was a problem.

But the worst thing was the light in the bedroom last night. He was right about that, too. *Somebody had been in the house.* Cleaning up with Clorox, fucking around with the vacuum cleaner. After he left with Sharon and before he came back. He could smell the Clorox. He'd gone over everything carefully before putting Richie in the bag. Found the basement door cut open. That was the clincher. Somebody had been there, checking Richie out, doing something no good, knew about what had happened.

Which is what Vic wanted to talk about with Ears now, in a general way. The baseball-field bleachers were the best place to meet again. In the open air. Safe, low-key. So he'd put in the call that morning, and now Ears appeared at the edge of the grass, shielded his eyes, and shambled slowly toward the bleachers. A big man with big ears and hands and knees. A gut that exploded. Fat-bango, your stomach is huge. The kielbasy and pasta and beer and steaks and clams marinara sloshing around in there like his stomach was a washing machine, with a little porthole window like Victor's mother's machine used to have. He'd put a cat in there once as a kid, and when it was dead, he cut off the head and slipped it into a kid's lunch box at school. Nice. You used to be a nice boy, his mother had said, but they both knew she was lying. I was never nice, Vic reflected, I never had the chance.

Now Ears climbed the bleacher steps.

"Hey."

"Fucking knees," said Ears, sitting down. "Since when do I come to you?"

"Since I asked."

"Let's say we ran into one another."

"You can say anything you like."

"What's the problem, why the attitude? I know I got to pay you tonight."

"Someone's on to me, Ears."

"Who?"

"Don't know. Your guy?" said Victor.

"Not my guy. If it was my guy, you'd be dead by now."

"Thanks a fucking lot."

"Those girls actually died."

"I guess they did," Victor said.

"But just two Mexican girls."

"You seen Richie around?" asked Victor. "He missed work."

"Nope."

"So I think whoever set this thing up is, like, getting anxious about it. Afraid it's going to come back to them."

Ears shrugged. "You think that, why?"

"Like I said, somebody is on to it."

"What's that got to do with your dear old friend Ears?"

"I want you to tell me who set this up."

"Originally? I don't know. It came down from above. The moon, the stars."

Victor stared at him. "Who spoke to you, Ears?"

"You know I don't have to answer that."

"I got my theories."

Ears shrugged.

"Some guy is hunting me. How did he find me? Somebody is setting me up. Maybe he wants my gas station for himself, you know what I'm saying?"

"Hey, Victor, this is sounding, what, a little wacko, you know?"

Victor sat still, not answering. Maybe Ears knew something, maybe he didn't. Somebody was nosing around. Not a cop, but someone else. Somebody working for somebody. Somebody you never heard of, Victor, which is exactly what you always were afraid of. Seemed to know his way around. Not good. Victor didn't like it. He had a feeling that Ears knew exactly what was going on, too. Whack Victor, grab the gas station for himself. Send the killer back to Florida or wherever he came from. Untraceable. Unsolvable, now that Richie was gone. It all made sense now.

"Know what?" Victor said.

"Yeah."

"You're right, I'm fucking wacko. Paranoid."

"There you go." Ears nodded. "I told you, don't worry."

"Anyway, we got a little date tonight."

"I'll have the cash. Some nice girls there tonight, too."

"What time, ten, eleven?"

"Hell, I can go late. Wife and kids are at her mother's."

"Midnight?"

Ears stood to go. "I'll see you then."

Victor shook his hand. Firmly, no bullshit. With a nod of the head. So Ears could relax. Solid. Reaffirming trust.

And the last time I'm ever going to do that, Victor thought.

17 **I like New York,** realized Chen as he walked past horse carriages waiting at the edge of Central Park for tourists. Now I understand why people visit here, even people from China. New York was not as good as Shanghai, of course, but everyone knew that. New York was old, now, losing strength, and Shanghai would soon be the world's greatest city. Want proof? New York hadn't even rebuilt the World Trade Center and it was many years since it had been destroyed. In Shanghai, the government would have rebuilt those buildings in a year and made them bigger. But of course that was expectable now, for China's economy was growing three times faster than any other country's and would be the leading global power within ten or fifteen years. Especially since America had wasted so many resources in the war in Iraq. And kept borrowing money, weakening the dollar year by year. He knew that some people said that Russia would come back up, because it had oil and because global warming would strengthen its agriculture, but he had been to Moscow and St. Petersburg and it seemed to him that Russians were weak and drank too much. They had problems with drugs, too. He had also been to Paris and London and Berlin and Rome, among other places, and it was his objective, well-educated opinion that these cities were slowly dying and could in no way compare to Shanghai. But of course the real reason was that Asians were smarter than whites. All the tests proved it! The Americans knew this, too, which was why they wanted Asian immigrants. To lift the average. To compete with China!

He walked along the southern edge of the park toward the Time Warner building. Later he would do some shopping at Saks. He had three girlfriends, each the same size, and he'd decided just to get three of everything and give one of each to each girl. Of course, anything you could buy in New York you could buy in China, but they would be excited to see the Saks box and wrapping paper.

Chen stopped at a park bench and pulled out his phone, which worked in America, of course. You could get that, you just had to pay more. He dialed Ray Grant's house, and a woman answered.

"Ray Grant, please."

"The older Ray Grant can't come to the phone," she said. "I assume you mean the younger Ray Grant."

"Yes, that is correct," he said, being careful about his pronunciation.

"Just a minute please."

"Hello?" came a male voice.

"Ray Grant?"

"Yes?"

"This is Chen."

"Well, hello there, Chen. I don't remember giving you this number."

"I am calling to hear from you how you are finding Jin Li."

"I am working on things," said Ray.

"I expect you will find her. I am now waiting."

"I told you I'm working on it."

"When do you expect to be finding her?"

"Soon."

"That is good. I need her for my business work."

"I'm sure she misses working for you."

"My men almost found her. She was living in a building filled with papers and old stuff."

"Sounds like you're doing fine without me."

"No, no. I want for you to find Jin Li."

"I want to find her, too."

"Maybe my men come to help you find Jin Li."

"I don't need them."

"They are hate you, and if I say to do it they will come get you, or come hurt your father."

"That would be a very bad idea."

He remembered the injuries to his men. They feared this Ray Grant now, he knew. "I will call you in two days. I want you to be a successful finder of my sister by then. Do you understand? Two days, I call."

Ray Grant hung up.

When Chen returned to the apartment in the Time Warner building, his men were in the living room watching television. They stood immediately when he came in.

"Boss, you had a delivery while you were out," one of his men said.

"What is it?"

The man shrugged. "The building guys say we have to give them very big tip so we did. One hundred dollars for each man."

"Get it."

The men pushed in an enormous wooden crate on wheels. Made of fine lumber, nearly fifteen feet long and six feet high, it carried elaborate markings written in both English and Chinese about how to dismantle it, as well as the tools necessary attached to the crate itself. The box itself was a piece of expert carpentry. The men set to work on it and a few minutes later the crate's sides dropped away to reveal a huge and magnificent bull with horns, ferocious eyes, and flared nostrils, one hoof lifted and long tail raised in aggressive passion.

The bull was plated in gold. Such a thing must have cost, what—hundreds of thousands of dollars?

A tasseled rope hung around the bull's neck, holding an elegant silk pouch.

"Bring me that bag," Chen ordered.

The pouch was removed and handed to him. He excused everyone, then opened the bag and removed a note written in flowing Chinese calligraphy on elegant yellow stationery with a blue border. The stroke work had been performed at a very high level. At the bottom was a New York address and phone number.

The note read:

Mr. Chen,

Imagine my pleasure when I heard that you were in New York. I have admired your recent accomplishments in China but have always been too shy to tell you. Please accept this modest gift as my way of welcoming you to New York, where we often hope for a "bull market." This term may not be well-known to you. It means we hope there is optimism in stocks and business. Of course China right now is enjoying its own "bull market." I am sure you are very proud of your country. I would deem it a great honor if you would be my guest to dinner so that we might discuss mutually beneficial opportunities.

Yours sincerely,
William Martz

Chen ran his hand along the raised backbone of the sculpture. He had to admit he was impressed that a New York businessman had found him, and so quickly. This was the way international business should be done, with a token of respect and graciousness. He would find out who this Martz was and whether the man was worth any of his time. The gift of the bull suggested the answer was yes.

Every city has bad places. And this is one of them, Ray thought as he drove right into the Victorious Sewerage yard, the smells of excrement and diesel exhaust coming in his window. He hopped out of his truck and walked up to the construction trailer set in the back. The sign said, BEWARE OF DOG. He pulled open the door. A middle-aged secretary looked up. She had a lot of makeup on, considering where she worked.

"Hey, I'm looking for Richie," he said.

"Haven't seen him."

"But he works here."

"I don't know where he is. Let me call." She picked up the phone. "Victor, there's a man out here . . . looking for Richie." She nodded, hung up. "What's your name?"

Ray didn't answer.

The secretary didn't like this, he knew. She picked up the phone. "Victor, maybe you should get out here now, you know?"

The door behind her desk swung open and out stepped a man taller and older than Ray, muscular and lean, a thumb inside his belt. He had thick black hair and was chewing cinnamon gum. "Yeah?" he said to Ray.

"I'm looking for Richie."

"He ain't here." He stopped chewing, frowned. "You call earlier?"

We're recognizing each other, thought Ray. That's what's happening. "No. Where is he?"

"Don't know. Should have reported to work."

"You know a girl named Sharon?" Ray ventured.

The receptionist watched Victor's eyes anxiously.

"Mister, we're busy here and it's time for you to leave." Victor took a step forward. "What's your name again?"

Ray shook his head. "Can't give you that. But I can tell you Sharon says she had a great time with Richie the other night. A great time. Hot. A smoking hot time."

Victor's mouth was frozen. He didn't blink, studying Ray, his body, his stance.

"What d'you mean?"

"Richie will know. Ask him."

Victor twisted his head as if looking at a bad TV picture. Ray watched as his chest rose and fell more quickly, the subtle enlargement of his pupils, his brain juicing him up for a fight.

"One more part of the message, if you don't mind."

"Yeah?"

"Tell Sharon's boyfriend he needs to work on his golf game."

Victor nodded coldly. "I see."

"Just tell him that."

Ray gave the secretary a polite smile and stepped quickly out of the office, alert to any movement behind him, and opened his truck. In the rearview mirror he could see Victor standing in the trailer window, talking into a walkie-talkie. Almost immediately a man stepped out of a shack nearby and hopped into one of the huge tank trucks. A blast of diesel smoke shot from his stack as he started up. But Ray was too quick for him, already had the pickup truck in third gear and gunned it across the gravel, slamming over the ruts, toward the turnout to the avenue. The green truck bolted for the same spot, but Ray got there first, even as the truck's bumper crushed the back panel of the red pickup, kicking it sideways. Ray fishtailed forward through the gap into the avenue, almost hitting an ice cream truck tinkling its mechanical ditty, and moments later was way down the avenue, gone but not forgotten.

■ ▦ ▦

He dropped the truck at his father's and walked to the subway with his old fireman's equipment bag. The train would be the fastest way to get to the East Side of Manhattan this time of day. Sitting in the rocking car, he studied the subway map, his eyes drawn to the World Trade Center site. It always made him feel strange taking the subway so close to what had happened. He'd never gone back, never stood at the site and thought and remembered. Something about the ceremonies and political speeches had made him uneasy. The pile had burned for one hundred days. A lot of the firemen and construction workers who worked the site were getting sick now, had breathed in all sorts of terrible stuff, pieces of plastic and bone tissue and chemical compounds no one had ever seen before. I don't think I've dealt with the whole thing, Ray thought. Maybe I just ran away. Maybe I felt guilty about Wickham. Things got a little foggy after he was released from the hospital. His memory wasn't even perfectly coherent. He'd lost weight, some of the skin grafts had to be redone, and his leg hurt still. He'd taken a leave from the fire department. And also attended forty-six funerals, some of them with his father. He felt guilty for not going to work; the department told him that he would always have a job. The FD desk shrinks made him come in six times, handed him a lot of printed materials. His personal shrink was a woman in her fifties with tired eyes. She wore no makeup. "Frankly, I feel like just drifting away," Ray finally told her.

"Why don't you?" she said.

"Well, the guys—"

"The guys will understand," she said. "And if they don't, who cares?"

He sat there in silence.

"Let me tell you something, Ray Grant Jr. I've read your whole file, of course. The FD doesn't want you back right now, not like this. You're deeply traumatized. By 9/11 itself, then by being trapped, then by having your partner die on top of you. Yes, I know about that. We don't know if you're a busted fireman. We don't know what you're going to do when it comes right down to it. And you know what? Neither do you. You don't know much right now. My suggestion is that you go on official indefinite leave. You're not disabled, although we could probably get some kind of mental health exception, though I don't recommend it. You could take a leave and when you felt you could come back, you could take the physical again, retrain and recertify, then get assigned to a company. The union will make sure that happens. But you need to drift away, as you put it."

He nodded uneasily. "You've seen a lot of guys like me?"

She shrugged. "Everyone is different."

"Yeah, but in general. Burns, falls, accidents, cave-ins . . . a lot of guys?"

The lady shrink nodded. "Couple of hundred, anyway."

He didn't know how to respond.

"Listen to me. Being a fireman is a macho thing. Sacrifice, heroism, the whole deal. Very male. But it doesn't allow for emotional nuance, for ambiguity. You got hit hard. Maybe you should accept that, not resist it. Let the hit carry you somewhere. Ever consider that?"

"My dad always told me I should be a cop."

"He was wrong, in my opinion."

"Why?"

"You interested in power?"

"Not really."

"Justice?"

"That's tougher."

"Something more basic. More elemental?"

"Life and death, yeah."

"Then go find it, Ray. You found some death, go find life."

She stood then. They were done. She gave him a direct look, like a mother to a son, woman to a man. Firm. With a profound human authority. He remembered it. She'd been right. Go find some life.

Within a week, he was on the other side of the world, everything he needed in a rucksack. In a little town in Indonesia. Unplugging. No cell phone, no Internet, no newspapers, no CNN. He met a skinny German girl, and they traveled for a few weeks. She was pretty but she had an intravenous drug habit. He wouldn't have sex with her. He'd seen two advanced AIDS patients coming out of a burning Harlem walk-up once, living skeletons. Besides, he hadn't survived the WTC just to get whacked a stupid way. His refusal to fuck had the effect of making the girl do more drugs. But he knew that if he stayed with her, he might eventually have sex with her, maybe shoot some of the heroin she kept in her knapsack. He told her he was going to leave and she tearfully admitted this was a good idea. He paid a man with a truck to take him to the next town. A few days later he was in the Philippines. In an outdoor restaurant, he saw some big blond guys who looked like sunburned surfers from California. They weren't. Aussies. Relief workers. Lounging around in their boots and sunglasses. He sat down and shared a beer with them. They asked where he was from. New York, eh? Long way from home? They'd just flown in, they'd said, were waiting. A typhoon was hitting the eastern islands. They would be dropped in by a C-5 military transport as soon as the trailing edge cleared the coast. Advance team with sat-phones, tents, water. He asked if he could join them, help out. No, they said, we don't take tourists. The tone of the conversation changed, became awkward. He didn't push it. When the bottles were almost empty, one of the guys asked him why he was in the Philippines. Drifting, said Ray. What do you do there in New York, mate? Ray took a last pull from his beer. Used to be a fireman, he said.

"Fire department, New York City?" said the Aussie, his voice more energetic. "Whereabouts?"

"Company Ten, 124 Liberty Street, lower Manhattan."

"Certified first aid?"

"Yes."

"Rope trained, rappelling, the whole bit?"

"Sure. Smoke-plunge and failing-structure rescue. Roof collapse, floor collapse, wall collapse."

"Construction analysis? Post-and-beam, masonry?"

"I can tell if it's going to fall down," said Ray.

"You can drive a lorry?"

"Lorry?"

"Truck?"

"I've driven a pumper and the hook and ladder."

The Australian nodded. "Gimme a minute, mate." He rose and found the others. They turned and looked at Ray.

Two days later he was in the top of a mangrove tree, trying to rescue a terrified eight-year-old girl clinging to a branch. She'd been in the stripped branches for thirty hours, after the waters had gone down. Her mother stood waiting. When he reached the girl, she clung to him so tightly he could feel her heart hammering against his chest. Her arms squeezing his neck for all she was worth. The best feeling ever, in his life. Ever. The best moment of his life. *I'm going to remember this until I die.* He struggled not to cry when the mother raced to her daughter. The crew spent three days digging out corpses from the mud. They directed airdrops of bottled water and foodstuffs and distributed them to thousands of hungry hands. They saw hundreds of people dying from dysentery. Three weeks later the crew was rotated out and given medical exams. His parasites were not unusual, but he'd lost twenty pounds. The scar on his stomach sank inward. They offered him a job. From there on it was six months in the field, off two weeks. All over the world. He didn't read many newspapers, he just lived—in the place, in the time, and with the people.

Was he finding life? Not exactly. Or yes, in the midst of a great deal of death. From time to time he saved someone again. Not that others would not have saved the same person, but it was Ray who happened to be there, with the rope, the oxygen bottle, the hand. He remembered these moments, tried to understand them but could not. Understood less and less, in fact. No continuity. He lived in a stream of moments. Smoked opium a few times, mostly drank beer to relax. He read the Bible, then the Koran. Then some of the Hindu texts. Most of the cities had a bookstore where you could buy books in English. He followed the news about the war in Iraq, the war in Somalia, the little wars everywhere. He saw UN workers selling pallets of tires to local middlemen. He saw a man holding a pair of pliers walking through a field of bodies, each thick with flies; the man searched for the bodies whose mouths were open wide enough to pull out teeth with gold fillings in them. In Somalia, after having his truck emptied, he was handed an AK-47 and told to keep watch for raiders seeking to steal more relief supplies. The gun felt strange in his hands, so light. Inevitably the crew's work intersected with war zones. They were held up at gunpoint a few times, their money taken. Sometimes local gangs needed to be paid off, warlords placated with gifts of medicine. It came to him that there was a certain futility to what he did. The more relief work you did, the more you saw how much there was to be done. Some of the aid workers got sick, or outright collapsed. Others just flaked, didn't make the flight, called in their resignations. But most of them kept going, not really knowing what else to do. No one in the rest of the world much cared.

I had some good times here, Ray thought, looking up at Jin Li's apartment, a walk-up in the East Nineties. He had with him a set of fireman's skeleton keys, which contained the master forms provided by the major key manufacturers as well as a variety of trial-and-error sets created by the fire department's research department. Using the keys was sometimes faster than breaking a door down, especially if it was metal and dead-bolted. You were supposed to turn them in if you left the FD, but no one ever did.

He put on his old fire department suspenders and boots, carried his bag of tools plus a water pressure gauge, and clipped his old ID to his shirt and figured this might help him. His father owned an old police radio that didn't work very well but crackled and popped convincingly, and he carried this in one hand, too.

At the front door he encountered a little old woman who had dyed her hair but forgotten to do the eyebrows.

"Ma'am, I'm going to follow you in."

She turned in alarm. "You are?"

"Yes."

"Who are you?"

"Fire department."

"Where's the fire?"

"No fire. Just checking something."

"What is it?" she demanded to know. "Why isn't the super letting you in?"

"Between you and me?" He leaned close. "I'm an inspector. We have a confidential tip regarding the building's automated sprinklers, and letting the super know I am coming would be potentially disadvantageous to the safety of the residents."

The woman nodded in keen understanding of such a stratagem and her eyes narrowed in conspirational pleasure. "I *see*. Just give me one detail so I can understand."

"Yes, ma'am. We require sprinkler systems to be on their own piping system so that a regulatory constant pounds-per-square-inch pressure may be maintained and so also that shut-down repairs to dwelling plumbing systems do not impair the readiness of the fire sprinklers. However, maintaining two water piping systems is more expensive, and—"

"Yes!" the woman exclaimed. "This building is so cheap you can't believe it!" She opened the door and pushed at him to go in, right past the mailboxes he was supposed to break into to find a telephone bill. "Come on, get in quietly," the woman insisted. "I won't tell anyone until it all comes out. We'll expect a full report to the tenants' association. What floor will you be on?"

Jin Li lived on the top floor, as he remembered. "The structure has five floors and we are required to start at the top to check the pressure there first."

"Yes, yes, hurry, please. I live on the third floor. I'll be waiting for you."

He followed her up the stairs, carrying a bag of groceries for her along the way. "How long will you be before you get to our floor?" she asked.

He showed her the water pressure gauge, as if that explained everything. She nodded eagerly. "Perhaps an hour, okay?"

"Yes, thank you."

He continued on to the fifth floor, the hallway of which corresponded to the L-shaped building, and followed it around to Jin Li's apartment, which lay at the end of the hall. He tried his fancy skeleton keys one by one. He found three that went in but none that worked. Which was why he was glad he'd brought the stubby and heavy gas-powered Saws-All. He would be making a lot of noise for fifteen seconds. Couldn't be helped. He started the saw, gouged the reciprocating blade into the door crack, and guided it downward, cutting two brass dead-bolt locks in about ten seconds. A hell of a skreeling racket, too, metal on metal, bright brass sawdust spewing onto the carpet. Wake the dead, for God's sake. He waited for a door to open along the hallway, a head to pop out, but nothing happened. People were at work, maybe that was it.

He turned the handle and pushed open the door. The apartment was dark, and he shut the door behind him before turning on the light.

"Let's remember a few things," his father had briefed him earlier. "People live different ways. Young people are often quite messy but have places where there is order. Their music collections, their spices, that kind of thing. A bed with the sheets on the floor means nothing. Women are not necessarily neater than men, although what will be neat and messy will usually be different. People say gay men are the neatest but not in my experience. Blind people living alone are. They have to be. Anyway, you are looking for three things, the way I see it. You are figuring out if she left in a hurry, you are seeing if the place has been tossed by someone else, and you are looking for information about what kind of trouble she's in. The faster she left, the more information is available."

He first checked the refrigerator, which was running. He opened the door. No mold on anything. Some Chinese vegetables in there. He sniffed the quart of skim milk—not sour. But that didn't tell him much. He needed a date stamp. She'd been gone at least five days. In the trash was a bill from the local supermarket, which included a quart of milk. The bill was marked the day before the murder of the Mexican girls.

He inspected the bedroom. The bed was unmade. What was missing? He saw no computer, no wallet, no cash. He checked the bathroom; her toothbrush and toothpaste were gone. He opened the cabinet; her birth control pills were there; this, as much as anything, suggested a hasty exit. She'd said she never missed a pill, ever. In the closet he saw her dresses hanging neatly, many with the dry cleaner's cellophane still on them. He recognized some of them, had run his hand over and inside them, too.

Had the place been tossed by someone else? Hard to say. The apartment was neither messy nor particularly orderly, just as he remembered. He checked the kitchen drawers, the living room table drawer, the dresser. He stared at the phone and then hit Play Messages. Nothing. That was in her nature. He tried scrolling through the numbers for incoming and outgoing calls; all had been erased. Come on, come on, Ray muttered. I'm not getting what I want. He went back to her dresser and opened up the underwear drawer. In a small silk box he found some jade earrings and a matching jade bracelet. He'd priced jade in Malaysia, and even to his unpracticed eye, this jewelry looked expensive.

Not getting much, he thought. He paced around the apartment a second time, peeking into the hall closet and under the bed, but found nothing. He crept out the door and pulled it shut, feeling defeated.

"I hope you have a good fucking reason for being in there," a voice said.

Ray turned around. A man of about fifty with a red cane stood watching him. He was holding his portable phone.

"Hi," said Ray.

"You hear me?" He pointed the cane at Ray.

"I did."

"So what's going on? I hit the number one here, this dials 911, and the cops will come."

Ray put down his bag of tools. "I just broke into her apartment," he admitted.

"I got that. What did you steal?"

"Nothing."

"Right."

Ray pulled out his pockets, one by one. He opened his tool bag and showed it to the man, who poked his cane inside.

"I'm her old boyfriend. She's in trouble. I'm trying to find her."

The man smiled. "Very romantic."

"It's true. I'm surprised I didn't run into you before."

"You've been here?"

"Lots. Nights."

The man nodded in disgust. "I *work* nights. I'm the light man on the Empire State Building."

Appeal to the man's pride, Ray thought. "All the colored lights, the reds and greens?"

"You got it. What's your name?"

"Ray Grant."

The man nodded suspiciously, as if this was an obvious lie. "You look like a fake fireman or something."

"I was a real fireman."

"Was? Can you prove it?"

"I got my old ID right here."

"Oh, fuck you," the man snarled. "That's bullshit. Probably can buy them on the Internet, eBay or something." He held up his phone menacingly. "Okay, asshole, unless you convince me otherwise, I'm calling the—"

"The Empire State Building is sheathed in eight inches of Indiana limestone," Ray announced. "It is unlikely to ever collapse in a fire because of the high ratio of its poured concrete to its structural steel, and because every floor has its own ventilation system, meaning fire cannot easily travel from floor to floor . . . and the building's steel columns and girders are enclosed in two inches of brick terra-cotta and concrete, not spray-on mineral fiber as is common and increasingly controversial today. Also, as I remember, the elevators and utility shafts are masonry-enclosed. The building has a smokeproof stairway with independent vent shafts, a safety feature eliminated in the 1968 revisions of the city's building code, due to weight issues and cost considerations. Old-timers in the Fire Department say that if the 9/11 airliners had hit it instead, it never would have collapsed."

The man nodded, even allowed a smile. "That's correct." He put the phone in his pocket and leaned on his red cane. "Okay, Ray whoever you are. You got me."

"You have any idea where Jin Li might be?"

"Nope."

"She moved out. Really fast."

"Scared?"

"I think so."

"Why don't you call her?"

"I did. No answer."

"No answer at work?"

Ray shook his head. The first place Chen had checked.

"That girl works hard. Long, long hours."

"You know about the office-cleaning company?"

The man hesitated, unsure whether to answer. "Well, she tells me sometimes, like how she works in midtown in the evenings at various locations but has to get out to Red Hook every day in the morning, to manage everything."

"Red Hook?" An industrial area in Brooklyn, on the water.

"Sure, where the company keeps its trucks. Tough to park a lot of big mobile shredding trucks in Manhattan. You need parking space, Red Hook is pretty good."

Ray had never considered this; it made sense. He picked up his bag. "You got that address?"

"Nope. But Christ, drive around. Can't miss those trucks."

Yes, there are a million great places to eat in New York City, the steakhouses, the celebrity chef halls of worship, the places to see and be seen (at Michael's: "There's Henry Kissinger! There's Penélope Cruz!"), the stuffy theater district joints with timed seatings, Italian-Chinese-French-Vietnamese-Indian-nouvelle-fusion-whatever trend is next, the taverns and bars and clubs and eateries and saloons and bistros and cafés and sushi places frequented by skinny women and coffee shops and bookstore cafés filled with geniuses and depressives and bodegas and snack bars and pizza joints and espresso bars and fast-food places and emporiums of fish and tearooms and Thai noodle shops, absolutely every possible taste catered to, not to mention the Oyster Bar, where businessmen have been knocking them back for decades before taking the train home—and be sure you try their New England clam chowder. Yet not to be forgotten and in fact to be specifically remembered is the Primeburger, on the north side of Fifty-first Street off Fifth Avenue. Not a high-class joint, but not a low-class joint, either, rather a real old-time Manhattan luncheonette. Hamburgers have been served there since 1938. Last remodeled in 1965. You enter to a long counter on the right, single seats with once-futuristic swing-trays on the left, a few crowded tables in the back. Tuna melt, Boston cream pie. Jell-O with whipped cream. Prune juice, if you want it, heh. All the waiters are older guys in white jackets and neckties, with their names embroidered on the jacket. The menu is not expensive. Your basic burger is $4.50. You heard right: $4.50 in midtown Manhattan. Gray-haired businessmen like the place, some of them rich guys who the world forgot twenty or thirty years ago. But they stayed on, oblivious to being disremembered, getting to their little offices by eight a.m. each day, making a few phone calls, watching the price of something on a screen: pork bellies, spot oil, the Brazilian crop report. Not retired, just working an easy schedule. Don't run anything anymore, no titles, no pressure. Take the early train home, money made. Men of habit, not only do they eat at the same time each day but generally eat the same thing, and thus the Primeburger waiters grunt intimately at them as they arrive, mouthing again the order that never changes. "Ham chee, Swiss'n'rye, Co-no-ice."

Sometimes these old men meet each other at the Primeburger, and if you pretend to be deaf and never look at them, you can hear their conversations. *He got a great price on that lot on 56th Street . . . They were once a very fine firm . . . I heard the painting might be available for a private buyer . . . The margins are way too tight, he needs to unload . . .*

Like that, millions being rearranged among the tuna salad sandwich, the coleslaw, the baked apple.

This was where Martz was headed. Far chair at the counter. He eased down on a rotating stool. An old black waiter drifted over, eyes unblinking. "Menu?"

Martz waved it away. "Turkey club, orange juice, apple pie."

The sandwich appeared in less than two minutes.

"You remember me?" Martz asked.

"Depends who's asking," said the waiter.

"I'm asking."

"Then yes, I do remember you."

"Thought so. You seen Elliot around?"

"Expect he'll be here for lunch in about half an hour."

Martz nodded. He knew this, of course, though it had been years since he'd seen Elliot. One of the consolations of age: your friends didn't change their habits. They *died* but they didn't change.

When he was done eating, he picked up a packet of sweetener, tore off the corner, emptied the white powder onto his plate, and then took out a pencil and underlined five letters in the word NUTRASWEET: the T, R, S, and double E, then drew an arrow from the S to the end of the word. What did you get? TREES. He handed the empty packet to the waiter. "I would take it as a great favor if you would give that to El-liot."

"Yes, sir." The waiter betrayed no reaction at the oddity of the item and instead tucked the packet into his breast pocket.

"Appreciate it," said Martz. He finished his apple pie, then slipped a fifty-dollar bill beneath his empty plate. He checked the waiter's face. But he was writing up the tab, which he set down on the counter, the big bill and the plate already gone.

As, a moment later, was Martz, toothpick in his mouth, shambling along Fifty-first Street, teeth set, hating everyone, especially himself.

Get your money fast. Across the street from the sewerage yard sat a check-cashing operation that was always busy on Friday nights. Because the place received two armored truck deliveries each week, and because workers walked out with wads of cash, the building had three security cameras trained on the outside. The windows were full of advertisements for cash-wiring services specializing in Latin America, Africa, and Asia. For all the immigrants sending money back home. This afternoon's customers, most Latino men in work clothes and baseball caps, stood in a neat line, responsive to the quasi-governmental spareness of the room, which was festooned with official notices about fees, currency rates, and identity theft—not to mention the threatening signs announcing that the premises were under twenty-four-hour surveillance and that all deliveries were made by armored truck drivers licensed to carry "and use" firearms. Victor pushed his way in, a paper bag from the liquor store under his arm. The Nigerian man behind the glass nodded at him in familiarity; half of Victor's laborers used the place.

"Violet in?"

"Upstairs."

"Tell her."

The man picked up his phone, spoke a minute, nodded at Victor. "She says five minutes."

He nodded. Sat back and waited, and by habit inspected the line of men and women waiting to cash their checks. You could tell a lot about them, especially the men, he thought. Male human beings, he'd come to learn, more or less fell into four categories by the time they had reached forty. There were the guys who had it made (done, game over) because they were professionals of one sort or another or worked for big companies or owned something so big and fabulous that made so much money that they could call whatever shots they wanted. They had money packed away in places most people never heard of. They had wives and children or maybe second wives. They didn't worry when they needed a new car; they just bought it. At very most 5 percent of men fell into this category, by Victor's reckoning. You saw them on the subway with their laptop computers, their good office shoes, their soft hands. Almost all had gone to college. No doubt this small group of men could be separated further in smaller categories, but for his purposes, the 5 percent was enough. Victor hated these guys. Then there were the guys who were industrious and smart and who were working every angle they could think of, guys with roofing companies that employed thirty men and who flipped a little real estate on the side, bada-boom, guys who maybe cut a few corners but were good with people, kept things moving along. This group included the local lawyers who took every piece of business that came their way, neighborhood accountants who did a little keep-it-vague bookkeeping as necessary, and so on. Lots of guys running restaurants fell into this category. Victor himself fell into this category, although once he had his gas station, got the money rolling, things would be different for him. Guys in this group worked too hard, considering. They might make it into the 5 percent category, except ten years later, and never with any peace of mind. Some of these second-tier guys were happily married, many were not. Many of them fucked around and hurt their momentum that way. Dissipated themselves. Drank or smoked too much, lost a lot of mornings. Victor, yeah you could say that about him, although he had that natural resilience and stamina most men could only dream about, weak motherfuckers. Then the third group was the guys who weren't going to make it. Instead of running roofing companies, they were still working on roofs, which by the time you hit forty was a very bad idea—the cold and heat and heavy work wore you down, busted your joints. These were the guys who had missed out, or restarted their lives so many times already that nothing was ever going to take. Too many women, jobs, apartments, nights that went bad. They lost stuff— they lost money, friends, jobs, car keys, their cell phones, anything they needed they lost. They were slowly sinking and maybe they knew it but probably they didn't, not yet, anyway. Richie had been one of these guys, two paychecks away from being flat busted. Tried to pick up work on the side, didn't much. Never got any momentum. Women were good at identifying these guys. Men with old pickup trucks, men who bought cheap beer by the case, men who couldn't remember who the vice president of the United States was. Often they had muscles from the work but had started to waste away from the smoking. Got those cigarette bodies, lanky, almost diseased looking. Fingertips always stained. Jacks-of-too-many-trades. Credit bad, prospects slim. One fall off a roof, one cracked-up car, one bad fight in a bar, and they were hanging on by their teeth.

And then, of course, there was the fourth category, the deadbeats and losers who were crashing on somebody's couch or living inside their truck or moved before the rent check was due or lived off a woman somehow, either a mother (pretending to "look after" her) or, more likely, some divorced woman who needed some kind of man around to holler at her children for her or, worst case of all, lived with one of the many different kinds of crazy women who usually ended up getting the worse end of the stick. Most of these guys were boozers or beaters, child abusers, freaks. Fucking animals.

Meanwhile, Vic had dreams and self-discipline. He made plans and stuck to them. Figured the angle, as he was doing now with Ears. He had to take the right line of action, trust no one, especially the people who said they were his friends. Richie was supposed to be a friend but got whacked because he did something wrong, drew attention. The way Vic saw it now was that Ears and whoever he was working for had done a favor for somebody big but also saw a way to work it the other way and create a blackmail situation. That's what Vic would have done, anyway. Somebody high up in some company had ordered something be done to these two Mexican girls, and Ears and his pals didn't want to share the gold mine. Thought they'd buy off Vic for a lousy twenty, twenty-five Gs. Then go back and blackmail the guy for a couple hundred grand. But they'd screwed up somehow or Richie had talked to somebody and now there was a problem, the guy asking around the yard. That asshole was on a suicide mission, too, and next time Vic saw him, he'd be ready. And Vic wasn't going to get fingered, sorry. Far as he was concerned, he did Richie a favor. Guy never felt a thing. If it had come from Ears, Richie would have suffered. But now Vic had to protect himself, get ahead in the game by a few moves.

"Violet says come on up."

The door buzzed and he pushed through. He passed the small window of the money room; inside, a currency-counting machine spun a blur of bills while an electronic readout kept the tally. Lot of money in a joint like this, lot of money in a neighborhood like this, lot of money in Brooklyn, guy. That's what the tiny-balled motherfuckers in Manhattan didn't understand. We've got some power in this part of town. Fucking Guineas built this city, brick by brick. Sure, the Irish, too. Now, of course, most of the Italian guys were fat and lazy and it was the new foreign guys who worked their asses off. No wonder they were getting all the good businesses. He climbed the stairway, hearing how heavy his footfalls were, a sound he knew well.

The upstairs apartment was owned by Violet Abruzzi, whom he had known all his life. They'd grown up two blocks from each other on Bay Ninth Street and he'd kissed her on the lips in third grade. His father might have porked her mother, though no one ever knew for sure. Which made them some kind of almost half cousins or something in his head. He'd played on the same Catholic school baseball team with Violet's older brother Anthony, a tall guy with a real curveball. Lot of good times back then. The next summer the two of them got beaten down by four newcomer Russian guys; Anthony had lived in a state facility ever since, wearing some kind of neck brace that kept his head from falling backward. One of the Russian guys had broken both of Victor's arms and punched him so many times they thought he was dead. The local detectives had asked Victor what had happened; he said he didn't remember. Of course the detectives didn't believe him. They knew how things worked. A few months went by, people started to forget. Not Victor. He planned, told no one. Bought a gun, made a silencer for it. What was left of the Russian guy was found under the boardwalk in Coney Island. Whoever did it—a real sicko—had used a fish knife and taken out his eyeballs and put them in the guy's hand. And his nuts in his eye sockets. Message: keep an eye on your balls, ass-hole. The other Russians, terrorized, moved away the next day. The detectives came back, went through every room of Vic's father's house, every square foot of the yard. Looked through the business records, the supplies, found nothing. But people in the neighborhood thought it was Vic. He was smart enough to say nothing. Violet got very friendly after that. They'd had sex in the local Catholic church a few times, lying down on pew cushions, kept quiet. All kinds of places. She'd gotten pregnant but he wouldn't get married. So she'd had an abortion, a big relief then. After that she'd gotten married a few times. Every time she got married she gained another twenty pounds. No kids, which was probably okay, knowing Violet now. The check-cashing operation had been left her by her late, latest, and probably last husband, a man twenty years her senior, and it was, by any definition, a money machine. They took 4 percent of whatever they handled. Victor knew that the deliveries from the armored car company dropped $350,000 on Monday mornings and $700,000 on Thursday evenings—but forget about holding the place up. He'd studied the situation, of course. The armored car company was mobbed up and Violet herself had a gun license, as did all her employees. And anyway, it was Violet. A few years earlier, a couple of young gansta-punks from East New York had cased the place, busted in screaming robbery, and been shot dead as soon as they came through the office door. It wasn't a bank, where you politely handed over a prepared bag with dye packs on a timer set inside. The police hadn't even picked up the spent shells.

"Hey, baby," came Violet's voice.

The apartment was dark, but he knew his way.

She lay in her bed, smoking, as usual. "You bring me anything?"

He pulled a bottle from the bag. "Drambuie, you like it."

"Sweet, I like sweet. Good for late at night."

Since her teen years, Violet had always had a terrible time sleeping. Now she reached her enormous arm over to her side table and found two glasses. Poured an inch in each.

"Here."

Victor took it in one shot. Then he pulled off his shoes, took his gun from his sock, slipped it into his shoe, took off his pants, folded them. He didn't know why he did this, came to see her. Well, yes, he did. The ugliness excited him.

"Come here," she said.

He stood next to the bed and she hung her head back off the side of the mattress. He moved over her.

"You take a shower in the last week?" she asked.

"The Drambuie will kill the germs."

"You're probably right."

She took him. She was quite good and sucked him hard quickly. She began to finger herself beneath the covers. She moaned a bit. After a minute she pulled him out of her mouth. "All right." He walked around to the other side of the bed. She rolled over and presented her enormous ass upward. This was the ugly part, the part he liked. He slipped in from behind. She had never had kids, so even though she was a size eighteen or twenty-two or whatever the huge size was, she was tight as a glove inside. And Violet was fucked ten or fifteen times a month, so she was really in shape down there. He gave it to her hard for a minute or so, sensed boredom in himself, and made a point of watching the traffic on the boulevard out the window.

"Come on, Vic," she instructed. "Don't lose interest."

He pounded her and it felt good. The hot jolt running toward the tip. She squeezed herself at just the right time and he heard a noise come out of his throat and as he shot it occurred to him that he'd enjoyed killing Richie more. You might be a sick fuck, Victor thought. Well, look where you are, you must be.

"All right now," said Violet, her voice amused. "Finally, a little emotionality. You and me. I think we got a chance at Oprah."

He sat back.

"Nice to see you enjoy yourself," she purred.

"Maybe I actually did, yeah."

"Oh, you did."

"Okay, I did. You liked it, too."

"I'm a woman of capacious appetites."

"What's capacious?"

"Big."

"Right. *Big.*"

"That's enough." She poured herself a glass. "You're lucky. Your real girlfriends wouldn't put up with this shit."

"My real girlfriends go out in the Brooklyn sunlight and interact with civilized society."

He wiped himself with the sheet. Violet rolled over.

"Something's bothering you."

"Nah."

"Hey, Victor. It's *me*, right?"

"Sure is."

"I'm just saying, is all. You seem like something's bothering you."

"You think you know me?"

She laughed and poured another glass. "I'm just saying, a woman can tell some things."

All right, his shrug said, I'll give it to you. He pulled on his pants and went into the bathroom.

"Plus I never complain about your girlfriends."

"How could you?" he called behind him.

"I *could*. But I don't."

He smiled. This was just play. "I got a guy messing with me, Violet. I don't know who he is."

He sensed her settling in for the conversation, pleased he'd opened up to her. "How messing?"

"Just came by the lot, asking questions." He flipped open the cabinet in her bathroom, reached his hand in the back and opened Violet's bottle of chloral hydrate, the same powerful sleeping pills that killed Anna Nicole Smith. Dissolved in both water and alcohol. He'd used five on Richie, explained to Sharon how to mix them in.

"Questions about what?" came Violet's voice.

"Just things." He poured out ten pills, wrapped them in a piece of toilet paper, and slipped them into his pocket.

"You doing some stuff these days now, Vic?"

He came back to the bed. "I'm always doing something."

She lit a cigarette. "What's he look like?"

"Regular guy. Built."

"Cop?"

"Doesn't have the swagger."

"Not confident?"

"No, no, very confident. But lone-wolf confident. Like that."

Violet was quiet. "I heard about those Mexican girls who got killed out by the beach."

He started pulling on his shirt. "Oh, yeah? I did, too."

She smoked her cigarette, wouldn't look at him. How did she know? he thought. How *could* she know? "Vic, they got killed with a load of sewage." She looked at him meaningfully. "Whoever heard of that?"

"Pretty tough to track sewage. Stuff degrades quickly."

"But the truck."

"Trucks can disappear. Guys in Queens buy them for scrap, crush them an hour later."

"But you said there's a guy—"

"Not a cop, like I said. Somebody's fucking with me."

"I can ask people," she said.

He found his shoes. "Don't ask. Just listen." He checked his watch. "Gotta go."

She looked at him. This was the moment when he used to give her a little kiss on the cheek, a momentary gentleness that recalled their shared childhood, her brain-damaged brother, the dead baby, the life together that never happened.

"Yeah," said Violet. She turned her back.

Downstairs he knocked on the glass. The Nigerian guy looked up from his freaky African newspaper.

"Hey, I forgot to ask you, you seen Richie?"

"He was here couple days ago, boss."

"Cash his check?"

The Nigerian shook his head. "Just paying us a social visit, Mr. Vic."

Fucking Richie, did he come and bang Violet twice a week, too? Did *he* tell Violet about the girls? It was quite possible.

Victor fingered the ten pills in his pocket, again checked his watch. The day had a plan. A goal. And to achieve that goal, he needed to go mix some chemicals.

She waited in the shadows, across the street from the truck bay on Fifty-first Street. She was dressed in the CorpServe uniform she'd last worn on the evening of the attack, yet now it was washed and pressed, all evidence of those events gone. She reached into her pocket and affixed her CorpServe ID badge. Straggling workers on their way home hurried by her, men and women thinking about dinner, the children, what was on TV tonight. A few minutes after seven p.m., the forty-four-foot CorpServe mobile shredder pulled up, #6 as usual, and the truck bay door was lifted by the security men. The truck was driven by old man Zhao, who always drove it. He had a perfect safety record, she remembered, not bad considering his age. His eyesight was excellent, too; she'd ordered him to be tested six months earlier. She had a soft spot for him; maybe he reminded her of her grandfather.

The two floor cleaners would have arrived by the service entrance already and would be upstairs at work in the Good Pharma offices. The truck was now parked for the evening in the truck bay, and Zhao had started up the actual shredder unit, which ran off an electric battery, not the diesel engine. The reason, of course, was that some trucks needed to operate within completely enclosed facilities and could not be a danger for asphyxiation by diesel exhaust of the operator as well as those nearby.

She darted across the street and found Zhao. He was surprised to see her, and she put a finger to her lips and drew him out of sight of the security camera.

"They said you were killed!" he exclaimed in Mandarin.

"Of course not," Jen Li answered him.

"They say all the operations must stay normal. Orders from the big boss in China."

Her brother, of course. "That's good."

"But everybody is nervous."

"Tell me, how did the other Mexican girls react to the news?"

Zhao shook his head. "Oh, they were very sad. I think some of the girls quit."

"What about on this job?" she asked.

"Well, they shifted some of the others. Just cleaning, I think."

"No one at the company upstairs said anything about the girls to us?" said Jin Li, scarcely able to believe it. "Did the police ask anything?"

"A detective came around last night." The old man pulled out a card and handed it to Jin Li. She fingered it, felt the hard edge of it. Detective Peter Blake, the lettering said, Brooklyn Homicide Division. The man who had called her. She slipped it into the pocket of the coveralls.

"What'd he say?"

Zhao straightened up, ready to make his report. It was evident he'd sought to memorize the conversation. "He asks if we saw anybody follow the little Japanese car with the two girls in it. I say no. He asks if you were in car with the girls. I say I do not know. He says why you do not know. I say I did not see where you go, I drive the truck. He says where does Jin Li go most nights? I say I think to her apartment. He says where is that. I say I do not know. He says does Jin Li have American boyfriend named Raymond Grant and I say I do not know but I think maybe yes. He says that he thinks I know. I say yes, I have heard about this American boyfriend but I have never seen him. He says did the Mexican girls smoke pot? I say that I think they did, because of smell in the car. He says how do you know smell of pot? I say this is smoked in China except in my village we called it the pig that floats. He laughed. I liked this detective, I know you are sorry to hear this. A very professional man. He says, where else did these girls work? I say well mostly in this building but sometimes other places, too. He says why and I say because sometimes we do not have enough people in each place. He says did these Mexican girls get in any trouble on the job? I say no, I don't think so. Very good workers. He says what about their boyfriends, do they sell pot to people in company? I say no, Jin Li will fire everybody who buys pot in company. He says can I read English good. I say no, just traffic signs and beer bottles. He likes that. He says he reads beer bottles, too. He says why do I think somebody kill some Mexican girls. I say I do not know. He says maybe Jin Li kill Mexican girls then run away. I say I do not think so. He says why not. I say you are nice to those girls. Everybody think you are best boss they ever had. He say he think Mexican girls sell some drugs to everybody, maybe drugs from their boyfriends. He say Mexicans getting big in the drug traffic in New York, most people think it is other people. I say I do not think so. He says he wants dog to sniff me and sniff the truck. I say okay. They bring in the dog and he does not say I have pot. He smelled me, he smelled this truck. I like this dog, very good number-one dog. He says he thinks Jin Li knows how come some Mexican girls died. I say I think you good person, not like that. He says why are you not very upset about Jin Li. I say I think she is okay, she is smart. He—"

"Okay," Jin Li interrupted. "Next time you hear something like this, you call me. Anything you think I need to know. You have my number. Leave a message in Chinese if I don't pick up. Okay?"

"If you say so."

"Now, I want you to take me upstairs."

"But you can go up."

"No, I don't think so. I don't want the elevator camera on me. Just put me in the roller bin, throw an empty bag on me."

Zhao did not like this, but he allowed her to climb into the bin. He dropped some empty garbage bags over her, then summoned the freight elevator. She heard him call one of the CorpServe workers on his radio. A moment later the elevator arrived and he wheeled in the bin.

"Floor number two-four," he said in English, then left.

Jin Li heard the doors close.

"MeezaJin?" came a voice. One of the Mexican girls.

"Don't talk to me," she answered. "The camera is on us. Don't look inside the roller, just look at the door, okay?"

"Okay, jes."

"Just roll it through the lobby, through the main door, and stop it next to the little kitchen."

Which the woman did. Jin Li climbed out into the kitchen, where there was no security camera. She knew this kitchen well, had used the coffee machine in it many times. The CorpServe worker stood there, waiting for instructions. Jin Li also knew that the security man moved ceaselessly from floor to floor, appearing on every floor once every half hour or so.

"In ten minutes I want you to be here with five or six full bags. You are going to put them on top of me and take me down, okay?"

"Jes."

"Leave the roller here."

Jin Li knew this floor, had walked it dozens of times, knew its layout, who worked where, and what the best sources of information were. The floor had four sections: executive, legal, fiscal, and research. The best information usually came from research and fiscal, but she figured that she would search in the executive section. She wanted an indication that someone at Good Pharma was worried about CorpServe spying on it. Then she could tell Chen to stop doing whatever he had done that had alerted them, or to cover his tracks, if possible.

But where, exactly, to look? The CEO of the company was a tall, elegant man named Lewis Henry who seemed never to be there. The people who seemed to really run the company were the vice-president, a man named Reilly; the comptroller, a woman named Moritz; and the director of research, a man named Brenner. She inspected Moritz's office first—not her trash but the papers on her desk. Nothing there but long printouts of manufacturing costs at a plant in Puerto Rico. What am I looking for? she wondered. A note, a report? It seemed unlikely she'd find anything like that.

She entered Brenner's office. His desk was piled with neat, spiral-bound research reports. She flipped one open. It had to do with a new product for "sexual response enhancement in females." Tested on 406 women aged twenty-two to sixty, median age forty-one, the results showed that "71 percent of the respondents had enjoyed an increased—" This isn't what I'm looking for, thought Jin Li, keep moving. She studied the papers piled on the man's windowsill. Apparently he was a pack rat of sorts. The reports were organized by clinical trial date and research product. I could spend a year reading in here, she realized. She retreated out of the office, looked at her watch. Four minutes.

Next came Reilly's corner office, a large room with a conference table to one side and matched set of sofa and chairs at the other. Four windows. Private washroom. Framed photos and articles on the wall. From the earlier papers she'd seen, it seemed clear that he was the public face of the company, did a lot of deal making and communication with investors. Was quoted in the newspapers. She examined the picture on his desk. A smiling, attractive woman looked back. Probably was a high school cheerleader or something, Jin Li thought dismissively. She pulled open his desk drawers. Nothing of interest. As with the other offices, a computer hummed to one side of the desk. She assumed that all the computers were shut down automatically, but to test this notion, she pushed a key with her knuckle. The computer beeped and a prompt for a username and password appeared. Forget that, she thought.

Not much on the desk. Printouts of sales figures broken down by region, research summaries, a copy of a legal settlement for a liability suit for one of the company's projects, a slim folder containing all the stories that mentioned the company in the major print media that day, and so on. And a call list on Good Pharma stationery, no doubt generated by his assistant. Next to each name and time of call received were several lines for him to record the essence of the conversation. She skimmed the names.

Recognized one. James Tonelli. The building operations man who had hired CorpServe in the first place. Next to his name, the message: *Knows you wanted to speak to him urgently.* Reilly trying to reach Tonelli—why? The list had other interesting names. One of the messages said, *We have received an inquiry from the NYPD regarding the death of the two Mexican workers in our CorpServe cleaning service.*

She folded the list into a small square, unzipped the coveralls, and slipped it into her pocket.

The CorpServe worker was probably back at the kitchen with the roller bin filled with bags now, wondering where Jin Li was.

I haven't found anything good, she told herself. She stole into the private bathroom. Flicked on the light. Tiled shower. Toilet. A small closet with an extra suit, several pairs of shoes, and a selection of pressed shirts and ties. Pretty nice life, she thought. She opened the medicine cabinet. One bottle of pills. Beta-inhibitors. Used to remove anxiety in public situations. Half the executives in New York probably took them.

She heard a noise and turned off the office light. Poked her head out the hallway. The security guard was walking away from her. The floor's layout had the lobby and elevator banks in the center, with rings of inner and outer offices circling it. The kitchen was at the other end of the floor, in the direction the guard was walking. But he was checking offices here and there, and Jin Li knew her way around. She ran as fast as she could down the hall in the opposite direction, turned left, ran that hall, and turned left again, working her way around the other side of the building to get to the kitchen before the security guard did. She turned left for the last time and saw the CorpServe worker standing there looking worried.

"Quick!" ordered Jin Li.

She lifted out five big bags of paper, then jumped into the bin.

"Put them on me, quick!"

"Jes."

The worker did as asked.

"Roll it to the service elevator."

Which she did. Jin Li heard her punch the call button.

"Hello," said the worker to someone.

"Evening," came a male voice, relaxed but firm. "Headed down?"

"Jes."

"We got transition procedures coming," the security guard's voice said. "Tomorrow we will be explaining them to y'all."

"Hokay."

The service elevator doors opened.

"Night now."

The doors closed. Jin Li waited. When the elevator reached street level, the worker pushed the roller to the mobile shredder. Jin Li wriggled up through the bags and hopped out. Had this been caught on tape? Probably. The roar of the shredder made it hard to think.

"He said there are new procedures coming?" she asked the woman.

"Jes."

The Mexican woman barely made eye contact. I scare her, realized Jin Li. She knows about the two dead girls.

"Did you hear about them already?"

"Jes. Yesterday they tell us."

"What did they say?"

"They say we no more do this building. They no want us anymore. So we go to other job. Something like that, I think."

Jin Li studied the woman. She had no idea what she was saying. She simply did what she was told and did not question why Good Pharma was getting rid of CorpServe. But Jin Li understood why. And now she needed to tell Chen to be careful, assuming the company did not know about him already, or even that he was in New York. If they know he is here, she thought, they will do something to him.

She'd been enormously patient. She'd waited a few days before talking with Tom about what had happened at Martz's party, not that she hadn't kept going over the interaction, trying to understand what it meant for Tom. As soon as the old man had shaken her shitty fingers in front of Ann's face, she had gone cold inside—cold toward Tom, certainly cold toward Martz, whom she did not consider as a patient or worthy of her medical opinion. In fact, no medical opinion had been rendered directly to him. He had simply let go of her hand and then hoisted up his pants.

"I know I got a fucking prostate problem," he'd grumbled.

She'd pulled off her gloves inside out and thrown them in the trash.

"Come on," she snapped at him. "Turn around, face me. I dare you to look me in the face!"

But he had, and wheeled to confront Ann. "Your husband is in a lot of trouble, lady. Focus your attention on him." He cleared his throat. "So, by the way, what's your medical opinion?"

What an asshole, she thought. And I just put my fingers inside it. "My *opinion* is that you should fear chaos—in all its forms—cellular, psychological, interpersonal, and existential."

Martz, an old warrior, smiled thinly in disgust. "That's it?"

"That's all I'm saying to you."

He grunted, seemingly irritated with himself as much as with her, then left the room, leaving the door ajar. She heard the tinkle of silverware and the murmur of party talk. She sat to collect herself, looked out the corner window. A beautiful view, the lights of Manhattan to the south and Jersey to the west. So high up she could see all the bridges and the Statue of Liberty. Money bought you a lot of sky.

Connie Martz hurried in. "He said you didn't tell him anything?"

Ann looked at Connie. How much did this woman know about her husband? How much did any woman know? And how much do I know about Tom? she thought.

"He seemed eager to get back to the party," she said diplomatically, her anger receding as she saw Connie's anxiety. "I'm supposed to tell him directly but I'm going to tell you."

"Please."

"Given the bit of history you gave me plus what I felt, I think he needs an immediate needle biopsy of the prostate, as well as a PSA test. I'm sure he's had one in the past, given his age. But the lobes of the prostate are lumpy, irregular, and show what we call differential firmness—hard here, soft there. Not good. This is very consistent with prostate cancer, though not proof of it. Only a needle biopsy can tell you for sure. But I would have this done tomorrow."

"Test for cancer tomorrow?"

"Once prostate cancer escapes the gland, treatment is much more difficult. The cancer seeds itself. Treatment is no longer confined to the organ but is systemic. From a theoretical basis, the escape of one cell is the tipping point into advanced prostate cancer. If you get it before that first cell escapes, then—"

"Yes, yes! I understand!" Connie's beautiful blue eyes became tearful, then she nodded in determination. "Thank you, Doctor."

Ann had found Tom when she rejoined the party and asked if they could go. He'd seemed relieved, but it took them fifteen minutes to extract themselves graciously. Connie noticed their exit, Martz did not. In the elevator, Tom asked her where she'd gone.

"I just gave your friend Martz a prostate exam."

"What? At a cocktail party?"

"His wife was very persistent."

"And?"

"He needs to have more tests," she said obliquely, somehow aware that this was not the time to violate doctor-patient confidentiality.

"He's not about to die or anything?"

"No," she answered tersely.

That had been two days ago, and she had watched Tom carefully since then.

Now, as they prepared for bed, she said, "That man Martz told me a few things the other night."

"What kind of things?" responded Tom, his voice calm.

Ann stood at the side of the bed, waiting for his full attention. "He said you were in a lot of trouble, Tom. That there were huge amounts of other people's money involved. He said you needed to give him some information. That you had lied to him! He's a very threatening person, even if he has prostate trouble. Maybe even because."

"He threatened you?"

"No, he threatened *you*, Tom. I'm just a doctor who pokes her finger into people. You're the corporate big shot throwing hundreds of millions of dollars around."

"All right, okay? I get it."

She watched him pull on his pajamas. Too much chub around the midsection; led to organ fat. We are now middle-aged, she thought. And no children. From a biological point of view, we've failed.

Tom swallowed an Ambien, as he did every night. "You said he might be threatening *because* of the prostate trouble?"

Ann sighed. This was Tom doing his bait and switch, stalling while he figured out what to say next. "There is a theory," she began, "just a theory, but a smart one, that when prostate cancer reaches a certain critical mass, it begins to affect the man's endocrine cycle. Messes with it. Prostate cancer cells like testosterone, live on it. This is why in advanced cases an orchidectomy is done, castration, in other words, or chemical castration is achieved through the administration of Lupron. Anyway, the prostate cancer cells may mess with a man's testosterone level. The disease itself stresses him, as perhaps does somatic awareness that he is ill—something I really believe happens, which is that we know we are sick before we really feel sick or are told we are sick—but in any case the level of free testosterone in his blood and hence in his brain fluctuates greatly. The system is sort of on the fritz. This can cause a bit of low-grade confusion, depression, and irritability. Or just sometimes inappropriate aggression, such as I witnessed. Sugar levels in the aged are also more volatile, and you get some interesting combination effects of sugar levels and endocrine levels. He'd probably had a drink or two, which both raises testosterone briefly and decreases inhibitions, of course. But I'd bet the other factors were at play. There's a lot of research on this being done. Decision making may be affected. It's subtle, especially because by the age of fifty the pathways of decision making in humans are highly determined. People largely think the way they always have, unless the general brain health begins to degrade, usually because of dendritic plaques and ministrokes."

Tom was listening closely now. Like his life depended on it. "Wait, take it back to Martz."

"Fine. I think you're in some kind of trouble, Tom, and you haven't told me about it!"

He was silent.

"And, based on my clinical experience, and a brief interaction, the man you are in trouble with cannot be depended upon to be highly rational! Or kind and decent! I don't care how much money he has! He's an animal under stress! He's got high cortisol levels, increased blood pressure, who knows what. He's also clearly an aggressor, given how much wealth he's accumulated. In fact, extreme wealth accumulation is, according to some people, an indication of pathological obsession, personality disorder, inappropriate aggression syndrome, grandiosity, nice things like that."

"What do you suggest, Dr. Wife?"

"I suggest you get yourself out of whatever goddamn mess you are in! Come on, Tom! What the hell else do you want me to say?"

He was deciding to tell her, she could see. "Tom? What is it? You can't tell me?"

He made a little biting motion. "It's a business thing."

"You won't tell me? You're actually *not* going to tell me?"

"It's—I just don't want to go into it, okay?"

He looked at her, plaintively, she thought, so far buried in the structures and agendas of Good Pharma that he was more or less inextricable from it. She turned off the light, settled into bed, her mind wide awake now, even after a long day of work. Tom, she knew, was the company, the company was him. He was not the Tom Reilly she'd married. *That* man had disappeared at least ten years ago. *That* man used to be good in bed, be fun to spend time with. God help her for even having the thought, but the plain fact was that Tom had become, what, a human information processor inside the information structure that was the company. Good Pharma manufactured pills and other medical goods, but those were the endpoint results. The company didn't even make the pills, actually. They were jobbed out to for-hire pharmaceutical factories, usually in Puerto Rico or India, increasingly with proprietary manufacturing contracts. The company was a huge matrix of human information processors both running and being run by the information technology. The levels of abstraction, from the chemical composition of the pills themselves, to the research protocols, up through the organization of each division, to the management of the company as a whole, to its interaction with the health-care market on the one hand, governmental regulation on the second, and the financial markets on the third, required people like Tom, supersmart human processors who could carry around enormous levels of abstraction, segue among them and choose the proper inputs of information to each and derive the correct output information from each. You had to have a highly compartmentalized mind yet the ability to reach from one compartment to another for a piece of information that was relevant. Tom was like that and had become more so in the years she'd known him, the overall functioning of his brain becoming, arguably, more specialized in the exact manner the company required. Classic nature-nurture feedback. Environment switching on and off genes in real time, which researchers were starting to understand was possible. Her proof? Highly subjective, admittedly. But she was *his wife,* after all. He'd lost his playfulness. His sense of humor was far less subtle, more brutal and dark. He read faster; she could see it in the morning with the newspaper. Certain of his mental functions were more highly developed. He retained numbers well, perhaps because they had deeper significance. He could articulate better in social settings. He was, in fact, very good with the social aspect of the job, glad-handing prospective investors, showing them a good time, negotiating when the time came. She'd heard him on the phone from home, listened to his voice, and been impressed with the instant affability, the somber tones of judgment—whatever the situation demanded. But these were not authentic responses, she'd come to see. They were mannered—no, that was not the right word—they were *algorithmic*. Most of the people Tom dealt with were coming to him from a position he understood. He knew more or less what they wanted and why they were talking to him. Under these circumstances, an algorithm of interaction was called for. It was conversation, yes, but not exactly spontaneous human contact filled with discovery and intimacy. Ann herself understood this, for it was how she dealt with patients. You tell someone she has high blood pressure a few hundred times, you start to do it the same way. So she understood that. But in Tom's case most of the conversation involved abstractions that were answered with abstractions. The people on the other end of the conversation were working within an algorithm, too. This meant that Tom had very few real conversations. He spoke to dozens of people a day but always within his corporate persona and within the appropriate algorithm. He was trapped. The man he'd been once was either buried under all of this behavior or even, perhaps, gone. Irrecoverably. We change in only one direction. We don't ever change back. She still loved Tom, she supposed, at least out of a kind of habit; her mind was trapped within its own algorithms, too, of course.

But in this overall perception about her husband, who was now brushing his teeth in their bathroom, came another one. Tom had made an error. A big human error. He had misjudged a human being. Maybe it was Martz, maybe it was someone else. The misjudgment was a serious one, full of huge personal and professional risk. This led her to another thought.

Tom was stalling because he didn't have an algorithm.

He'd never seen the problem before.

He didn't know what to do.

Big wad in the pocket. Victor fingered the flash roll of hundreds as he and Ears walked into the midtown place on Broadway, his favorite, better than the ones in Queens, Brooklyn, Jersey, Long Island, all skanky compared to the Manhattan clubs, which had to cater to an international crowd with bigger money. He nodded at the bouncers, wide men in suits with their hands crossed in front of them, feet spread, as they inspected every patron and made sure he felt inspected. They didn't scare Vic. He'd been a bouncer in a club when he was younger. Back in the eighties. Most of these guys were fucking one of the girls, maybe trading them some speed or crystal meth. Ears led the way, the music booming around them. In front was the live stage, where three girls were on the poles. The place had about a hundred tables, most of them full, and perhaps seventy-five girls either sitting next to customers, dancing for them, or walking around looking for the next job. Most were dressed in only a thong bottom and heels. Every one was beautiful, of course, this being New York City, girls from all over the world, black, white, Latino, Asian, tall, short, stacked, skinny, even a few fleshy ones for the guys who liked that.

He and Ears sat down. The waitress came over. She wasn't bad looking herself but nothing like the dancers.

"What you'll have?"

"Vodka on the rocks," said Ears.

"Make it two."

"So, listen, Vic, I had a little talk this afternoon," said Ears. "About you and your gas station problem. The guys, they understand, suggest, you know, we do a sit-down, talk it out."

Victor nodded. "Good, good, I appreciate that," he said. He didn't believe any of it. Best case, Ears had talked to nobody. Worst case, they knew there was a problem now and wanted to get Vic away somewhere, get rid of him. What was he, stupid? No. He was ahead of them, had a plan. And now he saw her, the one he needed, the kind Ears liked, and beckoned her over, a tiny blonde with big eyes and even bigger chest. Great nipples, too—small and firm, gumdrops. She looked about nineteen, under the makeup. She smiled at him, but he pointed at Ears. The timing was crucial here. She swung her hips as she advanced.

"Hi, fellas." She put her hand on Victor's neck, began a casual massage like she was his regular girlfriend and had done it a hundred times. He could smell her perfume.

Victor pulled out his roll, let her see it, let her think he was going to be stupid with it. "Miss," he said, "I'm buying my friend here a couple of dances." He pulled off two Benjamins and handed them to her. "Three dances, just to warm up the night."

"Well, that's a very nice thing to do for your friend."

The girl flipped back her blonde hair, sort of like a mental reset button, and took Ears by the hand and led him into the back, where the girls preferred to dance, with the guy sitting up against the wall. That way they could get down and dirty, work the guy for the big bills, get him into one of the private rooms and flip a couple of $900 bottles of champagne.

Victor watched. A good start, he thought. He knew Ears had the $20,000 in his pocket and, much as it pained Vic, he was going to have to let that go. Give it to the universe. A little life insurance policy. He saw the waitress bringing over the two vodkas on the rocks. "Hey, great. Thanks, babe." He gave her a twenty for her trouble. He sipped his drink, but not too much, and went over the plan. In a place like this there were security cameras all over, at least a dozen. Anything he did right there at the table on the dance floor was captured on tape. But he had that figured, too. Yessir. We're talking about the Big Vic here, folks, not some grab-nuts jerk from nowhere. He stood up with his drink, eased his way to the men's room, the bouncers not very interested. The men's room attendant, a tiny Indian man in a tuxedo so cheap it looked sewn out of rubber, smiled and arranged his display of candies, gum, breath mints, and the like. Victor went to the urinal. The rule was you didn't watch guys take a piss. Especially in a strip club. And it was the one place that the security cameras wouldn't be looking at, because if it ever came out that there was a camera looking at hundreds of guys unzipping their dicks, some big corporate guys, some famous sports stars, TV people, whatever, then people would get whacked, simple as that. As they should. As for the stalls, he assumed the cameras looked in there, too, in case of guys fucking each other, shooting up, drug deals, whatever.

But inside the urinals? That was good. He set his drink on top of the urinal and unzipped with his left hand. He slipped his right hand into his pants pocket and found the four-ounce glass vial he'd put there earlier. The mixture was perfect, he was sure, the recipe handed down and improved by certain practitioners of the art over the last twenty, thirty years. Ten of Violet's chloral hydrates, six Tylenol PM, two Xanax, all mixed with dimethylformamide, carbolic acid jelly, and methyl ethyl ketone. One ounce of this hot shot was enough to kill a horse. Dissolved in alcohol, virtually odorless. The Tylenol PM kept the pain down and the chloral hydrate knocked the guy out before he could tell anyone what he was feeling.

Concentrating on not spilling the vial, not spilling even the tiniest drop, Vic thumbed up the glass stopper. The Indian guy had his back turned, as was the protocol. Vic palmed the vial over the drink, emptying its contents into the glass, and set the drink on the top of the urinal. Now the glass looked like it had a full drink. He stoppered the vial and dropped it back into his pocket. Then he zipped and flushed, the sound of which triggered the Indian attendant to turn on the water in the basin.

"You got a mint?" Vic said to the attendant, who was now holding out a towel.

"Yezzuh."

Victor washed his hands, took the towel, dried, grabbed a mint, and said, "Oh, wait," and retrieved the glass from the top of the urinal. He handed the man a five.

Back on the floor he returned to the table, where Ears's drink stood, and set his own down right next to it. He saw Ears finishing up with the girl. She was leaning into him, her breasts an inch from his nose. A little chitchat would follow, then Ears would return. Victor picked up Ears's drink, slid his own over a few inches, and casually drank a good half of Ear's drink in one long slow gulp and put the glass close to him, making it look like he'd been steadily working through his drink. Vic's original drink, now laced with the contents from the glass vial, appeared to be Ears's untouched drink. Vic pulled out his cell phone, turned it on, listened to nothing, nodded a few times, then clapped it shut just as Ears and the girl arrived.

"What's up?" Ears said.

"Violet was looking out across her window, saw somebody in the yard," said Victor. "Guy inside the gate."

Ears sat down, glanced hungrily at the girl.

"You were born paranoid."

"Gotta check it out. Don't want the cops coming around, either. Fucking sucks."

Ears nodded. He'd already hinted to the girl how rich he was, Victor knew, not that the girls here didn't start trying to figure that out right away. Victor rose, tapped his fist to Ears's. "I know you think I'm crazy."

"I do, yes. Came out of the womb freakin' paranoid."

"We'll do that money thing later—"

"Got it right here, man," said Ears, tapping his breast pocket.

"Ahh, you got a good thing going here with this nice young lady," Vic said magnanimously. "No need to do business here. We'll do it to-morrow, what do you say?"

"Whatever you want, Vic. You better hope I don't spend it tonight. Could end up in Atlantic City, who knows what could happen."

"But I'm not forgetting my side of the deal." Vic turned to the girl. "He's a good man," he told her. "Guy's an old pal of mine, okay?" He tossed off the rest of what had originally been Ears's drink, drained it, ice and all. Then he pulled out his roll of hundreds, gave her ten. "So, listen, I'm buying him a really nice evening, okay?"

"Oh, wow," she murmured.

"Yo, Vic, this is above and beyond the call of duty," Ears said excitedly, hitting what he thought was his own drink hard.

"Not a problem." He touched knuckles with Ears and left.

At the door he beckoned one of the bouncers, who lurched over.

"I came in with my friend," said Victor, pulling out a hundred-dollar bill. "But now I got to go."

He handed the bill to the man, who accepted it as if it was his due even as he inspected its authenticity. "What's the problem?"

"My friend is taking that—he drinks too much, liver is bad, and he's taking that medicine that makes you throw up if you drink too much alcohol, makes you sick very fast."

"He's gonna get sick?"

"Maybe, maybe not," said Victor. "But if he does, I want you to drag him out of here and put him in a cab and send him downtown to the SoHo Grand Hotel."

"For a hundred?"

"No. That was just to have the conversation." Victor smiled and pulled out another hundred and slipped it to the man, who snapped it away. "What hotel?"

"SoHo Grand. Very cool hotel, man. Big time there."

"That's right."

"Cool."

Outside, Victor turned the corner, pulled the vial from his pocket and flipped it into the street, where it popped. The pieces would be crushed by thousands of cars into powder by the next morning. He'd seen Ears drink at least an ounce of his drink, which meant half an ounce of the mixture. All he needed to do was take one more good pull, and then he'd have an ounce in his system. The methyl ethyl ketone went straight into the bloodstream. The sauce killed you about three different ways. Maybe he should have popped Richie that way. But he hadn't because there would have been a chance that Sharon would screw it up and kill herself instead of Richie. Though it would have saved Vic a lot of trouble, the cleanup job, moving Richie's body. But no, that had been a piece of luck, he told himself, because it was while he was cleaning up that he discovered that someone had been there. Gotten the tip-off from the smell of Clorox and the light off in the bedroom. He kept walking. The night felt good, and he was going to go sit at the bar of the Plaza Hotel, talk to the bartender, and any lonely woman who might be there, be seen on about five different security cameras, proving his whereabouts if anyone wanted to know later, and, most important, think of a way to trap the guy who was hunting him.

When I get that guy, Vic thought, I'm done.

Inside the strip club, Ears took another big slug from his drink, finished it. He felt better than he had in a long time, relaxed, glad Victor and his freakin' paranoia were gone. Not that Vic was wrong to be paranoid, because the guys with the big shoes had noticed how strangely he'd been acting and were definitely not happy about it. They'd already decided to string him along on the gas station thing then make a move when he'd calmed down. Pop him when he wasn't expecting it. That way James Tonelli could move in on the pharmaceutical company exec, Tom somebody, who had requested the hit on the cleaning company. That guy was going to pay big for silence about the Mexican girls. *Big.* They'd stumbled onto a gold mine! No way were the big shoes going to let Vic screw this up, either. You could put a fork into Vic, because he was done.

Meanwhile, Ears planned to have some fun. He liked this girl and her hard little nipples and he was definitely going to get her into one of the private lounges and get Victor's money's worth out of her.

"Having a great time here," Ears said, nodding in self-confirmation. "And you are a hell of a classy babe."

"We could go in the back to the Champagne Lounge," suggested the girl, who had introduced herself as Barbi, a fake name of course, making sure her hand rested on his thigh, her pink fingernail scratching through the fabric atop his penis. "Get a bottle, and we can play show-and-tell."

"Show-and-tell?" said Ears.

"Yes," the girl said flirtatiously. "I show, and you tell me how good I look."

"Hey, hey, that does sound—"

Ears was looking at her strangely, *misunderstandingly*.

"You okay, mister?"

"Yeah, yeah, I just got this—" He fell to the floor on one knee, gurgling. His glass toppled to the carpeting. Barbi realized he was no longer good for any money, so she stood up and turned on her heel, retreating to the ladies' room. This was what the girls tipped the bouncers for, right? To deal with the pass-outs?

The bouncers saw a man go down, nodded to each other, and lifted Ears up by the elbows. He wasn't light. His mouth was wet and hung open.

"Okay, pal."

They dragged him out the front door as a Mexican kid vacuumed up the glass. A cab was waiting. A cab was always waiting at this place. Ears gurgled and thrashed his head.

"SoHo Grand," said the bouncer, pushing Ears inside and slamming the door shut. He gave the cabby a fifty, more than enough to shut him up, and meanwhile counted himself pleased with the easy money he'd just earned. The big guy had slumped over in the seat.

"He gonna get out by himself?" said the worried cabby.

"The doorman will help."

The cabby lifted his open palms. "Is this bullshit or what?"

"All right." The bouncer peeled off another twenty. Seventy dollars for a fifteen-buck fare.

The cabby nodded in disgust, took the bill, and let his foot off the brake. Thirty blocks south he turned off into one of the side streets. The SoHo Grand was a hot place, filled with movie stars and rich Europeans. The doormen wouldn't take this guy. Plus the cabby didn't like how quiet it was back there. Usually the drunk guys rolled around a bit, started to snore. He clicked off his meter. If anyone asked, which they wouldn't, the fare had told him he didn't feel well and wanted to walk, get some air. He turned off his lights and engine and just sat there.

Nothing. The street was empty. He noticed a smell in his cab, a bad smell, and pulled over.

He was about to yank the guy out into the gutter for shitting up his cab, when he decided to see if he had any money on him. A quick inspection of his coat pocket revealed an envelope with more than $20,000 in it.

I could buy myself a new car, the driver thought.

He slapped Ears, checking his reaction.

Nothing, just his head tossed back, panting, eyes open but unseeing.

Ears took nine distinct cab rides in the next three hours. The car's windows were down. Each was a plausible fare, uptown, downtown, crosstown, to and from the usual places. For each, the cabby made careful notations on his fare log, tore off the receipt and tossed it. He made sure to drive for a few minutes between fares, as if looking for a passenger. Finally, near the end of his shift, he pulled over on a dark off-ramp of the FDR Drive, in a spot where the long cement traffic control barriers ran parallel to each other, leaving a narrow three-foot-deep slot between them. It was a hell of a job, but he managed, hoisting Ears up over the traffic barrier to flop down into the gap, still alive but not for long. He made a rasping noise. Could easily be weeks before somebody found him. The driver flipped the man's wallet out the window forty blocks south, and an hour later had pulled into his driveway in Sunnyside, Queens, where he could be seen wiping down his passenger seat with Lysol scented disinfectant, as he always did, eager to make his cab fresh for the next day.

Please, God, make me rich is a prayer of the poor. The rich, of course, can afford to pray for other things. But it is a truth not widely known that as men become very wealthy, with a minimum personal net worth of, say, $100 million, they cease to worship their god in any of the usual places. They may well continue to attend church or synagogue or mosque, but if they do, the quality of their worship is diluted or even nullified by the attentions, welcome or not, from others. People are watching them, they know, for signs of happiness, torment, greed, sickness, health, greatness, generosity—anything. Genuine worship is difficult under the circumstances. The alternative is to worship in a place where one is unknown, but wealthy men prefer to be known, for to be known to be genuinely rich confers protections and advantages and identity un-available to those who are not. Of course, it is possible that such men do not worship at all, and many do not—especially the younger ones, thus far untroubled by disease or grief or bad luck. But as very wealthy men age, they generally choose to confront big questions in places of tranquillity. The best places to do this are either places where they may be alone or places where they appear to be doing something other than worshipping.

East Hampton, New York, one of the most expensive seaside vil-lages on earth, is loaded with men too old and too wealthy to bother going to houses of worship anymore. On weekends they are generally found on a tennis court or golf course, as might be expected. But not a small number of them may be found at Gooseman's Nursery a few miles outside of town. Very often they arrive having not necessarily set out to go there nor having told anyone where they were headed. They are drawn there, parking their Mercedes or Land Rover or whatever else they happen to be driving that day, and without speaking to anyone, set off on a private journey. The nursery covers eighty acres of the most beautiful specimen and ornamental trees to be found anywhere, trucked and flown in from around the world to decorate the ceaselessly changing face of the Hamptons. Where else may one wander into a grove of perfect Kwanzan cherry trees, then onto a beautiful miniature forest of blue atlas cedars, then among a nearly infinite array of Japanese maples, red, yellow, orange, then through a winding path of weeping birches, onward and onward through row after row of beautiful trees? Pin oaks, dogwoods, paper birches, Alaskan spruces, sycamores, dwarf pear, holly, Austrian pine, golden larch, weeping willow . . . it's all there. More private than a park, yet more orderly than a forest. A man wandering through Gooseman's Nursery confronts a godlike variety, an infinity of forms, the spectacular promise of growth. The power of time, expressed as a small tree. For the reality is that men can plant and move only small trees. A genuinely large tree, say higher than sixty feet, cannot be moved. So to confront small trees is to confront time future, and as everyone knows, trees may live much longer than any man. A wealthy man in his sixties, say, brushing against the soft needles of six-foot eastern white pines, knows that these trees will still be young when he is truly old and will be alive long after he is not. To look at trees is to apprehend time and death.

Martz loved Gooseman's Nursery. He drove there several times a year. Connie didn't even know it existed. Only his first wife knew and that was because they'd picked out some ornamental plantings there. Years back. Many houses ago. That first weekend place had been bulldozed and built over with an eleven-thousand-square-foot shingle-style monstrosity that was itself bulldozed and built over with a twenty-three-thousand-square-foot Tuscan villa. He didn't like to think about it, just enjoyed wandering through the cedars and spruces, in particular, sitting on a favorite bench to rest. Which is what he did now, enjoying the sweat of walking in the sun, the smell of the trees.

He looked at his watch. Time now.

"I got the wrong row," croaked a voice.

A man in plaid shorts and a white tennis shirt appeared from between the pine trees. He shuffled a bit, watching his footing in the sand, his thin calves spidered with varicose veins.

"Right here," Martz said, not bothering to stand but lifting his hand to shake the hand of Elliot Sassoon.

"How are you, Bill?"

"Worse than ever."

Elliot laughed as he sat down. "You always say that."

Martz nodded. "Hey, thanks for making the trip."

Elliot shrugged. "For you, my friend, the world. It's been awhile."

"Couple, five years."

"Still with Connie? Because if you're not, I want her number."

"Still with her."

"I figure if she'll look at you, she'll look at me."

"She's probably looking at a few other guys, not that I could possibly blame her. What about you?"

"I'm diabetic now, that's my big news. Just take pills. Can't have sugar."

"You look thinner."

Elliot shrugged. "We're old men now, Bill."

"I know guys taking human growth hormone, swear by it."

Elliot shrugged. Death stalked everyone. "So what are we doing today?"

Martz's gaze went soft as he seemed to peer into the cave of his own imagination. Things lived in there, monstrous desires, wriggling schemes, petrified memories. "I'm going to do a lift soon, and I'm looking for a little help."

"When?"

"Soon. I'm thinking we start Monday night."

"That *is* soon. What's the play?"

"It's Good Pharma. I came in for big shares. I'm negatively lever-aged at around three hundred million."

"Big position."

"It's down a lot, thirty percent."

"*Big* hole. I thought that was a good story. Promising stuff in the pipeline."

"It is. Or was, anyway. There's some kind of leak and some Chinese guys rode it down. Made a lot on shorts. I'm not short on it, though, I need that price to come up."

Elliot nodded.

"I need to do this one thing and then dial it all back, Elliot. I got Connie, health pressures, I just want to clean up this little problem, go out on top, hand it over to the young cowboys."

"Couldn't understand more. What's the total cap?"

"About thirty bil."

Elliot hummed through his nose.

"I think we can move it with four hundred million," Martz said.

"I don't have that kind of cash today. We can drop some things in the morning."

"It's going to come quick."

"Tell me the numbers? I haven't been following it."

"It's riding around thirty-one. I want to get it up to forty-five, I'll take forty-three. I'd appreciate help around thirty-four as it's getting started, and maybe you'd get out at thirty-eight?"

"I'd rather get in at thirty-two, get out at thirty-five, six."

Martz smiled. "Knew you'd say that."

"I knew you knew."

"Okay, fine. Thirty-two on one end, thirty-six on the other."

"Anything else to tell?"

"Get your money ready. Be ready to night-trade. We're going to run this against a bunch of Chinese bastards who won't notice until their normal day of trading."

"Volume or speed?"

"I'll let you know how it will work. I don't have all the pieces in place yet."

"But you will? Because if I'm really going to get the cash together, not wait until the next meeting . . ."

"I'm getting the pieces into place. Don't worry."

"I'm too old to worry. Instead I just mentally masticate."

"Masturbate?"

"That would be a most welcome sensation. I said masticate. You know, chew."

The two men rose and ambled along the sandy trail between the rows of six-foot pine trees. As they neared the busier section of the nursery, Elliot turned to Bill and shook his hand. "Okay, big guy."

Bill watched Elliot trudge along in front of him. He stood a minute or two longer, to be sure Elliot left first. Connie thought he'd gone out to get the newspaper. He didn't like to do lifts, had only performed four in the last fifteen years, all with Elliot. Each case involved a smaller company on the way up, where something anomalous had driven the share price lower, interrupted the story line. Lifts were risky: they might fail after a lot of money got spent. The share price could stay sticky, not move much, too many people selling into the artificial buying. It could even go down. That had been known to happen; the volume rose but the price dropped slightly as shareholders looked to unload big positions without getting whacked. A lift was also risky, if the SEC noticed. Elliot was the best in the business, but that didn't mean he was invincible.

I'm really going to do this, Martz told himself glumly. I'm fucking how old and I'm still doing this shit? He found his car and buckled himself in. He needed Tom Reilly in his back pocket and he needed Chen. Well, he had Chen, who had called him just a few hours after the golden bull was delivered. They were on for tomorrow night. A surge of aggression ran through him as he gunned the car into traffic. He flipped open his cell phone as he drove, in violation of New York State law, and dialed his executive assistant, even though it was Saturday morning. "Call Kepler in China and transfer me," he ordered. The connection took a moment.

"Bill?"

"What'd you get on Chen?"

"Good bit. Hooked in to the biggest guys. Banks, heavy industry. Fancies himself a master of the universe. He's in New York looking for his sister. We got that through his personal assistant."

He knew this already, of course. But he needed to learn more before their dinner the next evening.

"He's a principal investor in the Dwai Group, which is getting big now. Many of their members have seats or affiliations on the Shanghai Exchange. They are very tough investors. My gut feeling is that if he were to call up some big pals and green-light a major move on an American stock, then they would take him at his word. He's made big money for people, he'd be in the country, they'd think he was talking to guys like you, whoever, you know, and they'd probably sign up, take the shot. But he's very loyal to these people, Bill, he's not just going to roll over."

"He needs the proper motivation."

"Don't we all."

Yes, Martz thought after hanging up. That's the part I don't have yet. I'm an old guy with a bad prostate and a wife with beautiful fake tits and my happiness rides now on understanding a young scam artist who crawled out of the gutter in Shanghai. Utterly ridiculous, except that it made absolutely perfect sense.

Violet had called him, a most unusual event. He waited for the buzzer, then climbed the stairs. She was in bed, shades drawn, smoking, a pile of magazines on the bedspread.

"Jesus, Violet, why don't you kind of, you know, get it together a bit, you know?"

She shifted her large bulk under the covers. "Can't, baby."

"Why?"

"Got what I need, more or less."

"So, what did you want?"

"I heard something that's going to interest you a lot."

"What?"

"Just pour me one first, okay?"

He went to the dresser. The bottle he'd brought her the day before was still there, half empty.

"So listen, Victor, I was talking to some people and they were saying about those girls who were found out by the beach—"

"What's this got to do with me?"

"Maybe nothing, all right?"

He brought her the drink and sat down next to her. She sipped the glass.

"I just thought you should know," Violet said, her eyes worried. He hadn't seen her like this in a long time.

"All right, what?"

"There was a third girl in that car."

"What?" But of course that made sense. He thought there might be three people when he was following the car along the Belt Parkway, then later figured he'd been wrong.

"Yes, she came out of the weeds, the grass near the little parking lot they got. Mrs. Polanzi's cousin has a house over there, she doesn't sleep much because her husband uses oxygen. She saw a pretty Chinese girl come running up the road there. It was raining, hard to see. She didn't think about it until later. She told the police about it the next day at the scene and they said thank you for the information, kind of like they knew already. Then a couple of days later she saw a big white limousine out there in the lot with a bunch of Chinese men in good suits. She'd never seen *that* before. It made her remember the Chinese girl. She wrote down the name of the limo company when the car went past again. She gave it to her cousin Frank, and Frank mentioned it to me and—"

"Frank some other guy who plays hide the salami with you?"

She punched him. "What do you care?"

"Just curious."

"You want to know?" she dared him. "You want me to tell you everything?"

He stood to go.

"Listen to me, Vic. I'm trying to *help* you. My friend Ronnie, who runs the limo service over in Bay Ridge, I asked him to make the call to the limo company even though it was a Manhattan company, he's got some connections there, you know, and he got through to the manager and the guy said that particular limo had *real* Chinese guys, from China, I mean, and that the bill went to some kind of Chinese bank or something. He said he charged them three times the usual, just to see what they'd do, and they said fine, whatever, charge it to our company, and he asked his driver, who was not Chinese, where they went and stuff and basically the driver said he didn't understand anything except that they were really looking for the girl who was in that car." Violet played with the edge of her nightgown. "Vic, she's some kind of important person for some Chinese guy with a lot of money, okay?"

He sat on the bed, thinking about it, incidentally rubbing his hand across her large, soft breast. He didn't care if Violet could tell by his silence that this information was important to him. The driver would know more than he pretended, like where the limo went and who else might have been in the car. Vic leaned close and kissed Violet on the cheek. "What would I do without you?" he said.

"Oh, Vic." She took his hand and kissed his fingers. "I just kinda got worried, you know."

He let his other hand caress the back of her head. She liked this, he could see. Ah, his thing with Violet. It was a thing they had, no doubt about it. Sad but real. She was maybe the only person who actually cared about it him. And for all he knew, she might have just saved his life. I've got the advantage now, Vic told himself, I'm going to get this guy.

26 **His father was sleeping,** and Ray studied him, feeling a stillness come over him. He had known this sensation before, had felt it when he carried out the body of a seven-year-old boy to his own father on a hillside in Kashmir, and though the boy had been dead for more than a day, the weather had been cold and the body was stiff and smelled like the stone dust it had been buried in. Ray had watched the father collapse silently to the ground, struck unconscious with grief, and while someone else ran for water and a blanket, Ray had held the boy in his arms, watching the wind lift his beautiful dark hair. It was a privilege to hold the body of boy for a man who loved his son so much, humbling, too, and Ray had known then he would hold the child as long as was needed. In such moments he had seen that everything he had ever wanted or might want was deeply insignificant, and that the secret to whatever peace might be available was to want as little as possible for yourself and as much as possible for others, especially those who wished no ill toward anyone. In such moments, and others like them—when he spent forty-six straight days carrying the tsunami dead, when he built a city of tents on a Turkish mountainside—he felt old parts of himself disappear. His religious training as a boy, never more than halfhearted, had cracked and fallen away. And one night while having sex with a young Italian nurse, a lovely girl, bouncy and true and seemingly untroubled by the grim work of the day, he had understood that he was fucking a corpse, and so was she. Worms and dust and putrefaction, a terrible thing to know about yourself. Was his lust improved by the scent of death? He did not know. He did not know a lot of things anymore. He did not know, for example, whether he was an American. Of course others would identify him as such, and while he loved America, despite its ills and evils, his love was a sad thing to him, perhaps even an inescapable burden. Americans knew so little about the rest of the world. The expats whom he'd met who'd spent many years abroad admitted that their American essence had started to disappear, whether they wanted it to or not. And so too with Ray. Maybe this was why he had come home. He had come home to be with his father but also to find out if America was still his home. Or could be again.

His father groaned in his sleep, lifted his chin, eased downward again. Here lay the clever Brooklyn boy who became the beefy detective afraid of no one, who then became the near dead, the shade awaiting release. *Don't be haunted,* Ray told himself. He wanted to grieve but dared not, for if he began he might never stop. You cried for one, you cried for all.

Better to get going again, look for those trucks in Red Hook. He hopped on the Belt Parkway, then the Gowanus, and turned off on Hamilton Avenue. Red Hook, once a place of long wooden docks and brick warehouses, had been more or less abandoned to the disinterest of time. There were still a few old wooden structures on a block or two of cobblestone streets, sailors' and dockworkers' houses, two-story and reshingled a dozen times over the years. Except for some new stores, the urban adventurers hadn't really invaded in full force yet because there was no subway, no good parks, no decent schools. Red Hook was a place where you went if you didn't want to be in the heart of things, even in Brooklyn. One of the motorcycle gangs had a house down there, but things were quiet, very quiet.

He rolled his truck slowly along the streets, searching all the open spaces, until he came to a yard surrounded by twenty-foot galvanized fencing that was itself topped with another ten feet of razor wire. He had seen this wire in every country he'd ever been in, around military bases, police checkpoints, shipping yards, airports, relief camps. Nasty stuff. The lot held seven mobile shredding vehicles, each marked CorpServe and more than forty feet long. Big, new, well-maintained vehicles. Each a quarter million dollars a pop, anyway, and with this realization it was clear to him that CorpServe was a bigger operation than he had realized, than Jin Li had ever intimated. "Just office company," she'd said. "No big deal."

But to buy and maintain such vehicles, to pay the rent on the lot, to pay the insurance—just that portion of the business was a few million. At the end of the lot he saw a low brick building in poor repair. Something was written on the door. He pulled out his binoculars. The lettering was Chinese.

That was good enough for him. He parked and found his way to the gate. The padlock was a good one, would require industrial bolt cutters or a heavy-duty gas-powered saw, neither of which he was carrying around in his truck. He walked the perimeter of the lot, looking for an easier point of entry. There was none. A rotten old water tower stood just a foot outside the fence. He went back to his truck, retrieved an eighty-foot piece of nylon rope, a belayer's carabiner, and a long crowbar. He hung the rope around his neck and hooked the crowbar under his belt.

The water tower was probably condemned; the service ladder up one side looked rusted and weak, but it had to hold him for only a moment or two, he figured. He shimmied up the iron leg beneath the tower, caught the bottom rung of the service ladder, long since frozen in place, pulled himself up, and climbed another twenty feet. The catwalk around the circumference of the tower was rotted out and he jumped over the holes. You fell through, you broke both legs easy. The catwalk on the far side of the water tank rested above and just inside the concertina fence, and he set up a belay on a piece of iron that looked like it would hold and lowered himself down to the fence, where he kicked the concertina wire away from himself as he dropped past it. The rope reached the ground, and he left it hanging there, because that was his way out.

He walked slowly along the fence until he came to the red brick building. The front door was locked and he didn't want to go in that way. He checked the windows for alarm contacts but saw none. The glass itself had embedded chicken wire. Not impossible to get through but certainly a hassle. He found the electric meter on the outside of the building. The service was rated for a thousand amps, a considerable amount of power. Maybe they'd done light manufacturing in there at one point. The meter wheel itself was barely moving. Not much happening inside, from an electrical point of view. The windows on the back of the building were barred and the back door was padlocked from the outside, which, he happened to know, was a violation of New York City fire department regulations. He took the long crowbar and slowly pried the lock fixture out of the metal door. He pushed on the door. Locked from the inside too. But with the long bar he was able to get the door open enough to squeeze through. Not a pretty job, he thought, slipping inside.

The building was dark. He pulled out his flashlight and came upon a rolling bin full of paper. He found a light switch. The building was in fact filled with shredded paper, some in rolling bins, some bagged in huge seventy-five-gallon waste bags. The blue bags were tagged, he noticed. The identifying information was in Chinese. At the end of the building, underneath a large clock, stood a desk and lamps and some kind of schedule, all written in Chinese.

CorpServe appeared to have been set up atop a previously abandoned operation: there were yellow lines painted on the floor, which, again, suggested some kind of light manufacturing process—back when America still made things that people in the rest of the world wanted—and these lines showed a parallel series of operations, probably conveyor belts that arrived at the back of the building where the loading dock was.

On the wall, under bright lights, hung a large white marker board, showing about thirty midtown locations and gridded by date for vehicle, staff levels, time, in, time out, supervisor name, and net weight received. Another large board was gridded for vehicles by date, load weight, driver, time in and out, service requirements, and start and finish mileage. Quite an operation, Jin Li, he thought, why didn't you tell me?

He noticed an office, its door locked. Maybe this was the nerve center. He took the crowbar and made quick work of the door, broke it down. One large desk, with huge file cabinets. Each was devoted to a company in midtown. There was a lot of confidential information, he saw, sales reports, office memos, legal reports, all kinds of stuff. What was it doing here?

He continued to paw through the paper on the desktop. He looked quickly at every piece. Nothing much here—except, wait, a faxed form letter from a Norma Powell that said, "Your previous tenant, NAME: <u>Jin Li</u>, has applied to be a tenant in my building, and listed you as her previous landlord. Kindly confirm that—"

He checked the date. Sent just a few days earlier. An address? Yes, in Harlem. The street address was just off Adam Clayton Powell Jr. Boulevard. Jin Li was in Harlem? Okay, he said to himself, I'm coming. Maybe she'd already moved in. It was the best lead he had. He took the paper with him, so that no one else would find it, and hurried through the building, not worrying about turning off the lights, and wedged himself back through the broken door.

He hauled himself up the rope to the water tower, arm over arm, kicking away at the fence again, found the catwalk, and threw the rope and tools down to the ground, then he lowered himself down the rusty ladder and dropped heavily on the other side.

A moment later he was back in his truck, speeding toward Harlem, barely noticing the old Chinese man on a bicycle who had witnessed Ray's impressive penetration of the lot by way of the water tower. The man had spent a few minutes inspecting the truck, too. Seeing Ray's hurry, he wondered whether to pull out the phone in his pocket. Jin Li had told him to call her, so he would.

Oh, timing really *is* everything! Martz waited a second longer, looked back at Phelps, who nodded. Phelps had arranged their entry into the East Side hotel, knew the security manager. It was a very nice place but Martz was surprised that Tom Reilly wasn't using the Pierre, say, or the Peninsula. Or the Ritz Carlton. He'd used it a few times, back in the day. The women always liked that, were enthused by the atmosphere.

Martz knocked on the glossy white door.

No answer.

He knocked again, politely.

The door opened a few inches and the face of a beautiful young woman appeared.

"Yes?"

Martz pushed in.

"Hey!"

Phelps came quickly after him, shut the door, began to gently explain to the young woman that she needed to dress and leave quickly.

The big bed was empty. Martz saw steam coming out a doorway, heard the shower. He stepped into the bathroom, saw Reilly in the large glass-walled shower soaping his dick reverently.

"Not bad," Martz said.

"What? Hello?" cried Reilly at the sound of a man's voice.

Martz pulled open the shower door. "See what you've made me do?"

"Get the fuck out of here!" yelled Reilly.

Phelps stepped into the bathroom doorway.

Martz reached in and turned off the shower, getting his sleeve wet.

"I've been trying to talk to you, Tom. I've called many times. I've had you followed to Yankee Stadium. I've invited you to my house. Which somehow resulted in your wife sticking her fingers in my butt. She and I had a little chat. I'm sure she told you about that. Yes, I've done a lot to get your attention. But you know what?"

"What?" said Reilly in his naked misery.

Martz looked at Reilly's crotch. "You've lost a little of your exuberance. How come? I don't excite you, Tom? Even after all the trouble I've gone to? I don't make your heart go fucking pitter-pat?"

"What did you tell my friend? Where is she?"

"Gone," said Phelps. "Dressed and gone."

"What do you want, Martz?"

Martz looked back at Phelps. "You can leave and close the bathroom door now."

Which he did. Martz leaned into the shower stall. "It's very simple, Tom," he said quietly. "You know there's been a serious security breach at Good Pharma." He stepped into the shower, his eight-hundred-dollar shoes on the wet tile, forcing Tom backward, and then lowered his voice to whisper. "It affected the stock price. But you didn't tell anybody. That was very *illegal*."

Reilly studied Martz's sun-damaged face, the droopy malevolent eyes.

"The SEC guys in Washington would enjoy buttering their toast with you, Tom," continued Martz. "Take it from me, I've been around long enough to see it happen. Given your behavior, it wouldn't take much to get them started. They butter the toast and then they take a lot of careful bites until the toast is gone. But that's just the government lawyers, Tom. Think of the investors, the lawyers *they* can afford!" he hissed. "Think of the cost of the lawyers *you'd* have to hire! That lovely young woman who just left? Some plaintiff's lawyer will want to depose her. See what the pillow talk in the hotel room was. What corporate secrets got mixed in with the juicy stuff. Come on,

man, this is New York City! Where blood gets turned into money!
Think of the articles in *The Wall Street Journal*! Think of your *wife*!
The hit to her reputation and practice. The looks her patients will give
her. I mean, the multiplier effects just go on and—"

Reilly allowed a slow nod of his wet hair, his eyes never leaving
Martz's.

"But—to get back to my point—though it was illegal of you not to
immediately tell the many trusting investors who own thirty billion
dollars of Good Pharma stock, it was also smart."

"Why do you say that?" asked Tom, surprised.

"Because you have a good friend who can help you with your little
problem if only—if only you would talk to him."

"Who, you?"

Martz gave a silent nod. "Me."

Tom exhaled through his nose, studying Martz.

"It's simple," Martz continued. "You and I will revert to our anthro-
pological origins. We either hunt big prey together or we hunt each
other until one of us wins."

"You're hunting me now."

"Nope, this is just tracking." Martz smiled a big, fabulous, glad-
eyed grin, his teeth bright. "Hunting is when you actually make the
kill."

Once fair, now foul, someday fair again? The Gowanus Canal in South Brooklyn is a green vein of seepage, a topographic remnant of what was once a bur-bling creek, and the nineteenth-century brick factory buildings on either side slowly crumbling into its sluggish shallows are the source of endless speculation by local investors who dream that the canal will soon be discovered as the next hot zone in New York's real estate market. No less a man than the great American trickster Donald Trump is rumored to have bought up large swaths on the sly. Indeed, nearby neighborhoods have begun to draw people with trendy eye-glasses and laptop computers, but for the canal the question as to who will dredge and remove the thousands of tons of toxic sludge within its banks—mud laced with heavy metals, PCBs, and nearly every other cancer-causing chemical ever dumped by American industry—is a question that no one can quite yet answer.

Which is why the neighborhood is mostly still home to car repair businesses, carpentry shops, a casket company or two, and other not so well specified enterprises that may or may not be legal. A perfect place for a little conversation with the driver of the white limousine that had ferried around the Chinese men.

He was a small man named DiLetti, fat in the middle, thin in the arms, with a dimple in his chin. He sat in a wooden chair in a nearly empty room.

"We know you're nervous," said Victor, standing on the warped floorboards. "That's expectable."

"You guys grabbed me." He looked at Victor in abject bafflement. "What, what did I do?"

"You drive a limo, right?"

"Yeah. But you know that."

"We want some information."

"What?"

"Where you were driving three, four days ago? We know you were driving around in Brooklyn."

"I don't have the log in front of me."

"I do." Victor held out the sheet. It had cost him exactly $100. "You picked up a bunch of Chinese guys at the Time Warner building and then drove them around. I want to know exactly where you went."

The driver's slow response told Victor that he remembered the answer to the question. It had to have been a memorable night, not the usual clientele for a cheesy Manhattan limo company. Not fake rap moguls getting blow jobs from a hire-a-ho, no East Side private school girls in jeans and party shoes on their way to a sixteenth birthday party. But something odd, not hard to recall. "Well, you, ah, you discussed this with Lem?"

The owner of the limo company.

"Where you think I got this sheet?" Victor said calmly, feeling the game with DiLetti engage, the negotiation take bite. "Lem gave us the green light."

"You guys cops?"

This was an interesting question. Because it gave Victor an opportunity. "Let me answer you this way," said Victor. "We have the authority to do what we're doing."

The very ambiguity of the statement seemed to relieve the driver.

"Okay," he said, nodding as if he knew exactly what Victor was referring to. "The pickup was at the Time Warner, like you said. It was four guys, actually. Only one or two spoke any kind of English. One of them translated. So I pick them up and they tell me to go to an address in Bay Ridge. Most of the time they had the partition closed."

"Bay Ridge."

"Yeah. Three guys got out there."

"Tell me something about these guys."

"Big. Very big for Chinese guys, maybe six one."

"Then?"

"Then they go into the house," said DiLetti.

"Address?"

"I don't remember the address. Third or fourth house on the left on Seventy-eighth Street off Ridge Boulevard. Green door. Porch is green, too."

"We can find it." He pointed at his friend Jimmy, who was serving as muscle, the way Richie used to. "Call Violet, tell her to get that address. She can have somebody over there in five, ten minutes, then tell her to check it out." He nodded back to the driver. "Okay. Keep going."

"So the guys go into the house and then two of them come out a few minutes later with something in a cardboard box. One of them stayed in the house. The rest get back in the car. So now there's a total of three Chinese guys in the car. A lot of discussion in Chinese, let me tell you. Very interested. I looked in my mirror but really couldn't see it. Then we go to another address a few minutes away. There's a red truck in the drive—"

"Old—red Ford F-150?" said Vic, remembering the vehicle driven by the man inquiring after Richie in the company trailer.

"Old, yes, Ford, I didn't notice. I don't know trucks."

"Then?"

"Then the three guys go into one house and come out a minute later with nothing and then they go into the house next door, which has lights on, and a couple of minutes later they drag a guy out of there and put him in the car." The driver paused. "This was a white guy, spoke English, so I heard that. They called him Ray."

"This Ray guy, he was in his early thirties, dark hair, good build?"

"Yes." The driver paused.

"You get the feeling he's pretty tough?"

"Yeah, you could say that."

Vic felt a surge of fury go through him. "Go on."

"Yeah, yeah, I will. But I'm starting to wonder something about the information, why it's like, so valuable."

"You're wondering about that," Victor repeated.

The driver smiled nervously, resettled himself, and then worked up his answer. "Yeah, you know, this is something that's, uh, *valuable*."

"To us."

"That's what I mean."

"You want payment for the information?"

"Well, you know, I mean—"

Victor nodded sagely. "What do you think this information is worth?"

"Well, I don't know, couple of thousand, anyway."

"What?"

"I said, a couple of—"

"No, no, I heard you. I just disagreed with you."

"So—"

"It's not the right amount," said Victor.

"Well, then maybe a thousand, seven fifty?"

Victor shook his head. "Still not right."

"I think—"

"I think you're really selling yourself short here," Victor said, nodding with animated judiciousness. "I mean, we want to be fair, we do want to be reasonable."

"You do?" asked DiLetti, amazed at his luck.

"Oh, sure. Honestly, this information is worth a lot more than a couple of thousand bucks to us."

"It is?" the driver said hopefully, his voice echoing in the empty, dilapidated room.

"Oh, yeah. It's worth—well, maybe a million bucks, actually."

"*Really?*"

"If you can deliver it accurately."

"Oh, I remember everything, don't have to worry about that."

Victor pointed at Jimmy, who was already smiling, though the driver couldn't see it. "Get Mr. Dick-Leety a million bucks in cash." He waved his hand at the next room, where the ceiling had caved in and runners from vines had stretched across the floor. "Right there in my safe. Small bills, Jimmy."

"You got it, boss."

The driver looked around anxiously. "Wait, wait, I didn't—"

"So go on with your story, okay? We're going to compensate you for your trouble."

Now the driver was actively worried. "So, okay, we took this guy—"

"How's that million bucks coming, Jimmy?"

A voice from the back room. Indistinct. "Can't find it, boss!"

"What? Fucking Jimmy can't do shit," muttered Victor.

"Wait, wait, so we drove into the city—"

"Jimmy, where the fuck is the million bucks! We don't want to keep Mr. Dick-Beetle waiting!"

"I'm looking, boss!"

"What did you find?"

"I found some kinda garden hose and a bag of old charcoal."

"I thought I fucking told you, a million dollars!"

Victor yanked out his gun and fired it over the driver's head, seemingly at Jimmy, who was standing to the side, smoking a cigarette. "Get Beetledick his money or he won't tell us his story!"

He waved the gun around wildly. Fired again, upward. A piece of old horsehair plaster fell out of the ceiling.

The driver dropped to the floor weeping, holding his arms around his head. He told them everything, first about the conversation the Chinese men had with the guy named Ray about some Chinese girl, who it seemed was his girlfriend, how they threw his phone out the window, the arrival back at the Time Warner building, an hour wait until they all piled into the car a second time, then again back to the house in Bay Ridge, then the two Chinese goons taking Ray into the house carrying the thing in the box, then the first Chinese guy coming out of the house not a minute later holding the tip of his nose, another with his hand clapped to a bleeding ear, and the third blinded by paint in his eyes. How they shot into Chinatown to a doctor's office, moaning and cursing, all of it, blood all over the back of the limo. Victor was fascinated, exhilarated. This was *good*. He'd hit pay dirt! This was the guy! The guy he was going to kill!

When they were done with the driver, they stood him up on his feet and ignored the smell from his pants and made him drink five straight shots of whiskey at gunpoint. But in a congratulatory sort of way, with a slap on the back. You made it through the rain, pal. Nobody touched you, right? Not a goddamned hair on your head was hurt! The driver was hesitant at first, but by the third slug of whiskey he was enjoying himself again, even cracking a grin.

"We're going to drive you home," Jimmy told him, leading the man outside to the waiting car. Victor had seen this done before; the man's terror was quickly reduced by the drink, you dropped him off somewhere near his home, and if he spoke to anyone he barely made sense, then he fell asleep and when he woke up he felt weird and badly hungover but realized he was unhurt—and usually decided that it was better not to mention his encounter to anyone of consequence.

Victor's phone rang. It was Violet.

"I got that address over on Seventy-eighth Street. Owner's name is Raymond E. Grant."

"Anybody know him?"

"Sure. He's easy to look up, and a man like you will be interested to know just who he is."

"Who?"

"A retired detective. Something like twenty-seven years as a detective. The red truck's in his name."

He said nothing.

"Victor? That's the kind of thing that worries me, you know?"

A detective. The younger guy named Ray had to be his son.

Victor would know soon enough.

"This is very brave, very strong man." Zhao pointed his finger, as if talking to Jin Li in person, not on a cell phone. "He climbed down the rope very far and then climbed up, using just his arms."

Ray, Jin Li thought. Very few men were so strong. "What color was his truck?"

"It was red," Zhao answered. "A good truck, little bit old. I looked at it. He has funny yellow shoe on the dashboard."

"Like a tennis shoe but yellow?"

"Yes, that is exactly right."

Only a month earlier, she had been to Ray's house, sitting outside in that same truck while he went inside to check on his father. It'd been a warm day and she dangled her foot outside the window, feeling the sun. Maybe that was when she'd lost the shoe. She'd never gone in and met Ray's father, perhaps because she was afraid to do so.

"What do you think he was doing, Zhao?" Jin Li asked.

"Oh, I know what he was doing."

"Tell me."

"Looking for you."

"Why do you say that?" she said, testing him.

"Because a man only does something like that if he has a big heart, and you are the only person he knows in this company, so I think he does this for you. He has big heart for you, Jin Li."

■ ■ ■

So what if the cab from Harlem cost sixty dollars? She didn't care. But it took a while to get over the Brooklyn Bridge, and she looked anxiously out the window. Ray had called her and she had never called him back. Terrible. I think I made a big mistake, Jin Li told herself. I will make it better. He will see how much I missed him. We can talk to the police, maybe, to this Detective Blake. She had the cabby hunt around the neighborhood until she found the right street. The house had a green porch, she remembered, feeling excited. After circling a few blocks, she spotted the house.

"Keep the meter running," she told the cabby. "I forgot to do something."

"If you got the money," said the cabby, "I got the time."

She dug around in her purse and found some lipstick and a mirror. Her lips needed a little something. She fixed them, then kissed a tissue to get off the extra. She brushed her hair, put on just a little eyeliner, a touch of blush. Last, the perfume. She expected to kiss Ray—a lot, okay?

"Lady, you mind I say something?"

"No, I guess."

"Whoever he is, he's a lucky guy."

"Thanks."

"And I'm not just sayin' that for the tip."

She paid the man and got out.

Yes, this was the place, a two-story house with a sharply peaked roof and what Americans called dormer windows. She'd spent many hours looking at real estate ads, both in Shanghai and in New York. People forgot how much Western architecture was built in Shanghai before the Revolution. The Bund along the Whangpoo River was all monumental British, French, and German buildings, neoclassical, Art Deco. Anyway, this house had an enclosed porch, freshly painted. The grass and bushes looked neatly trimmed. Somebody was caring for the house, no doubt Ray, which had to mean he was still here, right? She poked her head around the side of the house, saw a locked shed and a repainted birdhouse. Oh, I hope he is here! Jin Li told herself. She stepped up onto the porch and knocked tentatively. No answer. She noticed an ornamental chime in the center of the door and turned it. A bell sounded inside. A moment later, she could see a woman walk through the cluttered hallway.

"Yes, may I help you?" the woman asked from behind the door.

"I came to see Ray," Jin Li said.

The door opened. "He's in here," the woman said. She had a stethoscope around her neck. "Please."

The house was surprisingly warm for a spring day. Jin Li followed the woman into the living room, where an emaciated man of about seventy lay propped up against some pillows, arms at his sides, tubes going into both wrists.

"Oh, I'm sorry, so sorry," Jin Li protested, "I meant Ray Junior."

"He should be back soon," the nurse said.

She stopped where she stood, unwilling to intrude. In China, a sick person's privacy was never disturbed. "I—I don't—"

"Please stay," the nurse said. "Mr. Grant doesn't get too many visitors, and he certainly doesn't get any like you." The nurse smiled. "He's going to wake up any moment now."

"Are you sure?"

"He's a charmer, I better warn you."

So she sat on the couch, trying not to appear like she was waiting, trying not to be intrusive. She looked at Mr. Grant and then around the room, down the hall, anywhere she could. This was the house where Ray had grown up. Not at all luxurious by American standards and yet a very beautiful home as far as she was concerned, with nice wood floors and big, simple rooms. He was a boy *here*, she mused. So different from where I grew up.

"I think I am being given too many drugs," croaked a voice, Mr. Grant's, his eyes open now and studying her intently, with alarm, even. "If I am not mistaken, though I *could* be mistaken, I am looking at an exceptionally beautiful Chinese woman who has got to be the most beautiful woman, except for my wife, Mary, who has ever been in this house in the last thirty-nine years, and let me tell you that is saying quite a lot!"

Jin Li stood up but wasn't sure she should go to the bed. He looked so sick, and smelled a little, too. "Oh, hello, excuse me, Mr. Grant, I am so sorry that I woke you up, I was hoping to come see Ray, your son. My name is Jin Li. I don't think that you know who—"

"Lady, I know I'm lying in my deathbed, but let me tell you something, I know exactly who you are!" Ray's father stole a look toward the kitchen. His eyes narrowed. "Please, I'm going to ask you . . . ," he said in a loud whisper, "she's in the bathroom maybe. Please go into the kitchen and get me a little coffee. It's usually on the stove. Wakes up my brain. Will you do it?"

She stood tentatively. She could, in fact, smell the coffee.

"That's the ticket. Quick, quick, though!" said Mr. Grant. "Just a little milk, no sugar."

She tiptoed into the kitchen. It was very dated by American standards, she saw. It looked like one in a television show she'd seen many times with the voices dubbed in Chinese, something called *The Brady Bunch*. She poured a little cup of coffee with milk she found in the refrigerator and brought it back.

"I know just who you are," said Mr. Grant when she returned.

"You do?"

"Of course . . . you're the girl my son is so worried about. Just terribly worried, doing everything he can to find you . . ." He took the coffee cup with both hands and took a sip. Then another. "Good," he pronounced. A machine next to Mr. Grant's side beeped, followed by a mechanical click. He turned toward it and licked his lips. "Sooner than I expected," he noted aloud. Then he nodded in satisfaction at something and returned his gaze toward Jin Li. Except this time his eyes barely blinked. Was he falling asleep? She could see he was about to drop his coffee and rushed to catch the cup before it spilled on his sheet. "Thank you . . . ," he said, strangely. She set the cup down on the floor near her feet, out of sight of the nurse, if she came back.

Suddenly an idea came to her. "Mr. Grant? Can I ask you something?"

"Yes, I suppose you can."

"What did Ray do all of those years he was away from the United States?"

"Do?" The machine next to Mr. Grant clicked again but he did not seem to hear it.

"Yes. Did he work in the military, did he fight in a war?"

Mr. Grant frowned. "Did he tell you that?"

"No."

"I didn't think so . . . he did not tell you anything . . . right?"

How did he know this? She felt humiliated. "Yes, that's right."

"He was saving them . . . helping . . . hurricanes and earthshakes, I mean, *quakes* . . . hundred of people, many countries . . ." He closed his eyes, as if better to see what he was describing, and she watched his eyeballs moving to and fro beneath their lids, searching, maybe seeing. "Sometimes I read about it in the newspaper . . . terrible things he saw, much worse than anything I ever . . . saw too much, oh, you can see too much!" Mr. Grant lifted his face upward, his cheeks hollowed as he opened his mouth. "Never would talk about it, broke my heart, you see, I wish he would get . . . it's good for a man, to have a wife and children . . . sometimes he went down into . . . deep into, where all the dead people were . . . he was supposed to find the people, the children . . . very very difficult . . . sometimes . . . he . . . it . . . my garden, did you see the roses—?"

His head swayed, a man seeing only visions now. "Mr. Grant, how did Ray get the terrible scar on his stomach?"

"Aaah, ha—" He groaned horribly.

"Mr. Grant?"

"—that was . . . God gave it to him!"

His eyes opened, then rolled up in his head. A foul breath came from him, from deep within him. Then his head slumped to the side. One eye was nearly closed, the other open. Jin Li looked away. Why was she thinking of her grandfather? I must look at him, she thought, I must see this so that I understand Ray.

A minute passed, in silence. Mr. Grant's meager chest continued to rise and fall, and his features were slack now.

The nurse came back in, looking at her watch.

"Did you get a chance to talk?" she asked brightly.

Jin Li realized she was breathing quickly. "Yes."

"And you got a little coffee?"

"Yes."

"He's a very nice man." She lifted the sheet a bit to fix it and when she did so Jin Li saw the half-full urine bag. "He'll sleep now awhile."

"Maybe I should wait for Ray outside—?"

"Whatever you'd like."

Jin Li nodded affirmatively and stood, suddenly wanting to flee the room. But instead she bent down and ever so gently kissed Mr. Grant's forehead.

"You're sweet," said the nurse. "I'll tell him when he wakes up. And he'll like knowing it, too."

Jin Li slipped back down the hall, idly studying some of the family pictures. She hadn't noticed them when she came in. There was a picture of Ray in a football uniform, then another of him in a New York City fireman's uniform, getting a medal in his hospital bed. With his father and mother to either side. And a smiling, bald man whose face she recognized. Mayor Giuliani. "FOR VALOROUS SERVICE TO THE CITY OF NEW YORK ON SEPTEMBER 11, 2001" read the gold-script caption.

Oh, she thought, oh. So he was *there.*

She stepped out to the porch. Why hadn't he told her? How she wished she had known, how she missed Ray now—loved him, even. Everything—everything made *sense.*

She wandered toward the sidewalk, a little dazed in the bright sun, wondering why she was crying. Perhaps the sight of Mr. Grant, the conversation about Ray, the pictures, it was all a little much . . .

Too much, in fact, to notice the battered service van that had pulled up next to the sidewalk. A large man in worn laborer's clothes stepped in front of her. His dark eyes fixed on her face.

"What, excuse me—!"

He grabbed her with one dirty hand, flung open the van door, and threw her inside. She hit her head on the metal floor. He reached in and took her purse. She glimpsed a piece of rope and an empty plastic bucket. The door slammed shut, was locked from the outside, and the van lurched forward. She put out her hand to steady herself in the dark.

A sliding sound. The driver's narrow rear window opened into the van body. Behind a metal mesh, she could see the face. "Don't you fucking scream," he warned her.

The van drove a few more minutes. She felt for the side doors and the back door. Locked. Crawling in the darkness on her hands and knees she found the rope and plastic bucket, nothing else.

The van stopped. She heard the driver's door open, then shut, the sound of him walking around the back.

"I'm going to open the door. Don't try anything."

The door opened, flooding the van with light. He stepped in, flicked on the roof light, and closed the door.

"Don't scream, I'm warning you." He was a big man. He grabbed her hand and twisted it, so that she was on her back.

She kicked him as hard as she could. He leaned his knee on her chest and she hit him with her fists. Her blows did not bother him. He pulled out a roll of duct tape, tore off a piece, then put it over her mouth. She punched at him but he was big and heavy and his knee was pressing down on her. He turned her on her side. With the next piece of tape he bound her hands behind her. Then the ankles, even though she kicked at him. When he was done she lay on her back, wriggling, trying to free herself.

He took one more piece and held it over her.

"Close your eyes," he commanded.

She did. The tape went right over her eyes, catching a few strands of her hair.

He seemed to be in no hurry. She could feel him straddling her, so close she smelled the gum he was chewing, something like cinnamon. "You escaped me once," he said, "but not this time."

His hand moved down her blouse, tore it open. She could hear him breathing loudly through his nose. The hand felt her breasts, mashed them. Then it was between her legs, pulling down her underpants, the dirty thumb hooking up inside of her, hurting her. It probed and wiggled, then slipped out. Again she heard him breathing through his nose. She wondered if he was smelling his finger.

She felt herself being turned over and tied up with the rope. It was tight, around her hands, arms, and legs. She could feel him cinching the knots.

Then came the bucket, right over her head, duct-taped to her clothes, her breath echoing in her own ears. Darkness upon darkness. He might have said something to her but she could not tell what it was. She went limp with exhaustion, her clothes soaked with sweat. She felt the van door close again and the vehicle begin to move, and she was jolted backward along the hard metal floor, trussed, helpless, with no hope that anyone knew where she was.

30 "A wheelchair *gigolo*?"

"Yes, he only—you know—does it with women in wheel-chairs."

Connie lowered her voice into the phone. She didn't want anyone to hear her, including the house staff, who knew too much about her, anyway. "Old women?"

"No, no. Young, thirties, forties, maybe fifties."

"They *pay* him?"

"Well, yes. They pay him a lot, I heard. But they don't mind. It doesn't seem like much, *considering*."

"Considering what?" she asked.

"Considering how good he is! You'd be surprised how many women with money there are in New York City who are in wheel-chairs. You know, from falls, back problems, multiple sclerosis . . . hundreds, anyway."

"I never see them, though."

"Most kind of *hide*. I've got one in my building. That's how I found out about him."

"And your friend, how often does he—?"

"Once a month, about. Her husband never touches her. Not in *years*."

"Did she tell you about what—oh, *God*, wait, just a moment." Connie listened for the sound of the men coming down from the roof. Her husband and the funny little Chinese man named Chen whom they'd just had to dinner were up on the terrace having drinks and smoking cigars. They'd been up there awhile already. What could they possibly be discussing now? It had been the absolutely worst dinner conversation ever—stilted and weird, mostly because the guy's English was so bad, not to mention his skills with a *fork*, with Bill acting as if the man was some kind of high-powered global chieftain. Well, *sorry*, she knew who all those guys were, especially the billionaires in Hong Kong and Singapore, and this guy didn't rate. Bill said some other men might join them later. She listened again, heard nothing.

"Sorry, go on," she said, "you were saying her husband never touches her and she and the gigolo guy do it and all that."

"The neighbor heard them one afternoon, heard *her*."

"Come on! Who *is* he?"

"Well, he's like this tall logger guy in a flannel shirt who lives outside the city. He's like maybe twenty-nine, thirty. Comes in for one week a month. Kind of just *does* everyone, then leaves."

"That's—isn't that kind of *sick*? Or weird?"

"Actually, I think it's sweet."

"Well, they do *pay* him."

"Sure, but he doesn't have to do this! I heard it all started because he used to deliver Christmas trees and firewood into the city each winter, just a regular job, and I guess one time it was a woman in a wheelchair and one thing led to, like, *another*."

"I say he's on a weirdo power trip."

"That's what I thought. Exactly. But I heard differently. He's supposed to be gentle. Firm but *gentle*. A lot of these women are in chronic pain, are very stiff in the joints, weird medical conditions, the spine . . . you can *imagine* some of the problems."

Connie felt an odd irritation and clicked her fingernails against the inlaid table she'd found in—well, wherever it had been, Portobello Road in London, Rue Jacob in Paris, maybe. "It's got to be—"

The bedroom intercom buzzed.

"Connie," barked her husband's voice. "When those guys get here, send them up to the roof. Right away."

"Yessir, Mr. Husbo." She clicked off, returned to the phone. "I was saying it's got to be a weird power trip thing."

"Connie, I'm telling you that's what *I* thought."

"Until—?"

"I saw him."

"*What?*" she gasped.

"I talked to him."

A gust of jealousy went through her. "You did?"

"He's nice. Very intelligent. Maybe even a little *shy.*"

Why did this information torment her? "Does he, you know, do *regular* women?"

"That sounds kinda desperate, Connie."

"It *is* kinda desperate."

"What happened to that guy you had?"

"He started getting close to finding out about Bill, you know, how much money there was."

"What's, you know . . . going on with Bill?"

"Well, I *do* love him. But, you know . . . did I ever tell you he pisses in the tub every morning?"

"*Oh*-migod."

"As long he's interested in something, one of his ridiculous deals or why some billion-dollar company is not doing well, he's bearable. He's got one like that right now, tonight. I try to encourage him, you know, give him *something* to do! Otherwise I'd—"

"You'd be out buying a wheelchair!"

"Don't tell anyone else about this guy! I'm *serious*! Pretty soon *New York* magazine will do a story on him and everyone will know and it'll be ruined."

"Won't tell, promise."

"You know how to meet this guy?"

"Sure. He comes by the building."

"When next? I want to—" She heard the building intercom buzzing. "Sorry, I got to go do this. Hold on."

The roof terrace was reached by a private elevator within their apartment. She'd insisted they put it in so that she didn't have to use the regular elevator, which, after all, had an operator in it all the time, and she liked to go up to the roof in a bathing suit to exercise or sunbathe. The intercom buzzed again and she opened the door and was surprised to see five men in business suits, each carrying a briefcase. One of them was that little old man named Elliot she'd met years ago.

"Must be quite a party you guys have planned," she noted as he politely shook her hand. "But I guess girls aren't invited."

Elliot smiled in distant amusement. "Your husband is a remarkable man," he said. "And I cherish his friendship."

"Bill is up on the roof with a certain Mr. Chen, who's here from China."

Elliot looked her in the eye. "Mrs. Martz, I can assure you we are very familiar with this Mr. Chen."

She took them inside the apartment and down the hall to the other elevator, watched them get in, then remembered—the wheelchair gigolo!—and hurried back to the phone.

Longest trip of her life. They'd lurched along some kind of avenue in Brooklyn—she could tell by the stop-and-go traffic, the honking and sirens—then made a turnoff across bumpy ground and then she heard a truck engine and smelled *shit*, a cosmic enveloping gust of it. Like the van was tunneling through a mountain of the stuff. Then the van stopped a few seconds later, a garage door of a building was slid upward, and the van pulled inside. Now she just waited. She had an uncomfortable feeling between her legs where his thumb had been, and she could smell her own sweat and fear. Her neck ached from the struggle. But it was the tape over her eyes that hurt most. It was stuck to her eyebrows and lashes, and every time she blinked, the tape pulled. She breathed through her nose, the sound of it in the plastic bucket close to her face. Tough to hear much else than that, but now she could feel the van's engine switch off, and she heard the van's front door open and close, then the side door slide open.

"All right," his voice came to her, low and mean and firm, "I'm taking you out. Don't fight me."

She wanted to fight but didn't have it in her.

"Nod your head to show me you understand."

She did this, the bucket hitting her chest.

She felt his big hands grab her like a piece of cargo and drag her awkwardly across the metal floor of the van.

Then he picked her up and flopped her over at the waist, his shoulder in her stomach. He was carrying her—*down*, she thought. She heard a creaking noise. A strange abrasive chemical smell filled her nostrils, sickened her.

He put her down on something, a bed or sofa.

"You're pretty light," he said. She didn't know what this meant. "Now hold still, I got to do something to you."

She tensed, expecting the worst. But he was only wrapping something metal and heavy around her waist that settled against her hips. She heard a key click.

"I'm going to take off the bucket."

She felt the tugging of the tape at her clothes and hair, and when the bucket came off she no longer heard herself breathing through her nose.

His fingers touched her face and she started to struggle and cry.

"Hey! I'm just taking the tape off your mouth!"

She forced herself to be still. The chemical smell really bothered her, made her want to vomit, actually. Or maybe it was him—how close he was to her. She felt his fingernails picking at the end of the tape and the tape itself pulling away from her left cheek, her lips, then her right cheek. Stung as it was pulled away. She worked her face muscles a bit.

"Here's a bottle of water."

Something touched her lips. She shook her head violently.

He cuffed her. "Drink it. Don't be stupid."

She did, opening her mouth blindly, trying not to choke. It was regular water, so far as she could tell.

"All right," he began. "I know your name is Jin Li, however it gets pronounced. But who are you, anyway?"

She cleared her throat. She wished she could see him. "Why should I tell you?"

"Because I fucking told you to tell me!"

"Who are *you*?"

"Me?" He followed the question with a snort.

In that one word she heard an entire philosophy: a combative pride, utter disbelief that the universe so ignored him, and beneath that, the unmoored fury of self-hatred.

"Yeah, who are you?" she said brazenly.

"Me, I'm one who wins. That's what my name literally means, in fact."

"What is it?"

He hit her, hard. "I'm asking the questions. Don't forget that."

Her head spun and she fell backward, expecting to be hit again. But she did not forget what he'd said, not for a moment.

"All right, I got some questions. Were you in that car with the Mexican girls?"

I don't want to be hit again, Jin Li thought.

"No."

He hit her again. "Yes, you *were*. Now I know you are a liar and now *you* know that *I* know it. Got that? Okay? Don't fuck with me, right? All right—the limousine. Who were the Chinese guys in the limousine looking for you?"

Oh, Jin Li thought, he knows things. I'm going to have to be careful about everything I say.

He didn't suspect yet. Still thought he was enjoying a social visit. Still thought this was a polite mating ritual between wealthy men. Brandy and cigars. Bragging about China's economy, its foreign-currency reserves, its deep-water navy, its planned moon shot. Well, this wasn't a mating ritual, but one of them was certainly going to get fucked. And it's not me, thought Martz. They were sitting out in teak lawn chairs, the Manhattan skyline blazing around them. Fifth Avenue, Rockefeller Center, the Chrysler Building, the Empire State, the bridges to Brooklyn, the lighted windows far and near both intimate and grand. Even Chen, with his pumped-up self-importance, seemed impressed.

"How much does this kind of building cost?" Chen asked.

An amazingly ill-mannered question. "The whole building?" said Martz evenly. "Tough to answer."

"I am having—I have apartment in Time Warner Center."

"Yes, I hear those are very good." Martz made sure he didn't appear to be mocking Chen. "The best in the city."

The elevator doors opened. The men filed out, one by one, carrying their briefcases.

Chen, surprised, looked back at Martz. "Who are these people?"

"Friends of mine."

"Yes, I see." But Chen had risen in his seat, sensing trouble.

And at that, in the moment that changed the tone of the evening, Martz leaned forward and ever so gently pushed him back down.

Chen froze.

"My friend," said Martz, "we have now arrived at the part of the evening that is most meaningful to me."

Chen sat quietly, senses alert, hands gripping both arms of the chair. His bodyguards were sitting around in the aforementioned Time Warner building, drinking beer and watching American cable TV, probably. He'd let Martz send a car for him and hadn't wanted his men to come along. A mistake, he seemed to understand now, a mistake that a genuinely rich man in America would never make.

Martz turned back to him. "Chen, you are here tonight for only one reason. Through my company I am a major investor in a small, very promising drug manufacturer called Good Pharma." He beckoned to the translator, a slim Chinese-American doctoral student at Columbia University, to come join them. The other men sat at a table near the elevator opening up laptop computers. "Start translating everything I say. I don't want any misunderstandings. I want him to get to know your voice and I want you to get to know his."

The translator greeted Chen with formality. Chen's eyes cut back and forth between Martz and the other man.

Martz resumed. "My friend Hua here has worked for me for eight years. He knows your regional accent. He will translate. You have recently been trading in Good Pharma, short selling it and driving the price down. And by you, I mean you and all the Chinese investors you advise. Very impressive, except that you did this using stolen information."

The translator repeated this.

"I am listening," Chen said in English, as if looking for a chance to negotiate.

"Tonight, you are going to call your fellow investors in China, one by one, and tell them to buy Good Pharma when it starts trading at ten a.m. local Shanghai time. They are going to buy in Shanghai, Beijing, Hong Kong, and everywhere else they do business."

"Why would they do that?"

"Because you will tell them to."

Chen shook his head. "That would not be enough."

"I suspect that you will make a convincing case."

"How?"

"Very simple. You will tell them that you have more inside information. Very good information that will make them a lot of money."

Chen said nothing.

"Hua will be sure that you tell them what you say you are telling them. In fact, we have a device here that creates a ten-second delay in spoken telephonic conversation. It was developed by radio stations for the purpose of blocking any accidental transmission of FCC-prohibited language." Martz pointed at the translator. "Got that? Did he understand that? This device is also used by unscrupulous traders to front-run major trades ordered over conventional telephone lines. It's illegal because it is so effective. Hua will listen to everything you say and if he feels that you aren't speaking exactly to them as we have instructed, then he'll hit a button on the unit and your voice will disappear.

"Furthermore, Mr. Phelps, one of the men at the table over there by the barbecue range, will be watching your voice on a stress analyzer, and if he feels that your voice sounds like you are lying, he will knock out the tones at the high end so that a stress analyzer on the other end, or the human ear, which in my opinion is just as good, will not hear any suspicious tones in your voice. Mr. Phelps had twenty-three years with the CIA and is well versed in these techniques. Mr. Phelps?" he called.

Phelps came and stood before Chen, with his hand out.

"You will now surrender your cell phones and electronic devices and so on."

Chen gave him two phones and a beeper.

"Please remain comfortable," Martz said. He got up to go see Elliot on the other side of the terrace.

"Everything okay?"

"Hi, Billy Martz. Yes, we're set up, more or less. I spent the day at the office getting everything ready." He had three screens open, powered off one of the waterproof exterior plugs that Connie used for her elliptical motion machine that she kept stored on the roof, spending hours climbing a little closer to heaven or wherever it was his wife ultimately planned to arrive.

"You have all your power, all your communications?"

"Yes."

"Is it technically very difficult?"

"This technology has been around for a while now. You want tricky technology, go play around with stem cells."

"If you say so."

"Bill, you're turning into a fussy old man." Elliot smiled, patted him on the back. "You go do your thing and I'll do mine."

But he lingered, looking over all the equipment, amazed at how small it was, except for the large white transmission cone on a ten-foot telescoping tripod that had been hauled in and positioned earlier in the day. The key to a successful lift, Martz knew, now that almost everything electronic was traceable, was to move the communication not just from place to place, and from government jurisdiction to jurisdiction, but across technologies. Moving across each of these boundaries made it harder for any interested authorities to re-create the sequence of illegal communications. From what Martz understood, Elliot's men would, that evening, be communicating directly with a boat about one hundred feet offshore in New York Harbor. The mode was a digitally compressed and encrypted microwave beam, which required line-of-sight transmission and was effective only up to a few miles. Did not travel with the curvature of the earth. It couldn't be used on foggy or rainy nights, either. You shot it at a receiver the size of an umbrella, the beam a quarter inch wide. But it was absolutely untrackable. It was so good Citibank used one to shoot data from its famous headquarters on East Fifty-third Street to its back-office operations facility in Queens, built for that purpose in a line-of-site location on the other side of the East River. He watched the men go about their business. They'd spent hours checking and rechecking the transmission vector. The boat, papered with a Liberian registry, had a phone uplink to a private Dutch satellite network used only by shipping companies, and the data packets were in turn relayed and downlinked to a Greek shipyard that was owned by Elliot. The yard was filled with rusty tankers needing overhaul, but the fiber-optic cables running under and around them were state of the art. With this arrangement, Elliot could speak more or less untraceably to anyone in the world. The many legs of the communication degraded the sound quality and added a little delay, but not too much, perhaps four seconds.

But this was not all that Elliot did, not by any means. After all, anyone with a few million bucks and an antisocial personality could set up an untraceable mix-tech, global com-link. Mr. bin Laden, for example, among other miscreants. Elliot's real value, and the reason he was effectively paid millions of dollars for what amounted to perhaps seven or eight hours of service, was that he made things happen that otherwise could not; he provided capital and the smarts to leverage it to the greatest possible illegal effect. He and his tiny band of infidels had researched several thousand stock price surge patterns and painstakingly built a proprietary trading program that followed the documented natural arc of these surges using best-fit modeling within a field of scattershot data points. He then started to buy the stock in question and drive up the price, of course. But that was not all; once Elliot's trading gambit began, he didn't just slavishly recapitulate the curve with simplistic buying and occasional selling; instead he created it organically, he *birthed* it, which was to say that he used several thousand linked trading platforms that he empowered with randomizing block-size choosers and let run autonomously, giving the platforms a buy bias but also letting them react in real time and differentially to spontaneous market information. This meant that he allowed some of his trading platforms to make "bad" decisions, very much the way real flesh-and-blood traders did, getting in or out of a market surge too early or late. He also employed a mix of the patterns typically utilized by day traders, retail brokerages, private wealth managers, investment banks, and big institutional players such as pension fund managers and mutual fund companies. His platforms traded not just with and against all the legitimate traders in the market but blindly against each other as well. The result was not a simulation of a real stock surge but a real-life, real-time rise that was, from a statistical point of view, utterly legitimate.

The trick was to induce enough other legitimate traders to buy with sufficient speed and volume that Elliot's platform trades were hidden within the general movement of the stock. He started a little trading fire, hoped it caught, then added gasoline to it. Which was also to say that were the SEC to examine the general trade data, it would be hard-pressed to filter out and reveal Elliot's platforms. It was that sophisticated. Which, again, was also to say he'd probably bought some wee black-market SEC software, when rarely available, and studied it closely.

Elliot had an excellent record. Never exposed or investigated. And he was picky as hell. Had turned Martz down a few times. In general his bias was toward industries or companies that were experiencing a lot of market volatility. Tweaking his model continuously, Elliot stealthily moved around among New York, London, Frankfurt, Paris, Tokyo, Milan, Shanghai, Johannesburg, Melbourne. Each exchange or bourse had its own wrinkles, of course, its own trading rules, national holidays, weather seasons, electoral cycles, and sporting events. Best time to do a British lift? When the World Cup was playing on the same weekend as the Wimbledon finals. Trading volume always light on that summer Friday morning in late June or early July. Best time in Japan? During the Japanese World Series with a typhoon predicted for Tokyo. And so on. The stock had to have a story that made the restoration of its price somewhat plausible. Couldn't be in a dying industry, couldn't be in a takeover battle, for trading patterns around those were heavily scrutinized. Couldn't involve weapons systems, a personal belief of his, and couldn't directly enrich any of a select group of people, including Rupert Murdoch, Donald Rumsfeld, or George Soros. Elliot had a *few* standards. If necessary, he was able to trade one stock simultaneously across multiple exchanges, his trading patterns customized by location. It made for mind-boggling computer research and programming ability. It also meant that Elliot performed only two or three lifts a year and no more. He didn't want to get caught, after all.

Although he was brought in to work for others, Elliot watched the rising stock price with his own goal in mind, which was to get out gradually before the top was reached. In essence, this concept was paradoxical, because every sell order put downward pressure on the price. The trick was to front-run the market's natural conclusion of the short-term, secular rise in the stock's price. Buy less and sell more simultaneously. By the time the stock had topped, Elliot had sold his shares back into the very same heated demand he had created, booked jaw-dropping short-term profits, and initiated a secondary, obfuscatory buy-and-sell pattern of trading, very often one that maintained an artificially high price that was itself 5 or 10 percent below the stock's high. This rear-guard action often resulted in minor short-term losses that shaved at the major gains yet confirmed and publicly ratified the overall movement of the stock. The whole game could take two or even three days to play out, but the essential gambit would transpire in the next five or six hours.

And then I can relax, Martz thought, and go get my prostate biopsied. Once the Good Pharma stock rose near his break-even point, his own trading specialists would reduce his holdings in it, leaving him if not in the black then having suffered a loss of only a few percentage points—good enough, under the circumstances. He was down about $107 million; if he could get back $80 or $85 million of that, he'd consider himself whole and make back the difference another way.

All of this sounded very good in theory. But it still came down to two men, Tom Reilly and Chen. They would need to get started soon, given when the markets opened on the other side of the world. He returned to where Chen was sitting.

Chen rose. "I am going to leave now."

Martz said, "You don't want to do that."

"Why?"

"Because you'll be arrested for illegal stock market transactions before you can leave the United States."

Chen smiled. "I am a Chinese citizen."

"So?"

"My government would not allow it."

"Chen," said Martz, sitting down next to him, "the Chinese government arrests foreigners every day in China, as you know. It's a concept they understand well. We do it, too. There are a lot of people who are very antagonistic toward China's rogue behavior. Mostly conservative politicians. Your arrest would be a matter of personal satisfaction to them. I can arrange for them to praise this event on the floor of the United States Senate. Fast. In a day or two. I'm a very well-connected guy, Chen. I contribute to all their reelection committees."

The translator said all this but looked a little amazed himself. Chen listened, then nodded, his dark eyes showing nothing, however.

"The last thing you want to do is be arrested for illegal trading here. This will launch an investigation into everything you have ever done, and like a fatal disease it will touch all of the people to whom you have ever given information. It will cause loss of face. All those businessmen and government officials. All those Western companies that have those nice special arrangements with you and your people. You know this better than I do, Chen. You will become persona non grata. No, *worse*. You will have cancer and be terminally ill." He looked directly at Hua. "Will that translate?"

"More or less."

He uttered a few more words.

"So," resumed Martz, waving at another man just now arriving by way of the elevator, "you are going to call your friends and tell them to start buying Good Pharma. We will explain everything. My friend Tom Reilly is here—"

"Number two at Good Pharma?" interrupted Chen.

"The one and the same."

A big, handsome man in a good suit came over, shook Chen's hand. Like it was a business deal. Which, in a sense, it was. Just business.

Harlem had changed, yo. Now *white people* lived there! He knocked on the door of Norma Powell's house on 146th Street. It was well past the dinner hour; he'd be lucky if someone answered. The traffic up the FDR Drive had been a disaster; nearly two hours from Red Hook to west Harlem. 1010 WINS radio said the body of a mobster had been discovered dumped between two cement traffic barriers. The roadway in both directions crawled with cops and evidence technicians. Now Ray saw movement behind the curtain, and a moment later an enormous black man came to the door, with some kind of delicious smell of Italian cooking following him.

"This Norma Powell's place?" Ray asked.

"She's my mother. What's up?"

"I'm looking for a Chinese girl. Name's Jin Li."

"We don't say who lives here, mister. Especially eight o'clock at night."

Ray held out the fax he'd found in Red Hook.

The man inspected the piece of paper, handed it back. Tough to argue with that.

"You a cop?"

"No."

"Then we ain't got something to talk about."

She could be in her apartment or room right now. "How about you call her for me, find out if she'll see me?"

"You got a phone?"

"No."

"Why not?"

"Long story."

The man pulled out his own phone.

"You have her number?" Ray asked.

"Do I look like a chump?"

"No, you do not look like a chump."

The man dialed, listened, a look of patient disgust on his face. "Message," he said, snapping the phone shut.

"You should have said that—"

"Wait a minute there, Cool Breeze. I thought you *answered* my question."

"What?"

"That I wasn't a *chump*. Didn't you say something like that? Just because I'm calling her don't mean some funky white guy gets to talk to her, especially on *my* dime."

Ray tipped back his head. He hates you, he thought. But it's not personal. Don't react. Seek the elegant solution. What next? Stalling, he looked up the front of the building. Which gave him an idea. "Fine. Good-bye and thanks. By the way, whatever you're cooking smells good."

Maybe because it was burning? The man frowned in worry and shut the door. Ray could see him hurry toward the kitchen.

Ray examined the name slots on the buzzer. The one for 5F was empty. That would be Jin Li's. Fifth floor front. He stepped off the stoop ledge right onto the fire escape. Norma Powell and her son seemed to run things by the book. The New York City fire code stipulated that every room in which a person slept had to have a least two forms of egress, which meant, usually, a door and a window. He knew Jin Li would never rent a room without a window; she was a bit claustrophobic. He climbed up the fire escape to the fifth floor, his boots kicking a shower of paint chips beneath him. The iron-slatted landing on the fifth floor stretched across three windows, and he peered inside each dwelling. In the first an old black man was in a chair watching a baseball game on television. He had his hand around a forty-five-ounce bottle of beer. The next window was dark; Ray saw no one inside. The last window revealed an overly skinny young woman in a bra, jeans, and an air filter mask waving one arm around. She looked like a human praying mantis. What was she doing? He leaned close. She was spray-painting a giant canvas. Dangerous as hell. He knocked loudly on the window.

"What? Who are you?" She seemed neither surprised nor scared that he stood outside her window.

"Fire department inspection."

She opened the window two inches, leaving a screen between them. "What?"

"Fire department. That's an illegal industrial use of aerosol propellants in a multiunit residential dwelling," he said. "But I'm not going to write you a violation if you promise me one thing."

"What? Sorry."

"Keep your room ventilated, miss. Keep this window open."

"Yes, sir. Thank you."

"Are there illegal activities taking place in the next door apartment?"

"The room, you mean? No, she just moved in. I don't know what she does."

"Where is the occupant now?"

"I think I saw her getting into a taxi like a couple of hours ago. She lives in Korea or something."

"Was she alone?"

"I don't know."

A couple of hours ago? In a taxi? Ray climbed down the fire escape and headed toward his truck. The fact that Jin Li left in a cab meant something, since reaching lower Manhattan from Harlem was a lot more easily done by subway. You would take a cab from Harlem to someplace more difficult to reach. Like the airports. Or Queens. Brooklyn? He had a bad feeling. I've got to be smarter, he told himself. He'd come to a dead end. But just because he hadn't found her didn't mean no one else had.

The profit margin on single-serving bagged potato chips was enormous. Most people had no *idea*. And that was the key to owning a gas station. You had to have the convenience store with it, because the absolute profit margins on pumped gasoline were very tight, perhaps four cents per gallon. The retail gas market was highly competitive and utterly transparent. People could see the price and literally look across the street to see who had the lower price. The margins on coffee, snacks, and other convenience store items—yes, he would sell porn, which was nothing compared to what kids were looking at on the Internet—were about five times higher. The Turk's place on Flatbush Avenue was a gold mine. Better than he expected. He had all the info now, thanks to the man who did the Turk's business taxes, a Pakistani guy who didn't mind selling out his fellow Islamic brother and making an extra thousand bucks just for photocopying a federal tax return. The accountant knew everything. The Turk was pumping about 125,000 gallons a month. His Dunkin' Donuts franchise, just started a few months earlier, was doing an average $50,000 per month, daily gross increasing every day. The convenience store on the other side of the property was averaging $23,000 per month, with additional income from the ATM, the AirVac machine out in the lot, the paid-in-place cigarette displays (the tobacco companies desperate to hook teenaged buyers), and the prepaid domestic and international phone cards. Two years into a ten-year lease. Blimpie sandwich shop additionally approved for the location. And best of all, it was a great Lotto spot, people coming in and buying a hundred dollars' worth of tickets at a pop, fucking Mexicans and Haitians and Gambians and goddamned everyone, except the Hasidic Jews with their freaky wigged wives, but also including the poor old Italian women living off Social Security. The place was a money *machine*.

He knew all about the overall business now, too. The big oil companies were getting out of the retail gas station trade. Chevron, Conoco-Phillips, ExxonMobil, all selling off thousands of stations. At the same time, the big-box stores were getting into the business. Wal-Mart and Costco. *But not in Brooklyn, folks.* Very tough to get new gasoline tanks going into the ground, thanks to the state's tough environmental laws. What you see is what you already got, and what he was going to get was the station at Flatbush and Avenue J.

And his new best friend, the Chinese chick, was going to help him—*a lot*. He had not expected to find her at the old detective's house, but hey, he got lucky for once, and as soon as she'd appeared coming out the door he'd known he needed her. Not only had she possibly seen him on the night that he and Richie had attacked the girls in the car, but, more important, he had a feeling that whoever had sent the white limousine looking for her boyfriend had the kind of money that Victor could use. It was just a matter of making a couple of phone calls to the guy and arranging a pickup for the money. He wasn't going to hurt her. A few whacks upside the head were no big deal, didn't count. He did like the way she looked, though, had trouble keeping his hands off her, and the idea that she was his captive, and that he could do *anything* to her, excited him. She had a legitimately hot body, and he knew what it would feel like beneath him. What a groaning good feeling to slide the beef up into her, especially if she struggled. Hell, she could bite him, kick him, anything. Eventually she'd just have to lie back and take it. Total domination. The idea of this sent some wood down south to where the wild thing lived.

But keep your eyes on the prize here, Vic. Be a businessman, not a sex fiend. His plan, formulated as he'd driven back to the lot, was simple. He had a dozen old clonephones—very hard to get these days because the manufacturers had gotten wise—and he was going to use them to call whoever and get the money from them.

Now he opened the floor door and climbed back down. The porcelain bathtub stood nearly full with the brown liquid, whatever was left of Richie's bones still dissolving away there. The odor was strong. He wondered how badly it bothered Jin Li. Well, she had other things to worry about. He'd loosened her up, and it was time to push things along. Jin Li lay curled in a ball on the mattress, the tape over her eyes. He'd put another piece of tape over her mouth.

What a nasty little room this is, Vic thought.

"Here's a bucket," he told her. "And a roll of paper. I want you to keep yourself clean."

He cut the tape holding her wrists together.

She pointed to the tape over her eyes, meaning that she wouldn't be able to see what she was doing.

This had to be some kind of trick. "You want me to take off the tape on your eyes?"

She nodded.

"That means you can see me. That might not be good for you."

She shrugged.

"You saw me before, however?"

She nodded.

"I'll think about it."

She shook her head. *Combative.*

He pressed the bucket and toilet paper into her hands. "I think you'll be able to figure out what to do."

She was silent. He leaned forward and ran his hand over her breasts. She jumped back in surprise and fear.

"You worried that I'll rape you?"

She didn't move. Not a muscle. But her breathing quickened. "Answer the question. Are you afraid I'll rape you?"

She nodded.

"Good. You should be afraid. It's a distinct possibility. I'm actively fantasizing about it. On the other hand, I need you to be mentally composed for my purposes."

She made no answer.

"Now, let's call your brother. You realize, of course, that no one, and I mean *no one*, has any idea that you are here or that this room exists." He watched her. He could see that behind the tape her forehead had lifted. She was crying—but making no sound.

He took the tape off her mouth in one rip. "Tell me the number."

She did.

"That's a weird freaky number."

"It's a global number," she said, coughing.

He dialed on the clonephone. A greeting came on, in Chinese. He didn't leave a message.

"He doesn't speak English," she said. "You need to speak in Chinese."

The language difference. *You didn't think of that, Vic. You assume everyone speaks English.* He could kick himself—or worse. But he was in it now. No aborting the mission. He redialed and handed the Chinese girl the phone.

"Tell him you are kidnapped and he needs to get his hands on five hundred thousand dollars by tomorrow morning at ten a.m."

When the message came on, Jin Li quickly said in Chinese, "Chen, I need help. I am a prisoner in some kind of sewage place in Brooklyn. The man's name is an English word for *winner*. I am in the place where the shit trucks are parked, I think. This guy wants a lot of money."

He snatched the phone away. "That's plenty enough." He tried calling back. No answer. "We're going to have to wait. Meanwhile we will explore other promising opportunities."

The Chinese girl fell back on the old mattress, dragged down there originally for sexual purposes. He and Violet, when they were seventeen, eighteen.

Yes, she was going to be *very* useful. He had by now emptied out all of the contents of the girl's purse and found, among other things, her business card. She was the vice president and manager, American operations, of some outfit called CorpServe. A big deal. Whoa! But more interesting was the call sheet that he'd found in her purse. It was on the stationery of a company called Good Pharma, which had headquarters in midtown Manhattan, close to where he'd waited for the car driven by the Mexican girls. Dated from the day before, the sheet had been generated by a specialized spreadsheet desktop application; at the top of the page was the recipient of the calls, one Thomas Reilly, and for him the secretary had typed in the name and a message; below it appeared the person's title, phone number, and identifying detail, such as the names of wife and children, and record of the last call made to or received from that person:

NAME: James Tonelli. *Apologized for not calling sooner. Knows you wanted to speak to him urgently.*

NAME: Ann Reilly [clearly the wife of Thomas Reilly]. *Calling from her cell. Bill Martz called for you at home, please deal with him, she says.*

NAME: William Martz, chairman and CEO of Martz New Century Partners Fund. Five calls. *Tom, he is insistent you call him. He was making the call himself, not secretary. Frankly, he sounded sort of abusive.*

NAME: Christopher Paley, in-house counsel, Good Pharma Corp. *We have received an inquiry from the NYPD regarding the death of the two Mexican workers in our CorpServe cleaning service.*

NAME: Ann Reilly. *Martz again.*

He was putting something together. The two Mexican girls had been employed by CorpServe, where this Jin Li also worked, as a boss of some sort. The two Mexican girls had serviced the Good Pharma offices. Jin Li had been in the Good Pharma offices *yesterday*. The Good Pharma big shot named Tom Reilly had been called by Tonelli and a guy named Martz. Maybe that was related, maybe not. All these folks, Vic knew, had access to a lot of money, and some of it was going to become his. He looked at Jin Li cowering. I'm going to turn this hot Chinese girl into a gas station on Flatbush Avenue, he told himself. He saw her watching him.

"Open your mouth," he said.

"Why?" she asked fearfully.

"Just open your mouth."

She did.

"Wider, all the way."

She did.

"I'm taking the tape off." He reached forward and pulled it away in one quick motion. "There. Keep your eyes shut!"

"I am," she breathed fearfully.

"Stick your tongue out."

She didn't.

"Do it!" he yelled.

The sound of his voice scared her, making her blink. But she did as he had commanded, eyes closed, mouth wide open, tongue out.

"Move your tongue, like you're licking something."

She did, tears appearing from beneath her eyelashes.

"Good," Vic said. "Very, very good."

A man likes a drink at the end of the day. Especially me, thought Carlos Montoya as he passed through the strings of red beads in the entrance of his Queens bar. How many loads of laundry can you supervise before going mad? If the number was knowable, he'd nonetheless passed it a long time ago. He sat down at his regular table. I'm tired and fat, he thought, what else is new? The place seemed quiet, muted. Someone had turned off the music. Where were all the regulars, the Mexicans and Guatemalans and Ecuadorians who came here to spend a few of their hard-earned bucks and drink beer?

His waiter, Manny, eased up to him with a glass and bottle. "Hey, boss."

"The place is dead."

Manny jerked his head down the bar where an older man, lanky and quiet, sat. "Boss, you got a new friend."

The other man slid over a few chairs. He handed Carlos a card.

"Mr. Montoya," he said, "my name is Detective Peter Blake."

"Good evening, Officer."

"Let's get to it. I know you've had a hard day pretending to be an upstanding citizen. California Highway Patrol picked up two of your boys a few hours ago, snagged them on the bulletin we put out when they left the city so fast."

"They didn't do nothing."

"Then why did they run after I questioned them?"

"I told them to go have a great adventure. They're good clean young men, need to see this great country of ours."

Blake chewed on a swizzle straw, apparently reminding himself not to argue with such an erroneous representation of reality. He's on duty, Carlos realized, can't drink.

"I can get those boys a much easier time of it," Blake said.

"If what?"

"If you tell me what's really going on."

"They didn't do anything. Why would they kill a couple of nice Mexican girls? It never makes sense."

"Actually, I'm starting to come around to that idea myself."

Carlos didn't like the cards he was holding. All cops lie, he reminded himself.

"Mr. Montoya," the detective continued, "I got a few old pals in the California immigration system. We can put those guys on ice in a detention center for six months easy and no judge is going to give us a problem. Or I could have them extradited back here and we could offer them a very interesting plea agreement in exchange for a complete description of the Mexican drug distribution channels in the great city of New York. If their information is good enough, helps snag some major players, we can even provide instant United States citizenship as further inducement to complete cooperation. Okay, Mr. Montoya? You don't have a lawyer and this conversation never happened, but you can see I'm not fucking around, right?"

Time to fold, he thought. This cop is hard core. "What I heard is that it was a guy who owns a sewage yard in Marine Park," he said.

"What?"

Carlos explained that his young "cousin" worked there and had seen some things that disturbed him. Sorry, there was no name. Anyway his "cousin" was back in Mexico now.

"Names, I need names," said Blake.

Carlos scratched his head. There was probably money in this somehow, but he didn't want it. You turn into a paid government snitch then go to prison and have everyone know that, then you end up with a sharpened toothbrush in your throat.

"The sewage guy's name is Victor. I spoke to him myself."

"You did?"

He sipped his cold beer. "Called him. Told him I knew. And he threatened to kill my family. I was thinking about what I was going to do to him for that, something he could never forget, you know what I mean?"

Blake touched his own nose with his forefinger. "Hey, Carlos, you gotta tell us these things, okay?"

"I had my utmost concerns, Officer."

Blake was getting up to leave. "I'm going to check this out right now, and if you're wrong, then—"

"Then God strike me down," Carlos interrupted, feeling relieved of his burden. "Because those beautiful girls are in heaven now, the special part, reserved just for Mexican angels."

What a rotten place to die. He'd let her open her eyes and so now she looked around at the small cement-walled room with no windows, perhaps fifteen feet on a side. Next to her was an old porcelain tub with some kind of strange piping going into it. But odder still was the thick brown mixture in the tub; that was what gave off that strong chemical odor, a bad smell that reminded her of the iron yard in Shanghai where she worked one summer in the office doing paperwork while boys just off the train from the countryside worked long hours stripping the paint from old sheet metal. A trickle of water dribbled from the tub hose and emptied into a floor drain. Above her was a solitary incandescent lightbulb, bright, too high to reach and turn off.

She was sitting on an old mattress, her legs still taped and roped at the ankles, as were her wrists again. A thick metal chain was looped tightly around her waist, secured with a lock, and the other end of the chain was locked to a steel ring set into the cement floor. There was enough slack in the chain that she could sit up on the mattress but not enough that she could stand.

This guy is going to rape and kill me, Jin Li thought. This is the kind of place that crazy men torture and slaughter women. There were plenty of these kinds of men in America, she knew, just as there were men like this in China.

She was hungry but, more important, suffered a terrible thirst, perhaps because of the chemical fumes. She needed more water, but the man had climbed up the stairs to go do something, leaving the ceiling hatch open. He was taller than Ray but older and not as fit. Yet she feared him, not just because of what he had already done to her but because he radiated a malevolent potency. He was studying her closely, she knew, like a safecracker trying to figure out the combination, and she had certainly not forgotten his hands on—and inside—her body while in the van. If he did that then, what would he eventually do in the safety and obscurity of this windowless cement room? She could see he was thinking about it. Sort of tasting the idea in his head, his mouth already filled with saliva.

Victor had left the hatch open but he knew she wasn't going anywhere. He needed to concentrate now and dialed the number for Tom Reilly's wife's cell phone.

It picked up. "Is this Mrs. Reilly?"

"Yes. Who is this?"

"I'm looking for your husband."

"This is not his number."

"I understand that," he said evenly.

"Who is this?"

"Someone who needs to reach your husband."

"I don't speak to people who don't tell me their name." She hung up.

Victor waited a minute. Then he dialed using another clonephone.

"Hello?" came the cautious voice.

"Mrs. Reilly, give me your husband's number."

"He's in a business meeting tonight."

"I don't care."

"He cares." She hung up again.

He called back on the first phone.

"Listen," she said, "I'm calling the police."

"I wouldn't," said Vic. "That's not a good idea, under the circumstances."

There was a pause as if she was considering something.

"Who shall I say is calling?" she asked, her voice laced with sarcasm.

"Tell him the following words."

"Words?"

"Yes. Here they are. Write them down. The first word is 'CorpServe.' C-O-R-P-S-E-R-V-E. The second word is 'Mexicans.' As in Mexico, the country. Mexicans. The third word is 'dead.' Tell him those three words. He will be *eager* to speak with me then. I will call you back in three minutes." Vic hung up. This, he told himself, was going to be good.

We are way outside the paradigm now, Ann thought. She looked at the phone in her hand. She'd written the three words on the front of a patient's file.

"Yeah," came Tom's voice when she called. "Ann?"

"Got a strange call, Tom."

"Strange how?"

"From a man who wants to talk to you. Wouldn't give me his name. He told me three words to say to you."

"What?"

"What's going on, Tom? I'm beginning to feel—"

"Tell me the words, Ann, and we'll fucking worry about your *feelings* another time!"

She hadn't heard that tone in years. "The words are 'CorpServe,' 'Mexicans,' like the country, and the last word is 'dead.' "

"Okay."

"Okay? Dead Mexicans is an okay thing?" she cried.

"Yes. What next?"

"He wants your number, Tom." Her voice rose in anxiousness. "He's about to call back."

"Give it to him," answered Tom. "I think I know who this is." The timing could not be worse. The fellow named Elliot had started some of his preliminary buying of Good Pharma stock, tightening up the loose supply of shares that were available right now, but they weren't getting any movement upward in the price because Mr. Chen refused to talk. Tom watched Martz looking at him from across the rooftop, then back at Elliot. This crazy attempt to lift Good Pharma's stock price wasn't going to work. He saw that now, as plainly as he could see the red and green lights on the top of the Empire State Building, once and now again the tallest structure in New York City.

Vic dialed back using a different clonephone.

"This is his number," said his wife, repeating it. "He's there right now."

"Thank you for your assistance," said Vic.

"Fuck you, asshole." The phone went dead.

He dialed Tom Reilly.

"Yeah, James?"

"What?" said Vic, wondering if he sounded like James Tonelli, one of the names on the list.

"Why the fuck you calling my wife's cell phone number? How'd you get it?"

Gotta move fast here, thought Vic.

"James, this is Tom Reilly asking you a question. Talk, man."

"Mexicans," said Vic.

"I know. I heard. Again, why you calling my wife, James?"

"This isn't James, Tom."

A pause. "Who is this?"

"This is someone who knows what you told James Tonelli to do."

"I didn't tell him anything to do."

"Bullshit you didn't. You told him to kill some CorpServe workers."

"Who is this?"

"I want money, Tom. Real money. I know what you do, I know where your wife is."

"Listen—"

"No, you listen. I'll be calling back in one minute. Think about how much it would cost to pay me or how much it would cost you *personally* if I told people what you told James Tonelli to do."

He waited three minutes. Then called back.

"Two million, Tom. I want that in cash by the end of the day to-morrow." He hung up.

Tom examined his phone. He knew that Martz was wondering why he was taking a personal call at a time like this. But he had to play ball with this other guy. If he didn't, then—well, *then* he's sitting in court listening to James Tonelli, witness for the state after copping to a re-duced charge, saying how Tom had ordered the cold-blooded murder of two Mexican girls. By then he would have lost his job, his wife, his whole world. He could get hold of $2 million easily enough; that was a quick call to his private banker. Maybe I should stall the guy, Tom thought. But he remembered that the guy had Ann's cell number, which she generally didn't give out. It was used for emergencies at the office only. And for talking with Tom. If this guy had her number, then maybe he knew where they lived.

"Tom?" called Martz from across the roof.

But there was another distraction. Phelps was holding a cell phone. "Our friend here Mr. Chen had a message, from a Brooklyn cell phone, I think."

"Put it on speaker."

They did. It was a woman crying frantically in Chinese, speaking rapidly. Maybe she said the word "Brooklyn," Tom couldn't tell. The effect on Chen, he noticed, was immediate. He became agitated.

"What'd she say?" Martz asked Hua.

"She says she is kidnapped in Brooklyn and she thinks it's a place with a lot of shit and the guy's name means he is a winner."

"That's right," said Chen. "Exactly. That is my sister!"

Chen's phone rang again.

"On speaker again," said Martz.

"Who's this?" came a man's voice. Tough sounding.

Martz answered. "Why are you calling this number?"

"Looking for a guy named Chen."

"What do you want to say?"

"Let me talk to Chen."

Martz shook his head. "Can't do it."

They heard a woman crying out in Chinese, shrieking, weeping.

"Jin Li!" yelled Chen. "I hear you."

"Shut the fuck up," the voice on the phone barked.

They heard the Chinese woman again, being struck.

"Chen, I got your sister here," came the voice. "I want money fast. You heard her message. She might not be alive much longer."

Martz held up his hand. "Who is this?" he demanded.

"Someone who wants to speak to Chen." The phone went dead.

Chen said, "Let me make a call. I have to use my phone."

"No. Nobody does anything." Martz had to think it through. Chen's sister worked for CorpServe, he remembered, supervised the cleaning of the Good Pharma offices. The lift had started but they were losing time, not getting anywhere.

"I think I know who this is," Tom said to Martz. He'd be careful to move the blame away from himself. "This is where our problem began, thanks to Chen."

A phone rang again, Tom's this time. "Yes?"

"Put it on speaker, Tom," ordered Martz.

"Hang on," Tom said. "This is a private call."

"Not right now!" Martz yelled. "Your nuts belong to me, Tom Reilly, I've had enough of your bullshit!"

Tom put his phone on speaker. "Go ahead."

"Listen to me, listen to me good," came the male voice. "I'm going to explain—"

"It's the same voice!" yelled Martz. "Same as the other phone! Calling you!"

"Who's that?" came the voice. "You were on the other call!" There was some fumbling and static. "Wait, you motherfuckers, you just wait."

The phone in Phelps's hand rang. Chen's phone.

"Put that one on speaker," said Martz. "Christ. Now we got both of them."

"Who the fuck am I talking to?" came the man's voice out of both phones. A weird screeling feedback infected his voice. "I'm talking to everybody?"

No one answered. The wind moved over the roof.

"Listen, motherfuckers, listen Thomas Reilly or William Martz or Christopher Paley—"

"Who's that?" Martz interrupted.

"Company lawyer," Tom answered.

"Listen, you motherfuckers, and Chen, if he's there, listen to this—" There was the sound of three gunshots, *pop-pop-pop*, and then the screaming of the Chinese woman, a horrible keening. Had he shot her? "Hear that? I want a million in cash right now. I will be calling back in ten minutes. Or this woman is dead."

Both phones hung up with a loud click.

"We've been hijacked," Martz said. "I don't get it."

Now it was Chen who had a question. "This is fake, this is to make me call China for you?"

"No, goddamn it," said Martz, looking at his watch. "No. Getting a million dollars in the middle of the night is not easy." He sighed heavily, the cost of business getting steeper. "Look, Chen, I don't know who this guy is, but a million dollars is not going to stop me now. You understand? I got a lot more riding than that. And you, you have your sister. We could go to the police—"

"No, no police," said Chen. "I do not like police."

"Neither do I."

Chen seemed calm, resolved. "You will let me make one phone call, and then I will call China for you. I will call everybody in China for you. This is my sister."

Martz looked around at the others, not sure if he'd been tricked. Tom Reilly shrugged. "We got to do something."

Martz stared ferociously at Chen. "Deal," he said.

They gave Chen his phone back. He dialed.

"Who're you calling?" Martz said, but Chen, intent on getting the digits correct, wasn't listening.

Where was the nurse? The phone was ringing. Raymond Sr. listened to it. He flung out his hand and found the phone.

"Yes?" he breathed.

"Mr. Ray Grant?"

A strange voice he'd never heard before. "Yes."

"Jin Li is in prison room. In shit man building. I do not have the language. Name is English word means winner. Very much danger. Do you understand?"

"No."

"Prison room. Shit man big building. His name means winner."

The phone went dead.

This time he was ready with a pad of paper and pen. He wrote: *prison place/shit man building/name means winner.*

Winner. Champion. Victor. Conqueror. He stared at the paper. There was a boy . . .

The Dilaudid machine clicked. The nurse had recently increased the dose, he knew. He stared at the piece of paper. Winner. The winner was the victor. Victorious. He knew what that meant. Yes. But his eyes went heavy and he was gone. There was a boy named Victor, he thought he told the nurse. But was he talking? He wasn't sure. Not much older than my son. He and a friend of his from his baseball team got jumped by some Russian guys. The other boy got it worse, got his head beat in. I talked to Victor in the hospital. He was pretty beat up.

We didn't have quite enough for an arrest. We'd started to question the Russian guys, one by one. Then one morning they find the biggest of them under the boardwalk in Coney Island. Shot. The killer had used a homemade silencer, a Clorox bottle wrapped with electrician's tape. Then had some fun with the corpse. Had put his balls in his eye sockets and his eyeballs in his hands. Vicious. The other Russian guys just disappeared. I didn't think it could be Victor. He was so young, sixteen, seventeen. Big handsome kid with dark hair. Eyes wild. But well spoken, intelligent. I watched him for a few months. I thought about bringing him in, and finally I did. I had nothing on him and I got nothing off of him. Father owned some kind of huge sewerage service in Marine Park. The night the Russian guy got killed, Victor was with his girlfriend, the sister of the friend who'd gotten the terrible beating. So she said. I talked to her by herself. She said that she and Victor had been having sex in some kind of secret basement room at his father's business. They had sex and then got drunk. Or maybe the other way around. That was his alibi. Her parents weren't around much, out of the picture. The girl's old man was depressed about his son. I didn't see Victor as the killer. He wasn't hardened yet. You don't usually have a drunk seventeen-year-old killing and mutilating a twenty-four-year-old Russian guy who weighs about 230. Didn't add up. I couldn't figure it. You getting all this? Am I making sense?

The nurse came into his room, heard Mr. Grant making his funny gobbling noises, talking in his sleep. She pulled up his covers and went back to the television room, enjoying the peaceful evening.

He'd left her there. After all the shooting and screaming into the phones. Maybe he'd been talking to Chen; it wasn't clear. Why did he leave, was he expecting someone? Meanwhile, something—an idea, a panicked fantasy—was eating at her, even as she felt despair about her circumstances. She found herself staring at the fuming tub filled with the brown liquid. All the canisters of chemicals. She'd remembered the smell and then she'd remembered something from an applied chemistry course at Harbin Institute of Technology. She needed to increase the density of the jellied liquid. Could she reach? She wriggled into a crouch, grasped her waste bucket, stood awkwardly, shuffled to the tub, and scooped up a bucket load of the scummy mixture. Take your time, she cautioned herself. She knelt and set the bucket on the floor then sat down.

She watched the liquid settle and ever so subtly separate, the water rising to the top. She took off her shoe and stirred the stuff with it. The shoe started to smoke, but the water was brought to the surface. She tipped the bucket and poured off the brownish water, and it trickled across the cement floor toward the drain. By the time the shoe was too floppy and eroded to wear anymore, she had refined the mixture enough that the bucket was one quarter empty. And much more odorous. Her eyes watered. Yes, when the mixture was drained of water, it seemed to evaporate more easily. Evaporation, she recalled, was the achievement of the gaseous state. I know what to do, she told herself.

She took the heel of her shoe and dipped it into the mixture. Then she flicked the heel at the lightbulb. A perfect shot. One of the flying globules spattered against the bulb, stuck, heated, and then, just as it dropped away, burst into flame, landing on the floor and producing a horrible black smoke until it burned into nothing but a carbon smudge.

Jin Li coughed a moment, then remembered to slide the bucket around the edge of the mattress, where he would be less likely to see it and discover what she had done.

I'm going to sell this guy, thought Tom, as Martz looked on. He sat next to Chen on the table. "Okay, what I have here is a document that reports on the effectiveness of Good Pharma's new synthetic skin program. This is legitimate." He paused to let the translator catch up. "It shows that the skin has proved viable in extreme burn cases, and increasingly effective in geriatric patients. As you know, everybody in the developed countries of the world is getting old, fast, and we feel this product will find ready acceptance."

Chen said something to the translator, who then turned to Tom. "He says his earlier information showed that this product did not work. Early trials showed it was a failure. He says he will be asked about this."

Tom nodded. "That's smart, that makes a lot of sense. Those early trials suffered from methodology problems, not product failure. We were applying the synthetic skin to patients on blood thinners and in keloid scar areas. Both of those issues were resolved and our success rates shot up."

The translator relayed this.

Chen nodded his understanding.

Tom pushed on. "In approximately one hour, a leak of this positive information about our synthetic skin product is going to occur in a website chat room given over to the care of nursing patients. It's not an investors' site. But the site content is syndicated to a number of other websites for nursing patients and their families. From experience we know that an embedded nugget like this will be noticed by investment bloggers and the like, soon creating a viral rumor that Good Pharma has something hot in the pipeline."

Chen nodded. He was a quick study, after all.

"I need to say big numbers," he explained.

Martz interjected, "Yes, let's give him those."

"With fast-track approval by the Food and Drug Administration, we will have product in the pipeline in eighteen months. We figure the first-year sales at eight hundred million dollars, second year one-point-nine billion, and so on. Remember the target consumer population is getting larger rapidly. Those numbers are domestic only, by the way, so they at least double internationally. With rapid market penetration and what we expect will be eighty percent market-share domination, plus per-unit margins rising on falling unit-production costs, we see pure net profit streams in excess of two billion dollars five years from now—"

"Wait, please," said the translator, "too fast."

"No," said Chen, "no, not too fast. I got it. I understand. My friends in China, they will like this."

40 **She abandoned me.** He called the nurse, but no answer came back. Watching TV, bored with waiting for him to die. He'd have a little talk with his son about this. Ray was due home soon but there was no time to waste. He examined his tubes. One for pain, one for hydration, three for piss—the kidney tubes plus the catheter in his penis.

One by one he pulled them out, except for the left kidney tube. Couldn't get it out. Didn't matter. He pulled the tip of the other end out of the piss bag, would let the tube trail behind him.

He yanked back his covers. Hell, there was the long incision, dried and puckered at the edges, not healed, mostly covered by a bandage. Got to think this through, he told himself. He took his pillows from behind his back and head and dropped them onto the floor. Then he rolled off the bed and fell heavily on them.

Was he hurt? No. He wondered if he could move along on his stomach. He tried to lift himself up on his hands and knees to crawl. Pain shot through his torso and he could feel adhesions and stitches pulling. No, that wouldn't work. He rolled onto his back and pushed himself along the floor, his feet paddling him onward as he used his hands to pull himself, grabbing table legs, the doorjamb, anything to help. My hands are still strong, he realized.

The basement stairs. He peered over them. He certainly knew how many there were—nineteen. He had painted them, repaired the treads, fixed loose boards. He slowly swung his feet around and set them in front of himself, like a boy getting into a toboggan, and pushed off the first step. The idea was to do a controlled slide down them, surf them one by one, easing his bony rear end down.

He did okay for the first step, then the second and third. But then he slipped sideways and rolled into a ball and couldn't catch himself— so much stomach muscle had been cut!—and tumbled, heels over head down the last ten steps, not even reaching the bottom but falling sideways under the stair rail where the steps were open to the basement, landing atop a cardboard box of furnace vent filters.

There was a boy named Victor . . .

I'm okay, he panted. It hurts but I didn't bang my head. His wound was open now, blood seeping into his pajamas in a line on his chest.

Easing to the cool basement floor, he confronted the wall of filing cabinets, organized by year and then within each drawer by letter. What year? What year had he talked to Victor? What did a sullen, beat-up teenage boy and a detective talk about? The Yankees. The Mets. The boy was a few years older than Ray. This would have been in the late eighties. He located the file drawer marked 1989. He stretched his arm upward experimentally. Too far, too difficult to open. He spied a broom and slipped the handle end upward through the filing cabinet's drawer handle and pulled. The drawer slid out an inch on its rollers. Good. But how could he look through the files?

He had no illusion that he would be able to stand. He'd have to haul himself up somehow. He used the broom to pull the wheeled stool from the workbench toward himself, his eyes watching the slow progress of the swivel wheels as they rolled over every minute crack in the basement floor.

Impossible to climb atop it and yet somehow he did, keeping one hand on the file drawer, kicking his feet at the right moment until he lay over the stool, chest down on the cushion, his head hanging over the side. With his left hand, he pulled his torso up and dropped his head atop the files. There they were, in perfect alphabetical order.

The name. How would he find it? Vic, Victor. That was the boy's name. But what was the last name? The case would have been filed by the victim's name. Anthony. Did you see them hit Anthony? Anthony Del-something. Depasso, DeVecchio. Del-something.

His head was in the middle of the drawer. The letter tabs on one side were hidden, so he just grabbed a file at a time and worked his way down the alphabet—H, G, F, E, D. He pulled out the D files—Delancy, Dingel. The next file was Charnoff. No Del-something. Had he got the name wrong?

No, probably the year. One year earlier. One file drawer higher.

An impossibility.

He was panting now, a sour sweat soaking his pajamas. Losing energy. I can't get high enough to read the files in the next drawer, he realized.

But he could open the drawer. And he did, reaching blindly above himself and pulling it out.

He knew what would happen. It did. The file cabinet, its two highest drawers extended with their heavy contents, was destabilized and slowly fell forward, toppling him and spilling its contents across the floor.

I'm okay, he thought. The 1988 D files—? He could see them. Depasso. There it was. He pulled the file. He remembered Depasso. Had a sister named Violet. Beautiful girl. Slim. The file looked extensive; he'd done a lot of work, throwing everything in there, including a copy of the murder file of the Russian found under the Coney Island boardwalk. All his notes on Victor, the DD-5 forms. About his house and the sewerage yard his father ran. The building was some kind of old factory. He'd been all through it with the boy, Vic. Checking on the alibi. Seeing if any of the other Russians might be in there. The father hadn't wanted a cop looking around. Some kind of hidden room, some kind of bunker. Described in his notes, location, everything.

He crabbed his way out from under the files and from beneath the cabinet. The left kidney tube was caught behind him, but he kept pushing, feeling the tube yank deep inside him then rip out. He pushed with his feet along the cool basement floor, making progress foot by foot. In his left hand he held the file.

The stairs. He looked up them—nineteen steps. A mountain. He lifted the file as far as he could go, up two or three steps. Called. Hollered. Screamed. No sound came out.

Not in his bed? She saw the dangling tubes, the pillows on the floor. Her first thought was that he'd gotten outside the house somehow.

Then she found the open door to the basement. Mr. Grant lay atop the bottom stairs, a file of papers in his hand.

"Mr. Grant!"

He heard her, but said nothing. Instead he lifted the papers in his hand and waved them, as if they might be important.

He had every number. In his phone, a directory of the private lines belonging to dozens of big players in China. Elliot's staff transferred the numbers to their communications equipment, so the calls would be untraceable, and after some consultation, they arrived at a sequence, with the men most easily convinced to be called first. They put a headset on Chen, hooked him into the voice delay device, and the translator listened in and more or less simultaneously repeated Chen's words to Martz, in English.

"Terribly sorry to inconvenience you, sir. Yes, I know this is all in a hurry. But I am over in New York and have received a very good tip about the same American pharmaceutical company we shorted about a month ago. Good Pharma, that was it. See it on your screen there? I've just heard something about a major market move up very soon. Big research project to be announced, entirely new markets. You're the first one I called. Price might have started to move already. It has? Good. I think it's going to go a lot more than that. That shows that I know what I'm talking about. How much? Back the truck up, that's how much. Double the usual bet, I'd say, maybe triple. Yes, yes, I see it moving, too. You might want to help your friends out on this, by the way, let them get a piece."

Chen listened intently on the phone, holding the report Tom Reilly had provided.

Hua, translating quietly, glanced at Martz. "This guy is good," he said.

But Martz already knew that. Elliot was at the other table, sipping his coffee and watching his computers. They'd seen a dramatic upward bump in the Good Pharma price. Four points already, with momentum building, the curve getting sharper as the early European traders woke up.

As for the million dollars and Chen's sister, wherever she was, that problem seemed a long time ago now. Phelps had taken Chen's and Tom Reilly's phones—the ones that the blackmailer had called—and turned them off. Chen, meanwhile, hadn't asked how Martz was handling the blackmailer's request for money. Fine. They'd deal with the blackmailer later. Or, given how fast the price of Good Pharma was rising, maybe never.

The weight of a father. Terribly light in his arms; he'd carried children who were heavier.

"Thank God you came back when you did," Wendy said.

"Is he hurt?" Ray took each step carefully, turned sideways when he came to the doorway. Settled him in the hospital bed. The nurse first hooked up the hydration IV. Then the Dilaudid. He was panting and almost unconscious.

She felt his father's bones, took his pulse.

"The bleeding around the chest?"

"That's mostly seepage. I don't see any serious bleeding. He's very dry, of course."

"The nephrostomy tubes?"

"One's easy to put back in. The other will be a little bit of work."

"What was he doing down there?"

"You didn't see?" she asked Ray.

"No."

"He got into the file cabinets, all those papers."

"Which papers?"

"His old work files, I think. He had one in his hand when I found him."

"Which one?"

She pointed to a green folder on the table. "This one."

Ray took the folder. But he had already found the notes his father had written down in his now spidery handwriting: *prison place/shit man building/name means winner.* He glanced through the file. Victorious Sewerage in Marine Park. With a hand-drawn diagram of the building in the back of the lot.

"He was in such a good mood, too, after the visit from your friend."

"Friend, what friend?"

"That drop-dead gorgeous Chinese girl. You do know who she is, don't you?"

"Yes—"

"Well, she was here, hoping to see you, and she ended up seeing him."

"When did she leave?"

"That was hours ago! She said she might go out, then come back, I could be wrong about that. She came to see you and I said you were out."

But Ray was already running toward the truck, police file in hand.

Only later, when he was almost to Marine Park, did he realize that he'd forgotten about the guns hidden under the fertilizer bags in his father's shed. Too late to go back now.

A visitor? Victor was standing in his lot trying one clonephone after the next and getting no answer when he saw a car pull in. Those fuckers had turned off their phones—he'd make them pay for that. But now he watched the car. He shouldn't have left the gate open. The driver slowed and looked around. Vic stepped back behind one of his trucks. The car drove up to the trailer, then made a slow, investigatory circle around it. It parked, and an old man, tall and lanky, unfolded himself from the driver's door and walked up the trailer steps and knocked. There'd be no answer; the business was closed today, everyone gone.

The man knocked again. Nothing. He pulled something out of his sleeve and slipped it into the door. Ha, thought Vic, that won't work; it's also chained from the inside. The man was able to get the door open just enough to poke his head in for a quick look before he turned and descended the steps. He walked around the huge sewage trucks, stopping to write each license number on a pad of paper. The kind of thing a cop might do, Vic decided, but then again, there were ways to look up license information if you were not in law enforcement; you just had to have a friend who was.

After a few minutes, the man headed toward the warehouse. Vic hurried to the door and unlocked it, and even opened it an inch, not only to entice the man, if he was a cop, but also to help him get past any anxiety about making an unlawful search. If the door was unlocked and open, then the guy would not be able to resist entering; he'd just cautiously push through the door and look around.

And that is what the man did, though now with his gun drawn. Fine, thought Vic. I can do that, too. I wasted a lot of bullets scaring the Chinese girl, but I have two left. Nobody is going to hear anything back here anyway.

I need to visit Ray Sr. one more time, thought Peter Blake. I'll swing by the house after I'm done poking around this shithole. If he found nothing, he'd go back and arrest Carlos Montoya.

The warehouse door, he saw, had been left open. Was someone inside? Blake slipped out his service revolver and kept it at his thigh. The sewage trucks and the trailer had been unoccupied. If anyone is here, then they are inside, figured Blake. He pushed the door open with his toe. Peeked inside.

Musty and gloomy in that big space. Truck parts, old junk, hoses, stacks of tires. Tough to see in the dark.

Jin Li heard the shot. A quick pop. Then a pause. Then one more. It took a moment for her to understand what she'd just heard.

Then she did. Oh, Ray, she cried.

The gate was open. Next to the trailer was what looked like an unmarked police car. He drove past all the parked trucks and straight to the large warehouse behind it. He got out and tried the door. Locked. He tried the big garage-bay doors. Locked. He walked around the entire outside of the building. No windows at all on the ground floor, and a door on the far side that was locked. The building was a fortress, when you thought about it. He could try to crowbar his way in, but the doors looked heavy. And there might be an easier way. Ray tied a rope to the end of his crowbar. The rope was one hundred feet long. He took the crowbar by the straight end and flung it tomahawk-style at the windows. The crowbar crashed into the cement block below the windows and fell harmlessly to the ground, the yellow nylon rope looping downward after it. Ray retrieved the crowbar and threw it again. And again, trying to get it high enough to break a window and go inside the building. On his fifth try, the spinning crowbar reached high enough, broke the window glass, and fell through. The yellow rope whizzed out of its pile, jumping upward.

The trick was getting the hook of the crowbar to catch on something secure. Ray tugged the rope experimentally. He let the rope back down, then tugged again. Nothing. This time he slowly pulled the rope hand over hand, hoping it would catch on something inside. It didn't. He pulled and tugged, and finally it caught on something—a light fixture, a piece of electrical tubing, a pipe, something like that. How secure it was, he didn't know. He tested it with his weight. Pretty good, maybe.

In a moment he was up the wall and standing in the busted-out window frame. He'd performed this exact same maneuver in a building destroyed by the tsunami. With one hand holding the frame, he released the upward tension on the nylon rope until its crowbar hook dropped free. Then he pulled the rope and hook up to where he was balanced, untied the crowbar, slipped it into his belt loop, then tied the rope itself onto the window framing, being sure to knot it to several frames, not just one. Unlikely they would all fail at the same moment. With the rope secured this way, he could perform a standard free belay down the inside face of the warehouse.

Which he did, landing on the floor of the second story. He frantically searched the open area, pushing over boxes and poking through debris. Where are you, Jin Li? he thought. In a minute he had satisfied himself that she was not there. That left the first story, which was reached by a set of concrete stairs. Ray searched each area. Loaded with tires, truck parts, old cans of chemicals and solvents. A terrible fire hazard.

"Jin Li!" he called.

Nothing. It was a big building; studying every square foot of the floor would take hours.

He looked at the floor for openings, trapdoors. Maybe there wasn't a secret room like the one in his father's drawing. Or maybe he wasn't looking for it the right way. The electric wire was trenched from the avenue and no doubt arrived in an electrical panel somewhere on the side of the building facing the street. And there it was, in the far corner. But any idiot could follow wiring from a service box. If you wanted to hide wiring to a secret room, you'd run it off an existing branch, not home run it back to the main box. Even sneakier would simply be to run any power in that room off a regular socket with an extension cord. In that case there would be no permanent wiring leading to the hidden space. The same could be done with water. You simply attached a regular garden hose to a hose bib and ran the water wherever you wanted. But this would have to be inside, at least during cold-weather months.

He ran up the cement stairs to the second floor and scanned the open rafters for clues. You'd have to vent a secret room because sooner or later the air would go bad. The basic vent stack rose up the north wall. This would be the exhaust for the heating system. The venting was old, wrapped in asbestos plaster. But it seemed that the elbow of a four-inch PVC pipe met it right before it pushed up through the roofline. Painted the same color as the old plaster wrapping, it was easy to miss. He traced the pipe back into the wall from which it came. It came right out of the exterior wall. How strange was that? The wall was concrete block and he saw no indication that the vent pipe had been buried within it. There would be a scar in the cement blocks going straight up to the roofline. But maybe the vent went through the wall. He rushed to the window, broke it with an elbow, and peered out.

The vent pipe disappeared into a regular aluminum downspout that was presumably draining water off the roof. Very ingenious.

Downstairs he climbed atop a pile of tires and broke the window directly below the one he'd just looked out of upstairs, and then, using his crowbar, hooked the downspout and yanked on it. The pipe bent toward him, and at the now exposed joint between sections he saw a green garden hose and an orange-colored, heavy-duty extension wire.

Now it was a matter of following the spout down the building with his eye. Five feet from the ground, it veered sharply toward the northeast corner of the building.

He knew where that was. He jumped down from the tires and threaded his way through the junk and along an unlit hallway until he found the building's northeast corner. A battered old van was parked inside. He looked around for any service tools, oil cans. Nothing. This wasn't a place where vehicles were serviced. Why was the van in here? Hidden?

He looked below the truck's underbody, the wheels. Then he saw the door in the floor, right under the left front wheel of the van.

"Jin Li?" he screamed. He rapped the door with his crowbar.

Did he hear her? He heard *something*.

The van's door was open. He checked the dash, under the seat, the glove box. No keys. He glanced through the rear window of the cab into the back of the van. A body lay there. Jin Li? He jumped out and slid open the side door.

Pete Blake, half his head blasted away. He got here before I did, thought Ray. How did he find out about Victor?

Now he returned to the trapdoor, banged on it hard again. This time he definitely heard her.

"I'm coming!" he yelled.

He needed to get the wheel off the door. That was easy enough. He found three six-by-six pieces of lumber and slid them under the van, right beneath the engine block, one atop the other. Then Ray took his knife and cut out the air valve of the right rear tire. The valveless tube shot a jet of stale, rubber-smelling air, the weight of the van driving down on the compromised tire. The tube sang as the air escaped and the van settled downward on the piece of lumber, which served as a fulcrum to lift the front wheels. He repeated the process with the left rear wheel, sinking it six or eight inches. Ray heard the body of Pete Blake roll to the back of the van. Now the front wheels were more than a foot in the air—just high enough for him to open the hatch door.

"Jin Li?" he called.

"Ray! Here!"

He was furious to get inside and opened the hatch to reveal a crudely built wooden ladder that descended into a dark space. He swung down the ladder, shined his flashlight around. Some kind of dripping tub that smelled terrible. That accounted for the need to vent the room.

On a mattress thrown in the corner lay Jin Li, trussed by tape and rope.

"Okay," he said, pulling on a lightbulb string, "you're okay."

With the light on, he could see better. She'd been hit in the face many times. She began to cry. He held her, kissed her head, felt her shaking in his arms. He used his knife on the ropes and had to work at the tape for a few moments.

She convulsed and he held her again.

"Oh, Ray," she cried.

"Let's get out of here."

"There's a chain," she said.

Yes. The lock and chain links were too strong to break, so he set upon the anchoring ring, making short work of it with the crowbar, and slid the last link off it.

"You're going to have to carry the chain until I can cut it off."

"Okay."

He lifted her to her feet; she could barely stand.

He caressed her cheek. "Are you thirsty?"

"No."

"Hungry?"

"Just weak, I guess."

Too weak to stand for long. He squatted down and had her lean softly over his shoulder, her head dropped over his back.

"This is called the fireman's carry."

"That makes sense."

"Why?"

"Because you're a fireman, even though you never told me."

He carried her straight up the ladder, and when his head poked up through the opening, Victor hit him in the temple with a shovel and he collapsed down the ladder, falling heavily, Jin Li dropping hard on top of him.

"Ray!" she screamed, seeing the huge gash in his head.

Victor jumped down, landing squarely on top of Ray, his boots on his chest. Ray groaned. The front of Victor's shirt was spattered with blood. He had the detective's gun if he needed it but wanted to have a little excitement first.

The Chinese girl screamed.

Victor swung the shovel at her to keep back. Then he lifted the shovel blade like a guillotine over Ray's neck, about to chop downward, but Ray spun to the side and the blow hit the cement floor.

Ray scrambled over toward Jin Li. She backed away and picked up the bucket of foul chemical jelly, handing it to Ray.

"Make it go on fire!" she screamed. She stepped in front of Ray just as Victor swung the shovel, and took the next blow on her shoulder. She fell to the floor.

Ray understood. He thrust the bucket up to the hot lightbulb, pressing the bulb deep into the mixture, and instantly it burst into flames. Victor was reaching into his pocket. Ray swung the bucket at Victor, its burning liquid contents leaping across the intervening space and splattering across his eyes and nose and mouth, adhering to him and burning blackly. Victor howled and lunged blindly at Ray, his hands grabbing him by the throat, and the two men stumbled backward toward the tub—which is where Ray tripped, and as he fell he twisted sideways and Victor sprawled awkwardly across the tub, sinking heavily into the lumpy mixture and simultaneously setting its contents on fire. The big man writhed beneath the burning jellied surface, his hands grabbing weakly at the edges of the tub, his feet kicking to make him stand, and for a moment he lifted the black shape of his head but then his movements ceased and he slumped into the flames, his clothes and skin charring rapidly.

The little room filled with black smoke. Ray took a breath at floor level, where the air was better, again hoisted Jin Li over his shoulder in the fireman's carry, and staggered his way up the ladder and out of the room, pushing her past the underside of the van and scrambling after her. He kicked the hatch door shut behind him, knowing that whatever was left of Victor would soon be a carbonized, heat-eaten, faceless husk.

He carried Jin Li outside, and as she panted heavily, he reflected that he, a fireman, had just set another human being afire. I never wanted that, he thought, feeling the blood on his forehead. He was dizzy but okay. And how strange that he had tripped and Victor had gone over him. You can't be luckier than that, Ray thought—as lucky, but not more so.

All pleasure ends. Thirty stories above Central Park, a man worth $1.2 billion pisses into his bathtub. His prostate-removal surgery is scheduled for the next morning. It's a bloody operation with a long recovery time. I can get you another ten years, the surgeon has said to him, and that's good enough. But it will be weeks on the comeback, and he suspects— knows—that he will never be the same again. He's going to be tired, cautious, weakened. *Older.* What a good thing that the Good Pharma problem is gone now, resolved, the stock restored to its rightful former price, his block of shares sold off, the $89 million in proceeds booked into the Martz New Century Partners Fund, where he is going to let the money sit safely. Yes, there was a little unpleasantness involving the Chinese speculator, but in the face of his coming operation, he doesn't quite wish to recall the particulars. And as for Tom Reilly, the guy came through in the end, and that's who you want as your captain. Lands on his feet! Wall Street likes the guy. Reilly's future looks very good indeed. Heard he was getting divorced, though. But a guy like that, getting remarried will be easy.

In the kitchen his wife scrambles some eggs, sprinkles in dried peppers, and realizes, as if for the first time, that she will never have children if she stays married to this man. I have been very stupid, she tells herself, rich but stupid.

A wave of grief passes through her.

A moment later she is thinking about how to redecorate the yoga room of their villa in Palm Beach.

In Shanghai a young man tells his fellow investors that he was late in his return from New York because he had important business meetings. They nod politely; they know he drinks too much and has a weakness for expensive prostitutes. And, after all, what happens in America stays in America. They are more interested in hearing about his new CorpServe manager, another Chinese woman. For his part, the young man has reflected on his experience in New York and suspects that he will never see his sister again. She had called him and said she was safe. And that she was done working for him. Where will you live, he had asked his little sister. Don't worry about me, she'd said, forget about me. Americans are more aggressive than I realized, he thinks. It seems certain that China and the United States, which is weakening every day, will someday be at war, and like many of his fellow investors, he looks forward to this moment in global history.

In her midtown law office a woman in her thirties remembers her afternoon tryst with the man who had an old red pickup truck. She has thought of him too often, and wonders, still, what happened to him after the men in the white limo took him away. She turns her attention to *New York* magazine, some article in there about the sex lives of women in wheelchairs. She reads a page then flips the mag aside. Enough already, she thinks. Tonight she is going to hit a bar or two.

In the Mexican pueblo of San Jacinto, five hundred miles south of the Texas line, a woman in her fifties, dressed in black, shuffles across the cool stone floor of the church and lights a candle to the memory of her daughter. Her sweet girl is buried safely now in the churchyard, the cost of bringing her coffin home paid by a Mexican man in New York named Montoya. The other girl was buried in her town, too. The woman reminds herself that she must buy corn flour. Also, her youngest daughter needs shoes today. She has made the decision to go to El Norte. Despite what happened. America is rich, *mami*, she says, and no one can argue with that.

In Brooklyn, the obese owner of a check-cashing operation sighs, not yet able to gather the courage to claim the body of Victor. She's

been told what is left of him. I'm the only one who will do it, she realizes. She has been thinking about the two Mexican girls and their
families and has arranged, at a most reasonable price, for the sale of
Victorious Sewerage—land, building, trucks, client list—to a very en-
terprising young man from New Delhi, and when the check arrives to
her care, she is going to send every goddamned blood-soaked penny to
the families of the Mexican girls. This act will not bring anyone back,
but she feels it is the least that she can do. Karmic restitution, she calls
it, if not for Vic then perhaps for herself, since she loved him. A terrible, heartless, paranoid killer. But she loved him, yes, she did. There is
still an inch or two in the bottle of Drambuie that he brought her not
long ago, and she reaches out for it, drains it off. The heavy sweet liquid settles in her, warms her, and she decides to phone another man, a
deep-voiced Nigerian she has come to favor.

Forty blocks away, a young man with an old scar on his stomach
holds a Chinese woman in his arms, her forehead resting against his
chin. The stitches in his temple will come out soon. She bathed afterward and happily wrapped herself in his warm bathrobe, and they
have spent the night talking and being together. She had to kiss him a
few hundred times, everywhere, just could not help herself. She is
asleep now and dreams of her grandfather and the apples he gave her.
The man listens to her breathing and wonders if the people in her
dreams speak English or Chinese. He will ask her when she wakes up.

Downstairs, the retired NYPD detective has told the hospice nurse
what she must do. He has said this to her many times, pleading, begging, ordering, but, she reflects, they all say that. She knows there is a
time that is too soon and there is a time that is right. It is better that he
has lived this long. Good things happened that otherwise would not
have. Though his friend, the other detective, was killed. But now this
man has suffered enough. She sees that the cancer has invaded his eye
and the roof of his mouth. Chances are very good that it is through his
brain. He doesn't have much time left as a human being, but he could
be a dying animal for many days to come. She loads the Dilaudid machine, punches in the right code, and, softly pressing the button every
minute, takes him down. His last movements are the nervous system's

misfiring response, which causes the man to jerkily wave his arms, as if conducting a great symphony. His eyes are closed, his mouth open, white head sunk into the pillow. But his skeletal arms wave wildly, with passion. This eerie sight would be disturbing, but she has seen it before and finds a beauty in it, the last moment of the life force being released. She presses the button again, and again, and soon his arms softly fall to the blanket, and if the man thinks of anything as he dies, it is of his son. The nurse gently kisses the man on the forehead, as she does with all of them. She wants to believe they feel this last benediction. Then she removes all his tubes and arranges him in the bed. She will read her Bible until his son comes downstairs.

A typhoon three hundred miles wide spins across the sea to Indonesia, soon to flood a hundred villages. Relief workers from around the globe will fly in as quickly as they can. They will find that they are needed. They will find death and they will find life.

A New York City fireman holds a Chinese girl.

The world is old, the world is new.

Acknowledgments

Every story is discovered in circumstances that will never come again—a mysterious undertaking, the writing of novels. But what is not mysterious is that one receives help along the way. I wish to acknowledge and thank:

Brian DeCubellis, Susan Moldow, Kim Schefler, William Oldham, my long-time agent Kris Dahl, Rose Lichter-Marck, John Glusman, Karen Thompson, Jennifer Joel, Nancy and Rich Olsen-Harbich, Suketu Mehta, Don and Janet Doughty, Nan Graham, Dana and Stephanie Harrison, Bart and Renata Harrison, Matt Kaye, Jonathan Galassi, John McGhee, Katherine McCaw, Roz Lippel, Carolyn Reidy, Marion Duvert, Joyce McCray, Jeff Seroy, Abby Kagan, John Fulbrook, Lisa Drew, Frances Coady, Chuck Hogan and Robert Ferrigno, Ted Fishman, David Rogers, Guy Lawson, Don Snyder, Cailey Hall, Françoise Triffaux, and Richard Schoch. Each helped me in his or her way.

My editor, the incomparable Sarah Crichton, guided and encouraged and sharply improved this book. She has both a great eye and an intrepid spirit. Thank you, Sarah.

My wife, Kathryn, and our children, Sarah, Walker, and Julia. All of me for all of you.

A Note About the Author

Colin Harrison's previous novels are *Afterburn*, *Manhattan Nocturne*, *Bodies Electric*, *Break and Enter*, and *The Havana Room*, which have been published in a dozen countries. He and his wife, the writer Kathryn Harrison, live in Brooklyn, New York, with their three children.